love is on the air

Jane Moore is a columnist for the *Sun* and *GQ* magazine. She regularly presents investigative documentaries for Channel 4's *Dispatches*, on subjects ranging from supermarket secrets and broiler chicken production, through to food labelling and Britain's obesity crisis. She is also the author of the bestsellers *Fourplay*, *The Ex-Files*, *Dot.Homme*, *The Second Wives Club* and *Perfect Match*. She lives in London.

Praise for Jane Moore

'What makes this a page turner is the skilful presentation of human relationships'
Daily Telegraph

'Intelligent . . . thought-provoking . . . wholly gripping'
She

'Every bit as satisfying as a gloriously gossipy night out with the girls' Daily Mail

'Compulsive' *heat*

'Funny, moving and at times tragic . . . Fabulous'
Company

'A brilliant read' *Sun*

'The characters are rounded, flawed individuals you'll empathise with' *Glamour*

'Another witty, warm novel from Jane Moore' *Closer*

JANE MOORE

love is on the air

arrow books

Published by Arrow Books in 2011

3 5 7 9 10 8 6 4 2

First published in Great Britain in 2010 by
Century
Random House, 20 Vauxhall Bridge Road
London SW1V 2SA

www.rbooks.co.uk

Addresses for companies within The Random House Group Limited can be
found at: www.randomhouse.co.uk/offices.htm

The Random House Group Limited Reg. No. 954009

A CIP catalogue record for this book
is available from the British Library

ISBN 9780099505532

The Random House Group Limited supports The Forest Stewardship
Council (FSC), the leading international forest certification organisation.
All our titles that are printed on Greenpeace approved FSC certified paper
carry the FSC logo. Our paper procurement policy can be found at:
www.rbooks.co.uk/environment

Mixed Sources
Product group from well-managed
forests and other controlled sources
www.fsc.org Cert no. TT-COC-2139
© 1996 Forest Stewardship Council
FSC

Typeset by SX Composing DTP, Rayleigh, Essex
Printed and bound in Great Britain by
CPI Bookmarque, Croydon, CR0 4TD

In memory of Robert Brown . . . Deborah's true love

Acknowledgements

Thank you to Susan Sandon, Georgina Hawtrey-Woore, Rob Waddington, Louisa Gibbs and everyone else at Random House who has helped with the book, particularly the sales team!

Thanks also to my agent, Jonathan Lloyd, and all at Curtis Brown, to Dominic Mohan and everyone at the *Sun* for their continued support and, in particular, to my family for putting up with the forced solitude of the long-distance author.

And most of all, a massive thank-you to all my readers. I couldn't do it without you.

Chapter One

'I want to look like her.'

The photograph, torn from the cover of one of the hundred and forty-five gossip magazines littering the salon, is of Cheryl Cole, with more head hair than Jedward.

Unfortunately, the woman thrusting the picture towards my face looks more like 'merry' Old King Cole, apart from the merry bit. A triumph of hope over reality would be a masterly understatement.

'I've just got over a messy divorce and my daughter says I need a new hairdo. You know, to mark a new start.'

Time may be a great healer, but it's a lousy beautician, I think, inwardly grimacing at the task in hand.

'She said I could get extensions.'

'Yes, we do provide those here, but they're *very* expensive,' I reply diplomatically. 'And I'm not sure they'd suit your face shape.'

'I want 'em.' Her mouth sets in a firm line, her voluminous arms resolutely folded in front of her large, clearly unfettered bosoms.

I toy with the idea of issuing the legendary retort of

hairdressers everywhere – 'This is a comb, love, not a bloody wand' – but think better of it and scurry to the back room to try to find what colours we have in stock.

I find Luca leaning against the sink, nursing a cup of coffee. His name's Luke, actually, but he added the 'a' in the hope it made him sound more mysterious. Trouble is, his accent is more Romford than Rome and he thinks the Leaning Tower of Pisa is a five-for-one offer at Domino's. I love him for it, though.

'The customer's always shite,' I grumble, as I start opening cupboard doors and closing them with a spleen-venting bang.

'Oh dear, got a bad one, have we?' He rolls his eyes, then yawns. 'When I eventually get my own salon, I'm going to ban anyone who gives me a hard time or is too ugly.'

'This one's both.' I find a clump of light brown extensions and hold them up to the light. 'Do these say "Cheryl Cole" to you?'

He pulls a face. 'They say "cheap nylon scrag ends", love, whichever way you look at it.'

'Thought so. A match made in heaven, then.' Clutching the extensions, I walk back to the client with a heavy sigh.

I have been a hairdresser for sixteen years now, starting as floor sweeper-cum-tea-maker and working my way up to the lofty heights of 'senior stylist', as I have rather grandly been referred to on the tariff sheet for the past five years, and salon manager.

As a trainee, I imagined I was going to cut a trail-blazing swathe through the world of hairdressing, culminating in an eponymous salon to which all the latest celebrities would flock for inspiration.

But then, just like so many others in my trade, I decided that creativity is great, but plagiarism is faster, so here I am giving the customers what they want by copying someone else's style. I'm not sure whether I consider it a career any more or merely a job that has gone on too long.

Most days, though, I still enjoy the combination of staff camaraderie and the unpredictable flow of clients, many of whom are delightfully chatty and thrilled with their transformation.

And then there are those I might even describe as friends, even though our relationships don't extend beyond the salon doors. I was there the day they got married, making last-minute tweaks to their hair. I have seen them arrive at the salon with their new-born babies, and watched their offspring grow from demanding toddler right through to surly teenager. I know what they love about their husbands; I know what they hate. I know some of their deepest thoughts and desires, all unleashed to little old me, someone who touches them intimately yet is still ostensibly a stranger, someone comfortably distanced from their home life.

Only yesterday, I led one of them into the back room where she could weep in privacy as she told me her husband was leaving her for someone else. There was little I could do except comfort her and lavish some TLC via my scissors and dryer, but by the time she left she seemed faintly stronger for it. So I'm a bit of a therapist too, I suppose, and I relish the privilege.

But on days like today, when first I had a one-year-old boy screaming the place down for the duration of his first ever haircut, and now a Gollum lookalike wanting me to work miracles with hair extensions, it's rather more challenging.

My name is Cam Simpson. I'd like to be able to tell you that it's short for Camilla, but it's not. Nope, it's Camomile, as in the poncy tea, or that shampoo that's supposed to lighten your hair but rarely seems to. Apparently, it's my mother's 'favourite' tea, despite the fact that I have never seen her drink it and she originally hails from Colchester, where most seem quite happy drinking PG Tips or similar.

'But, dah-ling, it's soooo exotic and mysterious!' she always witters, after one of my many challenges on the matter. 'Who wants a dull old name like Sarah or Jane?' For the record, *she's* called Liz.

So, thanks to a mother who, rather than cure cancer or even just dress quirkily to make herself appear interesting, saddled her only daughter with an 'unusual' name, I spent my school years thwarting piss-taking behaviour from my fellow pupils and being saddled with the oh-so-witty moniker 'Baggy'. And the majority of my adult years so far explaining it to people who think they're all being highly original when they ask why I have such a 'refreshing' name. Gee, thanks, Mum.

To compound the injustice of it, she named my younger twin brothers Josh and James, her argument being that their being identical made them unusual so they didn't need daft names as well.

'Right!' I force a smile for the client, who is now flicking through the latest edition of *Hair* magazine and lingering worryingly on a picture of some stick-thin model whose hair extensions are so big she's clearly struggling to keep her lollipop head upright.

'I've found your colour,' I say brightly. 'So let's get going – it's a long old job.'

By the time I've finished, waved goodbye to what resembles a transvestite trucker (albeit a happy, smiling one) and cleaned up my work station, I notice it's six fifteen.

'Shit!' Grabbing my coat and bag, I make a cursory wave in Luca's direction and rush out of the door, turning left towards the busier end of the High Street, where all the theme pubs and wine bars stand cheek by jowl, a binge drinker's paradise. It's an assault course of excessiveness, from signs saying 'Two drinks for the price of one' and 'Girls drink free' to bins overflowing with empty fag packets and junk-food cartons.

My favourite haunt used to be Corks, a sophisticated and consequently quiet little place that boasted an excellent wine list and unobtrusive music. But because hardly anyone except me went in there, it sold out to a corporate chain that renamed it the Brewer's Droop, piped in bangin' tunes all day long and, now, inexplicably, it's crammed most nights. Clearly, I'm getting old.

I'm walking past it now, glancing through the window where I spent many a peaceful moment nursing a glass of house white before heading home to the thrills of my boyfriend, Dean, more of whom later. Inside, one man has another in a headlock and a woman of indeterminate age, who has clearly never heard of moisturiser, is shrieking at them both to 'Leave it aaaaaaahtt'. A traditional scene one mysteriously never sees re-enacted in Disney's 'typical English pub' at the Epcot theme park.

Hurrying on, I head towards the less raw environs of

Strada, the pizzeria where I'm meeting two of my oldest friends, Saira and Ella, for a long-overdue girls' night. We've known each other since school, but of late, the 'Three No Degrees', as my dad scathingly referred to us because we all exhibited no interest whatsoever in attending university, have become the Three Degrees of Separation, forced apart by maturity and its accompanying baggage.

Since her 'sort of arranged' marriage three years ago (meaning *she* could have said no if she wished but, fortuitously, Abbas turned out to be gorgeous and successful) Saira has produced Rashid, thereafter always referred to among us as 'the Golden Child'. I swear he didn't learn to walk until he was two, because there was no need. He was carried everywhere – held aloft, even – by Abbas's horde of proud relatives, his mother bursting into tears of pride and joy every time she so much as laid eyes on him. Consequently, the demands of an ever-present family posse and a new baby meant poor Saira's spare time shrank to nothing.

Around the same time, Ella met her latest boyfriend, Philip, a man who takes playing hard to get to new levels, in that he is still firmly married to his 'first and last wife', as he pointedly describes her.

'Love is grand; divorce is a hundred grand,' he once quipped to Ella when she brought up the latest celebrity break-up in the newspapers.

To any sane woman, this would be a small clue that he has no intention of ever leaving, but no, Ella doesn't see it that way. As far as she's concerned, the phrase was coined before he met her, a goddess in human form, and she is going to be the one to make him see the error of his intransigency. And the band played

'Believe It If You Like', as my grandma used to say.

But, regardless, these days most of her time is taken up with sitting in love's waiting room, just in case he might ring and want to see her. I can't tell you the times I have called Ella to suggest meeting for a spontaneous coffee and she's replied, 'I'd love to, but Philip said he might be able to leave the office for a couple of hours to come and see me.'

Invariably, he won't show and yet another day is wasted. But, as she constantly reminds me when I question her sanity, he pays her rent, bills and 'a little pocket money', so the very least she can do in return is be there when he wants her to be.

'Personally, I'd rather be homeless and my own person,' I sniff, and we won't speak for a couple of days, but then I'll feel dreadful for being so judgemental and arrogantly trying to impose my own ideals on a friend, and I'll call her to apologise. It isn't that I'm miffed she isn't jumping to *my* tune, more that she is at the beck and call of a man who, at best, simply doesn't deserve her, at worst, treats her like a high-paid hooker. Ella is kind, funny and ridiculously beautiful, and, in my humble opinion, could do so much better. But hey, who am I to talk?

I live with the aforementioned Dean in a one-bed-roomed flat that's so small we sometimes have sex without realising it. Which is just as well, because our conscious sex life is practically at the point of flat-lining. The last time we even attempted it was about four weeks ago after a night out to celebrate Luca's birthday. As you may have guessed, we were both pissed and, emboldened by lager and red wine, Dean leapt on me before we swiftly realised that same alcohol had rendered him physically incapable. So that was that.

We've been together for six years, living under one roof for four. I have chosen those words carefully because, sometimes, it seems that's *all* we have in common: the same bricks and mortar.

When I get home later tonight, it's a given that Dean will be occupying his usual position in the centre of the sofa, watching either Sky Sports or reruns of *Top Gear* on Dave. On the rare occasions he vacates it (toilet break, always during the ads, or bedtime) there's a permanent dent there to remind me of his enthusiastic indolence. Such is my desperation to break the cycle that last Christmas, I even forked out money I could ill afford on a Wii, in the hope it might stir him to *some* level of action. But it's still gathering dust in the corner, waiting for the day when Dean can find the time in his busy TV-watching schedule to actually connect it.

It hasn't always been this way. When we met, he was a keen amateur rugby player, relieving the largely sedentary tedium of his working week as a mobile-phone salesman by throwing himself around a muddy pitch most weekends before heading off to the pub with his team-mates and, invariably, me. My previous boyfriend had been a 'street artist', something I deemed fascinatingly anarchic at the time before rapidly realising it was merely a cover for being an idle twat. He was also so tight that I swear he'd learn to limbo simply to enter a pay toilet for free.

So Dean seemed generous, dependable, manly and *active* by comparison, a *real* man who, coincidentally, never ate quiche. Well, not unless it was packed solid with Peperami.

Then, after a couple of years, he moved into my tiny flat and morphed into his father, Roy, a couch potato who thinks that holding down a job during the week entitles him to sit on his idle backside the entire weekend while Dean's mum, Paula, waits on him hand and foot. More fool her. The only difference is that, as someone whose idea of housework is to sweep the room with a glance, I refuse to run around after Dean.

'That's it. I'm officially stuffed.' Saira pushes her plate away, one small chunk of crust the only evidence that an airbag-sized pizza has graced it.

'I'm not surprised.' Ella raises a deftly plucked eyebrow. 'A family of four could have lived off that for a week.'

Saira pokes out her tongue. 'I won't eat again until . . . oooh . . . later tonight,' she grins. She's always had a good appetite but rarely goes above an enviably curvaceous size fourteen. The thing about Saira is that she has a teensy waist that gives her figure an hourglass shape she knows how to maximise to great effect with stretchy tops and tightly tailored pencil skirts that kick out into fishtail hems.

I, however, may be young at heart, but feel distinctly middle-aged in other places. I only have to glance in the direction of one slither of pizza and instantly put on three stone. If I even smell one, my jeans suddenly become a size too small. I'm currently hovering at around eleven stone, and it has taken me six long, painful months of iron willpower to get here.

Ella, you've probably guessed, is über-slim and toned. She likes to pretend it's effortless, but we know different and have the incriminating photos to prove it. At school, she had brown, frizzy hair to her shoulders, a mono-brow and a real-life bottom and stomach area that suggested she might actually have internal organs. That was Ella as nature intended, not this expensively high-lighted, carb-free gym bunny who is seized with an overpowering compulsion to do four circuits after so much as a salad, and has a concave abdomen.

I let out a long sigh at the thought of our school days back in the mid-eighties, making us all now thirty-four, or thereabouts. In real time, we all universally hated it, but the passing years have distorted my and Saira's memories and morphed life at St Nicholas's Secondary School into a fiesta of fun that makes *High School Musical* seem drab and staid. Ella rarely indulges our nostalgic reflections, perhaps not wishing to revisit her unadulterated self.

'I was thinking about that school camping trip to Wales the other day,' I murmur. 'How it was our first time away from our parents and felt so exciting.'

'God, yes, it took about two years of pleading for my dad to even let me go.' Saira smiles dreamily at the thought. 'It felt sooo liberating.'

Ella makes a small snorting noise. 'You . . .' she jabs a finger in the direction of Saira, '. . . spent all week snivelling because you missed your mum, and you . . .' the finger moves round to me, '. . . moaned non-stop that there wasn't enough to eat and how you couldn't wait to get home and raid the fridge.'

I let a few, dignified seconds pass, then lean towards her slightly and inspect her forehead. 'Darling, you really should be careful. All that frowning leaves terrible lines.'

Saira laughs. 'She's right, though. I think we have probably rewritten history over the years. But it *was* a rite of passage for me in many ways. When I managed to come back alive and unsullied by male hands, my father started to give me a little more freedom.'

'Those were the days,' I sigh. 'No responsibility, no commitments . . .'

'No money, no independence, no LIFE,' finishes Ella. I resist the urge to question whether her current set-up is any better.

Since the school trip, we have shared several, more exotic holidays, sometimes all three of us, sometimes variations of two. The Canary Islands are a favourite, so too the Costa del Sol . . . nothing long distance, mainly because of time and budget.

But the last joint holiday was four years ago, before Saira met Abbas and before Ella was put on permanent standby for Philip. I've suggested a week in Spain a couple of times, but it has never materialised. We haven't even managed a much-discussed spa mini-break in Britain.

'OK, so the camping memories may have improved with age,' I concede, 'but you've got to admit the week in Mallorca was pretty damn fine.'

'Ahhh, those really *were* the days,' sighs Saira. 'Before shitty nappies and early starts . . .'

'Before skulking around in obscure restaurants and spending Friday nights wondering whether he'll call . . .' says Ella.

'Before . . .' I falter, unsure of what to say now I've started, '. . . mundanity.' I recoil inwardly as soon as the damning word leaves my mouth. Is that how I see my life now? I don't have time to dwell on it as Saira's voice punctures my thoughts.

'Why don't we go on holiday again?'

'We've been down this road before.' I point out wearily. 'Then you can never find the right time to leave little Rashid, and Ella always has something she *might* have to do with Philip.'

11

'Well, Rashid's a bit older now and I'm sure the omnipresent in-laws can help look after him; in fact they'll positively relish it,' counters Saira. She glances across at Ella. 'What about you?'

Ella shrugs. 'Yeah, why not?'

They both look at me.

'Are you asking whether I'm up for it? Or have I just become our official travel agent?'

'If a job is worth doing, make sure you delegate it to the right person, that's what I say,' grins Saira.

'And I say that delegation is a sign of weakness. Let someone else do it,' quips Ella, adding hastily, 'and I don't want to go camping in bloody Wales. It has to be somewhere hot, with comfy beds and an all-day bar. That's my criteria.'

I raise my eyes heavenward. 'Leave it with me, Your Majesty.'

Chapter Two

'Only me!' I shout in the general direction of the living room. I close the front door noisily behind me and throw my coat over the banister.

There's a reason for my deliberately bombastic entrance and it lies in the fact that I once let myself in quietly and stumbled across my beloved sailing solo, if you get my drift.

Now, to many women, particularly our younger, more idealistic selves, perhaps this would be a devastating blow, a sign that we weren't satisfying him. But to older, more settled women, such as myself, particularly one knackered after a long day at work, it was a blessed relief to know that any sexual desire he may have been harbouring was sated and I could enjoy an early night untroubled by any cursory nipple twiddling.

At the time, Dean simply grinned and said, 'Oops,' but I felt mortified to have witnessed it, hence tonight's theatrically loud homecoming. Mind you, if it was a gun-wielding gang of six in balaclavas, I still doubt it would be enough to garner a response if there's a televised football match in progress.

'All right?' I walk in just as he changes channels from Dave to Sky Sports. Variety is the spice of life, I think wryly.

He manages a quick smile and small grunt, and I hover expectantly, wondering whether tonight will be one of those rare occasions when he actually expresses even the faintest interest in how my evening went. But no, he returns to staring at the screen.

'Anything to report?' I persevere, knowing that unless a news event was so catastrophic that it was actually flashed across all channels, Dean wouldn't even know if Lord Lucan was sitting in our kitchen right now, making himself a cup of tea.

'Nope. You?'

At last, a flicker, a faint pulse detected in this relationship. I seize upon it and sit next to him on the sofa, struggling to get comfortable on the raised edge of the cushion that's propelling me towards its Dean-shaped dent.

'Saira's fine, and Ella seems OK, but she's still flogging that dead horse Philip. I just don't get the attraction.' I'm speaking to the side of his head because he hasn't bothered to turn and look my way.

'We were reminiscing about holidays . . .'

He makes a scoffing noise, but I'm unsure whether it's directed at me or the TV screen, where Arsenal have just scored against his beloved Tottenham Hotspur in a repeat of a match which, by the way, he saw in real time yesterday.

'Are you listening to me?' I demand.

'Yes.' He turns slightly. 'You said Saira is fine but Ella is still with Philip.'

'And what were we reminiscing about?'

'Er, old times?'

'I *knew* you weren't listening!' I leap to my feet and stand in front of him, blocking the screen. 'For fuck's sake, you're more interested in a match you've seen already than you are in me. What does *that* say about us?' I flounce off into the kitchen and flick the kettle on, my heart pounding with the injustice of being ignored. Opening and slamming cupboard doors, I grab a mug and throw a teabag in it, imagining it's Dean's head as I pour boiling water over it.

As the anger begins to subside, tears well. Is this how it's going to be . . . for ever? A form of coexistence with little or none of the benefits usually associated with long-term relationships, such as constant support, shared interests, conversation and sex on demand?

If I were sharing a house with a girlfriend, I would have come in and she would probably have asked about my night. Then we'd open a bottle of wine and sit at the kitchen table, putting the world to rights until one or both of us decided to get some sleep. There'd be no sex, of course, but then again, I don't get much of it now. Mind you, that's probably just as much my fault as it is his. I let out a wistful sigh.

'You sound fed up.'

I swivel round to find Dean leaning against the kitchen doorframe, a sheepish look on his face. I notice he's wearing the T-shirt I hate, with 'Heinz Meanz Fartz' emblazoned across the front.

'Are you pissed off with me?' He moves across to the small bistro-style kitchen table and plonks himself down.

'A bit,' I mutter, squeezing out my teabag and lobbing it in the bin. 'Do you want tea?'

I ask this knowing that, despite having been home for a few hours, he won't have made one. I reckon the only thing he can achieve on his own is dandruff.

'Yes, please. I was about to make one anyway.'

As if you move off the sofa in my absence, I think, resisting the urge to say it out loud.

'So what have I done?' He looks at me expectantly.

I *hate* it when he says it like that, clearly making the point that the misdemeanour is so small that he doesn't have a clue what it even is. It's designed to make me feel hysterical and petty, and it works.

'You didn't ask me if I'd had a nice evening.' It sounds so ridiculous when spoken aloud.

He frowns slightly. 'I did. You asked me if I had anything to report, and I replied "no", then asked if you had.'

He's right, of course. But I've been here so many times before, when he recalls some lacklustre or one-word answer as a defence against my condemnation of his lack of interest in me.

'Yes, but you had to be prompted,' I say.

He purses his lips. It's written all over his face that he thinks the slight is either imagined or completely fabricated. 'Well . . . sorry if I offended you.'

Another phrase I hate. One that makes the recipient feel as though they're being oversensitive and need placating with an apology of an apology, one that bestows no blame on its messenger.

Wearily, I approach the table and sit opposite him, nursing my untouched mug of tea. To be honest, I'm dog-tired now and want nothing more than to crawl into bed, waking up to a brand-new day when life might not seem quite so humdrum. But I have done that countless times before, sweeping my concerns – however minor – under the carpet, usually through apathy and an unwillingness to enter an energy-sapping, in-depth talk . . . if there *is* such a thing with Dean. But tonight, I feel a compulsion to articulate what's festering inside me.

'It just strikes me as odd that you wouldn't ask me how my evening went. It makes me think that if you're not interested in *that*, then maybe the disinterest extends to me personally.'

Mild irritation flashes across his face. 'That's not the case at all.'

'I only have your word for that.'

'Isn't that enough?' His eyes fix on mine questioningly.

An awkward silence descends, one indicating loud and clear that, no, I don't consider it to be enough.

'I need to *feel* as though you're interested,' I say eventually.

'So what should I do?'

Again, he places the ball firmly back in my court, seeking my instructions on how to behave, as if he's my recalcitrant child rather than my lover.

'If you have to ask me that, then that's part of the problem,' I sigh.

'Problem?' He looks perplexed. 'Have we got one? Is that what you're trying to tell me?'

Dean is no idiot. He did well at school, securing eight pretty good GCSEs and B-grade A levels in English and history, and if his sales bonuses are anything to go by, he could sell air conditioning to the Eskimos. He's also in possession of a fine wit, when the mood suits him. But when it comes to emotional intelligence, he's so dim he could be hit by a parked car.

Trouble is, he grew up in a family with two emotional pygmies at its helm. His mum, Paula, is your archetypal Stepford wife, all big hair, fixed smile and, once Botox became available on the open market, fixed forehead too. She looks like she's stepped straight off the set of *Dallas*, though they live in a typical red-brick semi in an unremarkable side street in Croydon, in the shadow of a vast Ikea.

In her mind, Paula is a company director's wife, consistently keeping up appearances in case she has to throw a power dinner party at a moment's notice. But her husband, Roy, is a taxi driver who exchanges the seat of his cab for the seat of their sofa, with little movement in between. The only exercise he gets is jumping to conclusions.

He works days, by which I mean from about 10 a.m. to just short of 5 p.m., Monday to Friday. He used to work the occasional weekend when Dean and his older sister, Stacey, were young, but once they'd flown the nest, and less disposable income was needed, he'd cut back considerably on his hours.

I'd like to tell you that he fills his downtime with fascinating hobbies or worthy pursuits, but I'd be lying. He watches TV mostly, perhaps the occasional war film DVD given away with a Sunday newspaper. And that's it. Consequently, he looks like the 'before' picture in one of those medical ads about high cholesterol, all puce-faced and sweaty at even the slightest exertion, with the waistline of a Spacehopper.

Paula fulfils her wifely duties in that she makes sure Roy's clothes are washed and ironed and his vast stomach filled, but aside from that she does her own thing. Bingo with the girls on a Monday night, salsa lessons on a Wednesday and the occasional shopping and lunch trips to town with her best friend, Dorothy. If Dean came home one day and told me she'd run off with a salsa instructor called Miguel, I'd reply, 'It was only to be expected.'

She's a whirling dervish, fuelled by a ferocious coffee habit. She doesn't sweat, she percolates. Consequently, their life is like one of those movie sequences, where one person is speeded up and shown whizzing around the room from chore to chore, whilst the other – in this case, Roy – is motionless. It's my greatest nightmare that Dean and I become the same in a parallel universe: two people who just happen to share the same patch of real estate and rarely communicate beyond 'What's on TV tonight?' or 'What's for tea?' Perhaps we have already.

Dean is staring down at the table now, his attention diverted by a football supplement lying across the fruit bowl. I take the chance to study him closely, something I haven't done for a while. His stomach, once highly toned from playing rugby, has now slackened considerably, with a slight paunch. But his arms and legs have maintained their muscle definition, and the firm bottom I fell in lust with all those years ago is still just as eye-catching.

Typical, isn't it? Every time I lose weight, it finds me again. Yet I'm sharing my life with a man who constantly eats junk with no discernible consequences.

Facially too, he's barely changed, with just a few more laughter lines (few of them inspired by me, I fear) and perhaps the faintest beginnings of a bald patch on the crown of his head. But the kind features, shock of dark hair and piercing blue eyes that once attracted me so much are still there; it's just the chemistry that seems to have faded.

Given my inner irritation towards him, you're probably wondering why I stay, and it's a question I often ask myself. But the answer is always the same: many of our obvious differences are simply the gender-related ones experienced by men and women the world over, and fundamentally, he's a *good* man and I know he loves me. It's just that he doesn't express it very often.

I always think that perhaps I'm being my own worst enemy in needing more obvious manifestations of what I mean to him, that I'm being too insecure. There are plenty of women who are happy just *knowing* they're loved; they don't seek constant and obvious reassurance of it.

And maybe my apathy is a self-fulfilling prophecy: if *I* make more effort to recapture what we once had, then perhaps he will rise to the challenge. They always say a successful marriage takes hard work on both sides, and it's the same with long-term relationships. We've just slipped into a lacklustre routine, that's all. With a little thought and dedication, it's possible we can get ourselves back on track. It's at least worth a try.

My spirits lift at the thought and I stretch my hand across the table, resting it on his. It feels awkward, because any intimacy other than perfunctory sex is alien to us these days, but I persevere and take heart from the fact he hasn't moved away from me.

'I'm sorry for being a bit oversensitive in there.' I jerk my head towards the living room. 'It's been a pretty shit day in the salon and I'm feeling a bit frazzled.'

'Forget it,' he smiles. 'We all feel like that sometimes.'

This, of course, is the point where any normal person

would ask what had happened to make my day so stressful, but not Dean. Sometimes, I think I could burst in the door and announce I'd just been the victim of a hit-and-run and he'd simply ask me where the cereal bowls were.

Focus, Cam, I tell myself, we're about to enter a brave new world. It's just that you're going to have to be the one who takes his hand and drags him to the threshold of it.

I squeeze his hand and smile reassuringly. 'I was thinking, how about we do something at the weekend?'

I can almost see the football fixtures scrolling down each of his eyes. After a couple of seconds, he shrugs. 'Like what?'

'Oh, I don't know . . . the cinema perhaps?'

As soon as the words leave my mouth, I know this is a bad idea, highlighting as it will the yawning chasm between our taste in films. I like rom-coms and the occasional arty, subtitled number, if I'm not too knackered to concentrate, and Dean likes movies with minimal dialogue and lots of car chases. The notion there might be a film on that we *both* want to see is laughable.

'Or just drinks somewhere, followed by a nice dinner?' I start nodding furiously to indicate that this is my preferred option. 'We could try out that little Italian at the bottom of the hill.'

'OK.' He nods and yawns simultaneously. 'Book it for eight and we'll have a couple in the pub next door first.'

'It's a date,' I smile, feeling a swell of optimism, despite being the one to suggest and, now, book it.

Dean removes his hand from under mine and stands up, noticeably relieved that I'm no longer cross with him. He turns towards the sanctuary of the living room.

'One of the *Mission: Impossible*s has just started. Fancy watching it?'

I shake my head. 'Nah, I think I'll have a bath and read my book.'

Just as he disappears from view, I remember what else I wanted to say and follow him. By the time I reach the living room, he is already ensconced in his dent, flicking through the TV channels.

'By the way, I forgot to say . . . Saira, Ella and I are thinking of going on a girls' week abroad.'

'Great.' He carries on scrolling down the channels and switches to *Mission: Impossible* just as Tom Cruise is dangling by one arm from a clifftop. Some days, I know just how he feels.

I sigh inwardly, hoping that our night out on Saturday will inject a bit of life back into our relationship.

Chapter Three

The queue of bleary-eyed people is snaking round the corner, moving at a snail's pace.

'Bloody hell,' I mutter, 'by the time we get to check-in, it will be time to come home again.'

'Let's look at the positives . . . we're on holiday!' says Saira, far too cheerily for my liking.

As the mother of a toddler, she's used to interrupted sleep and early starts. As she once pointed out, 'Why do people say they've slept like a baby when mine actually wakes up every two hours?'

But I'm childless and struggling to function and, so far, Ella hasn't uttered a single word.

It's 6 a.m. and we're in the soul-destroying hellhole that is Gatwick airport, along with the forty-nine thousand other people either too poor or too tight to pay for flights that leave at a reasonable hour. Worse, as easyJet has a first come, first boarding policy and we're at the back of the queue, we're in danger of being seated *outside* the bloody plane.

'Where's Rashid when I need him?' says Saira wistfully.

'Eh?' Christ, I think, it's only been two hours and she's missing him already. This is going to be a fun week.

'You get to board first when you have a small child,' she adds. 'But I suppose boarding last is a small price to pay for a stress-free holiday.'

Phew, normal service resumed.

After forty minutes, we finally reach check-in, where a sullen man wordlessly extends his arm for our tickets and passport.

'Didyerpackyerluggageyerself?' he recites.

'Yes,' Saira and I both chorus enthusiastically.

He stares pointedly at Ella, who doesn't notice, so I jab my elbow in her side.

'He wants to know if you packedyerluggageyerself,' I parrot.

She nods wearily and returns to staring into the middle distance, leaving me to pick up her ridiculously large suitcase.

'You do know we're only going for a week, don't you?'

'It's to cover all eventualities,' she mumbles.

'What – such as a full wet suit, flippers and oxygen tank in case we're lost at sea?' I grimace as I haul it onto the weighing scales. 'Just because something's your size doesn't mean you have to bring it on flaming holiday.'

After tapping away at his keyboard for what seems like an eternity, Mr Happy finally hands over our boarding passes.

'Right, now to the next queue,' I say breezily, heading towards the International Departures area, where passengers are being given clear plastic bags before being herded into various holding pens.

'Baaaaaaaaaaa,' bleats Ella mutinously.

My and Saira's hand luggage consists of a small handbag each, containing the usual suspects of purse, mobile phone and door keys. But we watch open-mouthed as Ella places half of Boots's make-up counter into two plastic bags.

'Ye gods, woman, what do you need all that for? And why didn't you put it in your suitcase?' My own holiday make-up consists of an ancient mascara and clear lip gloss stuffed in the side pocket of my washbag.

'Because luggage sometimes goes missing, and when it does, I will still look glamorous and you two will resemble something even the tide wouldn't want to take out,' she replies archly.

Twenty minutes later, we are sitting upstairs, having grabbed a quick coffee before making the hundred-mile trek to the departure gate.

'God, this is nice,' enthuses Saira, clearly not referring to the fact that she has one buttock perched on a plastic bench full of someone else's screaming children. 'No buggy to lug around, no pooey bottom to wipe . . . just *me* to think about for a change. What bliss.'

Ella smiles for the first time today, despite having just put her cashmere-clad elbow in a blob of ketchup left on the table. 'I must say, it's nice to be actually travelling *with* someone. I'm usually on my own, heading off to meet Philip in some foreign hideaway that's a suitably safe distance away from his wife.'

Undoubtedly, I feel different too. It's not that holidays with Dean are particularly stressful . . . After all, I'm always the one who suggests, books and organises it all so I know what I'm getting. But they're not particularly exciting either. We simply transfer our mundane routine to hotter climes once, sometimes twice, a year, and the dent in the sofa is replaced by one in a sunlounger. If they made one with an inbuilt commode, I doubt he'd ever rise from that either.

But then again, putting myself in *his* shoes, he's sharing his life with a control freak who couldn't bear the thought of going with someone else's flow. As he's far more laid-back than I am, over the years it has just become easier for both of us if I organise everything and for him to happily go along with it. It's a pattern of my own making, so I can hardly moan about it now.

And what is a holiday for, if not lying on a sunlounger and relaxing? I've never been one for spending five hours on a coach to go to see some old building and buy a piece of craftwork from a supposed 'local peasant' in a Man Utd shirt and Nike trainers, and neither has Dean. So looking at it *that* way, perhaps we're perfectly suited.

It's the same story with Ella and me. In the past, Saira has ventured alone on various sightseeing tours whilst we remained largely inanimate by the pool, but something tells me that, since Rashid's birth, she'll now be joining us.

Whatever. For me, I know that whilst my body will be motionless, my mind will be in overdrive, trying to gain some perspective on the ever-decreasing emotional circles I seem intent on tangling myself in.

The heat hits us as we leave the terminal building, the uplifting sensation of Tenerife's finest warm air enveloping our bodies.

'Aaaaaah, that feels good.' Ella lifts her arms and removes her jumper, revealing her enviably pert bosoms straining against a teensy T-shirt.

Nearby, a group of tanned men disembarking from a minibus notice and start shouting, 'Keep going, love,' and, 'Get 'em off.' They are clearly part of a team tour of some kind, each wearing a red T-shirt emblazoned with a club logo and clutching a long, slim bag that suggests oboe or hockey stick. Given their blatant lasciviousness towards Ella, I'm guessing the latter.

'You've still got it,' laughs Saira. 'If that was me, they'd be shouting, "Put it back on, love."'

Saira has always been the most self-deprecating of us, perhaps as a defence mechanism because, despite her flirting skills, the boys at school had rarely expressed an interest in her beyond friendship. This, I feel, was because her father had strictly forbidden her from wearing any make-up or fashionable clothes, so whilst the rest of us had slavishly followed each and every trend of our teenage years, Saira had remained stoically frumpy and, consequently, written off in the desirable stakes.

I hadn't fared much better, even *with* the supposed advantages of make-up and trendy clothes. I'd had a couple of snogs behind the bike sheds and managed a two-month 'relationship' with Tommy Miles, which consisted of three cinema outings to watch films he wanted to see, and one Saturday morning hanging around 'town' before he dumped me for someone else, but other than that . . . *nada*.

Ella the mono-browed schoolgirl had been largely overlooked by boys too, but she had morphed into a stunning twenty-something, a veritable prom queen who always nabbed the coolest guy with seemingly little effort. Her friends might know that the toned tummy and pert buttocks were achieved and maintained via thrice-weekly hard slogs in the gym, and the blonde hair and glowing skin required monthly (and expensive) trips to her local hairdresser-cum-beauty spa, but the men in her life thought it was all God-given.

I say *men*, because Ella had several boyfriends throughout her twenties, all gorgeous and all enthusiastically monogamous. She was spoilt for choice, flitting seamlessly from one to the next when a relationship hit even the smallest stumbling block. All the signs were that she'd nab herself a doting multimillionaire and have lots of beautiful, high-achieving children.

Meanwhile, I had 'enjoyed' – I use the word loosely – a couple of short-lived, rather lacklustre dalliances before meeting Dean when I was twenty-eight and settling into lacklustre longevity, and Saira had gone underground for a couple of furtive 'everything else but strictly non-penetrative' flings away from the ever-watchful eye of her father. Then Abbas had come along and they were still blissfully happy.

Ignoring the slightly less blissful state of *my* home life, it's ironic that Saira and I ended up settled whilst Ella's undoubted charms are being frittered away on a man whose idea of commitment is to spend the night.

Yet whenever Saira or I have attempted to broach the thorny subject that the grass may be greener elsewhere, Ella always counters with, 'Really? And what if it's just Astroturf?'

As we sink into contented silence on the coach on the way to the hotel, I take the opportunity to really study her as she taps out a text message on her ever-present iPhone.

Her sleek, shoulder-length blonde hair is scraped back into an immaculate ponytail, accentuating her high cheekbones. She's wearing make-up, but it's so expertly applied that you have to look closely to tell, and her clothes are a chic combo of aforementioned tight T-shirt, nicely faded 7 for All Mankind jeans and pristine white Converse trainers. It's a seemingly effortless look, but she freely admits she pores over the fashion pages of magazines and simply copies any style she likes.

She looks up and catches me staring.

'Penny for them?' she smiles.

I was just wondering why someone as lovely as you is with someone as unremarkable as Philip, I muse, before smiling back and replying: 'Who are you texting?'

'Philip.' She looks faintly sheepish. 'He just wants to know that I've landed safely.'

Resisting the urge to grab her phone and fling it out of the speeding coach window, before declaring, 'You are now your own woman, answerable to no one,' I rummage in my handbag to find my own steam-driven mobile. Dean didn't ask me to text him, but I do so to make myself feel wanted.

Have arrived safely. It's boiling!! I type and send.

Ping. The rest of his body parts might be approaching rigor mortis through lack of use, but Dean's forefingers and thumbs are superhero-sized from texting and changing TV channels.

Have fun x.

OK, so it's not exactly Cyrano de Bergerac, but at least he replied. I gaze soulfully out of the coach window and ponder my life. Am I happy? Hmm, let's start with an easier one . . . Am I *unhappy*? No, not really, compared to those suffering some of life's truly devastating events. I'm not a mother weeping at the grave of her dead child. I'm not starving or homeless. I'm not even mildly troubled by something out of my control. I'm just a little numb, perhaps, wading through the motions, and notions, of what a relationship is supposed to be. I have companionship, I have security, I have comfort . . . all hunkydory if you're seventy, but thirty-four? Shouldn't there be *more* than that? Or am I being churlishly unrealistic?

'That's a big sigh.'

I turn and find Saira looking at me quizzically.

'A sigh of contentment,' I hedge. She knows I have misgivings about the predictability of my relationship with Dean, but I don't want to go back down that road during a bumpy coach ride. Besides, she always plays devil's advocate and says if I want unpredictability, I might end up with someone like Philip. But there must be a middle ground where comfort and passion can walk hand in hand.

Or at least, I like to think so.

'It's on a busy roundabout. Lovely,' says Ella matter-of-factly.

'It didn't show that on the website,' I mutter. 'Anyway, let's actually enter the bloody place before we start moaning, eh?'

Apart from her choice of bedfellow, one of the things that annoys me most about Ella is her reluctance to help organise any part of a holiday or even restaurant booking but her enthusiasm to criticise it. Not that I'd actually *let* her organise any part of it, of course, but her willingness to nit-pick still rankles.

The Hotel Jacaranda is indeed a behemoth of a place, casting its substantial shadow across a busy road junction and roundabout. But as we enter the foyer, I am relieved to see the building reaches far back, with plenty of rooms away from the noise. And if previous experience is anything to go by, Ella will move rooms at least six times anyway.

In the old days, we used to squeeze into one room, tossing a coin as to who would occupy the extra camp bed. But these days, older and less financially strapped, I have booked us two rooms, one for me and Saira, and one for Ella and her make-up.

The Jacaranda is classed as a four-star hotel and the foyer is impressive, with shiny beige marble floors and an ornate staircase curling down towards a vast dining room. The pool is large and clean, if a little chilly, and the bar situated far enough away from any rooms so the noise won't disrupt someone's sleep. Most importantly, Saira's, who announces she has two years of it to catch up on.

'Great, I'm sharing a room with Rip van bloody Winkle,' I puff, dragging my suitcase towards the lift.

We are in adjoining rooms on the second floor, quite a schlep from the foyer but equally removed from the potentially noisy communal recreation rooms, so we're happy. Our balconies overlook the pool area, empty now except for a hardy gentleman swimming back and forth in the twilight.

Saira flops onto the bed with her mobile phone pressed to her ear.

'Hello, darling, it's Mummy!' She waits expectantly. 'It's Mummy . . . M-u-mmy. Are you having a lovely time with Daddy?'

Out on the balcony, I roll my eyes. Rashid is only two, for God's sake: he's hardly going to have a coherent conversation. I wonder whether I should have opted to share with Ella instead, but she'll probably be reporting in to Philip every four seconds, so perhaps Saira's calls home are preferable.

I baulk slightly, shocked at my instinctive cynicism about my friends' personal lives. Sure, Saira is besotted with her son, but that's normal, and she doesn't endlessly bang on about him to her childless friends like some women do. And for all Philip's faults, at least he's *interested* in Ella's whereabouts, even if it is in a rather stifling, controlling way. If I didn't return home a week today, I muse, I wonder how long it would be before Dean noticed and reported me missing? A day? A week? When the fridge was empty?

I wander back into the room just as Ella sashays through the connecting door.

'How's yours?' I ask, knowing it is likely to be identical to ours.

'Not enough room to swing a kitten, but it'll do.' She plonks herself next to Saira, who has now finished her phone call and is lying with a pillow wedged against her cheek.

'So what's the plan?'

I peer out of the window and down towards the bar area. It isn't exactly humming, but there are a few people sitting around drinking and I can hear the faint tinkling of the in-house pianist.

'Why don't we go as we are, just for a quick drink? Radical, I know,' I say to Ella, who is looking horrified at the prospect of leaving the room without at least an hour's preparation time.

'Suits me.' Saira leaps to her feet. 'A quick brush of my hair and I'm ready.'

'I'll meet you down there,' says Ella hastily. 'I just

want to freshen up. You never know who you might bump into.'

'Yes, I hear Steven Spielberg is in there all the time,' I quip. 'Just hanging out, looking for unknowns to cast in his next blockbuster.'

She pokes her tongue out at me and disappears back through the connecting door, leaving Saira and me to lead the way.

Little do I know that *I'm* about to meet someone who will throw an emotional hand grenade into my ordered life.

Chapter Four

The pianist is murdering David Gray's 'Sail Away' as we saunter nonchalantly into the bar.

'Christ, I wish he bleeding would sail away,' I whisper, placing my palm in the small of Saira's back and propelling her to a table as far away from him as possible.

I pick up the drinks menu and peruse it. 'Right, we're in Tenerife and it's the *law* that we must start our holiday with some radioactive cocktail . . . the more obscenely named, the better. I'm having the Carpet Burner.'

'How is that obscene?' asks Saira, taking the menu from my extended hand.

'Well, you know . . . carpet burns.'

She looks at me blankly.

'Please don't tell me that in all my years of knowing you, I have been blissfully unaware that you didn't know about carpet burns and have therefore failed in my duty to enlighten you on all matters sexual . . .'

'You have indeed,' she says gravely. 'You forget, I was never a wanton slut like you. I've led a sheltered life.'

'Watch it, you.' I flick her ear. 'I've never actually had

carpet burns myself, but I know a woman who has . . . Ah, here she is now.'

Ella is doing her best Marilyn Monroe walk across the bar, attracting admiring glances from every man present and even a couple of middle-aged women with suspiciously matching short back and sides, and comfy shoes.

'For God's sake,' I greet her, 'tell the Virgin Mary here about carpet burns, will you? I'll get the drinks in.'

Clutching the drinks menu, I walk over to the bar and order my choice – specifying no ice as it always takes up the valuable space where alcohol should be – plus a Bit on the Side for Ella and a Virgin's Pleasure for Saira. I have no idea of the ingredients in either, but the names amuse me.

As I walk back to the girls, balancing the garishly decorated drinks on a small silver tray, I pass a table where two men are deep in conversation. One is big and stocky, of rugby-player build, the other slimmer with short brown hair and wearing one of the worst jumpers I have ever seen, a fine-knit aberration of red and orange squares with overlying green squiggles.

He glances up and smiles at me. At least, I *think* it's me, but I look back over my shoulder just in case. Nope, no one else in his eyeline, so I smile back uncertainly and carry on back to my table.

'Here you go. A Virgin's Pleasure . . .' I place it in front of Saira, who looks intrigued, '. . . and a Bit on the Side for you.'

Ella pokes her tongue out at me before eyeing it suspiciously and asking: 'What's in it?'

'Probably your entire calorie allowance for the week,' I quip. 'But we're on holiday, so to hell with it.' I lift my glass and they do likewise. 'Here's to a well-deserved week of fun and relaxation,' I toast, and we all tap our glasses together.

Out of the corner of my eye, I spot the man in the garish jumper walking past us, presumably on his way to the loo. On the way back a few minutes later, he smiles at me again and I respond with a pathetic grimace that suggests I have wind. I have always been woeful at flirting, if indeed that's what's happening here.

Saira, however, despite Abbas being the only man she's ever slept with, is a masterful flirt. From top-flight businessmen right through to mini-cab drivers who don't even have English as a first language, she has them all eating out of her hand. Even the blatantly gay air steward on the flight over was clearly in her thrall, catering to her every whim while I had to practically lie prostrate in the aisle to get his attention.

'There are only three times when a woman shouldn't flirt,' she always says. 'When she's sick, pregnant or on the witness stand.'

And Ella rarely has to bother making even the slightest effort with the opposite sex, because men are drawn to her regardless, but I need all the persuasive skills I can get.

He's gone now, back to his seat, where he'll no doubt tell his friend he's just seen a woman with heartburn and a lousy taste in cocktails.

Draining the remnants of my Carpet Burner, I clap my hands together like an overexcited holiday rep and declare: 'I'm ready to party!'

'I'm not,' says Saira resolutely, and even Ella looks doubtful.

'Exactly *when* did you two hit middle age?' I challenge.

'Cup of cocoa and a nice game of Scrabble on the balcony, is it?'

Saira widens her eyes to suggest that, yes, that does indeed sound like her idea of a perfect end to our fledgling evening.

'I actually heard my favourite song playing in a lift the other day,' she says as further proof of her advancing years.

'We're on ho-li-day,' I emphasise, 'and correct me if I'm wrong, but I don't *think* we booked through Saga.'

Ella makes a small harrumphing noise. 'Where do you want to go?' Her reluctant tone suggests I'm asking her to trek bareback on donkeys up the Himalayas.

'Well, apparently, the beach is just a few minutes' walk from here, so I thought we could go and have a drink with a sea view.' I look from one to the other. 'You can have bloody Horlicks if you want.'

'Go on, then,' agrees Saira, 'but I don't want to be long because there's a pillow up there with my name on it.' She jabs her finger towards the ceiling.

As we get up to leave, I notice the man in the atrocious jumper has gone.

'Now then, isn't this lovely?' I enthuse, gesturing towards the seafront just as an inebriated man stops right in front of us and vomits on the pavement.

'Really special,' drawls Ella, drawing her pashmina tighter around her shoulders.

Admittedly, the wind coming in from the sea is a little chilly, and certain other holidaymakers do leave a little to be desired, but other than that, I'm really enjoying myself. The bar we have chosen is buzzing and our front-row seats are positioned perfectly for a clear view of the passing 'promenaders'.

'All human life is here,' I smile, nodding discreetly towards a couple walking by. He's about sixty-five and wearing black leather trousers with red cowboy boots, and his wife – judging by the humongous diamond on her left hand – is about twenty-five, with bouffant blonde hair, breasts spilling out of a diamanté-studded corset top, and pneumatic lips resembling overstuffed cocktail sausages. They're a Beryl Cook painting personified.

'It sure is.' Ella jerks her head towards somewhere over my shoulder. 'I think someone got dressed in the dark.'

I swivel round surreptitiously, or so I think, to be confronted by He of the Dreadful Jumper, strolling towards the bar with his friend. I snap my head back round again, praying he hasn't noticed me staring.

Ella and Saira, of course, are oblivious to my discomfort, and are now reminiscing about the time Saira's grandmother knitted her a fluorescent green mohair jumper that made her come out in a rash.

I laugh heartily, pretending I'm absorbed in their conversation; then after a couple of minutes I pretend to look for the waiter whilst really scanning the bar for Mr Fashion Bypass. He and his friend are sitting on the second row of chairs, about thirty feet away from us. Far enough, I figure, for him not to realise that his choice of knitwear has sparked a 'worst clothes of all time' theme on our table.

Ella is now reminding me about my first and last 'boob tube', an electric-blue Lycra number claiming to be 'one size'. Unfortunately, the size was clearly ten and my size-fourteen left breast had popped out of it during a particularly frenetic dancing session at our local nightclub. At the time, just sixteen and painfully self-conscious, I had wanted the ground to swallow me up. For months afterwards, I wore clothes that made burkas seem revealing, such was my desire to see the whole, horrible experience put to rest. But I realise now that my acute embarrassment had the reverse effect, keeping it fresh in people's minds for far longer than if I'd just laughed it off. Funny how it's only age and your own experiences that teach you things no one can. The sad irony is that now I'm approaching thirty-five, I finally feel my head is together just as my body is undoubtedly starting to fall apart.

'I'm going to the loo,' I say. 'Let's have one more round of drinks, then head back to the hotel.'

I expect Saira or Ella to make noises about leaving immediately, but they don't. It seems they're finally getting into the holiday spirit, but then it *is* still only half past ten.

As I sit in the cubicle listening to the distant throb of music and chat outside, I wonder what Dean is doing now. Correction: I *know* what he's doing now – sitting in his dent on the sofa, watching football highlights or perhaps reruns of *Only Fools and Horses*, with the remnants of a takeaway at his feet. I wonder if he's missing me at all. Probably not. After all, it has only been a day so far.

I smile to myself for being so silly. Dean and I may not be love's young dream, but we *do* love each other in our own way, I'm sure of it. When King Edward VII died, his widow, Queen Alexandra, reportedly said: 'Now at least I know where he is!' Perhaps *I* should be thinking, At least I know where he is . . . and he's alive. In other words, be grateful for small mercies.

I return to the table with a spring in my step, determined to have a good time.

'I'm actually *excited* about going to bed,' says Saira. 'How pathetic is that?'

'Quite a lot,' I reply.

Before we came, Saira warned me that the relentless grind of caring for a young child from six o'clock most mornings had taken its toll. 'I'll party for a couple of nights,' she promised, 'but I need to rest too because I'm absolutely knackered. You'll probably think I'm a lightweight killjoy, but when you get round to having kids you'll understand.'

I probably will, but right now we're back in the brightly lit foyer of our hotel, where I'm staring wistfully at a group of young women nearby, clearly preparing to go out just as we're getting ready to retire for the night. Judging by their matching pink tiaras and T-shirts bearing the slogan 'Jade's last hurrah', I'm guessing it's a hen weekend.

I must look particularly melancholic, because Ella pipes up: 'I don't mind having a quick drink in the bar now I know my bed is just a short lift ride away.'

'Great!' My spirits lift. 'Let's go.'

We kiss good night to Saira and head down the staircase towards the bar, where the pianist has either been shot for crimes against music or has simply finished his shift and been succeeded by a woman now singing 'My Cherie Amour' rather well.

There are about twenty people spread around, mostly in couple formations, and quite a few of the women scan

Ella as she walks in before hastily glancing at their husband to see if he's doing the same. As ever, I feel invisible next to her, for ever condemned to be the clichéd 'fat friend'.

Opting for a glass of white wine this time, we sit at a table for four near the door. I'm halfway through a monologue about the advantages of Tenerife over Lanzarote when Ella's phone makes a beeping noise and she grabs it faster than Billy the Kid after a Red Bull, leaving me trailing off mid-sentence.

She looks mildly troubled by whatever it is she's reading, then taps away at the keys whilst I stare into space and resist the temptation to submerge the bloody thing in her drink.

'Sorry,' she smiles quickly. 'I'll just send this and then I'll be back with you.'

By contrast, my phone is lurking in the depths of my handbag, vying for space with the basics I carried on the plane. It's on silent mode and I check it about once every couple of hours for any missed calls. Is that another glaringly obvious sign that I'm just not in love with Dean, I ponder, because if I am, then surely I too would be pouncing on my phone the minute I thought it made a squeak? Or is it simply the difference between being in a relationship that's safe and comfortable as opposed to one rooted in emotional uncertainty?

'Who is it?' I ask, curious now.

'Philip. He just wants to know whether I'm back safely at the hotel.'

'*Safely?* We're in Tenerife, not frigging Afghanistan.'

She purses her fulsome lips disapprovingly. 'He worries about me, that's all.'

'What, and Dean doesn't care about me?' I snap.

'I didn't say that.'

No, but I did. Probably because, deep down, that's what I feel, whether it's true or not. Sensing I might be about to say something I'll later regret, I push back my chair, mumble something about needing a wee and head off towards the loo, where I brush my untangled hair and wash my fairly clean hands just to pass some time.

Walking purposefully back out to the corridor, I recoil as I bump straight into someone heading the same way.

'Sorry, entirely my fault,' I bluster, then instantaneously freeze as my eyes rest on a red and orange blur. It's *him*.

'Are you stalking me?' His face is deadpan but his eyes are smiling.

'I could say the same to you.'

'Damn, she's found me out.' He clicks his fingers in mock exasperation. 'Have you just landed on these fair shores?'

I make a tutting noise. 'You're a lousy stalker. Surely you should know *exactly* when I got here?'

He bursts out laughing. 'Good one.' He starts walking along the corridor, back towards the bar, and I follow.

'We arrived a few hours ago,' I say. 'I haven't even unpacked yet.'

'Been before?'

'Years ago. And it wasn't this area. It was the cheaper bit down the coast.'

'Well, in that case, you need to talk to an old hand who's been here, oooh, at least six days.' He holds the door open for me.

'Good idea. Where's the best bar?'

'Ah, a woman after my own heart.' He scratches his chin whilst I linger awkwardly, waiting for an answer.

42

'I'll tell you what. Tomorrow, me and my mate Jason are driving to a lovely, non-touristy beach we've been tipped off about. Why don't you and your friends join us, then if you're up for it, we can take you to a couple of decent bars around here tomorrow night?'

'Sounds good,' I reply instinctively and selfishly. Then I remember there are other considerations. 'But I'd better consult my friends first. One is already in bed, so I won't be able to let you know until the morning, if that's all right?'

He shrugs. 'Sure. We won't be leaving until about ten, I reckon, so if you want to come, meet us in the foyer just before that. If you're not there, I'll assume it's a no.' He holds out a hand. 'I'm Tom, by the way.'

'Cam,' I smile, praying he doesn't ask what it's short for.

'OK, Cam. See you tomorrow . . . maybe.'

I bound back to the table like Bugs Bunny after an espresso, grinning from ear to ear.

'Bloody hell!' exclaims Ella. 'You've gone from major grumpiness to hysterical joy in sixty seconds. Have you taken something?'

'No.' I laugh disproportionately to her mildly amusing comment. 'It's just my natural *joie de vivre*.'

She still looks suspicious but doesn't pursue it, and I say nothing about my encounter or the proposed plans for tomorrow.

I have a feeling Saira and Ella won't be keen, and I have no intention of going alone. So I will need a convincing argument and all my persuasive powers to pull it off. Which means I need to be sober. Which also means I won't broach the idea until the morning.

'Come on, then.' I drain my glass and stand up,

grabbing Ella's mobile from the table. 'I'll just text Philip and tell him you're making the journey from the bar to your room and that you'll text him in ten minutes to let him know you arrived safely.'

'Fuck off,' she says amiably.

Chapter Five

'Have you lost your mind? They could be a couple of serial killers who prey on gullible women,' hisses Saira under her breath, violently jabbing a fork into her fried egg.

I cast my eyes around the dining room, checking that Tom and Jason aren't lurking behind a potted palm, but there's no sign of them.

'I'm no criminal psychologist, but serial killers don't tend to hang around in pairs and book package holidays in Tenerife,' I hiss back, raising my eyes heavenward.

'That's what they *want* you to think.'

We lapse into silence, her wolfing down the rest of her vegetarian fry-up, me staring enviously at it whilst disconsolately stirring my low-fat yoghurt.

'Look, it could be a laugh,' I persist. 'And let's face it, the chances of us exploring another part of the island without the aid of someone else's transport are negligible.'

'To be honest, Cam, I just want to lie on a sunlounger and dribble. If the frigging Hanging Gardens of Babylon were just a bus ride away, I couldn't be arsed.'

'All you have to do is be driven to a nice beach, where you can lie and do nothing all day while your friend runs back and forth bringing you lovely cold drinks. How hard can it *be*?' I am in danger of sounding like I'm pleading now.

Saira stops eating, her fork poised in mid-air, and studies me suspiciously. 'Hang on, what happened after I went to bed last night?'

'Eh?'

'Did you cop off with this bloke? Is that why you're so keen to drag me off to some far-flung beach when there's a perfectly nice one a few hundred yards away?'

'Certainly not!' I protest huffily, my face flushing. 'I spoke to him for about three minutes, that's all.'

'And now we're all hopping in his car for an Enid Blyton *Five Go Mad at the Seaside* adventure?' She narrows her eyes. 'What's going on here?'

'Nothing!' I reply, a little too loudly. 'For God's sake, can't men and women just hang out together without everyone thinking there's an ulterior motive?'

'Er, not on this occasion they can't, no. We've come on a *girls'* holiday and on day one you're seeking the company of some bloke you don't even know and, by your own admission, have spoken to for only three minutes. It doesn't make sense.'

She's right, of course. It doesn't. And it's only now she's made me confront this fact that I even admit to myself that there may be another agenda.

'Look,' I sigh resignedly, 'I *like* him, that's all.'

'I like lots of people, but it doesn't mean I want to trot off and spend the day with them all.' She frowns slightly. 'What exactly are you saying here?'

Damn Saira and her finely tuned emotional intelligence.

I shake my head. 'I don't know. It's not a big deal, but I noticed him when we first went into the hotel bar last

46

night, mainly because he was wearing a toxically dreadful jumper. Then he was in that beach bar, and I saw him again back here after you'd gone to bed. We had a brief chat in the corridor outside the loos.' I pause and smile sheepishly at her. 'There was just *something* that clicked, I'm not sure why, and I feel compelled to see him again, that's all. Nothing deeper than that.'

Saira is now shaking her head and making a little siren noise. 'Uh-oh. What about Dean?'

'What are you *talking* about?' I gasp in disbelief. 'I am merely suggesting going to the beach with someone, that's all. I'm not bloody eloping.'

'You used the word "compelled".' She raises one eyebrow. 'I felt *compelled* to spend more time with Abbas after our first meeting and we've got a child now.'

'Are you taking the piss?'

'A bit,' she grins. 'But I still maintain that women in happy relationships don't feel *compelled* to actively seek the company of a virtual stranger they meet on holiday. Particularly when they have two perfectly good mates to keep them amused.'

She looks at me questioningly and I feel an over-whelming urge to share the thoughts that have been troubling me in recent weeks. My only fear is that by actually voicing them to someone else, I will make them real and have to do something about them.

She's looking at me expectantly, so I make a quick sweep of the restaurant to establish that Ella isn't looming into view, knowing this might be a long, complex conversation that needs time to breathe.

'I'm not sure if I'm happy,' I falter, unable to think of a better way to put it.

'Okaaaay,' she says slowly. 'In what way?'

'With Dean.'

She smiles. 'I kind of figured that's what you meant. None of us is reluctant to moan openly about our jobs, are we? Besides, we've touched on this before . . .'

'I know. But before it was a faint niggle and now it's a sodding great nag.'

'I see.' She protrudes her lower lip. 'In what way do you think you're not happy?'

'I don't really know.' I have the grace to look sheepish at my own emotional ineptitude. 'This is the first time I've really admitted it to myself, let alone anyone else, so I haven't figured out the finer details yet.'

Saira's expression darkens slightly. 'He doesn't . . . you know . . . *abuse* you in any way, does he?'

I'm utterly horrified I may have led her in any way even to think that. 'Oh God, no, not at all. He would never do that. He's way too kind and gentle.'

She looks faintly perplexed by my description of characteristics that many women would seek in their perfect man. 'So what is it, then?'

'I think I'm *bored*,' I blurt emphatically.

I expect her to view this pronouncement to be as earth-shatteringly grave as I do, but she simply shakes her head and smiles. 'We all feel like that from time to time. Life *is* boring sometimes, and so are relationships. You've probably just lost your spark, that's all,' she says soothingly. 'We all do occasionally. It gets snuffed out under the daily grind of trudging to and from work, paying bills, fixing that dodgy cupboard handle . . . whatever. But don't worry, it'll resurface again. You just have to work at it.'

'Let's have some new clichés, shall we?' I smile.

She pokes out her tongue. 'It's true, though. And I think you're thinking too deeply about it all. I'm happy in my marriage, but it doesn't mean everything is perfect, it just means I have decided to see beyond the imperfections.'

I'm unconvinced and must look it, because she lets out a frustrated sigh.

'Cam, it can't be hearts and flowers all the time.'

'I know, but *some* of the time might be nice. His idea of a romantic gesture is letting me watch what I want on the telly.'

She purses her lips. 'Have you said any of this to him?'

'What, "Oh, hi, Dean, could you be a bit less bloody tedious, please?"'

'Stop being facetious.' She pushes her empty plate to one side and fixes me with a stern look. 'What I mean is, have you tried telling him that things have become a little stale and that perhaps both of you could start making more of an effort? You never know, he might feel the same way.'

'Saira,' I say leadenly, 'you've met Dean. It won't even have crossed his mind that we're in a bit of a rut. He opens the fridge, it has food in it. He sits on the sofa, there's Sky to watch. He gets into bed, and I'm in it. What more does he need?'

She pulls a disapproving face. 'Come on, you're sounding bitter. He's a decent bloke; you have to give him a chance. If you haven't said anything to him, then he will assume you're happy with how things are. He's a mobile-phone salesman, not a bloody mind-reader.'

'Maybe.' I shrug. 'But even so, I feel like it'll be flogging a dead horse. You can't make someone something they're not. What did my grandma used to say? "Character is like a fence, it can't be strengthened by whitewash."'

'How very defeatist of you,' she counters flatly. 'It sounds to me like you've given up on him already, that you're not even prepared to try in case it works.'

'No, that's not true.'

'How long have you felt this way?'

I purse my lips in thought. 'Six months? Maybe slightly longer.'

'And you've been together six years, which tells you that there must be *something* you liked about him before now!' she declares triumphantly.

'I don't dislike him at all. I just don't feel like he's *the one*.'

'Ah, the ever elusive *one*.' She smiles indulgently. 'Cam, you're a bright woman. Please don't tell me you buy into the age-old crap that there's only one person on the planet that we're meant to be with?'

'No, I don't. But you can't talk. You always say that when you met Abbas it felt right.'

'Yes, as in he was *someone* I felt I could be with for the rest of my life, not the *only* one. If he hadn't been the cousin of a cousin, I'm sure that eventually I would have met someone else and married him. Sure, it's about a feeling you get, but it's also about making a decision and just getting on with it.'

'OK, well, I don't get that feeling with Dean.'

'And you do with the bloke you met in the bar last night?' She looks at me pointedly.

'Don't be daft. To be honest, he just seems a bit of a laugh and I could do with one right now.'

'Gee, thanks.'

I playfully punch her arm. 'I don't mean it that way, just that sometimes it's good to broaden one's horizons.'

'Hmm, well, let's see what Ella reckons about your proposed day out. Here she comes now.'

'Drive carefully! It's not just cars that can be recalled by their maker, you know,' booms Saira anxiously. Then, hissing at me out of the corner of her mouth, she adds: 'I can't believe I let you talk me into this.'

We're squished into the back of a rented Toyota Rav4 that was probably last serviced during the Boer War, and bumping our way along a dirt track leading to what, we hope, is a beach. Saira has already banged her head twice on the roll bar and is looking disturbingly mutinous.

Ella, by contrast, is having a wonderful time . . . back at the hotel pool, reclining on a sunlounger with the latest summer read. She flatly refused to come on our little outing, dramatically declaring that she'd rather dip her freshly manicured feet in boiling oil and feed them to wild coyotes. Reassuringly, she also demanded to know the safe code for our room, so she can access her passport and ticket home in the event that Saira and I have made a severe error of judgement and are about to star in the latest *Blair Witch* film.

To say I feel a surge of relief when we turn a corner and encounter a stretch of beach would be a masterly understatement.

'Ta-dah!' Tom leaps out of the front seat and gestures towards the glittering sea. The beach is about a hundred metres long and there are just three other people on it – locals, judging by the deep mahogany hue of their tans.

'Welcome to our own private paradise,' grins Jason, opening the boot and pulling out an ice box. 'There aren't any shops or bars nearby, so we've bought our own provisions.'

'And what about lavatories?' enquires Saira tightly.

'I reckon that clump of bushes over there is the best place,' he replies, peering into the distance.

'Charming.' Saira shoots me yet another dirty look.

'That looks familiar.' Keen to change the subject, I squint at the large blanket Tom is laying out on the beach.

'It's the bedspread from the hotel room,' he says sheepishly. 'I'll sneak it back in later.'

Sitting down and admiring the surroundings, I must admit it's a beautiful spot, unsullied by tourists and their residual rubbish. The sand is still the silvery, volcanic black typical of the area, but minus the fag butts, ring-pulls and occasional dog turd of the more accessible beaches. If *we* had a hire car, it's definitely somewhere I'd come to again, armed with nibbles and books, and relishing the peace, but I feel it's a little rustic for my two comfort-loving girlfriends.

But right now, I'm wondering how on earth we're going to fill the long silences that always feel so awkward when you're with people you hardly know.

'So how long are you here for?' asks Jason. Well, at least he didn't talk about the weather.

'A week,' says Saira. 'This is day one and I haven't even dipped my toe in the hotel pool yet.'

She looks at me pointedly and, yet again, I feel awful for persuading her to come. But then I look around me, taking in the beautiful beach, blistering sunshine and chilled white wine and think, How bad can it be? Methinks she doth protest too much.

'We've been here nearly a week already,' sighs Jason. 'It's back to dreary old Blighty tomorrow.'

Is that a pang of disappointment I'm feeling at the thought that Tom is leaving so soon, or is it merely a spot of tummy trouble from last night's comedy cocktail?

'Where do you live?' Saira drags a forefinger back and forth in the sand.

'Birmingham.' Jason's Midlands accent is very pronounced. 'You?'

'London. But my parents live in Erdington.'

As they start to share stories on the joys of England's 'second city', I tune out and make use of my mirrored sunglasses to appear as though I am staring straight ahead out to sea, but really I'm glimpsing sideways to study Tom more closely.

He's unpacking the ice box, laying out four glasses that also look suspiciously like hotel issue, and tearing open bags of crisps and peanuts.

I'm pleased to announce that the ghastly jumper is nowhere to be seen, replaced by a sky-blue polo shirt and faded dark blue cotton shorts. His tanned feet are bare.

I reckon he's about five feet ten, weighing about twelve stone. His eyes are hazel and he has a larger than average nose and full lips. Overall, he has a pleasant, open face that's enhanced greatly when he flashes his slightly uneven, but enviably white teeth. He reminds me somewhat of Christopher Eccleston, the ninth Doctor in *Doctor Who*, and a secret crush of mine.

Jason is now telling Saira all about his job as a motor mechanic and how it's a good career because people will always drive cars.

'Except her,' she smiles, jerking her head in my direction. 'She's failed her test six times. On the last one, she—'

'Saira!' I interject. 'They don't need to know that.'

'Oh, I think we do,' says Tom through a mouthful of peanuts.

'She hit a woman on a zebra crossing.'

Tom's mouth has now fallen open, revealing a mishmash of crushed nuts.

'Only a little bit.' I hold my thumb and forefinger one centimetre apart to illustrate how minor I feel my misdemeanour was.

'They found the victim's shoe *forty feet* away,' adds the woman I foolishly refer to as my friend.

Tom's mouth has now closed, but his hand is clamped against it. 'Was she OK?' he mumbles.

'Right as rain,' I trill.

'After a month of physio,' scoffs Saira.

'But luckily, I got top marks in my cycling proficiency,' I quip, 'so the world is safe.'

There's a stunned silence for a few seconds, then Tom clears his throat. 'Were you arrested?'

I wince slightly, anxious to move on from this uncomfortable subject. 'Yes, but I was never charged. There was some legal issue over culpability because of the dual controls the instructor is supposed to use in an emergency.'

'Watch what you're saying,' grins Jason, 'or it'll be taken down and used against you.'

'Sorry?' I frown.

'He's a policeman.' He nods towards Tom. 'Just made detective sergeant. He's going to go far, that boy.'

'Detective?' asks Saira. 'What, like solving murders and stuff?'

Tom laughs self-consciously. 'More of the "stuff", actually, and it's invariably mundane. I'm really keen to move across to the murder squad at some point, but thankfully murders are still pretty rare in my area. For now, it's minor burglaries and shoplifting, that kind of thing.'

He offers us each a glass of white wine, which we take. Jason has grabbed himself a beer.

'What do you two do?' he asks.

'I'm a hairdresser and Saira's a psychotherapist,' I reply, at which point Jason's eyes light up and Saira immediately raises her hand.

'If you're going to start telling me about some emotional issue you've had since childhood, please don't,' she says. 'I'm on holiday: the consulting room is closed.'

'Actually, I was going to ask Cam for some advice . . .'

'Never give yourself a haircut after three margaritas,' I quip.

'And what about an effective remedy for male pattern baldness,' he grins, tapping his receding hairline. 'I have tried a few miracle cures but, as you can see, they didn't work.'

'To quote the goddess that is Dolly Parton, "Just because you've lost your fuzz, don't mean you ain't a peach."'

I laugh, then notice that Tom is staring at me intently, causing a blindingly obvious blush to colour my other-wise pale face. He quickly looks away, leaving me wondering whether he *was* actually staring, or simply gazing in my direction, deep in thought about something, or someone, else.

'I'm married,' Saira suddenly announces apropos of nothing, 'and she . . .' She turns to look at me.

'. . . isn't married,' I interject swiftly, shooting her a quick glare that I hope the others can't see.

I can only assume she clocked Tom staring at me too and decided to intervene to save me from myself, in the annoying, ham-fisted way friends often do. She glares back.

'Guess what Cam is short for,' she says, surreptitiously poking her tongue out at me. She may have shut up about Dean, but she sure as hell isn't going to let me off lightly.

'Um, Camshaft?' jokes Jason.

'No! Try again.' She's loving this.

'Camilla? Or Camille . . . like in France?' volunteers Tom.

'Nope.'

They both shrug resignedly.

'Camomile!'

'Actually, that's rather pretty,' says Tom.

I could hug him. And not just because he's being so kind to me.

'But I take it you don't like it?'

I shake my head. 'It's not the name as such, just the tiresome effort of having to explain it to people all the time.'

'In that case, we won't add to your pain by asking,' he grins, smoothing out a corner of the blanket.

A comfortable silence descends, but before I can fully relax, Saira's back on her mission to destroy.

'What about you two? Are you married?' She looks pointedly at Tom, but he shakes his head and my insides flutter slightly.

'No, we're both single boys about town,' he smiles.

'Well, I am,' interjects Jason. 'And he's usually my arresting officer.'

'It must be hard having a policeman for a mate, though,' muses Saira. 'I'd feel I have to be on my best behaviour all the time.'

'Nonsense,' Tom scoffs, topping up our wine glasses in the process. 'Although, to be honest, I think it's probably what I *don't* know about Jason that makes us such good friends!'

He stands up and brushes the sand from his legs. 'Now come on, enough of this boring work talk, who fancies coming for a swim?'

Saira shakes her head and Jason lies down and closes his eyes.

'Hmm, think that's probably a no, then.'

'Nice work, Detective,' I grin. 'I'm not massively keen on cold water either, to be honest, but I'm more than happy to stand on the shore and make supportive noises while you immerse yourself in it.'

I stand up and start walking towards the water's edge about a hundred metres away. I don't look back but am convinced I can feel Saira's disapproval burning a hole in the back of my neck.

As I reach the shallows, wincing slightly as the cold water laps my toes, I feel a swishing sensation by my right arm as Tom runs past me, taking great strides through the shallows, then diving in head first when he reaches the deeper waters. I watch him swim a confident freestyle back and forth for a few minutes, then close my eyes and tilt my face towards the sun. It feels glorious, a world away from the grey predictability of my life back home.

Something cold hits my face and I open my eyes to find Tom flicking water at me. He sits down on the sand at my feet, patting the patch next to him. It's wet but I don't care.

'I love the sea,' he says dreamily. 'When I was a child, we lived in north Cornwall, just outside Bude. I was a bit of a surf dude and my dad kept a small sailing boat. He absolutely loved it.'

'So how did such a waterbaby end up in landlocked Birmingham?'

'Divorce.' He shrugs almost imperceptibly. 'Dad sailed off into the sunset with his best friend's wife. Literally. They went off to tour the Balearics, leaving Mum to cope alone with me and my younger sister. She went where she could find work, which turned out to be the production line at British Leyland.'

'How old were you?'

'Fifteen. I had to grow up very quickly.'

I nod. 'That's a tough age to cope with your dad walking out.'

He looks at me curiously. 'Am I sensing that's the voice of experience?'

'Kind of. Except I was early twenties and living away from home when he ran off with someone else.'

'I'll bet it still hurt, though . . .'

'All part of life's rich pattern, isn't it?' I say vaguely, not wanting to spoil this near-perfect day with sad memories from my past. 'Is your dad still with the woman he left your mum for?'

'Who knows? We kind of lost touch after a while.'

'I'm sorry to hear that. If he knew what you were up to now, he'd be really proud of you.'

Tom smiles suddenly, perhaps also recognising that this isn't a time for melancholy. 'I don't know why I'm telling you all this about people you don't even know.'

'I asked you, that's why.'

'Then it's your fault,' he says amiably. 'Don't do it again.'

'Aye, aye, Sarge.' I make a salute sign and hop to my feet. 'Come on, let's rejoin the landlubbers.'

As we stroll wordlessly back towards Saira and Jason, I realise that in the past few minutes I have just learnt more about a man I barely know than I have about Dean in the past few years.

Chapter Six

'OK, let's play guess the foodstuff.' Ella points at an amorphous blob on her plate, her lip curling in distaste.

Saira studies it for a moment. 'Um, something in aspic, perhaps? Or it could be insulation foam?'

They both look at me for comment, but I raise my eyes in frustration, feeling that yet again they are nit-picking about my choice of hotel.

'Look, the rooms are clean, the beds are comfy, the location is great, and yet all you do is bloody whinge about the slightest thing,' I snap irritably. 'Neither of *you* could be arsed to research and book the holiday, but you seem very enthusiastic about shooting it down in flames.'

There follows a heavy silence, during which they both exchange not-very-surreptitious 'she's lost it'-style glances.

'I saw that,' I mutter sulkily.

'We're not having a go at you, sweetie. We're just having a laugh, that's all.' Saira prods the round jelly thing, which wobbles violently. 'You have to admit, it's not entirely obvious what it is.'

'It's blindingly obvious, actually,' I retort, and they

both look at me expectantly. 'The waitress has mislaid her breast implant.'

Saira breaks into a broad smile. 'That's the spirit!'

We're sitting in the vast dining hall of the hotel, an all-you-can-eat buffet extravaganza synonymous with a multinational boarding school. There's everything from curry to ham and chips, all congealing slightly under huge catering lights. I have just had something labelled 'rost dinner' and the gravy didn't move. You help yourself, with waitress service for drinks only – in our case, a jug of sangria.

We have paid for half board, so we're getting our money's worth. Well, Saira and I are, having made several trips back and forth, filling our plates with varying forms of unidentifiable stodge. Ella, as usual, is displaying an iron willpower, picking at a small green salad with baked potato and, now, the quivering blob, which, on closer inspection, I believe to be a mandarin jelly.

As Saira and Ella start to talk about tomorrow's prediction of slight showers, my mind drifts off to other matters, most notably why I have just suffered a severe sense of humour failure over something so trivial. It's just not me, you see. World poverty bothers me, so too bullying, bureaucracy, paedophiles and traffic wardens. But harmless gags about someone's pudding? Never. Normally, I'd be laughing like a drain.

But ever since I returned from the beach this afternoon, I have felt unsettled, as if the axis upon which my humdrum old life usually spins has been tilted slightly, making everything I do feel a little off-kilter. It's like when something's troubling you in life – be it an unexpectedly large bill or a looming court case – and even if you manage to forget about it for a little while and enjoy yourself, invariably the nagging anxiety frequently resurfaces and spoils everything.

But I don't have a large bill or impending court appearance. In a way, they would be easier to deal with. I have an impending sense of doom about going home, back to Dean and his dent in the sofa. Back to *my* own personal rut.

It's not that I've fallen head over heels in love with Tom. I haven't, I'm sure of that. It's simply that my day at the beach has hammered home to me that I seem to have more fun hanging out with Saira and a couple of casual acquaintances than I do with the man I have chosen to spend the past six years of my life with. And it's just not the heady surroundings of sun, sea and sand, because I have done that with him too and *still* not enjoyed myself as much.

In other words, it's slowly dawning on me that I might not need the emotional prop of being in a relationship, that I might just be fine on my own. But the crucial question is, have I the inclination, or even the balls to do something about it?

'Tragedeeeeeee. Well, *the feeling's gone and I can't control, it's tragedeee. Well, it's been so long and something's, er, wrong, it's tragedeeeee.*'

Saira is spinning round and round on the dance floor, her arms windmilling so violently that other guests are having to swerve out of her way. In stark contrast to the woman who sloped off to bed early the night before, she's noticeably pissed, slurring her words and laughing hysterically at nothing in particular.

'Do you think we should go and get her?' asks Ella,

eyeing her dubiously as she ricochets into a middle-aged man and spoils his sterling display of dad dancing.

'Nah, leave her. She's having fun. And so are we . . . watching her.'

The bar is half full but still lively, with a DJ who is blissfully avoiding Eurotrash pop in favour of old disco classics. As the Bee Gees' 'Tragedy' gives way to Abba's 'Dancing Queen', Saira starts gesticulating wildly in our direction.

'Oh Gawd,' mutters Ella. 'Something tells me we can't get out of this one.'

She stands up and walks towards the dance floor. I go to follow and realise that I'm slightly tipsier than I thought, clutching the side of an empty chair as I suffer a little dizzy spell along the way.

After returning from the beach, I turned down Tom's kind offer to escort us to the island's best bars on the unspoken basis that I would probably face a mutiny from Saira and Ella if I did.

'But maybe we'll catch you later in the hotel bar,' I smiled winningly, hoping he got the message that it wasn't a brush-off. But as yet, there's no sign of him.

As I sway self-consciously to the music, I try to add up what I've drunk since the wine at the beach and the two glasses of sangria at dinner. There was the double gin and tonic in the same beach bar as last night, followed by another sangria and a glass of red wine. Then, since arriving back at the hotel, I have downed another white wine and am now halfway down a ridiculously garish-looking cocktail called Radioactive Rumdinger. I feel faintly sick at the thought.

Saira has pretty much matched me drink for drink, but Ella is her usual sober self, having had only two glasses of white wine. A wilful decision that has less to do with maintaining dignity than it does with calorie content.

I feel a wave of relief (or is it nausea?) as 'Dancing Queen' draws to a close and I stumble back to the table, leaving the others to soldier on valiantly through the twelve-inch version of 'Disco Inferno'.

I grab Ella's still water and down it in one, closing my eyes in an attempt to stop the room spinning.

'Are you OK?'

I open them to find Tom towering above me. I'd like to say his look was one of concern, but I'd be lying. He is definitely finding it amusing.

'Fine. It's jusht a bit hot in here.'

'Is it? I hadn't noticed.' He smiles indulgently.

'Would you mind getting me another water?' I ask. 'Tap'll do.'

'Sure.'

He ambles off in the direction of the bar and I try to compose myself, fishing an ice cube from the depths of my glass and pressing it against my cheeks. I then stupidly run my fingers through my hair, inadvertently wetting my fringe so it clings even more to my sweating forehead.

The white cotton dress that had looked so fresh at the start of the evening is now a crumpled mess, much like its occupant.

'There you go.' He places a large bottle of still water and a clean glass in front of me but remains standing. 'Mind if I join you?'

'Go ahead.' I nod towards the empty chair that Saira is unlikely to be returning to, judging by the wildly spinning figure now gyrating to the Village People's 'Y.M.C.A.' Even Ella is joining in the fun, albeit slightly more reservedly.

'Where's Jason?'

'Sunburn,' smiles Tom. 'He looks like Po.'

'Who?'

'Po. The red Teletubby.'

'How do you know that?' I frown. 'You don't have children.'

'I do, actually.'

I pause, my brain taking longer than usual to compute this rather startling piece of information. Had I imagined the 'single men about town' part of today's conversation?

'I thought you said you were single.'

'I am.' He looks faintly bemused. 'But I also have a five-year-old son. I split up from his mum about two years ago.'

If I was in charge of my faculties, I would probably now ask him intelligent, thought-provoking questions about how he copes as a single dad, how he worries about his son's future when he's on the frontline and seeing so much crime. But as I'm hopelessly sloshed . . .

'Oh.'

We lapse into silence, him taking a mouthful of his beer, me staring at the dance floor but not really seeing anything.

'So.' He breaks the deadlock. 'Did you enjoy today?'

'Very much. Thank you.' Oh God, I sound like a nine-year-old thanking her great-aunt for a hand-knitted jumper.

'Good. Me too.'

More silence. It feels so uncomfortable that, in desperation, I take a swig of what's left of my cocktail.

'He's called Daniel.'

'Sorry?'

'My son. He's called Daniel.'

'Oh. That's a nice name.' The rush of alcohol and sugar from the cocktail rallies me slightly. 'Does he live with you?'

Tom shakes his head. 'No, that would be a little tricky with the hours I work. He lives with his mum, but I have lots of access. It's not ideal, but it seems to work for us all.'

'I don't have children.'

'I know.'

'How come?' I feel stung, as if he's perhaps picked up on a lack of maternal instinct I don't yet know about.

'Because you didn't know who Po was. When you have kids, you'll be sick of the sight of him. Or her. Whichever it is . . . I'm never sure.'

'Ah, thanks for the warning.'

He said *when* you have kids, not if. Clearly, I am radiating vast waves of maternal suitability. My mind fills with images of me running through cornfields, laughing as my two picture-book children try to catch butterflies with large nets. OK, it's a bit Timotei-shampoo ad, but a girl can dream, can't she?

'Fancy a dance?'

My romantic reverie is broken by the ugly reality of Tom asking me to approach the centre of the room and make a complete tit of myself in front of him. Dancing is not my forte. Never has been, and no amount of watching *Strictly Come Dancing* is going to change that.

'Er, I'd rather not, if you don't mind.'

'Why?' he asks unblinkingly.

'Because I'm not very good at it.'

'Me neither.' He grabs my hand and pulls me to the

nearest corner of the wooden floor, just as 'You're the One That I Want' starts up.

True to his word, he's as bad as I am, his arms flailing awkwardly whilst his legs appear to be moving to a different tune altogether.

'Hardly John Travolta and Olivia Newton-John, are we?' I giggle.

'Speak for yourself,' he replies, deadpan, doing a twirl before chugging his arms like a train and circling me.

Suddenly, for the first time since I was ten years old, I find myself following my grandmother's advice to 'always dance as if no one is watching' and enjoying every uninhibited second.

Until Saira heaves into view, that is.

'I feel shick,' she slurs in my ear. 'Need bed.'

As cries for help go, it's a pretty succinct yet incisive one. Trouble is, she's chosen someone equally sozzled as her potential saviour.

'Hang on.' Holding her arm tightly, I look over her shoulder and catch Ella's eye, jerking my head to entice her over.

'Do you mind taking Saira up to the room?' I plead.

'Sure, no problem.' She lets out a world-weary sigh. 'I've had enough dancing for one night anyway.'

She grabs Saira's other arm and starts to move away, then notices Tom standing nearby and shoots me a suspicious look. 'Aren't you coming too?'

'In a minute. I just need the loo,' I reply lamely, affecting a cross-legged wince.

'OK.' She doesn't look convinced, adding ominously, 'Be careful.'

After they've gone, I decide a visit to the loo would

actually be a good idea, if only to splash water on my face and fruitlessly check my appearance.

'Won't be a minute,' I shout to Tom.

When I re-emerge a few minutes later, he's back sitting at the table with two glasses of white wine and another bottle of water.

'I wasn't sure which you'd prefer, so I got both,' he says. 'Assuming you have time for one quick drink, of course . . .'

'I can't, Officer. I'm driving,' I say sombrely.

'Of course. Silly me.' He hands me the wine.

The water on my face has refreshed me slightly and I take a sip of the alcohol, hoping it might help to dampen the fluttering sensation in my chest. Nope, it's still there. I know we're still in a room full of people, but we're alone in the sense that there's no one present who knows us, meaning we're uninhibited by the constraints of our friends' judgemental expressions. Particularly me.

'Is Ella married?' Tom asks idly.

'Why?' I demand irritably, all my 'fat friend' neuroses trampling each other in their enthusiasm to rush forth.

He shrugs. 'Just making polite conversation, that's all. I know Saira's married and that you're not. But we didn't get round to Ella.'

'She's dating a married man. He's called Philip and he's a complete arse.'

'In what way?'

'Well, he's married, for starters . . .' I pull a 'duh' face, '. . . and, in my humble opinion, he's overly possessive. He's always ringing up to see how she is, but really it's to see *where* she is.'

'You old cynic,' he tuts. 'He might just genuinely love her.'

I can't tell if he's deliberately trying to wind me up or not, but I take the bait anyway. 'No, because if he did, he'd leave his wife, wouldn't he?'

The corners of his mouth turn down. 'Depends on the circumstances. If there are children, it's a tougher call because it's not just the wife you're leaving.'

'He doesn't have any.'

An image of Po flashes across my mind and, with it, the memory of Tom's earlier revelation (well, as I saw it, anyway) and my woeful response. Now, marginally more in control of my faculties, I decide to revisit the subject.

'Did you leave your wife?'

He ponders the question, the briefest flash of sadness crossing his eyes. 'She wasn't my wife. We never married. She left me. I can't blame her, though. I was an arse, to steal your quaint expression.'

'A my-sized arse, or a teeny Ella-sized one?' I smile conciliatorily.

Bad idea, as he proceeds to tilt his head and study my rear end. I instinctively clench my buttocks to try to make them appear smaller.

'I'd say somewhere between the two,' he decides. 'I was working hideously long and unsociable hours in my attempt to get promoted—'

'No one can blame you for that,' I interject. 'You were providing for your family.'

'True,' he nods. 'But that wasn't the problem, as such, it was how I behaved on the rare occasions I *was* home. I was knackered and grumpy, and felt that because I'd been working, I was entitled to just put my feet up whilst she did everything.'

I frown slightly, unsure what to say. My instinctive

reaction is that it sounds perfectly reasonable for him to want to relax, but as he subsequently describes himself as an arse, he clearly doesn't see it that way.

'I made the mistake of thinking she was just sitting around when I was at work,' he continues, 'whereas I now know she was working just as hard as I was, maybe harder.'

'Did she have a job too?'

'Yes, a full-time one in the shape of our son. Until we split up and I had to have him for long periods on my own, I had absolutely no idea how you don't get a minute to yourself. It's relentlessly full on.' He takes a mouthful of wine and lets out a long sigh. 'So she'd have a tiring day of dealing with a hyperactive toddler and no adult conversation, then I'd come home and be mono-syllabic, expecting her to start running around after *me*. I realise now that I should have done a little more around the house and made an effort to take her out to places, just the two of us . . .' He peters off, looking wistful.

It sounds like Dean and me, I think, except we both work and don't have children. 'So once you realised the error of your ways . . .' I smile to show I'm half joking, '. . . did you try and win her back?'

'I thought about it . . . a lot. But I knew it would have to be for keeps because we couldn't go through another split, it was too painful. And by the time I thought that, maybe I'd like to give it another go, she'd met someone else.'

'Are you still in love with her?' I ask the question without thinking.

'Um, in love, no. But I'm still incredibly fond of her. She's a great mum.'

Whoopeedoo, I think mutinously. How would I be described on my gravestone if I were to drop dead from comparative inadequacy right now? 'Here lies Cam Simpson. She was a great . . . er, hairdresser.'

Tom drains his glass and stands up. 'Right, one more before bed. Join me?'

'That's terribly forward of you.'

'Ha-ha. I meant drink.' He waves his empty glass to prove it.

'Oh-I-couldn't-oh-go-on-then.'

Watching him walk to the bar – well, OK, watching his nicely firm bottom, actually – I fleetingly wonder whether Ella is waiting up for me on the other side of our connecting door, like some disapproving Edwardian chaperone. But I dismiss the thought immediately. So what if she is? I'm not answerable to anyone, least of all a woman with her complicated love life. And besides, I'm only having a drink with someone – where's the harm?

It lies in the next glass of wine, whispers the devil on my shoulder. It lies in yet more intimate talk. It lies in the short lift ride to his bedroom.

'There you go.' He hands me the wine and our fingers touch briefly, sending a discernible shiver up my arms. I notice he's actually bought a bottle, placing the remainder on the table in front of us.

'Can I ask you a very personal question?' I shoot him a serious look.

'Sure.' He fidgets uncomfortably.

'What was that hideous jumper all about?'

He looks momentarily nonplussed, then bursts out laughing, probably through relief that I haven't asked him if he likes to wear women's clothing.

'Ah, yes. That was a birthday present from Jason. He's a great mate, but he's lousy at buying gifts. My birthday was in February, but as we were coming out here, I thought I could wear it in front of him without the danger of seeing anyone we know.'

'Damn, wish I'd got a picture. I could have put it on Facebook for the delectation of a wider audience,' I grin.

'*You*, madam, are trouble.' He leans forward, his elbows on his knees, and pushes his face closer to mine until our foreheads are almost touching. I can feel his breath on my cheek.

'It's mah middle name,' I drawl in a lousy American accent.

'You're very attractive and funny, do you know that?' he murmurs, his breathing slightly more rapid now.

'Why, thaynk you, kind serrrr.' OK, probably time to drop the accent now. I might be imagining it, but he appears to move closer still.

'Do you mind if I kiss you?'

Save perhaps being trapped in a lift with a shirtless Matthew McConaughey, I couldn't think of anything I'd like more. But I reckon that's a bit of a long answer under the circumstances, so I say nothing and simply close my eyes expectantly.

The kiss, when it comes, is gentle at first, his lips surprisingly soft. His smell is a pleasant mix of fresh male sweat, white wine and aftershave.

I flick open my eyes and note his are closed as he increases the pressure against my lips. It's everything I remember from my first kiss with Dean all those years ago, that unmistakable combination of anticipation, excitement and lust, the feeling you want to bottle for ever but find evaporates as time moves on.

Dean. I start slightly as, with an accompanying rush of guilt, his face fills my thoughts. He doesn't deserve this.

Tom has stopped kissing me and is looking concerned. 'You OK?'

I nod and smile, feeling so in tune with this man that the urge to tell him the truth is almost overwhelming. But I sense he's a man of honour and that learning I have a boyfriend may prompt him to leave me alone, so for entirely selfish reasons I say nothing.

Forcibly pushing Dean to the back of my mind almost as quickly as he popped into it, I take both Tom's hands in mine and push my lips against his, losing myself completely in the moment.

For years now, I have let my head make the decisions, always taking the sensible, expected route, never wanting to rock the boat. Now, just for once, I'm going to put my heart in the driving seat and see where it takes me.

Chapter Seven

Gee, thanks, Heart. Here's a fine mess you've got me into.

It's dark, but a small shaft of light piercing the partially opened curtain tells me that, although the room is identical in décor to mine, I'm not in my own bed. It's facing the wrong way, for a start.

I tentatively lift my head from the pillow, then rapidly lay it back down again as a stabbing pain shoots from one temple to the other. My tongue feels like the cracked bed of a water-starved lake.

Attempting instead merely to move my head slightly to one side, I can just make out through squinting eyes the form of someone sleeping next to me. I know they're sleeping because the deep, rhythmic snoring is a bit of a giveaway.

OK, so clearly I am in Tom's bed. *With* Tom. But have I just behaved like a wanton harlot, or can I reclaim a teensy piece of moral high ground by telling myself that we didn't actually have sex?

Lifting the bedclothes with the painstaking care of a curator handling an ancient parchment, I bite my lip as I discover that I haven't got a stitch on. Caution was, it seems, thrown to the wind . . . along with my underwear, which I now have to try to locate.

I carefully edge my way out of the bed and towards what I assume is the bathroom. As I am bereft of clothing, I can only hope it's not the door to the corridor.

Once inside, I close the door, then fumble for the light, my eyes snapping shut in agony as I flick the switch.

The sight that greets me in the mirror looks like the 'before' shot of an *Extreme Makeover* contestant. My face is blotchy, my hair wild, and there's now more mascara on my upper cheeks than on my eyelashes. I also appear to have a cut lip, presumably a snogging injury.

I look at my watch and freeze with tension. It's freakin' 6.30 a.m., and perilously nearing the time that Saira awakes each morning. I know she's on holiday without Rashid, but from memory, I vaguely remember her whingeing that she's now indoctrinated into rising early and physically *can't* have a lie-in, even if she wants to.

So, in the unlikely event that she has so far slept through the night without the need to pee forty-eight times, I have precisely half an hour to find my clothes and sneak back to my bed before she wakes up and sees it's empty.

Carefully opening the bathroom door an inch or two, I do a swift risk assessment. If I open it wide, the light might wake him up, but if I don't, I'll never find my clothes.

Luckily, either the surfeit of alcohol has knocked him out, or he's a deep sleeper by nature. As I met him only about thirty seconds ago, I'm not in a position to know which it is, simply grateful that I don't have to face the awkwardness of the sober 'good mornings' after the drunken encounter.

Grabbing my clothes and flinging them over one arm, I skulk near the exit door, out of sight of the bed, and quickly get dressed. A cursory check of my handbag confirms I still have my room key and credit cards, so blessedly he's not a mugger. Then I'm ready to tiptoe out of Tom's life as deftly as I entered it.

The door creaks slightly as I open it, but his snoring continues unabated. I close it behind me and let out a long sigh of relief. At least, I *think* that's what it is.

Feeling myself starting to relax, I even hum a little as I wait for the lift to arrive. But when the doors open, I immediately tense again as I'm confronted by a middle-aged couple clearly on their way out for a walk, judging by the clutched guidebook and sturdy boots.

'Gosh, you're early birds,' I burble.

The woman is staring open-mouthed at this mop-haired, black-eyed apparition before her, her eyes betraying her disapproval.

'Good night, was it, love?' asks her husband, in a broad Yorkshire accent.

Of all the lifts in all the towns, trust me to get into one at 6.30 a.m. with a pair of insomniac British ramblers.

I sigh wearily. 'Yes, thanks, it was bloody great.' The doors open on my floor. 'And now I'm going to bed.'

Well, that's the plan, at least. On the other hand, I may be about to walk into Armageddon, with Saira and Ella wielding proverbial rolling pins and demanding to know where I've been.

Face screwed with anticipation, I carefully place the plastic card in the slot and wait for the green light. It's still red. Damn.

Five goes later, I'm wondering whether Saira has had the lock changed, such is her disgust at my behaviour. Or perhaps they are down at the beach right now, organising a painstaking search of every bar and rockpool for a sign of their missing friend? My heart lurches at the thought, because it's quite patently something they would do if they thought I may have come to some harm.

I rummage in my handbag for my mobile, fully expecting to find it exploding silently with messages of concern, starting with a casual 'Where are you?' and building through a crescendo to 'We're now organising a news bulletin in Spanish to appeal for help as to your whereabouts.' But there's not even one missed call. Phew.

One more try and, suddenly, the key works and I'm in.

Relieved to find the room in darkness, I creep along the small entrance corridor and tentatively pop my head round the corner of the main room. Saira is fast asleep, face down with one leg sticking out from the covers.

My bed, the one nearer the window, is still neatly made, a piece of evidence just waiting to damn me should Saira suddenly wake up. Or perhaps she's seen it already and gone back to sleep? I have no way of knowing.

As I start to slowly remove my cardigan, she stirs, moving from her front to her left side, facing my bed. Still fully clothed, I dive under my covers just as she opens her eyes and squints into the gloom.

'Cam?' she whispers.

'Uh-huh.' I do my best to affect sleepiness, but my heart is thumping with adrenalin.

'What time is it?' Her tone doesn't sound accusatory, but that might just be a double bluff.

'Too early to be waking me up,' I grumble, resisting the urge to turn away from her in case I reveal a fully clothed shoulder.

She stretches and yawns. 'I can't believe I've slept this long without needing a pee. That shows how dehydrated I must be.'

There is a God. I realise quite how tense my entire body must have been when I feel it relax immeasurably. It immediately stiffens again when my eyes drift down to the end of the bed and see my sandalled foot protruding from the bedcover. I pull it up out of sight, just as Saira stumbles past on her way to the bathroom.

As soon as I hear the door close, I'm on my feet, kicking the sandals into the far corner of the room and hoisting my cardigan and dress over my head in one swift motion before jettisoning them to a nearby chair.

I'm now in my bra and pants, but a hasty risk assessment of how much time it would take me to find my nightie means the concept is aborted and I fling myself back into bed just as the bathroom door opens again.

'What time did you come in?' she asks casually. 'I can't believe I didn't hear you.'

'About five minutes after you and Ella,' I lie expertly. 'About midnight, I think. Anyway, you were so pissed I doubt you'd have heard me if I'd been crashing cymbals.'

She grimaces. 'Ah, yes, the wrath of grapes. That explains the pounding head. How bad was I?'

'Let's put this it this way: when "Y.M.C.A." came on, you took out the eyes of several innocent people along the way.'

'Oops. Someone must have spiked my nineteenth

comedy cocktail. Still, at least I got a good night's sleep.'
She stretches her arms above her head, then sits on the
edge of her bed and places a hand on her stomach. 'God,
I'm starving. I need a good fry-up to counteract the
alcohol. Fancy it?'

I can't think of anything I want less, preferring instead
to lay my head on the pillow that resembles a paving
slab, but actually right now feels as though it's stuffed
with the finest goosedown. My cheek is welded to it,
but I know that having pretended I came to bed at midnight, I have to appear bright-eyed and bushy-tailed.
Well, a bit, anyway.

'Sure.'

Resolving to catch up on sleep later by the pool, I haul
myself onto my elbow first, then swing my leaden legs
out of bed, slipping my feet into the very sandals I
removed precisely thirty seconds ago. They're still
warm.

Tugging on a pair of denim shorts and a T-shirt, I
watch as Saira slips on a calf-length white kaftan, and I
follow her unsteadily to the door, pausing only to rush
into the bathroom and chuck a couple of Nurofen
Express down my throat.

'Do they have any other fruit in Spain than bloody
oranges?' Ella is holding one in each hand, like a peasant
girl from central casting.

'We're in the Canary Islands,' says Saira.

'Same thing.' Ella starts to peel an orange and a jet of
juice shoots onto my hand. I stare at it for a couple of
seconds before slowly licking it off.

'You seem a little slow on the uptake this morning,'
she says, narrowing her eyes at me. 'Late night, was it?'

My brain suddenly sharpens considerably and I sit up straight with what I hope is an alert expression. I have no idea whether she sat waiting for me to return, a water glass pressed against the adjoining wall. But knowing Ella and her obsession with getting beauty sleep, I very much doubt it.

'No, not late at all. Just a few minutes after you two.'

'Really?' Her tone suggests she is about to wrench one of the industrial-sized catering lights from the breakfast bar and shine it in my eyes. 'Because you looked pretty ensconced with what's-his-name when I left.'

'Who's what's-his-name?' asks Saira through a mouthful of mushrooms. At least, I *think* they're mushrooms.

'Tom,' I reply blithely, my heart rate increasing as an image of me naked in his bed flashes into my mind.

'Tom from the beach?' Saira looks baffled. 'Was he there last night?'

Ella raises her eyes heavenward. 'Yes, and I'm Ella and this . . .' she waves a hand in my direction, '. . . is Cam. We were there too.'

'I know.' She rolls her eyes. 'I wasn't *completely* pissed, you know.'

'Could have fooled me,' scoffs Ella. 'I presume you don't remember being sick in that fake palm tree by the lifts?'

'I wasn't!'

Ella's face indicates that she very much was and that if Saira contests the matter any further she will drag her over there and show her the evidence.

'Oh God, I'm never drinking again. The shame of it.'

Shame, I muse. I reckon I'm top of the league on *that* emotion. Miraculously, the rest of my body doesn't feel too bad, but my conscience is hurting like hell. I wasn't as drunk as Saira, yet I behaved like one of those ladettes you read about in the Sunday tabloids, who pick up the first man they meet and end up in his bed. I can feel my face flushing at the thought.

'So when did he pitch up?' Saira has now clearly recovered from her brief liaison with 'shame' and is staring at me accusingly.

'He came and said hello just after "Dancing Queen",' I reply casually.

'I love that song! I can't believe I missed it.'

Ella and I exchange glances.

'You didn't miss it. You danced insanely to every last, excruciating second of it.' Ella pops an orange segment in her mouth.

'Ah, that explains why I'm aching all over. So who put me to bed?'

I so know where this is going . . .

Ella raises a hand. 'I did.'

Saira arches an eyebrow at me. 'Leaving you alone with Tom, eh?'

'For about *three* minutes.' I roll my eyes theatrically. 'Then I went to the loo downstairs so I wouldn't wake you, and came to bed too. I was ten minutes behind you both . . . tops.'

I'm making the assumption that this fabricated timespan is enough to cover Ella getting Saira upstairs, undressing her for bed, then heading off into her own room.

'Hmm, well, I sincerely hope so,' mutters Saira, standing up. 'Now, I'm going up for seconds – anyone else?'

I close my eyes, mainly through relief that neither of them seems to have the faintest inkling that I woke up in a stranger's bedroom, but also through sheer exhaustion. It's now eight o'clock and I have no idea how much sleep I have had or precisely what I was getting up to in between times.

When we arrived in the dining-cum-breakfast room, I did a rapid scan of all tables to establish whether the co-contributor to my shame was present. Mercifully, he wasn't, and I deliberately chose a chair facing the entrance so I am forewarned if he *does* walk in. Though what I will say to him is anyone's guess. Perhaps, 'Hi there, how was it for you?'

The door opens and a brown-haired man walks in. It's not him, but my nerves short-wire anyway. I visibly jump in my seat and knock the table.

'Whoa!' Saira cups a hand over her spilt tea.

'Sorry. I thought I felt something on my foot,' I lie.

'Probably Stuart Little or one of his furry friends,' says Ella, her nose wrinkling slightly.

Saira starts telling an anecdote about the time a mouse took up residence in her house and Abbas became obsessed about catching it, setting traps laced with such treats as peanut butter, chocolate and even smoked salmon. Every morning the delicacy would be gone, but the trap would remain firmly set.

'It got to the stage where this bloody rodent was eating better than we were,' she mutters.

I smile but tune out as she and Ella exchange infestation stories, preferring to dwell on my own little problem. What *was* I thinking? I'm a loyal, monogamous kind of girl, always have been. And whatever Dean's shortcomings, he deserves better than to have a girlfriend who behaves like an oversexed mongrel at the first sniff of sangria.

82

'By the way, talking about what's-his-name, I saw him in the foyer just before I came in here.'

Even though she's gazing directly at me, it still takes me several seconds to realise that Ella is talking to me. When I finally compute what she's said, my face doesn't just faintly flush, Jane Austen-style, it actually throbs with panic.

'Oh,' is all I manage, my mind racing from nought to sixty in a nanosecond.

Please God, he didn't say anything incriminating. He wouldn't, would he? He's too classy for that . . . or is he? After all, I barely know the man. Perhaps he was just pretending to be sensible and mature so he could get me into bed, and perhaps he's really a complete bastard who beds women for fun, just so he can drop them in it with their friends the next morning. Or maybe Jason didn't have sunburn at all and they'd shared a bet on whether Tom could seduce me, and as proof, he'd filmed the whole thing for YouTube. Who knows, one of those biplanes could be flying over the hotel right now, trailing a banner declaring, 'I shagged Cam Simpson last night.' Shit, shit, *shit*.

'I didn't recognise him at first,' continues Ella, 'so I wasn't terribly friendly. I thought he was going to try and flog me a dolphin trip or something . . . you know, the ones where you spend forty-eight hours on a boat and only see dead seagulls and a couple of turds float by . . .'

I'm nodding like a lunatic, a rictus grin on my face. Did he drop *me* firmly in the brown stuff?

'Anyway, he asked me to say goodbye to you . . .'

I remain rooted to the spot, unsure if I can actually breathe normally now or whether there's more to come.

But Ella has started to peel another orange and is showing no signs of adding to what's already been said.

'Is that it?' I croak.

She arches an eyebrow. 'What were you expecting . . . a love sonnet?'

'No, no . . . NO! Gosh, no!' OK, that's enough hysterical denials. Rein yourself in, woman, even if the relief is all-consuming. 'You just looked as though you were about to say something else, that's all.'

'Did I?' She twists her mouth slightly. 'Nope, that's it. He was on his way to the airport, so there was blissfully little time in which to converse. You know how I *hate* small talk with people I don't know.'

She embarks on a whingefest about a particularly dull corporate function she had to attend recently, and I let out a long, deep breath, feeling my shoulders relax. But then a sixth sense prompts me to turn to my left, where I find Saira eyeing me with all the suspicion of an airport security guard encountering a passenger clutching a one-way ticket and a copy of the Koran.

Normally, I would confront her, demand to know what was going on in her mind. But in this case, I know I have too much to lose, so simply smile reassuringly at her and say nothing.

He has left the building. And in a couple of hours, he'll have left the country too, taking my sordid little secret with him.

Thank Christ for that.

Chapter Eight

'A fond good morning to all our listeners. It's ten o'clock on a beautifully sunny Saturday morning and we're with you for the next three hours, so sit back and enjoy today's selection of classic summer tunes . . .'

The DJ's voice gives way to the opening bars of Style Council's 'Long Hot Summer' as I munch disconsolately on a mouthful of dull muesli and stare out of the window. I *hate* this song. Well, actually, I love it, but I hate the feelings it evokes in me.

'*I'm all mixed up inside. I want to run but I can't hide . . .*' I sing along quietly, '*And however much we try, we can't escape the truth and the fact is, don't matter what I do . . . I'll end up hurting you.*'

I turn to look at Dean, but he's oblivious to the loaded lyrics, chomping on his delicious-smelling bacon sandwich as if it's the Last Supper. He's poring over the new releases in *Computer Games Monthly* magazine, as if he doesn't fritter away enough of his spare time already in front of a small screen.

'*I don't know whether to laugh or cry: the long hot summer just passed me by . . .*' I trill, thinking back fondly to the early days, not long after we met, when we spent many a wonderful afternoon idling in the sunshine on a pub lawn somewhere, me in a little floral number and 'natural' make-up, still making an effort to look nice for him. These days, it's a denim skirt, vest-top and, mood and time permitting, a smidgen of mascara.

Summer is such a seductive, quixotic time when you're in love and full of dreams, marvelling at the sights and sounds around you as if it's the first time you've seen them. Now it seems like any other time of the year to me, just a bit sweatier.

I have been back from holiday for two weeks now and, during the train journey from Gatwick airport back to home, I convinced myself that I'd missed Dean. I was actually looking forward to seeing him, though whether it was a genuine emotion or a forcibly enhanced one stemming from my abject guilt wasn't clear. But in my head, at least, he was going to hear my key in the lock and be waiting in the hallway, brimming with affection and tales of how it felt like I'd be gone for months. Then he'd carry my bags inside, telling me that he'd already planned and bought supper, before carrying me up to bed for wild sex. Well, my key went in the lock, so *that* bit happened. But the hallway was empty and, when I called out, a muffled 'Hiya' came back from the living room, where, shock horror, the TV wasn't on. But he was stretched out on the sofa, clearly having just woken up.

'What time is it?' he yawned.

'Nine. Two hours since my flight landed,' I replied pointedly.

'Oh, yes.' He stood up and gave me a swift peck on the cheek. 'How was it?'

'Well, we didn't spiral out of the sky and plummet to our deaths, if that's what you mean.'

I had gone through to the bedroom on the pretext of unpacking my suitcase, but instead I'd slumped on the edge of the bed. I felt a debilitating crash of disappointment that swelled to raw irritation when I finally sauntered through to the kitchen and saw the mess. Dirty plates were stacked up in the sink and on the drainer, and the kitchen table was strewn with three empty pizza boxes and an accompanying plate with crust remnants on it. I suppose I should be grateful he bothered to even *use* a plate, I thought mutinously.

'Sorry.' He smiled sheepishly when he saw my expression. 'I was going to get it tidied up before you got back, but I fell asleep and time kind of ran away.'

The desire to snap, 'I wish *I* could run away,' was overwhelming, but I stifled it, knowing that as the one returning from holiday, I was hardly in a position to castigate the one who had stayed behind and worked.

Also, I was feeling badly destabilised by what had happened with Tom. For the couple of days after his departure, I managed to relax, mainly through relief that neither of my friends had rumbled me. But on the third day, when Ella was at the spa having a massage, Saira had casually asked me if there was anything I'd like to tell her about Tom, and I had, I *think*, managed to convince her that nothing had happened.

But it brought it to the forefront of my mind again and, for the final two days of the holiday, I had thought about him a lot, each time prompting butterflies in my stomach. I told myself that this longing couldn't be trusted, that it had less to do with Tom as a person and more to do with the circumstance of subterfuge, sun, sea, sand, lie-ins and liberation from the daily drudgery of work. It couldn't even be feasibly described as a holiday romance, such was its brevity.

I knew all of this, yet when I walked back into my reality of an untidy flat and a boyfriend who seemed distinctly underwhelmed to see me, the emotional crash was huge.

Later on, Dean alluded to the fact he'd missed me, by saying something along the lines of 'It's been quiet around here without you', though it was hard to tell whether it was meant wistfully or not. So, as homecomings go, it was pretty low on the scale. Or perhaps my expectations are just too high.

A fortnight on, we've fallen back into our old routine of both traipsing off to work during the week, returning exhausted and unwilling to do much except flop, he in his usual place, me invariably in the bath or reading in bed. But for the past two weekends, I have persevered with my brave new world in which we would venture out and actually *do* things together. Trouble is, I feel I'm the only one participating.

The Style Council song has finished, replaced by Barry White's 'My First, My Last, My Everything', a track that always uplifts me.

'What shall we do today?' I ask breezily, taking away his plate, empty except for discarded bacon fat.

'Don't mind,' he shrugs. 'Arsenal–Man U is on at three.'

In other words, he wants to be back by then, immediately placing a time restriction on our adventure, for want of a better word.

Placing our plates in the sink, I go back to staring out of the window. Our neighbours Mr and Mrs Payne – I have never known their Christian names – are in their garden already, probably having risen at 4 a.m. Mr Payne is sanding down their garden bench, and his wife is brutalising a rose bush with secateurs. But what strikes me is that they're talking, and I mean *really* talking. Not the occasional remark here and there, but a full-on conversation. I can't hear it but can tell it's animated by the way she keeps stopping the trimming in order to gesticulate in her husband's direction. He, in turn, smiles at her, then rests his elbows on the back of the bench and adds his two penn'orth. They look so comfortable with one another, yet clearly so interested too. Mrs Payne once told me they'd been together for thirty-five years.

Is there really anything left to say that hasn't already been uttered a hundred times over? In their case, obviously.

Turning back to Dean, I feel a surge of loneliness, a pang for the life I can see out of my kitchen window but can't seem to touch myself. On the few occasions I try to engage Dean in scintillating conversation, or even a vaguely interesting one, he nods and grunts in all the right places but rarely offers an opinion of his own unless there's a tenuous link to sport or mobile-phone technology. Perhaps he finds *me* boring and simply can't be bothered to engage?

It's often said that a successful relationship means leaving three or four things a day unsaid, but in our case *most* things are unuttered.

I'm not an intellectual heavyweight, or even close, but as I get older I find myself becoming more interested in what's happening in the world around me, yet sharing a home with someone whose interest in anything beyond his own life appears to be diminishing daily. Sometimes, if I stand close enough to him, I swear I can hear the ocean.

Again, it hasn't always been this way. We used to have heated debates about everything from politics (he's firmly left wing, I veer to the right) through to whether Bounty or Snickers deserves the title of 'Best Chocolate Bar'. But maybe we've now said all there is to say, and every time a supposedly new subject arises, we both feel we've been there before in some form or other, that there's no fresh perspective to take. So we say little or nothing.

I become aware of the DJ speaking again, announcing his weekly 'Love Songs' dedications slot, where couples send in syrupy eulogies about each other. Great. Just great. All that's missing is a big neon question mark hanging over Dean's head. What would my eulogy for him be? 'Dean – always there' is about the best I could manage. And his for me? 'Always on at me' perhaps.

Someone called Rita tells someone called Alan that she loves him just as much now as she did twenty years ago, and a young man called Alfie tells his girlfriend, Julia, that even though it's very early days, he already knows that she's the one. I wish I shared his optimism.

Predictably, like so many people when expressing their love, they have displayed deep unoriginality in their choice of song, hence their requests have been lumped together as an introduction to Eric Clapton's 'Wonderful Tonight'.

I sit back down opposite Dean and take a sip of my lukewarm coffee, pondering what *our* song would be, should the need for us to name one ever arise. Probably something by Coldplay, I surmise, a favourite band of ours. Or perhaps Snow Patrol's 'Run'.

'What's our song?' I say aloud.

'Sorry?' He looks up quizzically from his magazine and tightens his dressing-gown cord.

'If we had to choose *one* song that sums up our relationship, what would it be?'

'Alesha Dixon's "The Boy Does Nothing"?' he grins.

I laugh. Despite the empty pizza boxes and the dent in the sofa, I still admire him for his sense of humour.

'*Does he wash up? Never wash up. Does he clean up? No, he never cleans up . . . He does nothing. The boy does nothing!*' I sing happily, suddenly feeling a marked rise in my spirits. The sun is shining, it's the weekend, and we're going to spend the day – well, most of it – doing something nice together. Time to start looking at the positives and stop dwelling on the negatives.

Over the dying seconds of 'Wonderful Tonight', I pick up my coffee mug and wave it in Dean's direction. 'Another coffee? I'm having one.'

He nods and smiles, pushing his mug across the table towards me. 'Thanks.'

'That was Eric Clapton,' says the DJ. 'What a wonderful record that is. Now for today's "Where are they now?" appeal . . . It's not a love story yet, but with our help it just might be . . .'

Waiting for the kettle to boil, I put my mind to what Dean and I can do today, particularly with the time cap imposed by the football schedules. Perhaps a walk along the river and a pub lunch? But money's a little tight at the moment, so maybe a walk and a pre-prepared picnic . . . or possibly a bus ride to a museum?

'OK, so someone called Tom has written in to the show. He came back from holiday in Tenerife a couple of weeks ago, and wants to trace a lovely woman he met there . . .'

My entire body stiffens with tension. Tom . . . Tenerife . . . two weeks ago . . . it couldn't be, could it? The co-presenter is now wittering on about when she went to Tenerife last summer, and how lovely it was, so I slowly look back over my shoulder and see Dean still seemingly engrossed in his magazine.

The radio is just a few feet away. I could just non-chalantly walk over and switch it off, just in case . . .

'But back to Tom,' continues the DJ, and my heart leaps into my mouth. It's just a coincidence. It has to be. After all, there are thousands of Toms in the country and Tenerife is a big place that thousands fly to every day. I'm clearly being ridiculously oversensitive, but I still move swiftly towards the radio, my hand out-stretched . . .

'He says the woman's name is Cam, short for Camomile . . .'

Too late. The truth is out there, but my fingers are now on the off switch and I'm praying that Dean hasn't heard . . .

'Leave it.' His voice is loud and firm.

My fingers recoil involuntarily. I feel nauseous. But the DJ goes on to say something about Tom really liking my company and repeats his line that it's not a love story yet, but with the radio station's help it just might be. Then the opening bars of the Three Degrees' 'When Will I See You Again?' fill the air and I allow myself to breathe again.

'He just said your name,' says Dean challengingly.

I turn towards him, trying to look puzzled. But the heat burning my face tells me that it's probably giveaway pink. My only hope is that he wasn't tuned in to the preamble about 'lovely woman', etc.

I frown, I hope convincingly. 'Yes I thought that too. But I didn't hear the first bit to know what it was about,' I hedge.

'I did.' He's staring at me intently. 'It's someone called Tom who was in Tenerife two weeks ago, looking for a . . . and I quote . . . "lovely woman" called Cam, short for Camomile.' His tone is flat. 'Apparently, it's not a love story yet but, and I quote again, "with our help it just might be".'

'Oh.' I step backwards and lean against the work surface, unsure what to do or say next. It appears that Dean is quite the multitasker after all, reading a magazine and absorbing every last word of a radio announcement at the same time. Damn.

'As coincidences go, it would be unprecedented.' His mouth sets in a firm line.

He's right, of course. Complete denial would be absolutely futile, but I swiftly assess the situation and decide that I don't have to admit everything.

'OK,' I sigh. 'It *is* me. But it's nothing, honestly. He's some bloke I met on the first night in a bar. We chatted for a bit . . . which is why he knows my name . . . then he flew home very early the next day. It's no big deal.'

'Well, clearly it was to him. You don't go to the extreme measure of contacting a radio station to find a woman you just *chatted* to,' Dean replies contemptuously.

'What are you suggesting?' I fish in desperation.

'I'm not *suggesting* anything. I'm stating categorically that it stinks.'

We fall silent, him glaring at me, me staring impassively back before finding it uncomfortable and staring down at the floor. I feel both cornered and duplicitous, not a pleasant combination.

But most of all, I feel paralysed with shame. The morning after my transgression was bad enough, but once Tom had flown home I was able to push the whole sorry episode to the back of my mind and, for the most part, leave it there. If I tried hard enough, I could almost pretend it never happened.

But here it is again, in all its sordid glory, confronting me in the supposed sanctuary of my own kitchen, and in front of the man I have shared so many years with. Whatever I feel are Dean's shortcomings, I know for certain I would never find myself confronted by some infidelity of *his*. He just wouldn't do that to me. Meaning that, fundamentally, he's a far more principled person than I will ever be.

A wave of misery and regret sweeps over me, but I know I must hold it together, more for his sake than my own. It was a fleeting, drunken aberration that won't be repeated, so why own up and cause him hurt?

'Look, I know it seems an odd thing to do, but I can't be held responsible for the actions of some nutter I met for about five minutes in a bar,' I say eventually. 'I don't mind admitting I'm as spooked by what we've just heard as you are.'

'Why didn't you tell him you had a boyfriend?'

I shrug. 'The conversation was so fleeting that we barely spoke about anything.' I pause as if trying to remember. 'It was just a bit about the weather and what the hotel was like. The usual polite stuff.'

'So you were staying in the same hotel?' he asks, his eyes narrowing with suspicion.

Oh God, I'm digging myself such a hole here. I feel my

face burning and can only hope that, outwardly, it looks normal.

'Yes. It was the hotel bar we met in. Quick chat, then gone.' I make a slicing gesture across my throat to accentuate the point.

'But long enough for you to tell him your full name . . . which normally you keep well under your hat,' he says accusingly. 'It took about six months for you to tell *me* what it was.'

'It wasn't me. Saira told him.' As soon as the words leave my mouth, I can feel a metaphorical size nine being simultaneously inserted. Now my friends are implicated in this supposedly brief encounter.

'So, if I ask Saira and Ella about this . . . quick chat . . .' the words drip slowly from his mouth, '. . . they'd back up your version of events, would they?'

I nod keenly. 'And it's not a *version* of events, it's the truth. I have a completely clear conscience.' Oh, how I wish.

'Or a bad memory,' Dean retorts.

Attack, some say, is the best form of defence. Whatever, right now it feels like my only option. My overwhelming urge is one of protection, to shield Dean from the ugly truth. The power of it takes me by surprise, suggesting as it does that my feelings for him are not as endangered as I have been telling myself.

'Look, Dean . . .' I feign a sigh, '. . . please feel free to question my friends if you wish, but *I'm* telling you that nothing happened, and if you don't believe me, then I think that speaks volumes about our relationship, don't you?'

Christ, I feel like such a heel. And a cheap one at that. Lying effortlessly has never been my forte, and when it's

95

over something I feel so inexorably guilty and cheap about it seems infinitely harder.

He doesn't speak but carries on staring at me impassively for a few seconds, clearly mulling things over. Eventually, he lets out a long sigh.

'OK, fair enough. If you say you only talked to him, then I'll take your word for it. But you really should be more careful in future, he sounds like a potential stalker.'

'I know!' I exclaim, jerking my head towards the radio. 'I was as surprised as you were when I heard that. It didn't even cross my mind that it was anything to do with me until I actually heard my name being read out. I mean, the notion that you'd put out a message for someone you met for a few minutes is *insane*.' I realise I am now over-egging it and resist the urge to go on.

Dean stands up and stretches his arms above his head. 'Right. I'm just going to get dressed, then we'll do whatever you've got planned. OK?'

'Sure!' I smile reassuringly.

His willingness to accept my version of events has flooded me with such relief and gratitude that I'd happily sit and watch the football match *with* him as our afternoon activity. But of course, as I'm claiming to have done nothing wrong, I have to be careful to keep my behaviour normal.

'I'll just tidy up here first, so let's aim to leave in, ooh, about half an hour?'

He nods and leaves the room. I wait until I hear him enter the bathroom and close the door, then let out a sigh so deep it feels like every last breath of air has left my body. Phew, that was close.

Chapter Nine

It's my birthday and I'm thirty-five. Or halfway to seventy, as Luca cheerfully pointed out earlier, hooting with laughter at the mere thought.

'But there are many advantages,' I retorted. 'Such as wisdom, serenity—'

'And absolutely no peer pressure!' Luca interrupted joyfully.

'Darling, you're thirty yourself – the same generation as me.'

I had lunch with him and a couple of other younger . . . grrrr . . . colleagues from the salon, and now I'm on my way to dinner with just my family, and very close friends, namely Saira and Ella. Luca is great company, but a little too much of an egotist for small groupings, always me-deep in conversation.

We're meeting at a cheap and cheerful trattoria near the flat, and as I enter the packed room, I can't see her but I can most definitely *hear* my mother's voice rising above the fairly muted throng.

'I brought Camomile up to be punctual, but with independence has come appalling tardiness,' she booms.

For the record, I am precisely four minutes late. My mother is a travel agent for guilt trips.

'Fear not. I am among you,' I say through a forced smile, kissing her on both cheeks whilst making a mental note not to sit next to or near her tonight. As it's my birthday, one of my brothers can take the hit.

Talking of which, there they are, propping up the bar either side of a blonde whose rear view I don't recognise. Presumably another customer's wife, girlfriend or perhaps daughter, but none of these would prove a barrier to my relentlessly flirtatious siblings.

'Sorry, are Dumb and Dumber bothering you?' I smile at her.

When she turns round, I see that she's about twenty-five and absolutely stunning, with baby-blue eyes and the kind of retroussé nose seen only on Barbie or in cosmetic-surgery catalogues.

'Not at all,' she drawls in either an American or Canadian accent; I never can tell the difference. 'In fact, they're offering to show me the sights.'

'And what sights would those be?' I ask Josh. I know it's Josh because he has a black fleck in his left eye, which his supposedly identical twin, James, doesn't have, as well as several other distinguishing features I can recognise. But most would struggle to tell them apart and the pair of them have hours of fun confusing people as to who's who.

'Debbie here hasn't seen much of our fair city at all,' he replies. 'So we thought we could start with the London Eye, then perhaps take in the Tower . . .'

Followed by a hotel bedroom, I think to myself. Actually, that's slightly unfair to James, who is flirtatious but monogamous when he's in a relationship, which he is at the moment. Josh, however, is a complete and utter tart, and shameless with it. Some men can take women or leave them – he prefers to do both.

'Lovely.' I beam at her, then turn to kiss each brother on the cheek. 'Is Jenny here?' I ask James pointedly.

'Nope. She had to work late. Sends her love, though.'

After swapping telephone numbers with Debbie and waving her goodbye, Josh turns back to me and wrinkles his nose. 'Sorry, sis, I haven't got you a present yet, but never fear, I'll find something.'

'How very thoughtful of you,' I say drily. 'But don't bother. Your gift can be to sit next to Mum and distract her so she's not on my case all night.'

He does a salute. 'Consider it done.'

'Have you bought me anything yet?' I squint at James, who winces and shakes his head.

'Good. Then you're the other side of her.'

He opens his mouth to protest but then clearly thinks better of it.

'And please don't drink too much either,' I add. 'I need you relatively sober for the task.'

This may seem rather overanxious, controlling behaviour, but last year's birthday still weighs heavily on my mind, when the twins were once again dutied with distracting Mother from her excesses and failed to do so from an excess of their own, namely too much alcohol. James fell asleep at the table, and Josh spent the latter part of the evening chatting up one of the waitresses, leaving Mum unattended and able to harangue me about everything from the choice of food in the restaurant to why hadn't I yet opened my own salon?

She doesn't *mean* to be so challenging, and I'm sure

she feels she's simply being a concerned, advisory parent. But, God, it's wearing.

'Sis, I swear I'm pacing myself tonight.' James's voice punctuates my thoughts.

'And I only judge myself to be drunk when a toilet seat is hitting the back of my head,' says Josh blithely.

'How very reassuring to hear,' I mutter.

It's funny, they are virtually identical in looks, and most people would think my brothers had similarly outgoing personalities too. But whilst I get on brilliantly with James, naturally gravitating towards him at all family gatherings, Josh and I repel each other like magnets, always sniping and being visibly irritated by one another. I have never worked out why. Saira once suggested it was because we are so similar, and I didn't speak to her for a week.

The restaurant is starting to fill up now, both with my friends and other customers. I see Saira and Abbas arrive, followed shortly by Ella and . . . oh my God, it's Philip!

'Is that who I think it is, or am I hallucinating from too many of these?' I murmur to Saira, lifting my Prosecco glass as I kiss both her cheeks.

She turns, none too discreetly, and squints in their direction. 'Bugger me, it *is*.'

We have both met him a couple of times before, but only fleetingly at Ella's flat, and *never* in other company. We have always assumed he'd be too nervous of encountering someone who, via six degrees of separation, might know his wife.

As he takes Ella's coat and vanishes in the direction of the cloakroom, I take the opportunity to sidle over to her.

'To what do we owe the pleasure?'

She looks baffled. 'You invited me.'

'Not you, you daft cow. *Philip*.'

'Oh, yes,' she smiles nervously. 'He took some persuading, but we figured this place was obscure enough that he wouldn't bump into anyone he knew.'

We both know that what she really means is that it isn't expensive or well-located enough.

'Great! Well, I'm really glad you're both here,' I enthuse. 'If you'll excuse me a minute, I'm just going to make sure there's a chair for him.'

As I'm waiting for the restaurant owner to rustle up another place setting, I hastily scribble Philip's name on a scrap of paper and place it between Ella and Saira. Even though it's supposed to be a casual dinner, I never leave seating arrangements to chance in case Mother plonks herself next to me for a night of her well-meaning but none the less interfering ways.

'What you up to?' Dean peers over my shoulder.

'Philip's here.' I pull a face to suggest this is extraordinary.

'Who?'

'Precisely. Ella's mysterious boyfriend . . . you know, the *married* one.'

'Oh.' His face darkens slightly. 'Well, don't put him next to me. I don't approve and might have to say so.'

He walks away and I close my eyes wearily. Why, when it comes to family and friends, are there always those who are incompatible, who have to be seated at opposite ends of the room, making matters difficult for the host or hostess? It's not supposed to be about *them*, yet time and again I feel like the Henry Kissinger of table planning.

Still, thank heaven for small mercies, I suppose. Since the potentially catastrophic matter of the radio announcement five days ago, there has been no further mention of it and Dean and I have fallen back into our normal routine. But for once, I'm grateful for the safe predictability of it.

He rarely sees Saira or Ella, but knowing my birthday dinner was fast approaching, I called them separately to relay what had happened and ask them please to back up my story of a quick chat in the bar, should Dean mention Tom to them. Under no circumstances should the trip to the beach be mentioned.

Ella seemed distracted when I called anyway, so had readily agreed, but Saira had been a little trickier to bring on message so smoothly.

'But *why* did he go to such lengths to find you?' she said yet again after I'd ignored the question twice.

'I don't know, he's probably a bit obsessive,' I replied.

'Really? He didn't strike me as the type.'

I was only glad we were having a telephone conversation and not face to face, or she'd probably have sussed out my guilty conscience straight away.

Eventually, she agreed not to say anything on the understanding that we would discuss the matter in greater detail another time. Saira would never drop me in it anyway, I know that. But being a highly moral person, she also couldn't let a perceived misdemeanour pass without pointing out the error of my ways. Repeatedly.

'Philip, how lovely to see you!' I enthuse as he returns from the cloakroom.

As I bellow his name, I swear he flinches instinctively, probably a nervous tic from a lifetime of furtive assignations and the fear of coming face to face with someone from his 'other' life.

'Happy birthday, Cam.' He smiles and shakes my hand as if we have just completed a business deal.

If you saw Philip sitting alone at a bar, and had to guess what he did for a living, you'd come up with 'businessman' of some sort. The first time I met him, at Ella's flat, he had come from the office so the expensive suit, crisp white shirt, single-colour tie and solid silver cufflinks were understandable.

But the second time was a Sunday afternoon and he was wearing similar, albeit minus the suit jacket, no doubt because he'd given his wife some old waffle about having to go to the office even though it was closed for the weekend.

And tonight it's the same ensemble except the shirt is pale blue and the blue silk tie is loosened slightly. I'd hazard a guess he even wears one with his pyjamas.

According to Ella, Philip is the chairman of a small private bank in the City, one that charted a steady, cautious course through the boom years and subsequently fared well when the bust came.

Yes, I thought, there is absolutely nothing adventurous or unbuttoned about Philip. He looks as though his entire life is going according to the plan he probably drew up when he was about fifteen, shortly after he bought his first suit.

Tall and slim, he has none of the middle-aged spread usually associated with a man in his early fifties. As we sit down to be faced with the set starter course, I discover why. It's deep-fried Camembert with cranberry sauce, chosen as an ironic nod to my seventies childhood. But Philip's lip visibly curls when he sees it, and he immediately pushes the offending item to one side, eating only the accompanying straggle of rocket leaves and half a tomato.

I toy with the idea of pointing out his fussiness, but figure that as it's such a momentous event he's even here, I'd better not rock the boat so soon into the journey. Instead, I quietly amuse myself with thoughts of how minuscule his and Ella's weekly shopping bill would be should he ever leave his wife and move in.

'What are you smiling about?'

I turn to my right, where Dean is looking at me with a quizzical smile, clearly wanting to share in my private joke.

'Nothing,' I reply, mindful that both Philip and Ella are within earshot.

'Well, for nothing, it was certainly amusing you.' His expression and tone are now faintly accusatory. 'Were you thinking about *him*?'

I know immediately who he is referring to.

'Him? Who's him?' I fire back, affecting bewilderment.

'Radio boy,' he says scathingly.

I roll my eyes. 'Oh God, not that again. I've already told you, I barely spoke to the bloke.'

'So you keep saying.'

His voice is low and ominous, unsettling me. So, as it worked so well last time, I take the usual refuge of the guilty and once again go on the attack.

'Look, Dean, if you *want* to ruin my birthday dinner by picking an argument where no cause exists, then go right ahead. But *I* won't be participating.'

Ah, yes, that *other* refuge of the guilty: the moral high ground. But it seems to work. His mouth tightens and he pointedly turns to his right and starts a conversation with Josh, who, clearly grateful for respite from Mother, swivels enthusiastically round to face him. Within seconds, they are engrossed in predicting the outcome of the next Rugby World Cup.

I tuck into my Camembert and ponder why Dean has suddenly brought up Tom's message again. I truly thought he had accepted my explanation and had forgotten all about it, but clearly it's still festering.

During our brief chat about it, Saira suggested I put the boot on the other foot for a moment and imagine that *I* had heard a similar message from a girl seeking Dean after he'd returned from a lads' holiday.

'Would you just accept that it was some nutter and forget about it?' she challenged me.

Thinking about it now, no, I probably wouldn't. Even though I had been smirking to myself about Ella and Philip's food consumption, it was perhaps only natural that Dean's imagination had run away with him, particularly as I had declined to share my thoughts. He was only human, after all. And besides, I *had* behaved appallingly, snogging and God knows what with a man I knew very little about.

I flush with shame again, both at the memory of my infidelity and the way I have just snapped at Dean, who, all things considered, is being immensely tolerant. After all, *he's* done nothing wrong.

I reach under the table and snake my hand across his upper thigh, giving it a tender squeeze. He carries on talking to Josh, but surreptitiously places his hand over mine and squeezes back.

I let out a small sigh of contentment. It's going to be all right . . . isn't it?

*

'Oh, are you the *married* one?'

My mother's disapproving tone cuts through the cordial chitchat like a knife through room-temperature butter. I find she has worked her way down the table and is now sitting in Saira's chair, adjacent to Philip and next-but-one to Ella. The pair of them are looking shell-shocked.

I turn back to the other end of the table and glare mutinously at Josh and James, who are both locked in deep, clearly drunken conversation with each other.

'Josh!' I hiss, never quite able to admonish James. 'Clearly you've forgotten our deal . . .'

'Clearly I have,' he smirks.

OK, I actually want to kill him now and there's a large cheese knife lying temptingly within reach. But in the meantime, I need to avert the potential crisis at the other end of the table.

'Mum, Mum!' I cry shrilly, patting Abbas's empty chair next to me. He and an exhausted Saira bailed out about half an hour ago. 'Come and chat to me.'

God, I must be desperate, but needs must. Knowing my tricky relationship with Mum, Dean frowns in my direction, clearly puzzled by my sudden volte-face.

'No, thank you, dear, I'm quite all right where I am,' replies Mother firmly, before turning back to the disruptive task she has in hand. 'So, Philip, isn't it?'

Ella fixes me with a 'help me or lose my friendship for ever' stare, so I hastily slide along to the seat next to my recalcitrant parent.

'Have you all enjoyed yourselves?' I ask brightly, like an overoptimistic holiday rep dealing with customers who've just endured an inclement and unprecedented week of storms in their supposedly sunny idyll.

Ella smiles wanly and is about to say something when Mother's determined voice cuts across her.

'Isn't it terribly stressful, conducting two relationships at once?'

The glass wall between Philip's married life and the one he shares with Ella is one that neither Saira nor I would ever dare peer through surreptitiously in his presence, let alone actually mention to him. And as far as I know, Ella doesn't broach it either, not wishing to be perceived as 'nagging' and therefore, in his eyes, wifely. But a mere two seconds after meeting the man, Mother has taken a claw hammer and smashed right through it.

'Mrs Simpson, I really don't think—' begins Ella politely, her expression betraying an altogether less ladylike emotion.

But Mother merely studies her with beady eyes before interjecting, 'And you, dear, should think more highly of yourself than to share a man with another woman. You're stunning: you could have anyone you want. Why are you wasting your life?'

And there it is, the ugly truth, dripping its glutinous, unpalatable blobs on all of us, but particularly Ella, who is now looking faintly sick. Mother has uttered the sentiments shared by both me and Saira, supposedly Ella's best friends and yet either too cowardly, embarrassed or polite to put it quite so bluntly. I've come close a couple of times, urging her to rethink her position as, I saw it, Philip's occasional plaything. But I would never have dared to voice my opinion in front of *him*.

After several awkward seconds of stunned silence, Philip gives a cursory glance at his traditional, silver-strap Rolex and declares sarcastically: 'Gosh, is that the time? I think we've had enough fun for one night and, besides, I have an early conference.'

'Ah, yes, a conference,' burbles Mother to no one in particular. 'In other words, a meeting to decide when the next meeting will take place.'

Ella leaps to her feet, scooping up her pashmina with one hand, her clutch bag with the other. 'Happy birthday again.' She smiles at me but it doesn't quite reach her eyes. 'Thanks for inviting us.'

'Yes, thanks,' parrots Philip, sounding like he's auditioning for the speaking clock. His expression clouds slightly as he turns to Mother and inclines his head in a small nod. 'Charmed.'

'That's it,' she says wearily. 'Run away from the truth, both of you. Life's so much easier when you bury your head in the sand, isn't it?'

'Mum, *stop* it!' I'm furious now. She's made her point; no need to drive the stake deeper.

She obliges, but her thin-lipped expression tells me that she feels no remorse whatsoever for driving my guests away.

'I'm so sorry,' I mutter to Ella and Philip as I usher them towards the cloakroom area. 'Did I forget to mention that my mother's role model is Edna the Inebriate Woman?'

Philip smiles wryly, putting on his coat. 'Forget it. Mothers are always a little unpredictable, aren't they? I remember when mine reported her car stolen from a multistorey and the police found it on the floor above, where she'd left it.'

I grin indulgently, but inwardly I'm thinking that an occasionally forgetful mother is infinitely preferable to one with full-blown social Tourette's, speaking her mind when her opinion is neither sought nor appropriate in the circumstances.

'Well, thanks for coming, anyway. Maybe the four of us could have dinner to make up for this?'

Philip's face visibly falls.

'With Dean and me, not Mother,' I add hastily.

'Oh. Yes, let's.' He smiles quickly, then places a proprietary hand in the small of Ella's back. 'Come on, young lady, let's get you home.'

As I stand and study their retreating backs, I'm put in mind of a protective father come to collect his little princess from the school disco.

I start slightly as I feel a hand on my shoulder and turn round to find Dean holding my handbag and coat.

'I know it's your birthday but can we sneak off home now?' he says sheepishly. 'It's all getting a bit ugly over there.'

I look over to the table, where James has his head on his folded arms, clearly fast asleep, and Mother is jabbing her finger at Josh, who is slurring back loudly: 'Mind your own bishness.'

I nod gratefully. 'Yes, let's.'

Dean casually slings an arm around my shoulder and we walk outside, both wincing as we hit the cold night air. He hails a passing cab, holding the door open for me, and I suddenly start to see the comfort in such small gestures of consideration, how it gives you the feeling of being cherished.

So what if it's not constantly exciting . . . or even occasionally? Safe familiarity has its charms too, particularly against the backdrop of my high-octane family.

'By the way,' I murmur, nuzzling his ear, 'I couldn't

tell you earlier because they'd have heard, but the reason I was smiling to myself was because Philip ate only a lettuce leaf as his starter. I swear he and Ella could survive on hamster's rations.'

'He ate only half his steak too, *and* pushed his strawberry cheesecake away untouched. So I grabbed it from the waiter and wolfed it myself,' he grins.

Smiling, I snuggle into his shoulder and close my eyes. Dare I say it, but I feel something approaching happiness.

Chapter Ten

Dean and I have just had sex. OK, so it wasn't mind-blowing or earth-moving, but it was sex none the less, and a welcome change from the usual routine of me going to bed early and alone whilst night-owl Dean stays up until the early hours before eventually sneaking in beside me.

Some people say that sex isn't important, but I disagree. It doesn't have to be Olympian, it can be a perfunctory 'quickie' and still elicit the easy intimacy so vital to a successful relationship. Without it, the little signs of affection don't flow so effortlessly . . . the hand-holding, the occasional 'just because' kiss, the caring back rub after a long day. They all gradually diminish to nothing in the absence of the main event. Sex lightens the mood, if you like.

Look at Dean now. He's humming to himself as he wanders through to the bathroom to clean his teeth, and I feel more relaxed than I have in a long time, more optimistic too. Not very romantic, I know, but perhaps if both of us agree to a prescribed timetable of intimacy for a while, it will help us to break the impasse until such a time as affection comes more naturally again.

As the post-sex adrenalin rush subsides, a wave of bone-tired weariness washes over me and I plump up my pillows in readiness for sleep, just as he re-emerges looking remarkably chipper and bright-eyed for 2 a.m.

'Think I'll just go and do some YouTube-ing and wind down a bit.' He kisses my forehead.

I could launch into my usual routine of how TV and computers are stimulants, not rest aids, but I don't, not wishing to disturb the good atmosphere. Besides, I'm desperate for sleep, and having the whole bed to myself for a while means I can stretch out.

'Night-night. Love you,' I murmur from the depths of my pillow. I realise it's been a while since I've said that.

'Love you too,' he replies cheerily from the hallway.

I silently vow to say it more often as I drift off to sleep with a beatific smile on my face.

When I wake, at 9.10 a.m. according to my bedside clock, Dean's side of the bed is empty. As in never been slept in, covers still flat and smooth, pillow undented. He's probably fallen asleep in front of the TV, I think. It would be unusual, but not unheard of, particularly given the amount of wine consumed.

Stretching, I yawn hard and contemplate turning over for another hour or so. But curiosity gets the better of me, so I decide to see where Dean has laid his head to rest, then make myself a cup of tea and return to bed. Perhaps with him for a repeat performance of last night.

Padding down the hallway, I peer into the living room but the sofa is empty, the television off. Frowning slightly, I carry on through to the kitchen and find Dean sitting at the table, staring down at the floor. His laptop is in front of him, but closed.

'Morning!' I chirrup, with the confidence of someone who doesn't yet fully understand the situation. 'Don't tell me you've been up all night on that bloody thing?' I tap my finger on the Apple logo, then move across to switch on the kettle.

'Something like that, yes,' he replies flatly.

I turn back from throwing teabags in two mugs and squint at him. 'You OK?'

'Not really.' He carries on staring at the floor.

Genuinely puzzled by what can have prompted this melancholy from the man happily humming to himself just a few hours ago, I place a mug down in front of him and sit in the adjacent chair, nursing mine. 'What's the matter? Remember, a problem shared is a problem halved.'

'Yes. But trouble is, *you're* the problem.' He looks straight at me, his eyes a mixture of anger and sorrow.

'Uh?'

I just don't get it. We have sex, we say we love each other, and go to sleep . . . well, in my case, anyway. And now he's glowering at me across the kitchen table. What on earth has gone wrong in the meantime?

He lifts the lid on his laptop and I snort in frustration.

'Dean, *please* talk to me. Don't just tell me there's a problem between us and then start playing bloody computer games.'

'I'm not,' he says quietly. 'I want to show you something.'

The screen flashes into life and he turns it towards me, twisting his body at the same time so he can reach the keyboard. Under the table, I'm channelling my irritation through my tapping foot, wanting just to take my tea back to bed and polish off another couple of chapters of the latest John Grisham, desperate for the normality I'm usually troubled by.

The computer screen changes suddenly from the distinctive white of Google to bright orange with 'Flame FM' scrawled across the top. Instantaneously, I feel as though a bullet of ice has just entered my body and is now coursing round every vein. It's the website for the radio station Tom contacted.

By some miracle, I manage to keep my face impassive except for a mild frown that I hope suggests genuine bafflement. Though it's rather pointless, as Dean is looking at the screen and not at me.

'Now then . . . here are the live messageboards,' he says calmly, moving the cursor across and clicking. A list of daft screen IDs such as 'ditsygirl' and 'bovverboy' fill the screen, presumably people with little or nothing to do except exchange banalities with each other all day.

I stare at him, still affecting puzzlement but inwardly knowing full well what's likely to be coming up next and feeling every nerve ending jangling at the prospect.

'I couldn't get that radio message out of my mind,' Dean explains matter-of-factly, 'so I went on the website, to the bit where you can make contact with the person trying to find you . . .'

It now feels as though the ice bullet has travelled upwards and lodged itself firmly in the back of my throat. I can barely swallow.

'I set up a temporary, subsidiary email address to mine . . . using your name.'

I raise my eyebrows when he says this, from instinctive shock, I think, but he clearly interprets it as wounded surprise.

'Sorry.' He smiles sadly. 'But suspicion makes people behave in underhand ways.'

He taps the keyboard some more, using his forefinger to point to a specific 'reply to on-air message' box.

'I sent a message to him . . . as if it was from you.'

I shiver, feeling my forearms breaking out in telltale goose bumps. As yet, I have eaten nothing, but the urge to rush to the sink and throw up is strong.

'And?' I shrug, trying and no doubt failing to appear nonchalant.

'And . . . he replied.'

He studies me intently for my response.

'Well, he would, wouldn't he? Maniacal obsessives tend to.' I know I'm kidding no one, least of all myself. But again, although I'm protecting my own back in the process, my primary objective is to prevent Dean from being hurt. Yes, I should have thought of that before I leapt into bed with Tom, but I didn't. So now it's damage limitation.

'Actually, his reply seemed pretty normal. Look.'

He tilts the screen towards me, where an email from Dean pretending to be me says: *Hi there. It's Cam. How you doing?*

Tom's reply reads: *I'm good, thanks. I hope you don't mind me contacting you this way? Best, Tom.*

I relax slightly, relieved at its innocuous tone. 'Big deal,' I shrug.

Dean is tapping again, closing the website. 'Once we had each other's personal email addresses, we didn't need the website.'

Big deal indeed. *Huge* fucking deal, in fact. The feeling is that I'm about to be confronted with my – and Dean's – emotional Armageddon.

The MSN homepage appears, then my temporary, fake inbox. It contains four emails from someone called Tom Jarvis. So *that's* his surname. After waking up naked next to him, I never hung around long enough to find out.

'I'm going to have a quick shower and put on some clean clothes,' Dean suddenly announces, standing up. 'I'll leave you to read through these. You'll find yours in the "sent" box.'

I nod slowly, feeling my well-practised attack mode now to be futile.

He pauses in the doorway. 'We'll talk when I come back.'

After he's gone, I sit motionless for a while, just staring at the screen and wondering what I'm about to unearth. Options hurtle into my head at breakneck speed, then rapidly out again, each replaced by another. Do I simply get up and leave, go clear my head somewhere before returning for the showdown? Or do I delete all the emails and deny they ever existed?

A girl can dream, but I have made this bed and now I have to lie in it, albeit with great reluctance and dread.

My scant knowledge of the email system tells me that, for chronological purposes, I need to start at the bottom and work my way up. As I click, I taste bile at the back of my throat. What am I about to face?

From: Cam Simpson
To: Tom Jarvis
Of course not! But I must say, your radio message took me by surprise. Good job I have such an unusual name, I guess.
Cam x

116

From: Tom Jarvis
To: Cam Simpson
Indeed! I doubt I'd have found you otherwise. I was
also a bit worried you might not *want* to be found
. . . you left pretty abruptly.
Tom x

Instinctively taking a sip of the lukewarm tea I patently
don't want, I sigh deeply. OK so far, I reckon, but
perilously close to dangerous territory.

From: Cam Simpson
To: Tom Jarvis
I know, sorry about that. I wasn't thinking straight.
But now you've tracked me down, I'm really glad.
Cam x

The cleverly feigned ambivalence, of course, of a
pretender who knows nothing of what really happened
and is desperately fishing.

From: Tom Jarvis
To: Cam Simpson
Phew! I was hoping you'd say that. I didn't want
things to be awkward between us, because I was
going to suggest we meet up sometime?
Tom x

From: Cam Simpson
To: Tom Jarvis
To carry on where we left off?
Cam x

OK, so the 'fisherman' has just become as subtle as a deep-sea harpoon embedded in the forehead of its prey. My sinking feeling approaches one of drowning.

> From: Tom Jarvis
> To: Cam Simpson
> Whilst that would be nice (!), perhaps we should reverse a little and start with an actual date first? I know we had our day at the beach, but we weren't alone so it doesn't count. I was thinking more cinema or dinner this time?
> Tom x

I close my eyes in despair. So now Dean knows that my story about a brief chat in the bar before going our separate ways is utter hogwash. He is all too aware that the woman he trusts has blatantly lied to him. Tears of shame prick at the corners of my eyes, but I blink them away and compose myself.

What else is there? I can hardly bear to carry on, but know I have to.

> From: Cam Simpson
> To: Tom Jarvis
> Good idea. I hope you weren't offended by me leaving so abruptly. It's just that, well, you know . . .
> Cam x

To me, it is now blindingly obvious that these emails supposedly from me are being written by a cyber-intruder who is even repeating Tom's own observations so as not to put a foot wrong whilst blatantly trying to glean further, more juicy information. But then I remember that Tom thinks I'm a singleton and the notion that a suspicious boyfriend is behind these exchanges wouldn't even cross his mind. With a thumping sense of dread, I open the latest email from him, dated yesterday.

From: Tom Jarvis
To: Cam Simpson
Don't worry, I was pretty embarrassed too. I just want you to know that jumping into bed with women I barely know isn't a habit of mine! But I'd like to get to know you better, which explains the message.
Tom x

'Shit!' I exclaim softly, a lump of emotion constricting the back of my throat. I look at the time of Tom's last email: 9 p.m. Right when we were mid-birthday dinner and Dean was bringing up the subject of Tom, seemingly from nowhere. Now I know why.

But even then, he only knew that we'd spent the day at the beach together. Nothing more. Then he must have logged on after I'd gone to sleep and found the incontrovertible evidence of my infidelity waiting for him. No wonder he didn't come to bed last night.

The tears come again and this time I let them, my wet cheeks the manifestation of my deep sorrow and self-loathing. What *have* I done? What must poor Dean be feeling right now? Given the evidence, his restraint so far has been admirable.

As I wipe my face with the back of my sleeve, my mind starts to race. Clearly, there's no innocent explanation for this and I have to confess all. But can I minimise any hurt to Dean by convincing him that my one night with Tom had simply been a drunken aberration from which I've learnt the important lesson that what I have *here*, with him, is what I truly want in life? I'm not sure if I can even convince myself of that, but it's got to be worth a try.

'Well?'

I swivel round to find him leaning against the doorframe, studying me contemplatively. His hair is wet from the shower and slicked back, making his red, sleep-deprived eyes seem more stark. I feel a wave of revulsion with myself over what I am putting him through.

If I'd been a certain type of man, of course, and my girlfriend had pulled the email stunt, I'd now be ranting and raving about *her* underhand behaviour in a bid to detract from my own. But I know pursuing that line would be futile. Besides, I don't want to.

'I'm so sorry,' I blurt after a few seconds. 'But I was pissed out of my mind and it meant absolutely nothing. I can't stress that highly enough.'

'It clearly meant more than just nothing to him.' He doesn't move from his position, staring at the ceiling.

'I think he just likes me, that's all,' I shrug. 'If you hadn't answered his message, I doubt very much that he'd have pursued it.'

'And you wouldn't have been found out,' he says worryingly calmly, now gazing out of the kitchen window, as if contemplating what to do next.

Suddenly, now this relationship seems as if it's clinging to a precipice, it feels like the most precious thing in the world to me. The thought of this familiar, safe old rug being pulled from under my feet is wholly destabilising and my overwhelming instinct is to try to save it.

My eyes are stinging with the urge to cry again, but I know I mustn't, that it would seem manipulative.

'Look, yes, we ended up in bed together. But I was far too drunk to actually do anything.'

'Gee, thanks. That's really comforting to know,' he snaps sarcastically.

As he turns back towards me, I see his expression has changed from one of icy calm to blatant anger. I'm not sure which I prefer.

'Am I really so *fucking* bad?' he spits.

I recoil in shock, mostly because Dean rarely swears. He may be a 'rugger bugger' but he's quite old-fashioned in many ways and thinks it's disrespectful to use foul language in front of women.

'It wasn't like that. Truly,' I protest, tears now welling with such force that I can't stop them.

'So what was it like, then? Tell me. I'm fascinated to know.' He glowers down at me. 'And don't you *dare* start fucking crying. You've no right.'

I blink furiously to try to stem the flow, but it's futile.

'I met him in the bar and he invited us to join him and his friend at the beach the next day. You had to drive there so we went in his hire car.'

'*We?* Who's we?'

'Saira and me,' I reply miserably. 'Ella wouldn't come.'

'So she has got some sense after all,' he mutters. 'And as for Saira, I thought she was better than acting as moral support for your infidelity. She always makes herself out to be holier than thou.'

I shake my head. 'It was just an innocuous day at the beach as far as she was concerned. She doesn't know about the rest.'

The urge to sob loudly is all-consuming, but as Dean is managing to hold himself together, I know I should too. Tears are pouring down my face, but frequent gulping manages to quell any accompanying noise.

'Then what?' he demands.

'Then I bumped into him in the bar again that night – I didn't arrange it, I promise.'

'But as he was clearly staying in the same hotel, it was hardly rocket science to work out he was going to be there, was it?'

'S'pose not, no,' I whimper. 'Although I didn't think that at the time.'

'And?'

'And I got drunk. We kissed, and . . .' I feel like I'm going to be sick.

'*And?*' he shouts.

'And I ended up going to his room. The next thing I remember is waking up in the early hours and sneaking back to my own room,' I continue solemnly.

'How convenient.'

'Sorry?'

'Your amnesia.' He scowls at me, his eyes black with anger, a small muscle twitching in his cheek. 'Were you naked when you woke up?'

'I still had my underwear on,' I lie.

'I don't believe you. But you're probably trying to save me from being more hurt than I already am, so perhaps I should seek consolation in that,' he says bitterly.

We lapse into silence, mine guilty, his sullen. My mind is racing with what to do next, but deciding nothing. Eventually, I settle on the coward's way out, putting the onus on him.

'So what do you want me to do?'

'*Me?*' He slaps a palm against his chest. 'Apart from wanting you *not* to have leapt into bed with another bloke, I can't think of anything right now.'

'If I could turn the clock back, I wouldn't have done it,' I cry. 'But as I can't, we have to deal with it.'

I pause, waiting for him to respond, but he doesn't, continuing to stare at the floor, his hands rammed in his jeans pockets.

'Dean, I'm so, so sorry. But surely it tells you something that *I* didn't contact *him*, not even after hearing the radio message?' I mitigate.

He merely shrugs quickly before resuming his motionless stance.

'It tells you that I'm not interested in him. On any level,' I surmise on his behalf.

The phone rings in the living room, but neither of us moves to answer it. I'm desperate to end this impasse and carry on as normal, but I know that's not my decision to make.

'It's probably Stacey about the wedding.' I smile weakly. His sister is getting married next month and I'm her chief bridesmaid. Or maybe not, the way things are going. Either way, she seems to ring about eight times a day to discuss every last, inexorably dull detail. Usually, I dread it, but right now I'd take a seemingly endless conversation about which colour napkins over this.

'She'll call back,' he mumbles, pulling out the chair adjacent to mine and sitting on it. He still seems distracted, inspecting the end of his fingernails instead of looking at me, but I take it as reassuring that he hasn't yet walked out.

'Cam, do you love me?' he asks suddenly, his eyes now boring straight into mine.

'Of course I do,' I murmur, resisting the urge to add the fatuous afterthought 'Whatever love means.'

'I mean *really* love me, not just saying so because you think you should?'

'Yes,' I reply, and right now, here in my kitchen, with Dean looking wounded by my unforgivable behaviour, I feel that I genuinely mean it. I wanted excitement – well, now I've got it.

'And do you want our relationship to continue?'

I nod enthusiastically, again convinced that, at this very moment, yes I do.

He straightens his back and regards me pensively. He's clearly mulling something over, but judging by his softer expression now, he's erring towards conciliatory. So I stay shtum and await the verdict.

'OK, then here's the deal,' he says eventually, splaying both sets of fingers out on the table in front of him and letting out a long sigh. 'You're not to make contact with him ever again.'

It crosses my mind to mention that it wasn't *me* who'd made contact this time, but now is probably not the moment for semantics.

'OK. Of course.'

I let out a quiet sigh of relief and wonder what we do now. An uneasy hug, perhaps? Shake hands on it? But he doesn't seem to have finished yet.

'I will delete the email address I created, so if he contacts it again, his message will bounce back as undeliverable.'

Up until now, I haven't allowed myself to think about Tom as a person, finding it easier to regard him as a two-dimensional, distant third party who has inadvertently caused trouble between Dean and me. But now I can't

124

get his face out of my mind, the kind eyes faintly perplexed as an email bounces back, the engaging smile twisting with uncertainty as he finds out 'Cam' isn't communicating with him any more. I have no plans to see him again – never did, perhaps – but I don't want deliberately to hurt him either. After all, none of this mess is his fault. He doesn't even know I have a boy-friend, let alone that he's the one he's been exchanging emails with. The burden of shame and guilt is all mine.

'Sure. Fine by me,' I nod. 'Totally fine.' Just to clear up any lingering doubt.

'Good.' Dean stands up and readjusts the belt of his jeans, smiling warily. 'Now I just want to put this behind us.'

'Absolutely.' I nod officiously, feeling my shoulders start to relax slightly for the first time since I walked into the kitchen an hour ago.

'One more question . . .'

'Yes?' I smile, assuming it's in the back-to-normal category of 'What do you fancy eating later?' or 'Have you seen my favourite blue shirt?'

'Have you done this before?'

'Sorry?'

'Have you slept with anyone else . . . other than this bloke . . . since we've been together?' His tone is so matter-of-fact that he could indeed have been asking about food choices or his shirt.

'Of course not!' My shoulders have tensed up again through indignation, though given my recent behaviour I'm smart enough to know I can't suddenly take the moral high ground.

'Sorry.' He shrugs apologetically. 'I needed to ask.'

The phone rings again and he seems almost relieved,

walking purposefully through to the living room to answer it. I hear him say, 'Hello,' then launch into an analysis of the big match earlier this week, so it's obviously one of his drinking buddies.

I sit stock-still for a few seconds, wondering if the little exchange we've just shared was real. I feel like an employee who has just been admonished for poor work performance and told that if I try better in future, my failing won't be mentioned again.

I've been around long enough to know that, when infidelity rears its ugly head, the expected reaction by the injured party is usually one of unbridled fury or, at the very least, tears of hurt and disbelief. God knows I saw enough of that from Mum when Dad left. But Dean's reaction seems so . . . measured, not a sentiment one usually associates with passion.

Does this confirm my deepest fears that he doesn't really *care* about me, that I'm merely a comfortable constant in his life that he'd be reluctant to lose, nothing more? After all, to err is human; to forgive so swiftly, unusual.

Or should I take the more grateful view that he *is* simply unusual, a rare soul who cares deeply about me but doesn't see the value in histrionics?

Putting the boot on the other foot, as Saira so wisely suggested I do, I would have gone into meltdown if those emails had been sent to Dean from another woman. Does that mean I care more than he does, or simply that we're just very different personalities?

Either way, some might say it's not exactly a ringing endorsement for our future together. But right now, after the reasonable, mature way he has handled my deceit, *I'm* choosing to see him as a calm, sensible person who tempers my emotional excesses and keeps us reassuringly steady rather than bouncing off the walls.

I pick up the laptop and tuck it under a pile of newspapers, out of view for now. But something tells me that the emails within it and the memories they evoke won't be quite so easy to block out.

Chapter Eleven

Saira is speechless for the first time in living memory. Her eyes are bulging and her hand is clamped over her mouth. She couldn't look more surprised if she had jump leads attached to each nipple.

'OhmyGod!' she eventually splutters.

'Indeed.' I raise my eyebrows.

Ella says nothing, merely scrutinising me through narrowed eyes.

I have just spent the past ten minutes filling them in on everything, and I mean *everything*. From what happened with Tom after they'd both gone to bed, or in Saira's case into a coma, right through to Dean confronting me with the emails. My abject humiliation is totally and utterly complete, although to be fair, neither of them has judged me in any way at all for it.

'And you give *me* stick about being with Philip,' scoffs Ella after a few seconds.

Correction: Ella is now metaphorically sitting behind a desk wearing a long, grey, curly wig and brandishing a gavel.

'I know, I know, *mea culpa*.' I feign thrashing a cat-o'-nine-tails across my back.

'And I'm not even the one being unfaithful!' she adds for good measure.

'All right, all right. You've made your point,' I smile thinly, although I'm feeling far from cheerful. As one of life's great control freaks, I'm feeling distinctly queasy at this uncontrollable and escalating situation.

Knowing I was meeting them for a drink after work, I spent the entire morning mulling over whether to tell them or not. At one point, I was so deep in thought that I forgot to wash Mrs Davies's perming solution off in time and she'd left the salon resembling Shirley Temple on a particularly windy day. Still, she'd seemed happy, but then she is suffering from early-onset dementia.

On the pro side, I felt I needed to tell someone or I might burst with the stress and strain of it all. But one of the cons was that once it was 'out there' it might lead to uncomfortable questions I'm not sure I can answer.

'Are you absolutely sure you've made the right decision?'

Like that one from Saira, for example.

'What do you mean?' I hedge, knowing perfectly well what she's getting at.

'Well, you know, maybe Tom *is* more your cup of tea than Dean.' She makes a face suggesting she wants to say more but can't, presumably alluding to our conversation in Tenerife where I confessed I was feeling bored by my current set-up and felt 'compelled' to go to the beach with a man I barely knew.

I'm considering my reply when Ella interjects.

'*Cup of tea?*' she sneers. 'Oh, puh-lease. How bloody twee and *English*. What she actually means is, was he better in the sack?'

'Actually, I don't mean that at all,' says Saira crossly. 'There's more to life than sex.'

'Speak for yourself,' laughs Ella. 'I happen to think it's the meat in life's sandwich, if you'll forgive the *double entendre*.'

'I think you'll find it's more a single one,' retorts Saira. 'And I'm not saying that it doesn't have some importance, just that it's not the be-all and end-all. If it was, then everyone would split up the second they have a baby.'

'I can't answer the question anyway,' I chip in, anxious to steer the topic back to me so I can seek their advice, 'because I don't even know if we *had* sex.'

'But you said you woke up in bed with him?' frowns Ella.

'I did. But other than that, I haven't a clue what happened.'

Ella snorts loudly. 'He's a man and there's a naked woman in his bed. What do you think he's going to do – tuck you up and read you a bedtime story?'

'Not all men would take advantage,' says Saira firmly. 'Some have principles.'

'If he had principles, he would have taken her back to her own room.'

I hold my hands up in a 'stop' gesture. 'I'm not sure that even *I* knew where my room was, the state I was in.' I wince slightly. 'Let's put it this way, without going into the finer details, it didn't *feel* like I'd had sex, if you know what I mean.'

'Hmm.' Ella looks unconvinced but lets the matter drop.

'The important question here,' adds Saira earnestly, 'is *would* you like to see him again?'

I purse my lips, the beginnings of a headache starting to pulsate between my eyes. Prior to the radio message, I hadn't thought about Tom much. He'd popped into my head maybe once or twice a day before I dismissed him as a holiday fling that's best forgotten. But since he tried to get in touch, he's been on my mind a lot, his obvious interest in me proving seductive. True, *I* haven't felt compelled to get in touch with him, but now I know Dean has, and that Tom has responded favourably, I'm feeling torn between the two emotional extremes of forgetting it ever happened or leaping straight on a train to Birmingham.

'Yes. And no,' I reply.

'Good. That's clear, then,' says Saira sarcastically.

I ignore her and press on. 'Yes, because a small part of me – and before either of you makes a cheap gag at my expense, no, not *that* small part – would like to see if there *is* anything between us, or whether it was simply one of those little dalliances artificially heightened by being on holiday. And no, because I promised Dean I wouldn't.'

Saira simply nods sagely, as if sympathising with my plight. But Ella arches an eyebrow and makes a small spluttering noise.

'Then you have to go and see him.'

'Didn't you hear what I just said about Dean?'

'He'll never know.' She makes a dismissive waving motion with her hand.

'But *I'll* know,' I counter.

'Oh Jesus, don't come over all Goody Two-shoes now. It's a bit late for that. Look, it's very simple: this is clearly unfinished business and that's a very dangerous thing to have hanging around in the background when

131

you're trying to make a go of something, that's all I'm saying.'

She looks from me to Saira and back again, perhaps expecting a contribution but not getting one.

'It's like a flesh-eating disease, festering beneath the surface of your skin,' she continues dramatically. 'Every time you have even the smallest of arguments with Dean, Tom will drift into your mind as a "what if?". It'll be a constant itch unless you scratch it.'

Taking a hefty swig of her wine, she gulps a couple of times, then gestures that there's more words of . . . ahem . . . wisdom on the way. Advice after mischief may be like medicine after death, but what she's saying is undoubtedly striking a chord in me.

'You might meet him and think, Ugh, what was I thinking?' She curls her lip to illustrate. 'Or you might really like him and want to see him again.'

'It's the latter that worries me,' I grimace.

'In which case, may I humbly suggest that it's already in the back of your mind that you *are* quite keen on him?'

I've never had Ella down as being particularly astute, but today she's excelling herself. I decide to come clean.

'The thing is, I have been feeling a bit . . . well, *bored* lately. Dean and I just seem to be in a rut. I think that's partly why I succumbed.'

Of course, this isn't news to Saira, who remains palpably unexcited by this devastating bombshell. But to my surprise, Ella's expression doesn't change either.

'I've suspected that for a long time,' she confesses. 'Don't get me wrong, Dean's nice and everything, but he's not very dynamic, is he? His get-up-and-go has got up and gone.'

132

'He has his moments,' I offer loyally. Even though she's voicing precisely what I have felt for so long, I still feel uncomfortable hearing it from someone else without saying a little in his defence.

'And life isn't always about fireworks,' ventures Saira valiantly.

'No, but the occasional sparkler doesn't go amiss,' Ella retorts.

'She's right,' I sigh heavily. 'There's no point pretending. I *do* feel there's something missing, but I'm not sure what.'

Ella nods encouragingly, but Saira is frowning at me. Quite fiercely.

'Cam, you're your own worst enemy, you really are. I sometimes think you'd find fault in a hybrid of Brad Pitt and George Clooney. Perhaps he'd be a little *too* good-looking, eh? Or what if his big toe was shorter than the next one along? Would that be grounds for separation?' She glares at me challengingly. 'Stop being so bloody *picky*. Try to celebrate the good things about Dean rather than constantly focusing on his faults. No one's perfect, least of all *you*, yet you seem to regard this relationship as a period during which you decide if you can do better.'

It's true, I do have a history of being über-fickle when it comes to men. I once dismissed a perfectly nice man who asked me out in a nightclub because, in the airless room in the middle of July, he seemed a little sweaty. Another time, one of Abbas's friends expressed an interest in me, but I decided that his eyes were too close together.

Saira's theory is that I don't actually think there's anything wrong with them at all; I'm simply looking for excuses to thwart anything or anyone that might upset my ordered world by making me fall head over heels in love with them. She fears I have a self-destruct mechanism that activates the moment I feel a situation is getting out of my control; that rather than deal with ups and downs, I abort.

The reason I'm with Dean, she says, is because he kind of crept up on me. There was no 'ka-pow', just a gradual getting to know each other that, before we knew it, had drifted into living together. She reckons I feel safe with him because I know he'll never leave me. And given his muted reaction to my misbehaviour, I think she's probably right. I'd have to walk down the local High Street firing a machine gun into every shop front before he'd even *consider* the notion that I might be an unsuitable life partner.

'Do you know what, Cam? There's a lot to be said for someone who's dependable,' adds Saira, breaking into my thoughts.

Ella affects a yawn. 'What, like a faithful old dog?'

'Faithfulness is something to be commended, not scoffed at.' Saira scowls at her. 'It's the bedrock of any successful relationship.'

'And *she* has been unfaithful.' Ella jabs a finger in my direction. 'So that should tell you that something's most definitely up.'

Saira shoots her a death stare and Ella shoots one right back. Meanwhile, I sit in the middle of them, more confused than ever and feeling that my inferiority complex is wholly justified right now.

Do I keep trudging along the familiar, well-trodden path of life with a man I'm undoubtedly fond of and, if pushed, probably still love, or do I step out into the great unknown with someone who, so far, doesn't extend beyond a one-night stand? The thought of either is enough to fill me with trepidation, and it hasn't even crossed my mind that there might be another option.

'You could ask Dean for a temporary separation and spend some time on your own,' suggests Saira. 'You've been together for so long, perhaps you need some time apart to fully appreciate what he means to you.'

I stare at her wordlessly for a few seconds, mulling it over. 'No.' I shake my head. 'He'd think I was hedging my bets, and he'd be right. After what's happened, it has to be all or nothing. I owe him that.'

Saira folds her arms. 'So what's it to be, then?'

'More drink,' I sigh. 'That's what's needed.'

I stand up and walk across to the bar. When I've ordered I open my purse to extract a twenty-pound note and a small piece of paper flutters to the floor. I stoop to pick it up.

It's Tom's email address, written down by me shortly after reading the emails and just before Dean took his laptop away.

If I truly mean what I say – that he was merely an aberration and I won't contact him again, then I have no need of this piece of paper. I should just chuck it away and, with it, any link to Tom.

Tearing it into small pieces, I place the remnants in the nearest ashtray and, taking our drinks, walk back to my friends.

Chapter Twelve

Saira says she can't go to the pub or a party without someone boring her with some long-winded story about how the death of their gerbil when they were four means they can't hold down a long-term relationship, then asking her advice on how to move forward with their lives. Consequently, when asked what she does for a living, she's been known to reply 'tax inspector' in the hope it gets rid of them.

Equally, the minute I say I'm a hairdresser, I find myself being asked for impromptu consultations on someone's cut and colour when all I want to do is drink my white wine in peace. Today is a case in point. It's Dean's sister, Stacey's, wedding and I'm chief brides-maid, which rightly means I should now be on my fourth glass of chilled Chardonnay and being chatted up by every single, and probably some married, male in the room whilst Dean sits in a corner somewhere discussing the 4-4-2 formation.

Instead, I'm upstairs at the hotel, in Stacey's bedroom, doing her hair. She wants an 'up do', unwise considering her plump face, but she's adamant, and consequently I've got about seventy-four kirby-grips in my gob as I struggle to coax her rather thick, unwieldy hair into the right shape.

Talking of thick and unwieldy, the groom is sitting in the corner of the room, contributing his less-than-helpful views on how *he* thinks the perfect chignon should look.

'Blake, isn't it bad luck to see the bride before the ceremony?' I say pointedly, though there's absolutely nothing that could be described as 'traditional' about this couple. Stacey has been married before, a short, ill-fated union that lasted just eight months before she found her husband in bed with her best friend. She punched them both, the police were called, and the story made the local paper, much to Paula's abject horror. Hard to keep up appearances when your daughter's love story would fit in nicely on *The Jeremy Kyle Show*.

Six months later, Stacey met Blake – apparently named after Blake Carrington from his mum's favourite TV show, *Dynasty* – when he did the MOT on her little Ford Ka, and they have now been on – and quite a bit off – for around three years. Last Christmas, when they'd announced their engagement and much drink had been had by all, she'd drunkenly confessed to me that she felt she could probably do better, but she was marrying him because she's thirty-seven, wants babies and reckons he'll be a good dad.

'You can't ask for more than that, can you?' she said.

Perhaps you can't, I think now, teasing the last few strands of her hair into place.

'There you go!' I step back to inspect my handiwork.

'Ooh, it's smashing, thanks.' Stacey twists and turns

her head in front of the mirror. 'What do you think, Blake?'

''Sall right,' he sniffs. 'But I prefer it like it usually is.'

For the first time since meeting him, I actually agree with Blake. It never ceases to amaze me how many women choose to have their hair one way for everyday life, then opt for something completely different on their wedding day, invariably a formal style that doesn't particularly suit them. Then, of course, it's immortalised for ever in the wedding photos, which mock you from your mantelpiece for the rest of your born days.

Stacey has made a similar mistake with her choice of dress too, opting for something 'trendy' instead of classic, meaning her wedding photos will always scream 2010 rather than looking timeless.

It's a knee-length, peach-coloured asymmetric dress that exposes one Amazonian shoulder and bingo wing, with an overly fussy frill around the bottom. She's wearing peach mules that appear too small, her fleshy heels protruding over the edge. But her undoubtedly pretty face is perfect, beautifully made up by her own fair hand, a triumph of subtle, 'natural' colours.

Blake is wearing a grey hire suit that clearly wasn't available in his exact size. The sleeves are too long and there are at least three folds of excess material resting on each black patent shoe.

'Come on, handsome.' She places her hands either side of Blake's face and leans in for a kiss. 'Let's go downstairs and greet our guests.'

Because Stacey has been married before, they did a quick flit to the local register office this morning, with both their parents as witnesses. Now there's to be a blessing on the lawns of this hotel, in front of sixty friends and family.

'I'll just get changed. Tell Dean I'll be down in about ten minutes,' I smile.

When they've gone, I reach into the little wardrobe and pull out Stacey's choice of bridesmaid's outfit, a peach satin bustier and mid-length skirt, with peach silk pumps, specially chosen so I don't dwarf her. Blake's two young nieces are the other bridesmaids, a vision in cute peach frocks with long ballet skirts, and I just know I'm going to resemble a flustered, stocky heffalump standing next to them. *C'est la vie.*

'It's not about me, it's about the bride,' I mutter to myself.

Wriggling around, inching my ample hips into the skirt and fastening the zip, I try to imagine how I'd be feeling if this was *my* wedding day. Excited, perhaps? Or ambivalent, knowing it won't change anything?

It's largely irrelevant, of course, because Dean has never even come close to proposing and seems unlikely to in the near future, given recent events.

'He's obviously a commitment-phobe,' Mother always says when she brings up the subject of my continuing spinster status. Funny, though, I muse, that if a woman doesn't want to get married, she is hailed as being 'independent'.

It's been three weeks since Dean showed me Tom's emails and I'd like to be able to tell you there's a new urgency to our relationship, borne out of the realisation that we might have lost it for good. But sadly I'd be lying. Normal service has resumed. No peaks or troughs to report, merely the flatline of a calm coexistence. But hey, he doesn't beat me or talk down to me, and he doesn't expect anything more than I'm prepared to give, so let's look on the bright side, eh? Or as Stacey put it, 'You can't ask for more than that, can you?'

With one last tug, I get the zip in place and turn to inspect myself in the mirror. Peach isn't really my colour, but putting that aside, I look pretty good from the calves up. The bustier accentuates my ample chest whilst cinching in my equally ample waist, and the skirt hides a multitude of sins. My hair is newly washed and blow-dried by Luca into a sleek, shiny mane, the perfect advert for the benefits of having a good hairdresser. The only downside are the flat pumps, which make my legs look stumpy.

'Right, come on. Where's that big bridesmaid smile' I tell myself, affecting a fixed grin. 'Let's get this over with.'

Downstairs, most of the guests have already arrived and are swigging their way through the Prosecco with an enthusiasm that suggests there may be a few ugly scenes later on.

'You look lovely.'

I swivel round to find Dean smiling at me, his eyes lingering on my impressive *décolletage*.

'Thank you.'

He snakes his hand around the back of my neck and pulls me towards him for a gentle kiss. It feels nice and I wonder why we don't do that more often.

'Right.' I pull away from him reluctantly. 'I'd better do a last-minute check of the bride's hair and get myself into position for the ceremony,' I smile.

'OK. See you later.'

He kisses me again and I wonder what's come over him. The romance of a wedding, perhaps, though this one is hardly the stuff that fairy tales are made of.

When I track Stacey down, she's in the middle of berating Blake, whose expression resembles a shame-faced dog being ticked off by its owner.

'You just can't help yourself, can you?' she shrieks. 'I ask you to do ONE thing, just one, and you fuck it up.'

'Stacey,' I grimace, 'keep your voice down. The guests will hear.'

'Good! Then they'll know what a twat I've just married,' she retorts.

Blake's crime, it seems, is to have been caught having a drink before the ceremony, something he had promised faithfully not to do.

'You can't even get our marriage blessed without being pissed first,' she continues.

'I'm not pissed. I've had half a—' bleats Blake, unable to finish his sentence because his new wife tramples over the end of it.

'Whatever. It still means my husband of a few hours has breath that *reeks* of booze.'

It's a vast overstatement, of course, but I reckon pointing it out at this juncture would be tantamount to a death wish, so I keep shtum. Instead, my mind fills with thoughts of other weddings I've been to and whether they've lasted. So far, two couples of the five nuptials I've attended have since split, a figure I feel may rise shortly after today.

At Saira and Abbas's wedding, a riot of colour and celebration, I just *knew* I was witnessing something special, a bond that would stand a strong chance of lasting for ever. Today, I feel I'm witnessing a union that will be lucky if it reaches a first Christmas. This likeli-hood certainly occupied my thoughts when assessing how much cash to shell out on their wedding present.

Whilst Blake sheepishly slopes off in search of someone in possession of extra-minty gum, I repin a strand or two of Stacey's hair for what I'm rapidly starting to view as a piece of theatre put on for the assembled guests, a romantic pretence of two soul mates being joined together in holy matrimony whilst indulging in some unholy bickering behind the scenes.

'All set?' I smile.

She nods and smiles back, though I'm sure I can see a flicker of doubt in her eyes.

'Then let's go knock 'em out.' I place a hand in the small of her back and gently guide her out of the door, towards the lush, primrose-covered garden of the hotel.

'You may now kiss the bride.'

As the throng erupts in a mix of applause and whistles, Stacey and Blake lean in for a lingering kiss that betrays nothing of their earlier tiff. They look for all the world like a couple deeply in love and, despite their differences, perhaps they are.

Gradually, we all troop towards the long, narrow table housing the drinks, and the mingling starts, creating a fevered buzz punctuated by the occasional guffaw or exclamation.

Dean approaches and envelops me in a big hug.

'Well done, you.'

'I tweaked a bit of hair and I held hands with Blake's nieces. Big deal.' I smile and shrug simultaneously.

'But you did it beautifully,' he grins. 'I'm very proud of you.'

I frown quizzically, faintly bemused by the attention he's lavishing on me. Perhaps the presence of his parents and family is a contributory factor, not wanting them to suspect there could be even the smallest of issues between us. Or perhaps it's alcohol consumption.

Here's Paula descending on us now, looking effortlessly stylish in a cream skirt suit and dainty snakeskin-effect sandals. She's an oasis of elegance amidst a husband and two children who appear to have had a style bypass. Dean's idea of up-to-date fashion is the latest Man Utd home shirt, Stacey seems to choose her clothes purely on the basis that they prevent her from being naked, and Roy is shambolic in the extreme. Today, he's wearing a decent suit – probably chosen by Paula – but his shirt is open at the neck and his tie loosened, giving him a dishevelled air, and his shoes need a good polish. His jowly, hangdog face doesn't help matters either, with bags that could house squatters and a permanent five o'clock shadow peppered with grey.

'Cam, you look exquisite!' lies Paula. God only knows what she thinks about her daughter's choice of wedding dress, let alone husband.

'Thanks. You look as stylish as ever.'

'Oh, *this* old thing!' she chirrups, casting an anxious eye towards Roy, who is talking to Dean. She moves closer to me and whispers behind her hand 'Actually, it's new and cost a bloody fortune, but I ate the receipt so old misery chops wouldn't find out.' She jerks her head in Roy's direction. 'He might want to waft through life as if he's covered himself in glue and dived into a Primark bargain bin, but I don't.'

I laugh. I like Paula. She might have a few airs and graces at times, but she's a good soul. And she absolutely adores me, thinking I'm the best thing that's ever happened to her son.

Now on the one hand, a girl could take a positive view on that, counting herself lucky that she doesn't have the mother-in-law from hell parodied in so many films and TV shows. But as I'm one of life's eternal pessimists, I wonder if her enthusiasm is more attributed to the fact that her low-key – to put it kindly – son has managed to land himself a hard-working girlfriend with a bit of fizz to her. Or perhaps I'm just being monstrously egotistical? It wouldn't be the first time.

As Paula drifts off to do her mother-of-the-bride thing around the room, my brother James suddenly materialises at my side. As my and Dean's families have crossed paths on several occasions over the years, mostly Christmases and New Years, mine were invited today. But only Josh and James are here, plus James's girlfriend, Jenny. Mother has a prior bridge weekend engagement she said she 'simply couldn't get out of'. For which read, didn't want to. She's always perfectly pleasant when she encounters Dean's family, but she told me she finds Roy a bit of an oaf, and I suspect she feels a little intimidated by Paula's unerring glamour and the fact that she looks fifteen years younger than Mother when there's actually only two years between them.

'Talk to me,' says James urgently. 'Make it look like we're having a really intense conversation.'

'Er, *why*?'

'Because Jenny has been dropping very heavy hints about marriage, that's why.'

I raise my eyes heavenward. 'I'm sure you're imagining it.'

'No, Cam, I'm not. She said, and I quote, "Do you think we'll ever get married?"'

'Ah. Then I see where you're coming from.' I pull a

face. 'Haven't you only been together, what, about eight months?'

'My point exactly. And that's what I told her. But she said she's picking up some vibe that I might be anti-marriage and she wants to know whether I am or not.'

'And are you?'

'I don't think so. It's not something I've really thought about, to be honest. Maybe in five years.'

James is twenty-nine and clearly feels he still has his whole life ahead of him, still plenty of time in which to sow his wild oats before making such a grown-up decision as marriage and fatherhood. However, Jenny is also twenty-nine and probably worrying about the threat of diminishing fertility. I'm sure she too would like to feel laid-back about her future with James, just seeing where life takes them and making spontaneous decisions when they see fit. But lurking in the back of her mind will be the possibility that by the time James is ready to commit and start a family, her eggs will have shrivelled to dust.

Whoever created us has a warped sense of humour, I smile wryly to myself. Men with a natural inclination to play the field and able to conceive well into their old age, sharing the same planet as women with a natural inclination to settle down, who invariably struggle to conceive past forty. Little wonder you see so many thirty-something women tripping down the aisle with fifty-something men. That's the moment their mindsets collide.

'If you have no intention of ever marrying her, then you must tell her,' I say aloud.

James wrinkles his nose. 'But then she'll dump me.'

'Yes. And find someone who wants the same things

from life that she does. In other words, not a bachelor who enjoys the chase but clearly has no intention of eating the game,' I say pointedly. 'You owe it to her to be honest, so she doesn't waste any more time.'

'Time spent with me isn't wasted.' He affects a hurt expression. 'We have great fun together.'

I could spend the next ten minutes explaining to him that the majority of women want fun in the context of something serious, but I know he just wouldn't get it. And besides, Jenny has just returned from the loo and is heading in this direction with a determined look on her face.

'Hi!' I kiss her on both cheeks, but can feel her shoulders are rigid with tension.

James starts wittering on with some anecdote about Josh's ill-fated first date with an air hostess last week, and Jenny fixes him with a leaden stare that suggests she knows she's on a hiding to nothing trying to pin him down on any serious detail about their future. James's idea of commitment is to book a mini-break in a fortnight's time, so I can see the end of this latest relationship might be in sight. But if so, he'll bounce back, he always does. And compared to Josh, he's positively monastic. Sometimes, I look at the pair of them and can't believe that out of a hundred thousand sperm, they were the quickest. Josh doesn't have relationships, as such, more fleeting dalliances with a succession of leggy, usually posh blondes with names so far including Araminta, Thomasina and, inexplicably, Fig. All similar in their stunning beauty and distinct lack of grey matter. Of those actually introduced to one or more of our family, the girlfriend with whom he had the shortest relationship lasted one week, the longest a whole four months before she wised up to the fact that Josh has a roving eye that would turn even the most secure of girlfriends into a jibbering, self-doubting mess.

He's currently single, but clearly not for much longer judging by the way he's moving in on, yes, you've guessed it, a leggy blonde across the room.

The sound of a finger being tapped against a microphone brings the room to something approaching silence, save for Dean's granddad asking a passing waiter for another pint of bitter.

'Ladies and gentlemen,' says the hotel manager, 'if you would kindly make your way through to our function room, food is being served.'

I'm on the top table, with Blake on my right, Dean to my left. Blake is now clearly three sheets to the wind, with a speech still to make, but I reckon a pink-cheeked Stacey isn't far behind him on alcohol consumption so she doesn't seem to care any more.

After the last of the plates have been taken away by a succession of flustered, underpaid teenagers from a local catering company, Roy stands up and coughs into the microphone.

'Welcome all,' he booms, waiting for the last of the noise to die down, 'to the wedding of my daughter, Stacey, and now son-in-law, Blake.' He unfolds a tattered piece of paper and falteringly starts to read a collection of prepared jokes.

'When Stacey was born, she was so ugly they fitted tinted windows to her incubator. She looked just like me . . . then they turned her the right way up . . .'

Everyone laughs obligingly and I tune out, surveying the room for several minutes before Dean nudges me to share his obvious delight at one of his father's observations.

'. . . Boy, did she love to eat. So much so, we had to get her baptised at Sea World.'

Stacey's smile is so thin it's almost transparent, and I mentally tick off another reason never to get married – so I won't have to endure the same from my father, who would, undoubtedly, make Roy seem understated.

'But seriously, ladies and gentlemen,' he booms, 'our Stacey's such a bad cook, she won't even lick her own fingers!'

A mixture of the audience's goodwill and alcohol ensures his speech is a hit and he finishes off with the usual father-of-the-bride fare of how he hopes they'll both be very happy, but at least it's a welcome slice of sincerity after the relentless comedy act.

Then Blake stands up, slightly unsure on his feet and clasping the microphone as if he is about to sing the closing bars of 'My Way'.

'I think you'll agree that my *wife*, Stacey, looks absolutely gorgeous today,' he says, and we all dutifully cheer on cue. 'In fact, so much so that I'm thinking of proposing again.' We all laugh wearily.

It's one of those heartfelt but not particularly original, one-size-fits-all speeches that betrays how little he really knows of his wife.

'People say it's obvious we're in love because we're always holding hands,' he continues, 'but that's because if I let go, she shops.'

I take a furtive look at my watch and note that it's five to eight. The 'party' part of the evening – in other words, Blake's erstwhile DJ brother and his 'bangin' tunes playlist' on his iPod – are set to start at eight o'clock. My plan is to do a couple of high-visibility dances, work the room a bit, then sneak off home when no one's looking before the night deteriorates into predictable mayhem.

I lean to my left and impart my cunning plan to Dean, who looks a little apprehensive.

'Let's see, shall we?' he whispers. 'Don't forget it's my *sister's* wedding. Besides, there's a surprise lined up, so it might be fun to stick around a bit.'

My heart sinks. It's bound to be Stacey's best friend, Gemma, a singer who got through to the boot-camp stage of last year's *X Factor* before her mentor, Cheryl Cole, decided she didn't own the stage after all and her 'journey' had come to an end. But even getting that far has been enough to turn her into a local celebrity, opening the new Costcutter on Marden Road and warranting posters outside pubs saying things like, 'Tonight, hear *X Factor* star Gemma Clarke sing a medley of your favourites. Tickets just £5 and the first drink is free.' She's very fond of belting out 'classics' such as 'I Am What I Am', 'Hey, Big Spender' and 'New York, New York'. In fact, I'm getting a headache just thinking about it.

Suddenly, I'm aware that Dean has stood up and now has the microphone in his hand. Ah, I think, that's why he knew about Gemma: he's been landed with the dubious task of introducing her. I stretch my neck so I can see round the table decoration, looking for signs of old lusty lungs lurking at the back of the room, waiting for her big moment. But she's still sitting down at her table, looking the worse for wear.

'As you all know,' Dean's voice booms around the room, 'my girlfriend, Cam, and I have been together now for just over six years.'

Hey? What's this got to do with Gemma?

'She's an incredible person. She's kind, loving and tells a great joke. Like Stacey's, her cooking skills leave something to be desired . . .'

There's a ripple of laughter around the room and I notice that everyone is staring at me with a knowing smile on their face. What the *hell* does he think he's doing?

'. . . but it doesn't alter the fact that I love her dearly and can't imagine life without her . . .'

Oh God. A stark thought has just punctuated the fog of alcohol swirling around my brain. This isn't what I think it is, is it?

'. . . So that's why . . .' He unclips the microphone from its stand and lowers himself to one knee.

Oh fuck, it *is*.

'Cam Simpson, love of my life . . . will you marry me?'

A woman nearby starts to clap her hands like a deranged lunatic and someone hisses, 'Sssssh,' rendering her instantly silent.

You could hear a speck of dust drop, and all eyes are boring into me as Dean kneels at my feet, staring up at me with smiling eyes that the longer my hesitation goes on are turning to pleading.

'*Will* you marry me?' he repeats plaintively into the microphone.

I can't think straight, other than the very clear emotion that I want to kill him for putting me on the spot like this.

The obvious answer is 'maybe', giving me more time to weigh it up in my mind before making such a big decision, but we've been together six bloody years so the needing-time-to-think argument doesn't really hold water. Then there's 'no', of course, but as his entire family are just yards from us in a state of high expectancy, I can't do that to him. So . . .

'Yes I will,' I say formally.

Dean leaps to his feet and grabs me, pressing my face against his chest as the room erupts in collective applause and general whooping.

'Thank you,' Dean murmurs gratefully in my ear. 'For one horrible moment there, I thought you were going to say no.'

'Talk about stealing Stacey's thunder,' I hiss at him, channelling my irritation into a side issue.

'Don't worry, she gave me permission to do it. She loved the idea,' he smiles, pushing his arm through mine. 'Here she is now.'

I turn to find Stacey descending with open arms.

'Congratulations!' she shrieks. 'Me and Blake are soooo happy for you. It's about bleeding time, isn't it?'

Oh, I don't know, I muse, I could have gone a little while longer.

'Yes, I suppose it is,' I reply quietly, but she doesn't hear me as the DJ's voice suddenly crackles across the room.

'Will Stacey and Blake please come to the floor for the first dance,' he booms.

'Come on, Blake!' She gestures frantically towards her new husband, who is rapidly downing another drink. 'It's our song!'

As Christina Aguilera's 'Beautiful' fills the room, an 'our song' I feel may have been forced upon Blake rather than mutually chosen, Dean takes my hand and tugs me towards the dance floor.

'Come on, let's join them.'

'We can't! It's their song, not ours.'

But as the words leave my mouth, I can see Blake gesturing wildly in our direction, encouraging us to share his very public pain.

A small ripple of applause breaks out as Dean leads me to the edge of the floor, which I sincerely wish would open right up and swallow me.

Swaying slowly to the music, I bury my head in his shoulder and close my eyes, trusting him to lead me.

Chapter Thirteen

The first thing I'm aware of is that my head is pounding so hard that it obliterates all other thoughts. Then one seeps through the fog that makes the discomfort seem twice as bad. I'm engaged. To be married. 'Happily' ever after. To the man merrily snoring beside me as if he doesn't have a care in the world.

Nausea and an anxious fluttering sensation in my gut have now joined the head pain in my medley of ailments. Oh joy. I'd like to just close my eyes and fall into a blissfully brain-numbing coma for the next twelve hours, the Land of Nod, where all is well and life-changing decisions don't have to be made, but sadly my bladder has other ideas.

Swinging my legs out of bed, I place my feet on the floor and catch sight of myself in the mirrored wardrobe opposite. Yuck is the only apt description. My face looks slightly grey and waxy, and I have a *Something About Mary*-style fringe, though thankfully without the aid of . . . ahem . . . nature's hair gel. Mine has clearly just hit the pillow at an awkward angle and stayed there.

I'm naked, and now it's official: when sitting down,

my unfettered breasts touch the upper swell of my distinctly pot belly. Bloody great.

In which case, perhaps I should be thrilled to bits that Dean has chosen to overlook my obvious physical imperfections and ask me to be his wife, but as I pad gingerly through to the bathroom, I can't say I'm feeling grateful.

If anything, I feel ambushed, placed in the unenviable situation of having to answer one of the most important questions ever posed to me whilst being gawped at by a roomful of virtual strangers.

Why, of all proposal scenarios, did he have to choose *that* one?

Perhaps, I muse, sitting on the loo with my aching head in my hands, he suspected I might say no if he did it privately. That an audience might shame me into accepting, which, of course, in a way, it did. What would I have replied if it had been done in private? To be honest, I genuinely don't know. And now I'm never likely to.

I hold my left hand up, just to double-check that a glittering engagement ring hasn't appeared overnight. Nope, still bare. Telling me loud and clear that Dean's proposal hadn't been planned in advance and had probably only been hatched in his mind earlier the same day, a kneejerk response to my infidelity and a feeling that a bit of spontaneous romance on his part might fix us.

Flushing the loo, I grab my dressing gown from the back of the door and head for the kitchen and a much-needed cuppa. Things always seem clearer after a brew, I feel.

But any thoughts I have of solitary contemplation are

shattered by the sight of Dean, my *fiancé*, wandering in two steps behind me, his eyes diminished to mere slits by lack of sleep, his hair mussed.

'Morning,' he yawns. 'Count me in if you're making tea.'

Instinctively, I reach for the mug that has a picture of Kermit and the words 'I'm a Muppet' emblazoned across it, lobbing in a teabag and haphazardly shovelling in one spoon of sugar. I slam the kettle on its moorings with such ferocity that he looks startled.

'You OK?'

'Sort of,' I harrumph.

'Which means no,' he sighs, sitting down at the table. 'Come on, out with it.'

I ponder for a moment, choosing my words carefully in my head, filtering out anything that might fall into the 'ungrateful bitch' category, which I undoubtedly am. I have never been one to choose my battles or think now, speak later, as the relationship experts are always advising us to do. I always wade in without knowing quite how deep the water's going to be. I'm one of those 'when all else fails, read the instructions' type of people.

'It's about the proposal,' I venture.

'Oh. Have you changed your mind?'

He looks so crestfallen that I instantly feel like a prize shit and instinctively seek to reassure him.

'No, no. Not at all,' I enthuse, immediately forcing myself into a dead end.

'Thank goodness for that,' he smiles. 'For a minute there, I thought you were backing out on me.'

Is it me, or has the air in the room been suddenly sucked away to virtually nothing? My lungs feel constricted, my heart is fluttering, my tongue dry.

'So what's the problem, then?' he asks amiably, looking straight at me.

'It's just the way you did it,' I reply lamely. 'I just felt a bit . . . well, ambushed.'

'Ambushed?' He looks perplexed. 'Is that really how you see it?'

I nod. 'A bit, yes. I always envisaged that when we got engaged it would be a private thing . . . you know, just between us.'

With a look of disbelief, Dean shakes his head and makes a muffled snorting sound. 'Cam, you amaze me, do you know that?' He stops speaking for a moment and stares down at the table, clearly composing his thoughts. 'You weep your way through soppy films all the time – remember when *An Officer and a Gentleman* was on one Sunday afternoon? When he walked into that factory and carried her off, I thought I was going to have to call an ambulance, you were sobbing so much.'

I nod silently, remembering it well. In fact, the sides of my nose are tingling just thinking about it now.

'You have told me so many times over the years that I'm not romantic enough, that you want some spontaneity in our relationship,' he continues, 'yet when I go completely against my character and stand up in front of a crowd to propose, you *still* pick fault. I can't bloody win, can I?'

He has a point, of course. In fact, more than a point, he's a hundred per cent correct in his observation. I am being ridiculously fickle. But I don't have the guts to tell him that the reason has nothing to do with the circumstances of the proposal and everything to do with the fact that I'm not sure if I want to marry *him*. Equally, I don't want to hurt him unnecessarily by voicing my doubts now when I might, given time, come round to the idea.

I console myself with the thought that, having taken six years to propose, Dean is unlikely to rush into wedding-organiser mode just yet, and a long engagement inevitably beckons. Plenty of time for weighing up the pros and cons and, if so inclined, backing out.

'You're right,' I sigh, leaning forward and kissing the top of his head. 'I'm being a twat, sorry. It's just that it took me by surprise.'

'Er, isn't that the idea of proposals?' He grins, clearly relieved that the threatened 'deep and meaningful' has turned out to be shallow and pointless.

'I know, I know.' I am feeling genuinely churlish now and starting to wonder how he puts up with me. He's a nice, uncomplicated person and I'm . . . just not. But rather than mark this down as another incompatibility in my mental 'con' box, I make a conscious decision to view it as a 'pro', that I'm lucky to have someone who's so accepting of the cow that I can be.

I sidle up to him and squeeze myself onto his lap, wrapping one arm around his neck and waving the other hand under his nose. 'Now then, where's the bloody ring?'

'Ah, yes,' he replies sheepishly. 'Well, as you're such a control freak, I knew that if I chose it alone, it would be completely wrong in every way, other than being circular. So I thought it better to involve you in such an important decision.'

'In other words, the proposal was a bit of a last-minute thing and you haven't got round to jewellery shopping yet.' I raise a quizzical eyebrow.

'Er, that too!' he laughs.

'What's the budget?'

'Up for discussion.'

'Hmm, interesting.' I wrap the other arm around the back of his neck and nuzzle his ear. 'In that case, let's go back to bed and negotiate.'

Lying in bed half an hour later, I idly study Dean as he rushes around the bedroom, grabbing clothes from the chest of drawers and wardrobe, hopping on one foot as he tries to tie his shoelace. As well as working full time during the week, he has to work one Saturday a month at the mobile-phone store, and this is it. He's already late. I, on the other hand, am one of the few hairdressers in the world who doesn't have to work on the busiest day of the week. This is because we also open on Mondays and, as manager, I'm there all week, so weekends are usually my only time off, and Luca steps in as 'Saturday supervisor'.

'Shit!' Dean stubs his toe on the edge of the bed as he stoops over to give me a quick kiss on the forehead. 'I'll see you later. I'll be home about six thirty.'

'Don't forget, I'm out with the girls tonight,' I shout as he retreats from the room.

There's a Champions League match on tonight, so I knew I was on safe ground when I told them I'd be free for drinks and a curry in Saira's local tandoori.

That's one of the good things about Dean and me, I think, swinging my legs out of bed and into my Bart Simpson slippers. We have our separate interests and are quite happy for each other to pursue them, without feeling insecure or excluded. The fact that Dean's pastimes don't extend much beyond the sofa helps, as I always know where he is.

As I pad through to the bathroom, I set my mind to pondering the other good things about life with Dean, determined to focus on the positive.

'Love is a decision, not just a feeling,' Saira is always telling me, though I have to confess I rarely take much notice. But thinking about her words now, I decide she's right. There are good and bad points about all of us, and we can either go through life eternally searching for the 'perfect' partner who quite obviously doesn't exist, or we can find someone who is fundamentally kind and decent and just get on with it. I know I have the tendency to overanalyse things and actively look for incompatibilities to fret about. Time then, perhaps, to relax a little and just go with the flow, ignoring the inconvenient fact that I currently feel like I'm oarless in a dinghy heading for churning rapids.

The phone rings and I know for sure it's going to be Mother, because no one else would have the audacity to call me before 10 a.m. on a Saturday. I toy with the idea of leaving it, but it's only delaying the inevitable so best to get it out of the way now.

'Hi, Mum,' I answer wearily.

'How did you know it was me?'

'Because no one else would call me this early on a weekend, unless it was an emergency.'

'Why on earth not? Life is to be lived, Camomile. It will simply pass you by if you spend hours idling in bed.'

I raise my eyes heavenward and inspect a patch of damp breaking through the ceiling, making a mental note to tell upstairs, yet again, to watch their overspill when having baths.

'How can I help you?' I enquire with all the shiny, new politeness of a call-centre worker on her first day.

159

'Can't a mother simply call her daughter, without there having to be a reason?'

'Usually, yes. But in your case, no. You're calling about the engagement, aren't you?' I sigh, wondering whether it was Josh or James who enlightened her.

'Well, dear, as *you* have brought it up, how are you feeling about it in the cold light of day?'

'Fine,' I lie, not wishing to tap the rich vein of my misgiving with someone who would undoubtedly broadcast it to the world. 'Why wouldn't I?'

'No reason,' she also lies. 'It's just that I know you very well and I hear you didn't look particularly overjoyed afterwards.'

'Really? And which of the twins have you been gossiping with?'

'The difference between gossip and news is simply whether you hear it or tell it,' she replies pompously, not answering my question. 'The point is that, yes, *one* of your brothers who cares about you felt you were less than thrilled by the turn of events.'

'It just took me by surprise, that's all. I felt a bit cornered,' I acquiesce. 'But I'm cool with it now.'

'Cornered?' Typically, she immediately seizes on the negative. 'That's a curious choice of word after being proposed to.'

'Is it? Which word would you *like* me to use?'

'Ecstatic? Or even just pleased?'

'Those too,' I remark drily.

'Are you sure?'

'Yes. Truly.'

I'm glad this conversation isn't taking place face to face because she'd clock my uncertainty immediately, but as it is, I seem to get away with it.

'Well, I'm glad you're happy, darling, really I am. I just wanted to make sure, given your muted reaction. I was worried your demons might be about to muck up what I'm sure is going to be a for-ever marriage.'

Her words hit me like a thunderbolt, not because I seek my mother's advice or approval over my relationships – far from it – but because she has never struck me as a particularly perceptive person. So her declaration that I have 'demons' has taken me by surprise as well as striking a nerve.

'Demons? What demons?' I long to snap, but deliberately keep my tone casual.

'Oh, nothing major, dear, just the usual stuff.'

OK, I'm even more wounded now. Not only do I have demons – according to my mother, anyway – but to add insult to injury she reckons they're *normal*, humdrum ones.

'Like what? Be more specific.' I can't believe I'm even pursuing this. Talk about masochistic.

'It's classic insecurity, darling. Because you come from a broken home yourself, you're afraid to commit to someone in case it all goes wrong.'

'Mum, I was twenty-two and self-sufficient when you and Dad broke up, not eleven and living on a sink estate with a drug-addicted mother. Believe me, I have no problem with commitment.'

'If you say so . . .'

'I *know* so.' I'm officially irritated now, almost to the point that I might elope with Dean tomorrow, just to prove her wrong.

It's not marriage *per se* that scares me, I want to scream, it's the thought of walking down the aisle with the wrong person. Or *are* my misgivings about my relationship with Dean merely a front to cover up a commitment-phobia that's so entrenched that even I haven't recognised it yet? Oh God, something else for me to torment myself with.

'Well, whatever, I'm absolutely thrilled for you,' she continues. 'He's good and reliable.'

'You make him sound like a car,' I mutter.

'You could use a worse analogy,' she trills. 'I mean, what would you rather have, a trusty VW Golf that starts every morning and delivers you safely to your destination, or a showy, temperamental sports car thingy that lets you down all the time?'

'Are they the only two options?' I say flatly.

'You know what I mean. Dean loves you, in his own way, and more importantly he *needs* you. Don't underestimate the value of that.'

'You mean he's unlikely to ever leave me.'

'Why do you say that like it's bad thing? Believe me, there are plenty of very successful marriages based on one person being needier than the other. You're a little insecure and Dean being so reliable is good for you. I have no doubt you'll be together for ever.'

'For ever.' I gulp instinctively. 'Those are big, scary words.'

'They are, darling. But it's what marriage should be, or the *intention*, anyway. Otherwise, what's the point?'

It strikes me that I've never really had a proper, grown-up conversation with my mother about how she felt about Dad suddenly leaving her for another woman after twenty-five years of seemingly happy marriage. Sure, I witnessed her initial devastation and tears which eventually morphed into anger and bitterness, but what does she feel about it now, thirteen years later?

Occasionally, the signs of residual damage are apparent, like her outburst to Philip and Ella. But for the most part these days, she seems happy in herself, and I now wonder whether that *is* the case or whether she has simply learnt to give the illusion of functioning to the outside world whilst secretly still struggling to cope?

'Mum, can we have dinner together?' I blurt, almost subconsciously. 'Just us, not the boys.'

'Of course we can, darling. I'd love that.'

She sounds so pleasantly surprised by the suggestion that I instantly feel guilty for not being a more attentive or even confiding daughter. My tendency has always been to block her out of my personal life for fear she'd take it upon herself to get involved. I'd like to be able to tell you I was shielding her, but it's more that I seek out good listeners to my problems, knowing that once I have voiced them aloud I am perfectly capable of finding my own solutions. In other words, I simply need a sounding board, whereas Mother is a sounding-*off* board who would be full of high dudgeon on Dean's behalf, lecturing me on what to do and endlessly reminding me of my criticisms for evermore, challenging me to do something about my fickleness.

But, I wonder, perhaps I can elicit a closer relationship between us if *I* become *her* confidante? And also, given my current 'engaged' status, I'm suddenly fascinated by other people's marriages, good and bad.

'Great. How about next Saturday?'

Even now, she blusters about various bridge nights, naming a date in a few weeks, but at least I've pinned her down.

After I put the phone down, I feel better. This is the new, maturer me, who addresses the issues in her life face on rather than merely burying them and hoping they never resurface. Just as Saira said, in so many words, you can't rely solely on feelings, your mindset has to be a positive one too.

So I have made a decision to forge a closer relationship with my mother and, from now on, I'm going to view my engagement to Dean with a self-prophetic enthusiasm. This is the dawn of a brand-new, decisive me. Now, if I can just put it into practice and decide what to wear . . .

A strange, slightly warped sound filters through from the hallway, the result of the doorbell batteries being on their last legs. Hopefully, it's the postman with my latest diet-book delivery from Amazon. I have an entire shelf of them in the living room, some barely opened, some half read, some voraciously consumed in one sitting in my eternal quest to have, as I see it, the perfect body. Though I suspect that until someone publishes *How to Eat Chips and Cream Cakes and Still Stay Slim*, bikinis and I will remain strangers.

Smiling, I throw open the door ready to greet our regular and über-surly postman with my usual cheery 'Hello!' that he subsequently ignores. It's one of my favourite sports.

But as my eyes alight on the figure standing there, my expression freezes to one of disbelief, my hand instinctively covering my mouth, my skin prickling with the sensation of instantaneous icy coldness.

'Hello, Tom.'

Chapter Fourteen

'Hi, Cam.' He smiles uncertainly.

My heart rate has accelerated to full gallop at the sight of my guilt-inducing foreign assignation now standing on the threshold of my home. Holy effing Moly, what do I do *now*?

Then I remember that Dean is at work and I instantly feel calmer. OK, this situation can be dealt with in a grown-up, sensible way . . . or at least, I hope.

'Come in.' I step backwards to let him in. As he passes me, a faint waft of his aftershave floods my mind with memories of that night, evoking a fluttering sensation in my abdomen.

'Go through to the kitchen,' I croak, clearing my throat nervously as I gesture towards it. From our demeanour, an outsider viewing this little scenario would surmise Tom's a conservatory salesman come to give me an initial estimate.

He hovers against the wall next to the kitchen door, clearly uncertain whether to sit or stand.

'Take a seat.' I gesture formally towards a chair. 'Tea? Coffee?'

'Tea, thanks. White, one sugar.'

The irony is not lost on me that I have slept naked in the same bed as this man, yet have absolutely no idea how he takes his hot drinks.

Turning away, I busy myself with opening cupboards to retrieve mugs and canisters for teabags and sugar. All the time, my mind is racing with what I'm going to say when he asks the inevitable.

'How come you stopped replying to my emails?'

Damn, he's asked it already. I don't feel in control of this situation yet; I need to stall for time.

'I'll answer that in a moment. But first, I'm interested to know how you found out where I live.' I deliberately keep my tone and expression serious, as if I'm genuinely bothered about how he tracked me down.

'Er, you're on the electoral register and there's only one Camomile Simpson in the London area,' he replies simply.

'Ah. Not much detective work involved, then.'

'If you mean using tracker dogs and an unwashed Tenerife hotel pillowcase, or consulting the criminal underworld as to your whereabouts, then no.'

'Good to know,' I add lamely. Not for the first time, I silently curse my mother for saddling me with such a stupid and overtly unusual name. It seems there's no hiding place from the damned thing.

'So, are you going to answer *my* question now?' He fixes me with a cool stare that suggests he's pretty pissed off with me.

'It's a long story.' I hand him his tea along with the age-old cliché.

'No matter. I've got all day.'

Sighing lightly, I place my mug on the table and pull out the other chair, once again busying myself with the exercise so I don't have to look at him. In fact, I have barely glanced at him since he walked in the door, not trusting myself to do so. I know that I'm going to have to tell him the truth. I'm not quick-witted or devious enough to come up with a convincing alternative at such short notice, and it would be obvious to even the most cerebrally challenged, let alone a policeman, that I was lying. Besides, as he's come all this way, I feel I owe him some clarity.

'I have a boyfriend,' I say softly, stirring my tea even though there's no sugar in it. 'We were both sitting here, at this very table, when your message came on the radio.'

'A boyfriend?' he repeats.

'Yes. He's called Dean. I should have told you.'

I look at him properly for the first time and see perplexity etched across his face.

'So why did you string me along with those emails?' he demands eventually, his eyes turning dead with distaste.

'I didn't. He did.'

As I tell him the whole story, of how Dean set up a fake email address and used it to correspond with Tom before confronting me with the evidence, his expression changes from anger to disbelief, then, finally, undisguised hurt as he hears how Dean gave me the ultimatum that I must never contact him again.

'And clearly you agreed to it,' he says quietly.

I nod, then shrug. 'What else could I do?'

'I see.' He takes his first sip of tea, which must be lukewarm by now. 'So on that basis and the fact that you yourself didn't make any effort to contact me after the radio message, it seems I have made a wasted journey, then.'

'I'm really sorry. I should have emailed you to explain

everything,' I acquiesce. 'But I didn't want to go back on my word.'

'Don't apologise. It's good to have principles.'

I'm unsure whether he's being sarcastic, given the wholly unprincipled circumstances of how we met.

'I mainly came here because I was worried when you, or what I *thought* was you, stopped replying to my emails. I thought something might have happened to you.'

A wave of gratitude sweeps over me that this man I barely know cares enough about my welfare that he would make this trip into the unknown. Followed by a small, demon-driven crash of disappointment that perhaps it's simply his protective, policeman's sensibilities that have brought him to my door rather than any strong desire to see me again.

Despite repeatedly and, for the most part, successfully, burying any desire I have had to see him, now he's here in my kitchen I'm feeling very affected by his presence, though I'm unsure exactly why. It could simply be apprehension rising from something I had compartmentalised as being in the past suddenly crashing into my present.

He seems slightly taller than I remember, and better-looking, somehow. He's wearing faded jeans and a simple, crew-neck, white T-shirt with short sleeves that reveal nicely toned upper arms. With the unrelenting light from the kitchen window illuminating his face, his eyes seem green rather than hazel, his lips fuller than memory serves me. The image of me leaning in to kiss them flashes across my mind and I snap my eyes shut to blot it out.

'Are you OK?'

When I open them again, his forehead is furrowed with concern. Extending a hand, he lays it on my forearm and I recoil as I might from an electric shock.

'Fine, thanks. But it does feel a bit hot in here.'

Standing up abruptly, I move across to the window, fiddling with the catch, then opening it to let in a cool breeze.

'Do you want me to go?'

The simple answer is yes, then this would all be over. He'd go home to Birmingham, back to his life and whatever future it holds. And I would carry on as if this visit never happened and marry Dean.

But I can't bring myself to say it, and I don't know if my reticence stems from pity for Tom or raw fear that I might be about to say goodbye for ever to someone I will die wondering about.

'No, stay a bit longer. As you've come all this way, it seems daft not to,' I add, trying to convince myself, let alone him, that this is the only reason for extending hospitality. 'That tea looks a little sad now. I'll make you another.'

I force a faux jolly smile and return to fussing around the kettle area, using the time to try to collect my thoughts. If I move the conversation to more neutral ground, I figure, we might both be able to escape this little episode unscathed.

'How's Jason?'

'Yeah, he's good, thanks,' he smiles half-heartedly. 'He's got a girlfriend now.'

'I hope she's worthy of him!' I joke, acting for all the world as if I've known Tom and his friend for years.

'She's very nice, actually. They've only been together a couple of weeks, but he seems really serious about her.'

I wrinkle my nose. 'That's a bit quick.'

'I know what you mean, but he's not like that usually. He says he just knows that she's different from all his other girlfriends.'

Marvellous. Yet another example of the 'when you know, you just know' theory.

'And how's Daniel?'

'You remembered his name!' His face lights up, but I'm not sure whether it's the mere mention of his son or that fact that my sharp recall might signify I'm more interested in Tom than I'm letting on. To be honest, the fact that the boy's name just popped into my head with no effort has taken me by surprise too.

'He's doing great, thanks. He *never* stops talking, though. It's exhausting.'

I hand Tom his fresh mug of tea and sit back down. 'Here you go. You didn't drink much of the last one.'

'To be honest, it was pretty lousy,' he grins sheepishly.

I burst out laughing. 'Bloody cheek. Though I admit making tea has never been my strong point. Now if you'd asked for coffee . . .'

Oh, what witty, Oscar Wildean banter we're sharing, all utterly dreary but conveniently diverting, filling the time between now and when he exits my life as swiftly as he entered it. I'm not sure what the next topic of conversation will be, but the weather must be a strong contender. Or perhaps tonight's television schedule?

'So how long have you been with your boyfriend?'

Blimey, wasn't expecting *that*.

'Um, just over six years,' I reply hesitantly, as if I can't quite remember.

'Six years?' His eyes bulge slightly and he glances around the room. 'So you must live together?'

'Yes. He's at work until six,' I add, to remove any doubt that he's not about to axe his way through the kitchen door and declare, 'Honey, I'm home.'

Tom raises his eyebrows. 'That's longer than Daniel's mum and I were together.'

'Just in case you're wondering, I haven't hidden any children from you,' I smile sheepishly. 'It's just him and me.'

Leaning across, he picks up my left hand and I get those electric shocks again.

'I'm guessing you're not married, then?' He makes a nodding gesture towards my bare finger before letting go.

'No.'

Again, I know I don't have to, but I feel compelled to tell him the whole truth. 'But funnily enough, he proposed to me yesterday.'

'Congratulations.'

The word may be a celebratory one, but his expression remains impassive as he scrutinises my face and perhaps picks up on my underlying reticence about this supposedly seismic event in a girl's life.

'And you said . . .?' He looks at me expectantly.

'Yes.' I smile weakly. 'But it was at someone else's wedding, in front of loads of people.'

'So?'

'So I felt a little ambushed.'

I don't know why I'm telling him this, but I just feel I want to, *need* to. Perhaps because I'm trying to mitigate any disappointment he might be feeling upon hearing about my engagement, or perhaps, far more dangerously, I don't want him to give up on me just yet.

He looks faintly bemused. 'It sounds romantic to me.'

171

'That's what he said when I brought it up.'

A small spluttering noise escapes his lips and his eyes are clearly mocking me. 'Hang on, did you *complain* about the circumstances of the proposal?'

'Not complain exactly . . . more a gentle grumble.'

He bursts out laughing and I find myself smiling along, despite the joke being very much on me and my churlish, controlling behaviour.

'Poor bloke. It sounds like I've had a lucky escape!' he exclaims.

'Escape from what?'

The atmosphere turns from light to deadly serious with the speed of a trapdoor slamming shut.

Tom studies my face for a few seconds, obviously mulling over what he wants to say, then lets out a heavy sigh. 'It's pointless denying it, because I've gone out of my way to find you. As I said in my emails to your boyfriend . . .' he shakes his head at the ludicrousness of the situation, '. . . I was hoping that we might start again . . . you know, go out on a date or something. But that was before I knew you were with someone else.'

'And now you've changed your mind?' I know I shouldn't, but I *have* to ask it.

'Well, it's a bit of a nonsense question, isn't it?' he replies exasperatedly. 'You're engaged and I have a young son, which means I need to know where I stand.' Shrugging, he adds: 'And never the twain shall meet.'

He's right, of course. But I still find myself rapidly considering my options and coming to the conclusion that there are only two.

Option one: stay with Dean and forget Tom, something I was trying valiantly to do before the latter pitched up on my doorstep. Or . . .

Option two: leave Dean and take my chances on someone I have barely spent a few hours with.

There *is* a third option, of course, and it's going it alone. In my twenties, the thought of solitude didn't bother me, but at thirty-five, and knowing that, in theory, I want marriage and children, it seems daft to give up on a relationship in which I have invested so much time, if not energy, simply to be on my own.

'What a mess,' I declare, unsure what else to say.

'Indeed,' he agrees wryly. 'To be honest, if I'd known you had a boyfriend, I wouldn't have come near you with a bargepole. I've never been one for complications.'

'Can I just point out that it was very out of character for me to behave like that,' I mutter. 'I wouldn't like you to think I make a habit of it.'

'Me neither. I blame Tenerife's generous alcohol measures,' he smiles.

We fall silent for a few seconds until I seize the opportunity to clear up something that has been troubling me.

'Did we . . . you know?'

'Did we what?' It's obvious that he knows exactly what I'm talking about.

'Did we have *sex*?' I squirm.

'Um, now, let me see . . .' He places a finger on his chin and looks up at the ceiling before staring straight at me and shaking his head. 'No, we didn't.'

I must look patently relieved because his brow furrows slightly.

'What do you take me for? You were absolutely blotto and, even though I find you very attractive, I'm not so desperate that I have to molest comatose women.'

Find. He said 'find'. Pathetically – worryingly too – my spirits lift slightly at this.

'Well, thanks anyway,' I smile gratefully. 'A lot of men might have taken advantage.'

'Yeah, well, I'm not like a lot of men.' His expression starts out deadly serious, then morphs into a smirk. 'But I did take a good look, though!'

I gasp with mock outrage and instinctively fold my arms across my breasts. 'Oh my God! I'm so self-conscious these days that I don't even take my clothes off in front of Dean.'

'Well, you shouldn't be worried. You're beautiful.'

And suddenly, for the first time in years, I actually feel it.

'Thank you,' I whisper, blinking furiously as I sense that I'm about to cry. I reach across and tear off a piece of paper towel to dab my eyes. 'Bloody hayfever,' I wince, but his expression tells me that he knows the truth.

'Cam, you don't have to answer this . . . in fact, tell me to piss off if you like . . . but do you *love* Dean?'

'God, don't you bloody start,' I sniff. 'A couple of people have asked me that recently, not least of all me. But what does it actually mean?'

He widens his eyes slightly, presumably surprised that I have to ask. 'It means that when you're with him, you feel content, as if it's the only place you want to be. It means that you argue occasionally – everyone does – but for the most part you get on well, complement each other even. It means that when you go to a party, you're happy to mingle apart, but take comfort from the fact that *he's* the one you'll leave with. It means that when you feel weak, he's strong, and when he feels weak *you're* strong. It means you feel part of a team, cherished, supported, but given your space when you need it . . . Shall I go on?'

I shake my head, biting my lip in an attempt to control the swell of emotion now threatening to engulf me. He's just described all of the things I *don't* feel. But then again, perhaps that's down to me and not anything Dean does or doesn't do. Perhaps I'm incapable of feeling those things about *anyone*.

'So, I'll ask again. Do you love him?'

'Not in *all* the ways you've just described, no,' I hedge. 'But love comes in many different forms, doesn't it?'

He nods. 'Yes, love for a parent, love for a child, love for a friend . . . etc. But none of them can be confused with the love you should feel for the person you're planning to spend the rest of your life with. It's different.'

'But presumably you felt all of those things for Daniel's mother, yet you split up.'

'Yes, but looking back, I'm not sure we *did* feel like that about each other,' he says regretfully. 'We were young and idealistic when we met, hooked on late-night clubbing and long lie-ins. Then Daniel came along and the shared responsibility was a big reality check that put us at each other's throats about who was doing the most around the house, working the hardest and so on.' He smiles ruefully at me and pushes his untouched tea to one side. 'Plus, it was easy to split up because we had never married. I didn't feel grown-up enough to make that decision and Daniel was a happy accident, not something we planned. But I'm older and wiser now and, as much as any of us can ever truly know,

I think I have a better idea of what a relationship needs to last.'

'I've already lasted six years with Dean,' I counter, 'so that must count for something?'

'Yes, it absolutely does,' he nods thoughtfully. 'But you have to ask yourself, is it through a basic compatibility . . . or just habit?'

And there it is, from an almost stranger: the question I have been playing over and over in my mind for the past few months.

'I don't know,' I sigh. 'It's something I think about a lot.'

Somehow, it feels easier, less disloyal perhaps, to unburden myself to someone who doesn't know Dean and is never likely to meet him. Someone removed, someone objective, though I admit Tom's presence in my kitchen after a holiday romance might compromise the latter slightly.

'Do you want to talk about it?' He looks at me questioningly. 'I'm not sure if I can be any help, but I'll give it a go.'

'There's not much to say really,' I reply hesitantly, now feeling inexorably awkward, given our previous circumstances. 'There's nothing about him where I can say he's this or he's that. It's just a *feeling* I get or, rather, don't get, if you know what I mean?'

He purses his lips. 'It sounds a bit like pre-wedding jitters to me. People get them all the time, apparently.'

I start shaking my head before he's even finished his sentence. 'No, I was feeling this long before the proposal. It was very much on my mind in Tenerife.'

'Ah.' He widens his eyes.

'Don't get me wrong. He's a really *nice*, kind bloke,' I

mitigate. 'But . . . but I'm not sure if that's enough.'

'Sounds good to me.' He leans his head to one side thoughtfully. 'If I was that way inclined, of course.'

I raise my eyes heavenward and give him a weary smile.

'Look, Cam . . .' he spreads his palms out on the table, '. . . I reckon you need to do some serious thinking. Far be it from me to pretend to know the answer here, but one thing I do know is that as you've already been together six years, you don't have to make any hasty decisions.'

He stands up, his chair scraping noisily against the wood floor. 'But you must have loved him once. Give it a bit longer and you'll probably find things will settle down again.'

'Are you going?' I feel deflated, wishing he would stay a little longer.

'Yes.' He glances at his watch. 'I've got a long trip home.'

'What happened to "I've got all day"?' I ask wistfully.

'That was before I found out you had a boyfriend.'

He walks across to the kitchen door and I follow him, gesturing for him to go in front of me. As we reach the front door, I pause with my hand on the latch, ostensibly blocking him from leaving.

'So what happens now?'

'Nothing.' He shrugs. 'I think we have what the Yanks refer to as "closure".'

'Do we?'

His eyes are sad. 'As I said, it's all a bit too complicated for me. I came here because I thought you were single . . .'

'And now you know I'm not?'

'It doesn't change the fact that I like you a lot, but it *does* mean that I won't be getting to know you better, to maybe change that "like" into something more.'

'Not even a friend?'

'No disrespect, Cam, but I have all the friends I need.' He places a hand on my shoulder and kisses me gently on my right cheek. 'Now I really *do* have to go.'

'OK. Well, thanks for coming,' I say formally, feeling leaden and deflated.

'Nice to see you again,' he smiles, stepping outside. 'Have a happy life. It's yours for the taking.'

I stand expectantly in the doorway, but he doesn't look back. Within a few seconds, he's out of sight, gone from my life.

Returning to the kitchen, I pour his tea down the sink and instinctively clutch the empty mug to my chest, crying my heart out without really knowing why.

Chapter Fifteen

At my occasional suppers with Saira and Ella, the conversation rarely extends beyond the mundanities of our lives. For example, Saira might bring us up to speed on Rashid's new tooth or tell an amusing anecdote about a particularly odious client she's encountered that week. Or Ella may reveal that Philip had said something that *could* be (if you suspended disbelief) construed as him thinking about leaving his wife, and we'd each analyse its possible meaning over wine and a simple pasta.

But tonight, instead of bemoaning Dean's latest housework transgression or a client's blatant rudeness, I know I'm bringing some real meat to the table, something we could chew on for the entire evening. So I'm letting the others vent their spleens first, patiently waiting for my moment in the spotlight.

'Do you know what? I meant to say, I could have hugged your mum the other week,' says Ella.

'Really?' I would be surprised anyway, but particularly so given my mother's disgraceful comments to them both and Ella's seemingly mutinous expression at the time.

'I know she was rude to me as well, but it was worth it just to hear her put Philip on the spot. Of course, I had to pretend I was furious, but I was secretly willing her to carry on, because I've been with him for two years and never dared do that.'

'So did it trigger a meaningful conversation when you got home?' mumbles Saira through a mouthful of bread.

'Meaningful is probably overstating it a bit, but interesting, certainly. He came as close as he's ever come to admitting he finds it quite stressful having an affair.'

I purse my lips, wondering if I've heard her right. 'But isn't that a bad thing?'

'Not if he decides to simplify his life and get rid of *her*.' She rarely mentions Philip's wife, Sally, by name.

The alternative is that he might choose to drop Ella from his adulterous equation, but neither Saira nor I mention this startlingly obvious fact.

'Are you sure that's what you want?' asks Saira eventually.

'Why wouldn't I?' Ella looks genuinely perplexed by the question.

Saira shrugs. 'Oh, I don't know. Smelly socks, grumpy moods, having to fill a fridge for two instead of one, having to take someone else's wants or needs into account. I love Abbas dearly and would never want to lose him, but I can also see that a part-time relationship must have its charms.'

'True.' Ella nods slowly, pushing a sundried tomato around her plate. 'But you also spend much of your time in a state of expectation, feeling disappointed and sometimes even bitter when nothing happens, feeling apprehensive when it does, and constantly wondering if or when it's going to end. You never just relax and enjoy the moment, always looking for telltale signs that he's about to leave, like a furtive glance down at his watch or becoming agitated as the light outside starts to fade . . .'

She peters out and stares into space as Saira and I exchange a quick look of 'ooooer'. It's the first time Ella has even come close to admitting such doubts about her arrangement with Philip.

'Yes, if you put it like that, then I suppose smelly socks are a small price to pay,' says Saira.

Ella doesn't show any signs of continuing so I take a deep breath and plunge into the void of silence.

'Well, *I* have some news.' Pause for dramatic effect. 'Dean has asked me to marry him.'

Such is my fixation on the dramatic, surprise element of my announcement that it hasn't even crossed my mind that it's not the most sensitive of leaps from one subject to another. Ella's face couldn't be more crestfallen than if I'd suddenly announced, 'Well, never mind your pathetic excuse for a relationship, *I* have a man who wants to spend the rest of his life with me and only me. Ha, so there!'

I lift my leg and remove my mock-snakeskin mule, clamping it between my teeth. 'Solly, Ella,' I mumble, before taking it out again. 'I have just realised that my timing stinks.'

'Don't worry about it.' She smiles, but her eyes remain wistful. 'I'm really happy for you. Honest.' She half stands and leans across the table to give me a hug.

'Assuming that you said yes, of course . . .' says Saira, staying firmly seated.

'Well, of course I bloody did. I'd hardly be announcing the fact with a big grin on my face if I hadn't, would I?'

Now Saira stands and hugs me too, but it's a lame one by comparison to Ella's and when she sits back down I can see her expression is a long way from unbridled joy.

'You're a dark horse,' she says matter-of-factly. 'When did this happen?'

'Yesterday. At Stacey's wedding. He proposed in front of all the guests.'

'Wow.' Saira raises an eyebrow but her voice remains flat. 'Pretty romantic stuff.'

I pick up her scepticism and run with it. 'No, I didn't know he had it in him either.'

'So, presumably you said yes straight away?'

I nod at first, my speech hampered by the large glug of white wine I've just taken. 'Yes. As there was a roomful of expectant faces, it was hard not to,' I laugh.

Ella reciprocates with a smile, but Saira's expression stays ponderous.

'Did you feel ambushed?' she asks.

Damn. I should have known this might happen, particularly from someone who often seems to know me better than I know myself.

'A bit at first.' I shrug nonchalantly. 'But I'm fine about it now.'

'Really?' She doesn't look convinced.

'Yes, really.' And I mean it. Sort of.

'Then I'm really happy for you. Congratulations.' Finally, her face breaks into a warm, genuine smile.

I smile back and give them the finer details of the proposal, but inside I'm feeling slightly destabilised by my best friend's initial hesitance. Surely, if Dean and I were meant to be, it would be a no-brainer that everyone in my life would instinctively jump for joy? But so far, only my mother seems to think it's great news. Hell, even my one-night stand saw fit to bloody question it. Ah, yes, *him*. And so to my next hand grenade of the evening.

'And whilst you're still reeling from the first revelation, I may as well throw another one in for good measure,' I say matter-of-factly. 'Tom turned up on my doorstep this morning.'

'What, *Tom* Tom?' Saira raises a questioning eyebrow.

'Isn't that a sat-nav system?' asks Ella, clearly oblivious to the import of my statement.

'Yes. Tom Tom,' I parrot.

'Will someone please tell me what's going on?' Ella pleads, throwing her hands in the air.

'The man called Tom that Cam met on holiday,' says Saira, as if talking to a small child with attention-deficit disorder, 'he turned up at her flat this moooo-rning.' She may be speaking for the benefit of our mutual friend but her eyes never leave my face, clearly scrutinising every inch of it.

'Bloody hell!' Ella's eyes widen. 'You've let me witter on about Philip and all the while you're harbouring two absolute corker pieces of gossip. What are you going to announce next . . . that you're pregnant with triplets?'

I'm trying to form a witty riposte in my head, but Saira slices through my thought process.

'What did he want?'

'Now there's a question,' I smile wistfully. 'First and foremost, to find out why I had stopped emailing him, I think. When I seemingly veered from chatty and keen to dead silence, he was worried something might have happened to me. He *is* a policeman,' I qualify.

'Human nature,' nods Saira. 'So did you tell him the truth?'

'Yes. The lot. How could I not when he was actually sitting in the kitchen I share with my long-term boyfriend?'

Both their expressions morph into mock horror, but I anticipate what they're about to ask.

'No.' I shake my head quickly. 'Dean wasn't there. He was at work.'

'So how did Tom take your, um, news?' says Saira.

'Remarkably well, considering.'

'But before knowing that, he'd come all that way to ask you out?' Ella scrunches her nose in disapproval. 'Isn't that a bit, well, *weird*?'

'Not when taken in context.' I could, of course, agree with her and be done with the matter, but I find myself wishing to defend Tom from the label of 'nutter' even though I'm unlikely ever to see him again. 'Don't forget, he thought I'd been emailing him, so it must have seemed out of character when they just stopped.'

'Well, I still think it's a *bit* odd,' sniffs Ella, standing up. 'Excuse me, I'm desperate to hear all about it, but I'm also desperate to pee. Hold that thought and I'll be back pronto.'

My heart sinks, knowing what's coming now I'm about to be left unattended. Sure enough, as soon as she's out of sight, Saira pounces.

'So how did you feel when you first saw him?'

'Surprised?' I offer.

'Don't be facetious. You know *exactly* what I mean.'

'Pleased,' I admit sheepishly.

'Pleased as in pleased to see a friend, or pleased as in gut-wrenching pleased that the man you're wild about cares enough to turn up on your doorstep?'

'That's probably overstating it a *little*,' I laugh. 'Somewhere between the two.'

She lets out a heavy sigh. 'Then may I humbly suggest you shouldn't be getting engaged just yet.'

'Why not?' I bristle.

'Cam, you know I have never been one of those friends who throw your confidences in your face, God knows we have mothers to do that . . .' she lets out a sigh, '. . . but in these circumstances I'm going to make an exception. In Tenerife, you told me you were bored with Dean.'

I purse my lips but don't respond, a sign she obviously reads as silent agreement.

'Now, when someone argues with her other half and says she hates him, I fully accept that it's a spur-of-the-moment emotion and that, one week later, she may well be madly in love with him again. Similarly, when someone says she's madly in love with a "perfect" man, I know there's no such thing and that, inevitably, there will be temporary fall-outs along the way that may cause temporary discomfort but probably won't change the bigger picture. But when a friend tells me she's *bored*, and has been for some time, that worries me. Particularly when that same friend becomes engaged to the source of that boredom.' She stares at me challengingly.

'I guess I realised that it was *me* who had to change.' I shrug. 'That if I was feeling bored, it wasn't his fault, but mine for being too pernickety and defeatist and that I should do something about it.'

'And have you?'

'Yes. We're doing more things together, or at least trying to.'

185

'Is that it?' She doesn't look impressed.

'It seems to be working,' I huff, annoyed by her obvious scepticism. 'Dean has been much more attentive lately. And he proposed in front of loads of people, for God's sake. He *never* would have done that before.'

Saira glances in the direction of the loo to check if Ella is returning. Even though we share many things together, there are certain, more intimate matters, that she and I keep just between ourselves.

'Look, I don't want to piss on your parade, Cam, really I don't. But don't you see? He's merely reacting to what happened in Tenerife with Tom. He's fighting another man for your affections and being territorial, getting a ring on your finger . . .' she glances down at my bare hand, '. . . or not, as the case may be, to prove you belong to him.'

I laugh nervously, not keen on the way this is going. Being a psychotherapist, Saira has an enviably good knack of nailing the reasons for people's emotions and behaviour, but on this occasion I don't even wish to *contemplate* whether she might be right, let alone fully accept it.

'I think that all sounds a little deep for Dean. I genuinely think he's trying hard to make things right.'

I can see Ella returning out of the corner of my eye and turn to smile broadly at her, anxious to move the subject away from such uncomfortable territory.

'Then at least wait until they *are* right before getting married,' she mutters. 'Don't say I didn't warn you.'

'Warn her about what?' asks Ella, sitting back down as a waft of freshly applied Chanel No. 5 assails my nostrils.

'About having a pudding,' I lie. 'A moment on the lips, a lifetime on the hips.'

'God, tell me about it!' Ella knows the calorific content of absolutely everything. If you were fighting for survival in deepest, darkest rainforest and chanced upon a rare, lesser-spotted something or other, Ella would be able to tell you the *exact* fat content and how much further you'd have to trek to work it off. 'I had a couple of mouthfuls of that delicious pudding at your birthday dinner and I swear I put on half a stone.'

I swear her pudding remained untouched until it was taken away (and probably devoured) by the waiters, but say nothing.

Saira simply raises her eyes heavenward, used to Ella's warped relationship with food.

'Coffee?' A waitress appears, pen poised, face impassive. Or is it simply miserable? Hard to tell.

'Yes, please,' replies Saira. 'With full-fat milk *and* chocolate sprinkles,' she adds pointedly.

'Mint tea for me,' says Ella. 'Absolutely *no* sugar.'

I order a standard cappuccino and the waitress slopes off, leaving me with the awkward proposition of where to take our conversation next. But Ella pipes up first.

'So, have I missed anything? When are you going to get married? Is there a date?'

I sense she's mentally dieting already to fit into some size-zero designer frock.

'No, not yet,' I smile. I would prefer to talk about something completely different, but innocuous chitchat about the wedding is better than returning to the subject of Tom's surprise visit. 'I'm letting the proposal bit sink in first before I submerge myself in wedding magazines.'

'Going to be a grand affair, then, is it?' asks Saira lightly.

'God, no. I doubt we can afford it. To be honest, I'd be happy just sloping off to the local register office and having a few drinks in the pub afterwards.'

'As you've waited this long,' says Saira pointedly, 'it seems a shame not to make a big song and dance about it. Why don't you let Ella and me help organise it, as our gift to you?'

'What a great idea!' Ella's eyes light up. 'I'm never likely to be planning my own wedding so I may as well throw myself into yours.'

'That's really sweet of you.' I manage a smile but, being an unashamed control freak, I can think of nothing worse than having others plan my big day for me. Besides, I'm not even sure I'm ready to plan it myself just yet. 'But as I say, we haven't got any further than the proposal yet.'

'And no ring, I see?' Ella jerks her head towards my left hand. 'So clearly, it was *very* spontaneous.'

'Or even reactionary,' mutters Saira, just loud enough for me to hear.

I turn my shoulder towards Ella, blocking Saira slightly. 'To be honest, buying jewellery isn't Dean's forte, so I'm rather glad he hasn't got round to it yet. It means I can steer him in the right direction!'

We all simultaneously take a sip of our drinks and silence descends. As there's no ring or wedding date, I realise I have rather hampered any further avenue for discussion.

'Right,' says Ella sheepishly, glancing at her watch, 'I'd better go. I think Philip might be popping round.'

This has happened before and Saira and I usually hang

back, relishing time alone to haul the minutiae of our respective relationships over the coals.

But this time, I lift my coat from the back of my chair and start to put it on. 'Me too. I'm cream-crackered after Stacey's wedding and need to get an early night.'

We both know it's a lie, but I simply can't face further interrogation about my feelings on Tom, Dean and marrying. Not until I've worked out what they are myself, anyway.

On the way home, staring out of the bus window, my mind drifts to Tom and whether he got home safely. Even on a friendship basis, it feels odd to think that I'll never know.

Chapter Sixteen

Luca has excelled himself this morning, resembling someone who has attended an all-you-can-wear designer flood sale. His tight green neon T-shirt ('Hilfiger, darling') is maximising the pecs he spends hours in the gym perfecting to full effect, and his drainpipe, black and white Gucci trousers ('They're *real*, you know, not from the market') are accentuating his equally pumped-up thigh muscles. But whilst his physique is a temple to masculinity, the rest of him screams a rampant homosexuality that makes Bruno seem in the closet. You've got to love him.

On his feet, he's wearing fuchsia-pink platform flip-flops that match the streaks in his otherwise dark brown hair. In one ear he has his customary two diamond studs, in the other a small chandelier of pink glass, cascading down to just above his shoulder. He's also wearing eyeliner and a smidgen of mascara.

Luca doesn't do subtle.

'Darling!' He minces across the salon floor, his arm extended. 'Let me see the ring.' He grabs my hand, looks at it, then drops it again as if it's a hot turd. 'Where is it?'

'He hasn't bought it yet.' I shrug sheepishly.

'Never mind, sweetie,' he drawls. 'A butch man like him should probably baulk at jewellery shopping anyway. Why don't you and I just go shopping for one with his credit card?'

'Because I will come back with an engagement "bling" that wouldn't look out of place on a drag queen,' I tease.

Luca *loves* Dean, though whether his affection for him lies entirely in what he feels is his suitability for me is unlikely. Luca is one of those gay men who adores straight men – the butcher the better – seeing them as a challenge, so Dean's penchant for sport and his emotional paralysis only serve to heighten his ardour. If only they had the same effect on me.

Last night I called Luca to discuss the possibility of him covering for me if I take yet another Friday off and had casually mentioned the engagement.

'Darling, that's fantastic news!' he enthused. 'You've nabbed yourself a good one there.'

Unlike my mother, who I regard as too subjective, here was a largely *objective* viewpoint I felt pathetically grateful for amidst the maelstrom of my own contradictory feelings. Hearing someone express genuine pleasure at my engagement news prompted an overwhelming rush of relief . . . as long as I didn't dwell too long on the fact that it was *Luca*, a man so adept at choosing partners that his last boyfriend turned out to be wanted for armed robbery.

Angela, the junior who washes all our clients' hair, is pleased for me too, though she has never met Dean so that doesn't really count. But right now, I'll take solace where I find it.

Mrs Cashman has just arrived, a lady of 'a certain age' who has been a client of mine for about five years now.

191

She's married with two adult daughters, both of whom come to me for a cut and blow-dry every so often.

'Did I overhear that you're celebrating?' she smiles as I tie the salon tunic at the back of her neck.

'Yes. I've just got engaged.'

'Congratulations! That's wonderful news. You've been together a while, haven't you?'

'Six years.'

She raises her eyebrows. 'Oh, well, in that case, you're absolutely sure you're making the right decision, then. I feel that some young people rush into things these days, but you certainly can't be accused of that!'

'No.' I smile to reassure her, but inside I feel my spirits sinking once more. There it is again, that recurring belief that normal people just *know* when they're making the right decision, no doubts whatsoever.

'How long have you been married?' I start to snip at her hair, knowing she wants exactly the same trim she has every six weeks.

'Twenty-five years! We celebrated our silver wedding anniversary only last month.'

'I'll be lucky if I get to paper.' I mean it as a joke . . . or do I? 'Has it all been plain sailing?' I deliberately keep my voice light in the hope she won't sense it's a loaded question.

'Not always,' she smiles warmly, 'but pretty much. There's always the occasional challenge that life throws at you, but it would anyway, married or single. And somehow, any problems seem easier when you have someone else to share the burden with.'

'Ah, but what if your husband is part of the problem?' I say idly, snipping her fringe carefully to ensure it's straight.

'In what way?' She's looking at me curiously now, probably because I have hitherto shown little interest in her marital set-up and am now asking pertinent questions about life, love and the universe. 'Do you mean infidelity?'

I shrug. 'Maybe. Or perhaps just falling out of love with each other.'

She purses her lips. 'I haven't experienced either of those so it's hard for me to say. Infidelity is something you deal with in your own way if you have to, but I don't really buy into that "falling out of love" thing if you once loved someone and have been with them a long time. I think people just stop making an effort with each other and let things slide. You just have to work hard at nurturing those things that made you fall in love in the first place.'

'Like what?'

She shrugs. 'Shared interests, being alone together, taking time to have proper conversation . . . that kind of thing.'

'And how do you *know* that you're in love in the first place?'

I'm doing my best to keep my tone and demeanour casual, as if I'm simply making vague conversation with a client out of politeness, but she's looking at me *really* strangely now.

'You just do. You don't even have to think about it.'

'And if you don't?'

'Well, if it's because of your own scepticism or inability to commit, then that's something only you can change, but if you *genuinely* don't know if you love someone, or could grow to, then you shouldn't be marrying them.'

*

'How do you think he'll react?' asks Dean nervously, turning down the narrow dirt track that leads to my father's cottage.

We've pretended that we just happen to be popping in on a Friday afternoon for no other reason than a desire to see him, but of course it's to break our news to him and his second wife. And as I only ever pay a flying visit just before Christmas, I suspect they already know something's afoot.

'I'm sure he'll be thrilled,' I reply. I know that even if he had reservations, my father, Jim, wouldn't dare express them after everything he put me through.

Since he walked out on Mum she hasn't spoken to him. Neither have the twins, siding with her as the injured party. So there's no way Dad will know about my engagement unless *I* tell him, and I feel it warrants a face-to-face announcement. Since the admittedly traumatic break-up of my parents' marriage, my relationship with him has never been quite the same. As a child, I utterly adored him, was a real daddy's girl. Every Saturday morning, we'd walk to the local common and buy a drink and a muffin in the café there. It was *our* precious time together, no one else's. On Sunday, he'd take the boys there to play while I stayed home with Mum.

At twenty-two, I moved out to a shared flat with friends, but came home a lot, still taking the occasional Saturday morning outing with him. The boys were expecting to head off to university the following year and finally Mum and Dad would have their lives back.

I had joked regularly with them about starting night classes or joining a rambling association to fill their time, but then, in 1997, he had waltzed off with Ava, leaving Mum's utter devastation filling *my* every waking hour.

At first, I couldn't bring myself to see him. I felt betrayed, abandoned and disillusioned by a man I had worshipped as infallible and now realised was just as flawed as everyone else. But after a while, and a few of my own short-lived relationships, I began to accept that there are two sides to every story and that it wasn't necessarily *his* fault that I'd placed such high expectations on him. Also, I missed him like crazy.

When I eventually contacted him, about a year later, he was overjoyed. But I made him promise he wasn't to tell Mum or the twins . . . not that he spoke to them anyway. I wanted to do it in my own time.

We met in a central London park, somewhere I felt certain that I wouldn't bump into anyone I knew, and had tea and cakes just like the old days. It felt good, if I ignored my nagging guilt. That's one of the worst things about some divorces: the children – however old they are – suffer torn loyalties, feeling that if they enjoy the company of one parent, they are somehow betraying the other.

After that, it was a discreet lunch here, a quiet drink there, all in fairly obscure locations, all without *her*, as I used to refer to Ava, whom he has since married. Much of the time it was so clandestine that I felt as if *I* was having an affair with a married man.

About a year passed before I plucked up the courage to tell Mum, who reacted pretty well and said she'd never expected me to sever contact completely.

'Whatever he did to me, he's still your father,' was her only utterance on the subject, and she's never asked me about him since. Whether this is because she is protecting me from having to play the eternal diplomat, or whether it is simply self-preservation, not wishing to cause herself upset, I don't know.

On the couple of occasions I broached the subject with the twins, suggesting that perhaps they too might like to reconcile with Dad, they both dismissed it out of hand. But for me, seeing Dad was one thing, agreeing to meet Ava quite another. When he first suggested it, I resisted, feeling it was a step too far and wholly disloyal to Mum. But over time, although Dad stopped mentioning it, I could tell my intransigence was causing him pain. He loved me and he clearly loved her, and for us to meet and get on would mean the world to him.

I didn't attend their wedding in 2000, but around five years ago, I finally offered to go for Sunday lunch at their house, an awkward first encounter, given that here was the woman who had conspired to cause my mother so much pain. But Dad was the one we'd had the relationship with, so if I'd managed to forgive *him*, then perhaps I should stop blaming her too.

Since then, I've seen her sporadically but still prefer to meet Dad alone. It feels better that way, less uncomfortable.

'There it is.' I point to the archetypal English country cottage right in front of us, with its thatched roof and wisteria-clad porch. It is exquisitely maintained, thanks to Ava, with not even the faintest flaking of paint on the cream sills and every window smudge-free. Dean has met Dad a couple of times in town, and Ava once over dinner at ours, but he's never been to their home before.

'Blimey, it's a bit twee, isn't it?' He pulls a suck-a-lemon face.

'It's Ava World,' I smile. 'Wait till you see the cuddly-toy collection.'

Sure enough, as Dad throws open the front door with a big smile on his face, Dean visibly baulks at the sight before him.

The hallway is fuchsia pink with a cream shagpile carpet that demands all guests remove their shoes and leave them in the porch. On the wall to the left is a modern oil painting of a naked woman, her pendulous breasts exposed, her head turned away. I have often wondered if it's Ava, but have never dared ask. To the right is a mirror festooned with crystals. 'Boudoir chic' best sums it all up.

'Darlings, you're here!' Ava sweeps majestically into the hallway, squishing Dad to one side as she plants a kiss on each of my cheeks and envelops me in a cloying cloud of Poison perfume in the process.

She was christened Ava after her mother's favourite film star, Ava Gardner, and has been trying to live up to it ever since. She has the same wide-set eyes and enviable cheek-bones of her famous namesake, and deliberately styles her hair like her. So in a darkened room by the light of a cigarette, there's more than a passing resemblance. But in daylight, Ava's skin has suffered the ravages of both her chain-smoking and refusal to leave the bedroom without an industrial amount of what can best be described as terracotta-coloured foundation. Consequently, she's more a bargain-basement Ava, glamorous but in a brassy way.

Glancing in the mirror, I now resemble a Toby jug, with a bright pink lipstick smudge on each cheek. Dean, lucky thing, merely warrants a handshake.

'And you must be Dean,' she says. 'If not, who on earth are you and what the *hell* are you doing here!'

Dean recoils slightly and shoots me an anxious glance before Ava descends into raucous laughter at her own joke, my father joining in. He always did have a curious sense of humour and now it seems he's found his comedic soul mate.

'Yes, I'm Dean. Er, nice to meet you.' His nervous expression suggests anything but.

We shuffle our way into the small corridor and the four of us stand awkwardly for several seconds, grinning inanely at each other.

'Come through, come through,' says Ava eventually, making small circling motions with her hands towards the living room.

There are two floral sofas, straight from Ikea's 'chuck out your chintz' ads, and a small plasma TV in the corner, the most modern thing about the whole place. The mantelpiece and bookshelves either side are covered with Beanie Babies, the soft toys fanatically collected by young girls in the early nineties but long since overtaken by myriad other fads.

And for the record Ava is fifty-four and doesn't even have children as an excuse.

Picking up a tartan one, Dean rolls it around in his hands. 'What's the significance?'

Ava shrugs. 'None. They're my babies.'

Dean shoots me a surreptitious look that suggests he's expecting to find one of them boiling on the stove, but I merely shrug in an 'I told you so' kind of way.

Ava *is* high octane and a teensy bit bonkers, and I have to admit that when I first met her I wondered if we'd ever find anything in common. But time has altered my opinion of her and I now realise that, yes, she is still all of those things, but she's also great fun and immeasurably generous in spirit. Although I have never breathed this thought to a soul, I can understand why Dad left his rather measured marriage for one of life's great, slightly eccentric adventurers. To me, who goes through life fretting about what others might think of me, Ava appears liberated, clearly not giving a fig about keeping up appearances. Which probably explains the Beanie Baby collection.

'Right!' Dad claps his hands together. 'Who wants tea?'

Five minutes later, we are all gathered around a particularly low coffee table, our knees pressed against it, such is the positioning of the armchairs.

'Dean and I have some news,' I venture between slurps.

'We thought you might, didn't we, Jim?' Ava looks at him but doesn't wait for a reply. 'I said, "She's got some news."' She stares at my stomach. 'Is there a little one on the way, then?'

I instinctively suck in my abdomen whilst my father has the grace to look embarrassed.

'Ava, darling, let's not make wild guesses. Let Cam tell us.'

'Dean and I are engaged,' I beam.

'That's fantastic news!' Dad jumps up and bangs his knee against the table. 'Ouch! Ouch!' He moves to one side and starts hopping around with an expression of agony, leaving me lingering with my arms in mid-air.

Ava fills the space, her ample bosom pressing against mine, her hair pressing against my mouth and sticking to what's left of my lip gloss.

'Oh, we're so happy for you both!' She leans away from me towards Dean, who looks visibly alarmed at the sight of the vision descending upon him in a theatrical hug. 'So when's the big day?'

The thought of Ava in a gargantuan lime-green hat flashes into my mind, along with the very real and present danger of her and Mother throwing bread rolls at each other across the top table.

'Um, we haven't got that far yet. One thing at a time,' I smile warily.

'You youngsters! So laid-back these days, aren't they, Jim?'

As I didn't go to their wedding, I can't comment on the finer details of it, but I *can* tell you that the wedding photograph I'm now staring at over Dad's right shoulder indicates that it was every bit as flamboyant as the bride, who's wearing a low-cut dress in pillarbox-red lace.

'You're right. We *should* name the day.'

At the sound of Dean's voice, I jerk my head round to face him, just to double-check it was actually he who said it.

'How about spring sometime?'

Yep. It's him all right. Looking right at me. Wanting to make our engagement *really* official. And once again doing it in front of other people so I can't bloody wriggle out of it.

'Spring, summer, whenever,' I bluster.

'These things need organising, Cam. We can't be too casual about it,' he ploughs on.

'Summer, then,' I smile, reaching for a Bourbon biscuit and hoping that's the end of the matter.

But Ava is rummaging around in her vast handbag and pulls out an A4 desk diary. She flicks to the 'looking ahead' page at the back and runs a red manicured fingernail down it.

'July the ninth is a Saturday,' she says brightly. 'Or the sixteenth? Or the twenty-third?'

Yes, yes, I think murderously. We can all bloody count.

'Any of those sounds good to me,' says Dean, looking at me questioningly.

A small fist of anxiety has formed in my chest, but I tell myself it's just the obligatory nerves that routinely accompany any momentous occasion in our lives.

'July the twenty-third, then,' I nod. 'Let's aim for that. Hopefully, there'll be less chance of rain by then.'

'Excellent!' Dean looks genuinely pleased. Or is it relieved?

'That's better,' smiles Ava. 'Now you can both enjoy planning the big day.'

In other words, I'll be the one doing the organising, with Dean taking his usual 'whatever you want' stance. Mind you, after years with a woman who won't let him buy loo roll without consulting her first, who can blame him?

The conversation moves on to Dean's job and I drift off into my own world, my mind filling with matters of great import such as what's on TV tonight and trying to remember if the salon schedule for Monday is a busy one.

'It's nice to finally see you settled,' says Dad, smiling at me as we take a short stroll around the garden. It has to be short as the garden is only thirty feet by twenty. But in that compact space he's managed to create a wonderfully colourful array of plants that would undoubtedly win a prize at even the grandest of flower shows.

Funny, isn't it, how when we're young, we can't think of anything duller than the creative or nurturing pursuits of, say, cooking or gardening. We open packets and reheat, thinking any other level of food preparation as a waste of time, and we're more than happy to look out over a concreted back yard that houses little more than dustbins and maybe a couple of rusting student bikes.

But then the inevitable happens and we inexplicably find ourselves drawn to the more leisurely pursuits of life, or wearing clothes purely for comfort rather than because they make a statement about our quirkiness or edge. Saira reckons it's simply part of Mother Nature's grand plan because there isn't room for all of us in the nation's nightclubs.

Dean is in the kitchen, helping Ava with the lunch by peeling potatoes and carrots, a skill I didn't even know he'd mastered. Again, perhaps it's up to me to delegate more and take what comes, rather than arrogantly assuming no one can do a task better than me and thereby doing everything myself.

'Dean seems really nice,' says Dad casually, tending to an overgrowing lavender bush.

'You've met him before.'

'I know. But only a couple of times, and I wasn't sure if it was serious.'

'Not serious? Dad, we've been living together for four years! How much more serious can it get?'

He shrugs nonchalantly. 'From my point of view, living together isn't anything like as serious as marriage. Living together, you can have an argument, pack your bags and leave. It's not as easy to leave a marriage.'

I resist the urge to snap, 'Well, you managed it easily

202

enough.' Besides, something more important than petty point-scoring is occupying my thoughts.

'Why didn't you think it was serious?'

'No particular reason.' He purses his lips in thought. 'Just a feeling, I guess.'

'What sort of feeling?' I demand. 'Like a heavy doom, or an "uh-oh", or just a faint twinge?'

He's looking at me closely now with an undisguised expression of bemusement. 'Um, none of those really. I didn't think about it deeply, it was just an almost subconscious feeling I had, I suppose, that he wouldn't be the one you'd end up marrying and having kids with.'

I am actually feeling properly sick now, as if this morning's bacon butty, consumed in a weak moment, is about to re-emerge. I swallow hard, trying desperately to stay in control of my bodily functions.

'Cam, are you OK?'

I must look rather green around the gills as Dad has now laid a hand on my shoulder and is viewing me with great concern. I simply nod valiantly.

'Look, it doesn't matter what I or anyone else thinks, what's important is what *you* feel about him,' he murmurs in a reassuring tone. 'For obvious reasons, just about *everyone* in my life was against the idea of me marrying Ava, but *I* wanted to, and that's what mattered.' He removes his hand from my shoulder and pulls me towards him in a full hug. 'This is about you and Dean and the rest of your life together. You'll find that all sorts of people will have an opinion on it, but ultimately they won't be there with you, walking in your shoes. So it's not their decision. It's yours.'

Undoubtedly, he means this as a pep talk, but it only serves to deliver me right back at the door of my original dilemma, of whether this whole wedding business is what I really want. If *Dean* is what I really want.

'Tell me about Ava,' I say, sitting down on their two-seater garden bench and patting the empty space next to me. 'How did you know?'

'I just did.' His whole face has lit up at the mere thought of her. 'For the first time in my life, I felt I was with someone who understood me, who accepted my little foibles and didn't want to change me.'

Dean doesn't want to change me either, I think. That's a good thing.

'And I presume you didn't feel that with Mum?'

He looks apologetic. 'Perhaps we shouldn't continue this conversation.'

'No, it's fine. I'm a big girl now,' I smile. 'Besides, as you're divorced, I've kind of worked out for myself that something wasn't right.'

'Good point.' He lets out a small sigh and glances towards the kitchen window, where Ava is still standing at the sink, chatting animatedly to Dean, who is out of sight. 'Your mum and I got married very young . . . that's what you did in those days. And it's very difficult to make a "for-ever" decision when you're only twenty-two and twenty-three.'

'And what about when you're thirty-five?' I smile wryly.

'It should be a lot easier. And if it isn't, well, that should perhaps give you pause for thought. I just hope that nothing I did has affected the way you view relationships.'

I wrinkle my nose. 'I don't think so. And even if it did, in some small, subliminal way, I can see that you're very happy now . . . so I know it can be done.'

'I'm very happy.' He stands up and brushes down the back of his trousers, before looking down at me with a warm smile. 'And I'm sure you'll be happy too. At the end of the day, you have to trust your own judgement. Now come on, let's go help lay the table for lunch.'

I follow him inside, wishing that I shared his optimism.

Chapter Seventeen

It's nine thirty on a Sunday morning and I'm standing at the bus stop at the end of our road in the driving rain. Don't ask me why.

In an uncharacteristic outburst of energy and spontaneity, Dean set the alarm for eight thirty, insisted I got out of bed, and made us a hasty couple of pieces of toast each before bringing me here.

It's a 'surprise' apparently, a mystery outing he's organised, presumably in the hope of bringing the spice of variety into our lives that I often complain is missing. So I can't moan, but boy, do I want to.

On the bus, frequented only by an elderly man and his grey-muzzled Jack Russell, which growls menacingly as I walk past, we sit near the back in total silence, each staring out of the grubby window. It's not awkward, it's one of those comfortable silences between two people who know each other very well.

I idly wonder where he's taking me. The theatre, perhaps? Although it's a little early and I have made it plain on several occasions over the years that, aside from a few notable exceptions, I *loathe* going to the theatre. Particularly to musicals. All that singing does my head in.

A boat trip down the Thames, then? Followed by lunch? I don't mind the last bit, but I'm not keen on any form of water-based activity, to be honest. In fact, on the one occasion I agreed to go on the ferry to France, as it was cheap, the sea was uncharacteristically rough and I spent the entire journey vomiting into a paper cup, which Dean had to keep emptying in preparation for the next regurgitation. So I can't imagine he'd risk a repeat episode.

Which leaves me completely stumped.

'What are you thinking about?' I ask him, hoping the answer might offer a clue, or he might simply feel now is the time to tell all about our destination.

'Spurs' chances in the Cup,' he replies, grinning sheepishly. 'I'm not sure the team is at full strength.'

I jokingly roll my eyes and we return to staring wordlessly out of the window until I feel his elbow jab my right forearm.

'Come on. This is our stop.'

I look around me and see we're disembarking on a main road running through the middle of Earls Court, an area of London with a mostly transient population of young travellers and asylum seekers awaiting permission to stay whilst whiling their time away in soulless bedsits or B&Bs.

The only landmark building is the Earls Court Arena, which hosts various concerts and exhibitions such as the Ideal Home Show. There it is now, in front of me, its vast frontage covered with a banner declaring . . . Oh God, no . . . it can't be . . . Yes, it is . . .

The National Wedding Show.

I turn and look at Dean, who is grinning from ear to ear, his eyebrows raised in expectation. 'Ta-dah!' Like a magician's assistant, he swivels his arms towards the sign. 'Surprise, surprise!'

Jesus, he's acting as if he's put the flaming show on himself, I think mutinously, clamping on a weak smile to cover my true thoughts.

I had seen this advertised in the newspaper about a fortnight ago and had hurriedly turned the page, horrified at the thought of traipsing round a load of stands whilst exhibitors try to tell me that their grotesque meringue dresses are just what I'm looking for. Particularly as I'm still in denial about even having to plan a wedding at all.

'I thought we might get a few useful tips.' Dean looks at me expectantly, clearly seeking approbation that he's done the right thing.

His faintly needy expression brings out the nurturer in me, and I suddenly feel like a prize cow for being so inwardly grumpy and outwardly unresponsive. Whether I like the choice of event or not, this sort of spontaneity is precisely what I have been demanding of him, and he's making a big effort to deliver it.

'Great, let's go!' I grab his arm and pull him towards the small queue already gathered at the front doors. At the very least, I hope, we might get a few laughs out of it.

Inside, the first stand everyone sees as they walk in is selling barbecues.

'What the hell's that got to do with weddings?' Dean wrinkles his nose.

I affect the stance of an exhibitor. 'Ah, sir, you see, if you get married in the summer, you might wish for an outdoor reception and our barbecue centre is just the thing to slowly grill food to perfection whilst you and your guests enjoy the big day . . .'

'. . . in a cloud of black smoke whilst the bride and groom argue about whose job it was to turn the Turkey Twizzlers,' finishes Dean, and we both laugh.

'Yes, in other words, it has nothing to do with weddings. It's just that they thought they might flog a few and were happy to pay the organisers to be here,' I hiss out of the corner of my mouth.

As we saunter round, we take great delight in pointing out other stands with similarly spurious links to the show's theme. Mobile phones ('So you can call the bride-to-be and find out why she's late,' suggests Dean), computers, garden furniture, hot tubs and various 'miracle' cooking utensils to alleviate the domestic drudgery that manufacturers consistently associate with getting hitched.

Eventually, we come across a wedding-dress supplier.

'Come on.' Dean puts a hand in the small of my back and pushes me towards it. 'Let's have a browse. It'll be a laugh, if nothing else.'

On the basis that he's clearly not taking it seriously either, I allow myself to be steered towards the racks of mostly cream frocks, billowing forth in a tsunami of silk, taffeta and, frock horror, what looks like shiny nylon.

'Can I help you?' A hatchet-faced middle-aged woman is standing at my side, one heavily plucked eyebrow arched upwards.

'I'm looking for a wedding dress,' I smile, trying to ignore Dean's hand pressing really hard in my back. I know if I look at him, I will collapse into giggles.

'We want something that will really stand out from the crowd,' I hear him say. 'We're marrying in a stately home and we need a dress that lives up to it.'

'I see,' she says crisply. 'Which one?'

'Er . . .' he frowns, '. . . isn't that what we need your help for?'

'No, I mean *which* stately home?' she persists.

Dean is not in my eyeline but I can tell from the pause that he is now in full panic mode, his mind blank of the paltry few stately homes he might faintly know of, all of them probably occupied by members of the Royal Family.

'Chuntsworthy Hall,' I interject quickly. 'Do you know it?'

She purses her lips, her eyes narrow with suspicion. 'No, I don't believe I do.'

'It's not one of the better-known stately homes, but it's a real find,' I babble, warming to my theme. 'It's in rural Northamptonshire but easily accessible from the motorway, and sooo beautiful. You should mention it to your clients.'

'Indeed.' The other eyebrow is arched now. She really is the most disdainful woman, though probably with good reason on this occasion.

'So, then. A dress.' Dean has found his voice again.

Despite her obvious suspicion of us, I can tell she doesn't know for sure that Chuntsworthy Hall doesn't exist and therefore can't risk upsetting a potentially lucrative client. After a small but none the less dramatic pause for thought, she swivels round to face the rack and runs her finger along the top until it reaches a certain gown.

'Assuming you want grand but traditional, this would be a good starting point,' she drawls with bored professionalism. 'There's a changing room over there.'

Dean settles himself on the purple satin banquette situated in the centre of the stand and glances over the exhibitor's shoulder to where a side cabinet is covered in champagne flutes.

'Ah, I see you have fizz,' he declares, looking at her anticipatively.

'Yes. Would you like one?' Her tone suggests the 'one' is in fact a slap around the chops.

'Lovely, don't mind if I do!'

She pours a glass and hands it to him. 'Your wife-to-be can have one later. We don't want it spilling on the dresses.'

'No, we don't, do we?' enthuses Dean, taking a sip and pulling a faintly disappointed face. 'Oh, not the best year, but *c'est la vie*.'

'It's Prosecco actually.'

'Ah, that explains it. Times hard in the wedding business, are they?'

Throughout, Dean is keeping an admirably straight face, though I am failing miserably with a woefully suppressed smirk that I hope the woman is mistaking for bridal joy.

This is fun. The show I wrote off as being über-dreary is flying in the face of my rather dismal expectations. As indeed is my gung-ho fiancé, who I'm now seeing in a rather new light. Perhaps it could always be like this and I just haven't bothered to find out.

I almost skip into the changing room and re-emerge about three minutes later swathed in a pure white dress, the bodice peppered with tiny hand-sewn sequins and a skirt that resembles a giant cotton-wool ball. I sweep out as if on castors and Dean splutters so violently that Prosecco dribbles from both sides of his mouth.

'I don't feel this design does you justice,' says the assistant with masterly understatement. 'I know you wanted a statement dress, but I'm afraid this rather swamps you.'

She means, of course, that I don't have the stature, both physically and socially, to pull it off. But that aside, it's hideous anyway.

'Oh, I don't know,' I counter. 'It could be just what we're looking for. What do you think, darling?'

Dean turns his head this way and that, studying the vision before him. 'Bigger,' he declares eventually. 'We need something bigger, perhaps with a long train? This screams small country estate, not palatial stately home.'

Doing little to disguise her impatience and suspicion that we're taking the piss, the assistant strides over to the racks and pulls out the most voluminous dress of the lot, judging by the way it's bulging forth from the others. The style is indeterminable because of its plastic shroud, but an industrial amount of cream lace is visible.

'Now we're talking,' grins Dean, proffering his empty glass for a top-up.

This one takes five minutes for me to wrestle myself into, and I struggle to get through the changing-room door, turning myself sideways for ease of exit.

How do I describe it? Imagine the most fairy godmother-esque full skirt, padded out with eight layers of netting and topped with a layer of fine silk studded with Swarovski crystals, and a skin-tight satin bodice that forces your bosoms to sit like two plum puddings just under your chin.

Dean gives the thumbs-up, his mouth twisted from the sheer effort of trying not to laugh. He starts to cough violently, presumably for the same reason, and his eyes well up.

'I'm sorry.' He flaps his hand in front of his face. 'I'm getting emotional.'

A small crowd has gathered nearby, some putting on a fine attempt to appear impressed, others less so. One woman is blatantly pointing straight at me and laughing uproariously.

'How much is it?' I ask.

'That one . . .' the assistant stoops down and looks at the label under the hem, just to make double sure, '. . . is three thousand pounds.'

'Is that all?' Dean affects surprise. 'Then I think that's the one, honey, don't you?'

A flash of alarm crosses my face. What the bloody hell is he doing? Even if we *could* afford it, I wouldn't even wear this monstrosity for a bet.

'We don't have the money on us today,' he continues. 'Do you have a website?'

'No,' she says firmly. 'I prefer the personal touch.'

'Ah. A business card, then?'

'Yes, I have one of those. But I'm afraid three thousand is the special show price. If you don't put a deposit down today, it will be the usual price of three thousand five hundred.'

'Oh, that won't be a problem.' Dean gives her his most charming smile. 'Will it, darling?'

I shake my head mutely and head off back to the changing room to extricate myself from the grip of this bridal aberration.

Gratefully handing it back to Cruella, we promise to be in touch. Once we have walked about fifty yards and cleared the next corner, we both burst into gales of laughter, Dean bent double, me clenching my thighs together for fear I'm about to wet myself.

Once my bladder is under control, we adjourn to a nearby coffee shop and spend the next half an hour dissecting what just happened and discussing what each of us was thinking at any given time.

If Saira or Ella walked past now, they'd think, Oh, there's a couple that look like Dean and Cam, but they can't be because they're laughing too much.

This is the most fun I've had with Dean since the early days of our relationship, when we were still getting to know each other and desperately trying to make good impressions.

Perhaps the prospect of marriage has inspired both of us to make more of an effort, to try to recapture some of that old mojo that clearly drew us together in the first place. And just as my client Mrs Cashman had suggested, no relationship can be successful without a bit of hard work on both sides. Perhaps, finally, we are both coming to understand that.

Smiling warmly at the thought, I extend my hand out and affectionately rub the side of Dean's face, taking heart from the fact he beams back at me with naked pleasure.

'We should do this more often,' I say. 'Well, not *this* again, but do stuff spontaneously, perhaps take it in turns to surprise each other.'

'Absolutely.' He grabs my hand and kisses it whilst staring into my eyes. 'I do love you, Cam. You know that, don't you?'

'Yes,' I smile. 'Yes, I do.'

Chapter Eighteen

Mum doesn't really do restaurants, so it's taken a lot of persuading to entice her out to her local French bistro. She's aware that it's there because she walks past it on her way to Tesco every other day, but she's never actually been in it.

The reasons for this are two-fold. Firstly, she's of the generation for whom 'dining out' is a treat reserved only for special occasions. As a child, I remember going to a restaurant to celebrate Mum and Dad's tenth wedding anniversary, then after that, an outing to celebrate – if that's the right word, given my lacklustre performance – my GCSE results. But other than that, any suggestion to venture out is always pooh-poohed with flapping arms followed by, 'Don't be silly. I'll cook.'

Secondly, post-divorce, her money has been a lot tighter.

So, though she offered to cook this time, I repeatedly insisted we eat out until she finally relented.

'What's the special occasion?' she demanded.

'There isn't one.'

But the truth is that *is* rather special in that I can't

remember the last time Mum and I ate together, properly, alone, with absolutely no distractions.

Usually, I'm sitting at her kitchen table, attempting to engage her in . . . ahem . . . scintillating conversation, whilst she fusses around with pots and pans, stirring various concoctions and punctuating our discussions with 'Just a minute' or 'Hang on, that sauce needs a little more seasoning.'

This time, I want her undivided attention so we can chat about 'stuff', by which I mean awkward stuff, namely Dad and Ava.

For many years now, I have compartmentalised my life, with Mum and the twins in one section, and Dad – and latterly Ava – in the other. And never the twain have met or been spoken about to the other. When out of earshot of Ava, Dad would occasionally enquire after Mum's welfare, but I sensed it had more to do with feeling he should than actually wanting to.

I have always juggled these two separate lives with practised ease, but lately it's been troubling me. I don't know if it's my age and the maturity that comes with it, but suddenly it just seems, well, *daft* that I have largely to pretend one parent doesn't exist when in the company of the other.

In fairness, Dad's not so bad in that I often mention Mum to him in passing, and he resists the urge to pull a face if, indeed, he would actually want to. After all, *he's* the one who left.

But in Mum's company, his is the name that cannot be spoken, and it's starting to grate on me. After all, we're all grown-ups, aren't we? Come hell or high water, I'm planning to address the issue tonight.

'Ooh, this is very expensive!' Mum is studying the

menu disapprovingly, her finger running from top to bottom.

'It's average for London,' I sigh. 'And besides, I'm paying, so don't worry about it.'

'You can't afford this.' She peers at me accusingly over the top of her half-rimmed spectacles.

'Mum, I'm thirty-five.' In other words, I think irritably, stop telling me what to think and do. But I don't say it, anxious to keep the atmosphere on an even keel.

'Five pounds fifty for tomato soup!' Her mouth falls open and she shakes her head theatrically. 'It must cost all of one pound to make, *if* that.'

'Then there's the staff wages, the overheads such as electricity and so on, the laundry bills . . . That all has to be paid for.'

She's still shaking her head from side to side, like a Wimbledon spectator in slow motion. 'Precisely. You're paying for all that when we could easily have eaten at mine for far cheaper.'

'And then you wouldn't have been able to relax and talk to me properly,' I say firmly, picking up the menu and studying it in the hope it puts an end to the matter.

'Talk to me properly about what?' she asks suspiciously, obviously deducing that as I usually spend most of my time trying to avoid time alone with her, there must be a matter of great import to impart.

'Let's order first.'

Once I have persuaded her to order a starter *and* a main course ('Just one course will suffice') and damn the cost, she watches as the waitress retreats towards the kitchens, then swivels back and fixes me with a penetrating stare.

'So what's this all about, then?'

I was hoping to have an organic conversation that eventually drifted towards what I wanted to say, but given her directness I decide to follow suit.

'I've met Ava.'

Silence descends with the swiftness of a drawbridge and her mouth purses into a tight circle and stays there. Seized with the compulsion to fill the void, I battle to resist it, wanting her to speak first. Eventually, she does.

'I see.' Her mouth is a firm line now, her eyes boring into me. 'When?'

This is the question I was dreading most of all. The most acceptable answer would be 'yesterday' or, at the very least, sometime in the past week, suggesting as it does that no sooner had the 'crime' taken place than my guilt and commendably honest nature propelled me into confessing as soon as possible. But that would be a big fat lie.

So do I tell the truth and admit that for the past five years I have been withholding this revelation, and effectively deceiving my mother all that time? Or do I fib and risk her finding out the truth further down the line?

'Five years ago,' I blurt instinctively.

Despite the low lighting, I see her face flush bright red and her eyes blinking rapidly. Whether it's through incomprehension or simply trying to hold back tears, it's hard to tell.

'Five years?' she mumbles, looking so meek and bewildered that I instantaneously feel like a prize shit.

I shrug sheepishly. 'There never seemed to be the right time to tell you . . . I thought it might upset you and I didn't want to do that.' I pause and affect a wince. '*Are* you upset?'

She contemplates the question before eventually shrugging. 'I'm shocked more than upset, I suppose. But it will probably progress to upset.'

'Don't *force* yourself to take it badly.' I raise my eyes heavenward, smiling lightly. 'You could just take it in your stride.'

'I could, could I?' She narrows her eyes at me, her body palpably stiffening. 'I could choose to ignore the fact that my only daughter has been in cahoots with the woman my husband left me for . . . that you have happily colluded in me being deceived yet again. Is that right?'

Her voice is hissy now, her jaw set. Her pupils are the size of pinpricks, giving her eyes a steeliness that betrays her utter fury with me. Suddenly, I'm starting to regret the choice of such a public arena for my confession.

'Mum, it's not like that. *Truly*,' I beseech. 'I just didn't want to hurt you.'

'That's what *he* said when I found out about his sordid little affair.'

Her voice is louder now, prompting a man on the next table to cast an inquisitive glance in our direction.

'It's not the same thing at all,' I mitigate. 'This isn't about what happened between you and him; it's about *me*. You're my mother, but he's my father. I love both of you and want to have a relationship with both of you.'

'Fair enough,' she accedes, though her tone is anything but conciliatory. 'And I knew you were still seeing your father occasionally and that was fine. But I didn't know it included *her*.'

'And it didn't, for a long time,' I reply wearily. 'But eventually it just became too awkward to ignore her.'

I inwardly brace myself for another onslaught but it

doesn't come. She simply stares down at her lap for a few heavily loaded seconds.

'Did you go to their wedding?' she asks in a quiet but deadly tone.

I shake my head and her chest visibly rises and falls in relief.

'And have the twins met her?'

'No.'

'Well, at least some of my children have remained loyal to me,' she sniffs.

Usually, I'm pretty mild-mannered in dealing with the natural turbulence in life, but on this occasion I feel the anger of injustice bubbling inside me.

'Are you just being deliberately pejorative, or is that genuinely how you see it?' Even in the midst of my fury I give her a chance to retract, but she's already nodding solemnly.

'Yes, it is.'

Something snaps. 'Oh, for God's sake, grow up, will you? You're fifty-nine not nineteen. Life goes on. There are people suffering untimely deaths all over the world and you've got your health and that of your children. Isn't it time to start counting your blessings for a change?'

I have never spoken to my mother like this in my life, and it's etched on her face. Her mouth is frozen open in shock, her eyes locked on me.

'It's been thirteen years, Mum. *Thirteen* bloody years!' I gasp. 'Just think of all the things you could have done in that time. The greatest revenge you could ever have on someone is to simply move on with your life and be happy, to show them that they don't define you, but instead you've chosen to remain locked in the aspic of your own bitterness.'

I stop suddenly, knowing I have already said enough, that to continue further with this character assassination might risk a permanent rift between us.

Her mouth is closed, her features morphing before my eyes into a twist of sarcasm.

'Quite the relationship expert, aren't you?' She arches an eyebrow.

'No, I'm not,' I sigh, now anxious to turn down the heat on this conversation. 'Far from it. I just hate to see you behaving as if your life ended the day Dad walked out. His presence doesn't validate you, it never did.'

'Oh, suddenly you *care* about me, do you?'

'Mum, you're being juvenile again. Stop it . . .'

We lapse into silence, seething on her part, weary on mine. This little confessional is veering wildly off course from how I'd planned it in my head.

'Cam, you've had *one* serious boyfriend in your life,' she bristles, 'and even that doesn't come close to marrying and having children.'

The light catches the corner of her eye and glints, but I can't tell if it's a tear or just the natural moisture of age.

'I know it's been demeaned in recent years, but when *I* stood at that altar and made those vows, it meant something,' she continues, her tone noticeably softer now. 'We entered a contract together, an agreement to stick at it, no matter what. On that basis, I sacrificed any working life *I* could have had to look after him and our children, to run the engine room of home, if you like, whilst he sailed about enjoying the relative freedom of the outside world.'

'Freedom?' I interject. 'Holding down a job to pay all the bills is hardly liberating.'

She gives me one of those rueful smiles that suggests I

still have a lot to learn. 'Believe me, compared to the repetitive drudgery of the school run, weekly wash, daily cooking, it's a doddle. He had coffees made for him, adult conversation on demand and time to himself.'

'But surely you knew how it was going to be?'

'Yes, I did. But on the understanding that when you and the twins grew up, it would be *our* time again. We were going to travel the world, go to quirky little cinemas and watch obscure foreign films. That was my light at the end of the tunnel; then he flicked the "off" switch.' She raises her forefinger in the air and bends it.

'You could still do all of those things,' I urge.

'On my own?' She stares disconsolately into the middle distance. 'It's not the same.'

'Then I'll come with you.'

She smiles thinly. 'Once or twice maybe. But it's not just that. It's waking up in the morning and chatting about something you see in the papers or on the news. It's about moaning to someone that there's nothing good on TV. It's about the comfort of a *shared* silence. You can't be there for all of that, can you?'

'True.' I pause and purse my lips. 'But a lot of people love their own company.'

'And a lot don't. Besides, I loved my own company when it was in the context of my marriage, but once that was *all* I had, the charm wore off pretty quickly.'

We lapse into one of those shared silences she has just spoken so fondly of, the void filled by the arrival of our starters: mine, a 'tricolore' of tomato, avocado, and mozzarella, hers, a rustic minestrone. The only localised sound is the clatter of our cutlery and her occasional slurping.

Once the plates are empty and pushed to one side, the silence becomes awkward again.

'So . . . although it pains me to admit I'm interested, what's Ava like, then?' Mum's voice is still faintly churlish but her expression has softened.

'A bit eccentric,' I smile. 'Not really my cup of tea, but she's harmless enough.'

I'm walking the tightrope of not wanting to upset my mother but not wishing to appear disloyal to my father either.

'Look,' I venture bravely, 'I know it must seem like disloyalty on my part, but it honestly wasn't meant that way. What can I say? He's my dad and I missed him. If I could have carried on seeing him alone, believe me I would have. But it just became untenable.'

'Sticks to him like glue, does she?' She gives me a wry smile. 'Women who've stolen men from their wives tend to behave like that because they know that one day the boot might be on the other foot. As they say, if you marry a man who cheats on his wife, you'll be married to a man who cheats on his wife.'

I decide to ignore this sweeping generalisation and persevere with the next point I wish to make.

'Do you think it's right that the twins don't see Dad?'

She sighs heavily. 'It was their choice.'

'But was it? They were still teenagers living at home, and saw you distraught and in pieces. They lived with it every day.'

'What are you trying to say?' Her shoulders visibly stiffen. 'That I should have bitten my lip and acted as though nothing had happened for their sake?'

'No, not at all. I'm saying that if you gave the twins

permission to have a relationship with Dad, they probably would.'

'*Permission?*' she scoffs. 'They're nearly thirty, for God's sake.'

'Mum,' I say reproachfully, 'don't be facetious. You know exactly what I mean. He misses them dreadfully.'

'So why did he walk out on them?'

'He didn't. He walked out on *you*. That makes him a lousy husband, but it doesn't mean he's a lousy dad.'

Now it's definitely the glint of tears I can see running along her lower eyelids. She blinks in an effort to control herself and I feel a rush of sympathy.

'You really loved him, didn't you?' I grab her left hand and give it a reassuring squeeze.

She nods miserably. 'What's the old saying? Never put all your eggs in one bastard.'

I smile, allowing her unflattering description of Dad to go unchallenged, given the circumstances.

'What does she look like?' She can't let it go.

'A bit Rita Fairclough,' I reply charitably.

'Brassy, eh? ' She looks wistful. 'That figures. I always suspected he liked that sort.'

Having made my point about the twins, I'm keen to move on to a different subject, away from the bitter confines about the past.

'I'm so glad we've had this chat.' I use the past tense to indicate that, as far as I'm concerned, the matter is now closed, for tonight at least.

'Is it my turn now?' she asks matter-of-factly.

'Sorry?' I haven't a clue what she's talking about.

'Is it now my turn to dispense a few home truths . . . seeing as this seems to be turning into a night of confessions?'

She gives me a loaded smile and my mind starts to race with what she might be about to say. Am I illegitimate? Or perhaps Dad left because *she* was having an affair?

'Go on . . .'

A small flutter of apprehension rises in my chest, swelling to a pounding sensation as she lets out a sigh so heavily laden that I imagine she might be about to tell me I was actually born a man.

'There's no easy way of putting this, so . . .' she pauses theatrically, '. . . if you don't marry Dean it will be the worst mistake of your life.'

No sooner have the words left her mouth than the waitress arrives between us, a main course in each hand.

'Thank you.' I manage to act normally and smile, but it feels as though my centre of gravity has exited the building. I discreetly clutch the sides of the table for support.

'Lovely, my dear, thank you. Do you have mustard, please?' says Mum brightly, as her blood-red steak is placed in front of her. It's so rare that a good vet could resuscitate it.

The waitress produces a pot of Dijon from her apron pocket and plonks it on the table before asking robotically, 'Anything else?'

'No, thanks,' we reply in unison, and she makes herself scarce. Thankfully, her brief interruption has allowed me to regroup a little.

'Now where were we?' I say sarcastically. 'Ah, yes, you were giving your forthright views on my future.'

'Well, as you were being so vocal about *my* marriage, I felt it wouldn't be taken the wrong way.'

'Your marriage involved me, making it partly my business. The same cannot be said of you and mine.'

225

'Yes it can.' She looks at me challengingly. 'I'm your mother, I care about you, and I don't want you to throw away the best chance you have of enjoying a happy marriage.'

'What makes you think I'm about to throw it away?'

'I don't for sure. I just get a gut feeling that you're unconvinced that Dean is the one.'

'Unconvinced is a little strong. But I'd be an idiot if I wasn't giving *some* thought to whether we'll last the course or not. Having seen what happened with you and Dad, I don't want to end up like that.'

What I mean, of course, is that I don't want to end up like *you*, embittered and lonely. It's nasty and I know it, but I can't help myself. However, she simply closes her eyes for a couple of seconds, as if absorbing the impact, then opens them again and forces a smile at me.

'If you're suggesting that *I* rushed thoughtlessly into marriage with the wrong person, you are sorely mistaken,' she says firmly but quietly. 'Your father made me feel alive. He was energetic about life, go-getting, kind and, most of all, incredibly funny. Whenever I was with him, I felt at the centre of things. Having him in love with me, as he was for many years, was like being swept off by a tornado. It was exciting . . . there was nowhere else I wanted to be.'

She pauses a moment and runs her hand back and forth across her napkin, smoothing out the creases.

'I was the quiet one, the social dead weight, if you like. We would go to functions and he would sparkle whilst I sought out the shadows. But he would drag me out of them, forcing me to speak to people. He taught me so much.' A solitary tear falls from her face and splashes on the side of her plate.

'That's why he was a sitting duck for Ava . . .' she says her name without a trace of acrimony, '. . . because she's vivacious like him, grabs life with both hands. At home, he had boring old me, who was naturally shy and used her children and chores to hide behind and become a dull drudge.'

'You're not boring,' I murmur, thinking of all the mother-centred dramas I have endured over the years. 'You called your first-born Camomile, for God's sake!'

'All a front, dear,' she smiles. 'He grew bored of me.'

'That doesn't make it right, though.'

'No, it doesn't. But it perhaps makes it more under-standable.' She lets out a dainty sigh. 'Though it pains me to say it, *I* married the right person who made me feel alive, but your father married the wrong person because I dragged him down and, despite many clues along the way and opportunities to change the way I was, I didn't do anything about it. I effectively handed him to Ava on a plate.'

'But how does all that relate to Dean and me?'

She smiles wistfully. 'He's a lovely, decent and, more importantly, *uncomplicated* man and I doubt he'd ever leave you. That's what you need, Cam, because sometimes I think you're your own worst enemy.'

'Meaning?' I bristle.

'That you have so much of Dad in you – bright, funny, the life and soul of any party – but also his self-destruct button, which doesn't seem to allow you just to be happy with what you have. You both always seem to be looking for something else.'

The obvious observation to make here would be that Dad seems perfectly content with what he has now, but I desist.

'Just because someone isn't quirky or difficult doesn't mean they're boring,' she continues.

'I never said Dean was boring.' Well, not to her anyway.

'I know. But I do get the impression that *you* feel slightly bored by his dependability, and I'm just saying that perhaps you should start seeing it as a positive rather than a negative. Your dad may have been a live wire, but he's not here with me now, is he?'

'So if you had your time again, what would you do? Still choose Dad, on the basis that your marriage would be exciting but not last the course? Or would you choose someone who's less of a live wire but more likely to hang around until old age?'

She smiles sadly. 'Would that life were so clear-cut. The ideal would be your dad exactly as he is, but also with the ability to stay faithful. Men like that do exist, you know.'

'In which case, why judge me for even wondering – and that's all I'm doing – whether there's someone like that for me?'

'I'm not judging you. All I'm saying is that maybe Dean is that man and you're just not seeing it.'

I nod thoughtfully and let out a long, heartfelt sigh.

'Do you know what I think?'

'Er, yes I do!' I tease. 'You've just spent the last few minutes telling me in no uncertain terms.'

She ignores my teasing. 'I think that once you actually get married and have a child, all this deliberation will stop. You'll just get on with it and you'll find contentment will just follow. Right now, you're over-analysing everything and thinking yourself into a bit of a funk.'

'Maybe. But what if I do the marriage and kids thing and *still* don't feel content?'

'Then may I humbly suggest that it will have more to do with your fickle nature than anything Dean may or may not do,' she replies firmly. 'And don't under-estimate the fact that you have been together this long. There must be *something* that makes you stay with him, and it's not as if someone "better" . . .' she makes quote marks with her fingers, '. . . has come along.'

'Noooo,' I say slowly, 'but I have . . . did . . . meet someone I like.'

The words fall out of my mouth before I have the chance to weigh up the pros and cons of saying them. But Mum doesn't register any sign of shock, simply inclining her head towards her left shoulder and viewing me quizzically.

'I see. Like? Or really like?'

'Not sure. I don't really know him well enough to say.'

She looks momentarily puzzled.

'I met him on holiday,' I clarify. 'We kissed, that's all.' As it's my mother, I feel it's best to leave out the naked-in-the-same-bed bit.

'A holiday romance, eh?' She nods knowingly. 'Darling, they always seem so glamorous – sun, sea, no dull old work to go to – it's not *real*. Place it in the context of everyday life and it would have its mundane moments too, just like every other relationship.'

She's right, of course, but it doesn't stop me from feeling overcome with my conflicting emotions. Tears start to cascade down my cheeks and splash onto my untouched seafood risotto. The only saving grace is that I'm making no sound, so no one in the restaurant notices.

'You OK?' Mum grabs my hand now, clasping it between both of hers. I nod silently. 'You seem terribly upset. Are you in love with this other man? Is that really what all this uncertainty is about?'

I shake my head. 'I don't think so. It's just that I felt very happy in his company, we had fun.'

She indulges me with a small smile. 'Darling, I have a laugh with my local newsagent, but I'm not about to run off with him. There has to be a little more than that to sustain oneself through the many travails of a shared life. You have a *history* with Dean, hundreds, if not thousands, of memories together. Don't mistake familiarity for predictability; they're not the same thing at all.'

She fumbles around in her handbag and extracts a tissue, handing it to me.

'Of course this other man is going to seem exciting by comparison. You don't know him one little bit; there's so much still to learn. But eventually, you'll know everything there is to know about him and it will boil down to the same comfort zone you're in with Dean. We can't go through life just chasing the chase.'

'I know, I know.' I nod emphatically.

It crosses my mind that I could give greater context by filling her in on everything, from the radio message, to Dean's emails to Tom and the subsequent confrontation, but I know it won't change her view and, besides, I'm feeling inexorably weary now. It's been an emotionally draining hour.

'What do you think I should do?'

It's rhetorical really, as I already know the answer. But I need to hear Mum's reply as confirmation.

'Either way, make a decision and stick to it,' she

230

replies firmly. 'Marry Dean and embrace it whole-heartedly, or tell him it's over and let him get on with his life.'

'He's such a nice person . . .' I sob, loud enough for the man on the next table to look over again and whisper something to his female companion. They both laugh and I feel like tipping my risotto over their smug heads.

'He is, darling,' she smiles ruefully. 'And if you let him go, he'll probably find another girlfriend very quickly and you may regret it for the rest of your life.'

Or not, I think to myself. But which is it to be?

I push my untouched plate to one side, my stomach feeling clogged with the nausea of indecision.

Chapter Nineteen

I won't be making any life-changing decisions today, that's for sure. It's Rashid's third birthday and 'Uncle Dean', as he's known, is a valued guest as the unofficial-for-religious-reasons godmother's long-term partner.

That's the problem with ending significant relationships, isn't it? There are all sorts of other factors that come into play, so many other people who get caught up in your residual mess. Relations who have grown close to your other half, perhaps even like them more than you, and friends who feel their loyalties are suddenly divided. It's a big sodding tapestry that has to be unpicked, and you're the one holding the scissors.

I'm sitting in Saira's back garden, perched on the edge of a dark green plastic garden chair that has rendered both my buttocks completely numb, quite an achievement when you consider the inbuilt padding on them.

Ella is here too, but without Philip because, apparently, he doesn't 'do' children's parties. What a tosser. Just as well he didn't have any kids of his own, or they'd be celebrating their birthdays in a gold-plated highchair in some poncy, à la carte restaurant.

'Er, isn't that supposed to be for the children?' I point

towards the bouncy castle in the shape of an old-fashioned fort, lurching from one side to the other under the strain of Abbas's weighty bulk.

'Yes.' Saira smiles wryly. 'But I'm enjoying the peace. If he asks me one more time whether the chapattis are cooked just the way his mother likes them, I'm going to jab a kitchen knife into that bloody thing and send it farting off to space with him on it.'

At that precise moment, a blue 'Happy 3rd Birthday' balloon floats past us, hotly pursued a couple of seconds later by Abbas's septuagenarian father waving his hands in despair.

'Lucky I bought some spare, isn't it?' Saira comments to no one in particular, following it up with a world-weary sigh. 'Social etiquette: the art of making your guests feel at home when you wish that they were.'

As Rashid doesn't go to nursery and therefore hasn't yet made any friends his own age, it's a gathering of Saira and Abbas's extended family, as well as friends and, if applicable, their children.

'Have you thought any more about when he might start nursery?' I ask, watching Rashid giggle with delight as Ella holds his chubby little hands and bounces him on her knee in a nostalgic rendition of 'This Is the Way the Farmer Rides'.

'Hopefully soon.' Saira's voice falls to a whisper and she glances anxiously in the direction of Abbas, who is now vacating the bouncy castle, drenched in sweat. 'It's a nightmare getting him to agree to it, because he thinks his family should carry on doing the job until Rashid legally *has* to go to school.'

I shrug. 'Is that necessarily a bad thing?'

'Not as such. But because they do absolutely *everything*

for him, I feel he's learning to be a little too reliant on others, and demanding, even. He needs to learn a little bit of independence, to play on his own once in a while without constant interaction.'

'I guess it's nice they want to help, though,' offers Ella. 'A lot of women have no support network around them.'

'I know, I know.' Saira moves her head from side to side in acquiescence. 'But as I say, it can have its drawbacks too. Sometimes – in fact, *most* of the time – I don't feel in charge of my own child's destiny.'

'Like when?'

'Like forking out for a bouncy castle for a three-year-old; like the continuing battle over getting him a bloody dog, which, of course, *I'll* be saddled with looking after. The other day, I found myself actually saying, "A puppy isn't just for Christmas."'

'No, if you're lucky, there's enough left over for Boxing Day,' I quip.

She smiles as Rashid lets out an excited shriek just as Ella lowers him between her knees for the finale of the song.

'He also needs to interact with children his own age,' Saira continues. 'He needs to start having some of his own little experiences, away from the rest of us.'

Abbas bounds up and tickles Rashid under each armpit, before lifting him in the air and swinging him back down again.

'Hey, little man,' he smiles. 'Come see what I've got for you!'

'Actually, Rashid,' laughs Saira, 'I think you'll find that it's *Daddy's* toy and he's just letting you play on it.'

Abbas grins, then leans forward and kisses his wife

affectionately on the lips. 'I was simply testing it out, to check it's safe.'

'Yes, dear, of course you were.'

I have no idea what Ella is thinking as she watches them, but she's smiling beatifically. For me, I feel I'm seeing the relatively mundane but innermost workings of a successful union between two people for whom marriage isn't just about romantic love but the bigger picture of their shared devotion to their child and wider family, even the slightly mad, irritating ones.

The three of us sit in silence for a few seconds, watching father and son playing together on the bouncy castle.

'He's such a great dad,' says Ella eventually.

'Yes, he is.' Saira takes a sip of her 'sparkling water', secretly laced with white wine to anaesthetise her against the inevitable stresses and strains of any young child's birthday party. 'I'm very lucky.'

'But are you?' Ella demands suddenly. 'Lucky, I mean. Or have you just chosen wisely?'

Saira stares blankly at her for a couple of seconds. 'OK, I know it doesn't take much these days, but you've completely lost me.'

'I mean,' sighs Ella, a little exasperatedly, 'that there are lots of nice, family-orientated men out there and it's just up to us whether we choose them or not . . . isn't it?'

'And you didn't. Is that what you're saying?' I peer questioningly at her.

'Exactly.' She affects a rueful grimace. 'For some reason, rather than join the real world, I have actively chosen to occupy the murky shade of some half-arsed existence.'

235

'That's a bit harsh,' I protest feebly, secretly agreeing with every word.

'No, it isn't. Look at you guys. Here you are . . .' she nods towards Saira, '. . . enjoying your son's birthday party in the bosom of your extended family, who, even if they get on your nerves from time to time, at least give a damn about you. And you . . .' she jerks her head in my direction and I recoil slightly, '. . . you're about to get married and will probably start your own family soon after.'

A faint feeling of queasiness rises from the pit of my stomach and I instinctively gulp to try to quell it. A child's birthday party is probably not the time to enlighten my friends about the doubt plaguing my supposedly blissful state of mind.

'But what have *I* got to show for thirty-odd years on this planet? A few fleeting relationships, and the past two years spent with a man who's married to someone else and refuses even to contemplate the thought that I might want to have children.'

'Do you?' I've never had Ella down as the maternal type, remembering the time when Saira handed her the newborn Rashid and she held her arms out stiffly, as if handling contaminated goods.

'Yes,' she nods. 'I didn't at one point. But now I do.'

'So what's changed?'

'I genuinely don't know,' she shrugs. 'It's just a feeling . . . My biological clock has finally started ticking, I guess.'

'Does Philip know?' Saira releases her hair from its elastic tie and instantly redoes it again, even tighter.

'No. But when I still thought I didn't want any, we had a conversation about it and he was transparently effusive in his agreement of my viewpoint. There was absolutely no effort on his part to talk me out of it; I got the impression that it suited him very much indeed for me to feel that way.'

'But he might change his mind if he knew you'd changed yours,' I counsel, knowing that this is utter cobblers. It was *always* Philip's way or the highway.

'Even if hell froze over and he did agree . . .?' She looks at me questioningly. 'He's still married and I'd either be virtually a single parent still living in the shadows and waiting for the precious few times when *Daddy* pops in, or he'd have to leave Sally, and God only knows what unholy mess *that* would create. She's not known for being low-key.'

This damning character assessment is based on just one occasion when Philip was at Ella's, and Sally left a message on his mobile saying she had crashed her car. She was so loudly hysterical that Ella heard everything, despite sitting several feet away from Philip as he listened. At the very least, she pictured Sally in traction and Philip being unable to get away for a while, but he turned up the very next day with the news that the only damage was a slightly dented front bumper.

Luckily, Rashid suddenly bounds over at that very moment, so neither Saira nor I have to comment on the blindingly obvious fact that, yes, procreation and an overt life with Philip would indeed be a very arduous, stressful affair.

'Mummy . . . bouncy castle . . . *now*,' he demands, his bottom lip protruding.

'Darling . . .' Saira pats him on the head, '. . . Mummy *is* a bouncy castle in her own right. She doesn't need to go on yours to show everyone how her flesh jiggles about.'

Ella and I laugh, but Rashid's expression doesn't change, his lip set stubbornly as he grabs the crook of her arm and starts to tug.

'OK, OK,' she smiles, turning to us. 'And you two aren't allowed to watch.'

'Brownie promise.' I hold three fingers aloft. 'But can I take photos?'

'Ha bloody ha.' She slopes off, her gait as reluctant as a coach trip of the morbidly obese leaving an all-you-can-eat buffet.

I turn back to Ella, who seems in a world of her own, staring in the direction of where Dean is standing in a portable goal whilst various of Abbas's nephews and nieces fire footballs at him.

'You guys seem really happy,' she says.

'We had a great day last week,' I smile, desperately focusing on something I don't have to gloss over. 'Dean took me to a wedding show as a surprise and I tried on some really outlandish dresses. It was a real laugh.'

Ella smiles wistfully. 'Sounds fun. Philip wouldn't be seen dead at something like that. And even if he did go, which he wouldn't, he'd spend his entire time in a state of high anxiety, worrying about bumping into someone he knew.'

I'm about to tell her about the ridiculously bling dresses I tried on, but notice that tears are welling in her eyes.

'Don't cry, sweetie.' I lean forward and squeeze her arm. 'Everything will come good in the end. Promise you. It always does.'

If only I believed my own advice, I think ruefully, I probably wouldn't be enduring this emotional quandary that I'm coming to recognise as entirely of my own making.

'It won't.' She shakes her head and rummages up the sleeve of her cashmere cardigan, extracting a pristine tissue, which she uses to dab her eyes. 'God, what a fucking waste of time.'

Ella *hardly ever* swears and I'm aware of flinching slightly in shock as I scan the nearby area for any small child that might have overheard. But it's all clear.

'You have your memories,' I console. 'They must be worth something, surely?'

'I could have had *better* memories,' she fires back bitterly, 'if I hadn't chosen to behave like a bloody doormat.'

Quite where this new, faintly feminist Ella has emerged from is anyone's guess, but she's here now, eyes burning with indignation.

'What are you going to do?' I'm picturing her chained to the railings outside Philip's marital home, or burning her bra in his front garden as Sally peers curiously through the net curtains.

'End it. I have to.'

'End what?' pants Saira, flopping back in her chair, a bead of sweat running down her nose.

I try pulling a 'this is serious' expression without Ella noticing, but Saira doesn't get it either, her brow furrowing.

'What's the matter? Why are you pulling faces at me?'

'Nothing.' I raise my eyes heavenward.

'I was just saying that I'm going to end it with Philip.' Ella seems to have composed herself now.

'Hoo-flamin'-rah,' enthuses Saira. 'He doesn't deserve you. Never has.'

Ella blinks a few times, looking faintly confused. 'Why didn't you say so before?'

'You can't really, can you?' Saira still sounds breathless as she bends forward to retie her shoelaces. 'I mean, it's a dangerous business . . . telling your friends what you *really* think about their boyfriend or husband, because if it all blows over and they stay with them, there's then this awkwardness because you're still thinking that he's a twat, only this time, your friend actually *knows* that's what you're thinking.'

'And you think Philip's a twat?' asks Ella impassively.

'Honestly, honey? Yes, I do.'

There follows a pause, with Saira looking faintly uncertain – perhaps feeling she may have overstepped the mark – and Ella looking at her thoughtfully.

'Me too!' she says eventually, breaking into a broad grin. 'God, it feels good to say it.'

Saira and I burst into slightly hysterical, overreactive laughter, both obviously relieved that any potential awkwardness is now unlikely.

'And what about you, Cam? What do you think of him?' Ella looks at me questioningly and I feel the niggle of uncertainty again. Saira is so much better at direct talking than I am, but in the current climate of honesty, I feel empowered to speak the truth too. Well, about *her* relationship, anyway.

'I'm not a fan . . .' I wince apologetically, '. . . but as long as you seemed happy with him, I didn't feel it was my business to say so.'

Ella leans towards the table and picks up her glass, raising it in front of her face. 'To a brave new world of honesty,' she declares, and Saira and I both clink our glasses against hers before taking a quick swig. I try to ignore the swell of turmoil inside me, knowing that I will tell them everything in due course, once *I* know exactly what I'm going to do.

Placing her glass back on the table, Ella stands up and smoothes down her skirt. 'Now, if you don't mind, I'm going to sneak off. I haven't seen Mum and Dad for a couple of weeks, so I promised I'd pop in for a late lunch.'

We say our goodbyes and 'good lucks', and watch her sashay across the lawn and through the kitchen door.

'Do you think she'll do it?' I say, still looking in the direction of the house.

'Um, not a hundred per cent sure, but probably, yes. I think she's finally realised she's wasting precious time with someone who is never really going to make her happy.'

I turn back to face Saira and find she's looking at me pointedly, her eyebrows raised.

'I'm sensing we're still firmly embedded in the brave new world of honesty,' I smile wearily.

'Cam, come *on*,' she beseeches. 'I know your situation isn't quite as easy to dismiss as Ella's, but what are you doing with your life? A man doesn't have to be married to someone else to be wrong for you.'

'I know, I know, but we can't talk about this now,' I whisper, glancing anxiously over towards Dean. But he's oblivious, standing several yards away in a circle of men clutching beers.

'When, then?'

'Tomorrow lunchtime?'

'Done,' she says firmly. 'I'll be all ears.'

Chapter Twenty

The salon is empty and dark when I arrive, an apt metaphor for my mood.

Last night, Ella sent Saira and me a simple text, stating, *Have done the deed! Will tell all when I see you face to face.*

After years of wondering why she was wasting her prime years on Philip, I don't mind admitting that the news she's finally dumped him has completely side-winded me. Not because I feel it's the wrong decision, or because I have one iota of sympathy for Philip. Believe me, I don't.

No, my discomfort is far more selfishly rooted. It feels like a mirror is being held up to my own life, the only difference being that Ella has acted whilst I remain knee-deep in my own cowardly indecision, seemingly unable to decide what best to do for both Dean and me.

Unlocking the door, I flick on the lights and tap in the salon code set by Luca – 1977 – 'the most glorious disco year *ever*, darling'.

I let out a small sigh. Despite my sombre mood, there's something comforting about coming to the same place every day, a satisfying solace in the same routine, punctuated only by the occasional new customer.

So why don't I feel the same way about my relationship? Why can't I find satisfaction in *its* familiarity?

The question to myself goes unanswered as Luca chooses this precise moment to bowl through the salon door like Road Runner after a double espresso. And I'm not just talking about the speed, it's the hair too.

'Fuck! Is she here yet?'

'Is who here?'

'Mrs Shaw?'

'Nope.'

He instantaneously deflates like a pricked balloon. 'Thank Christ for that. She *hates* me being late.'

Mrs Shaw is Luca's most prized client, solely because of her generosity. She has two simple rules, that her hair should be done exactly as she likes it, at a time dictated by her. If so, she has been known to cross Luca's palm with a fifty-pound tip. If not, there's a very clear and present danger she'll go elsewhere. So here is the naturally tardy Luca, who usually claims nothing is worth getting up before 9 a.m. for, all bright-eyed and bushy-tailed at 8.33 a.m. precisely.

As he busies himself getting everything in place for the royal arrival, I saunter over to the appointments diary to see who the day has in store for me. A couple of familiar names leap out at me, as does two hours of emptiness after lunch, followed by a four o'clock full head of highlights that will take at least a couple of hours. I scowl, wondering if our inherently idle receptionist, Angela, has even bothered to ask the client if she could come in earlier. My 9 a.m. is a Mr Clark, a name I don't recognise.

'Tea?' I ask Luca.

'Do bears shit in the woods?'

'I'll take that as a yes, then.'

But our communication is bluntly severed by the sound of the salon door creaking open, meaning Luca has now swivelled his head in that direction, his best, welcoming smile bolted in place.

'Mrs Shaw! A pleasure as always!' he gushes, swooping over and deftly removing her coat from her shoulders. 'You look so well!'

Mrs Shaw was clearly a great beauty in her day, with cat-like green eyes and pronounced cheekbones. But her eyes now have dark shadows under them and the cheekbones are counteracted by sagging jowls. Despite this, she might still be considered an attractive, middle-aged woman, were it not for the ageing frown that seems to be her default facial setting. Consequently, an entrenched furrow runs from the bridge of her nose, forking off each eyebrow and giving her the permanent look of someone who's just been told their supposedly winning lottery ticket is actually void.

Not that money is an issue for her. Luca tells me she's married to Archie Shaw, the property developer. No small flats or terraced houses for him – he deals in luxury apartment blocks and swanky hotels. Apparently, they fly everywhere by private jet and have more staff than my nearest Sainsbury's Local.

To the outside world, this woman would seem to have the perfect life, so why does she look so bloody miserable all the time?

Luca reckons her husband is always having affairs, so perhaps that might explain it. Whatever, hers is a face that suggests a life half lived, a skin clearly riven with the fault lines of unhappiness and dissatisfaction, a woman who has made a pact with the devil and clearly hates herself for it.

'I'm making tea, Mrs Shaw, would you like some?' I smile.

Luca scowls at me over his shoulder, as if I'm an interloper trying to muscle in on his prized tipper.

'Darjeeling. One sugar,' she barks, returning to reading *Woman and Home* magazine.

'You're welcome,' I mutter, retreating to the back room, where she clearly feels I belong.

Pouring water into the cups, I ponder the conundrum of rich and miserable or poor and happy . . . Which would I choose? Rich and happy isn't allowable as there'd be no competition.

Poor and happy, I conclude, stirring in Mrs Shaw's sugar and using a dirty teaspoon for my own private little piece of oneupmanship. After all, happiness is the holy grail that money can't buy, isn't it? It's the glittering prize, unattainable to those who don't work hard at finding and, most importantly, keeping it. Am I one of those it will forever elude, the architect of my own misfortune?

Carrying the cup carefully across the floor, I place it in front of the sour-faced old bag, who doesn't even look up to acknowledge my efforts, let alone say thank you. I linger pointedly, hoping to shame her into doing so, but Luca is hovering protectively over his client.

'Angela is pointing at you,' he mutters, jerking his head towards the reception area. I turn to see her talking to a man with his back to me, presumably my first client of the day, Mr Clark.

'Good morning,' I chirrup to his back, extending my

hand in preparation for when he turns round. When he does, the shock prompts me to withdraw it again immediately and overtly gasp.

'What are you doing here?'

Standing in front of me, with a sheepish grin, is Jason, Tom's friend from Tenerife. He looks slightly tubbier than I remember him, with even less hair.

'Ah, you *do* remember me, then! I wasn't sure if you would,' he smiles nervously. 'I hope you don't mind, but I was in the area and needed a quick tidy-up.'

Given the neatly trimmed strips of hair either side of his balding head, we both know he's lying through his teeth.

My bemused expression has clearly stirred Angela from her usual cretinous reverie and she's peering curiously at Jason now, taking in the lack of hair and my obvious discomfort. Time to move away.

'Do come over,' I smile stiffly, gesturing towards my work station on the left-hand side of the salon. 'We can discuss what style you'd like.'

'Ha-ha. I don't think there are many options!' he grins.

Once he's safely deposited in my chair long enough to have lost Angela's interest, I place my hands on his shoulders and give them a pointed squeeze. 'Now then, given that what little hair you have is already looking newly clipped, why *are* you here?'

He smiles apologetically. 'Yes, sorry about that. If I'd planned it, I would have turned up with a full beard and Catweazle hairdo, but as it's a spontaneous visit . . .' He looks at me via the mirror.

'So spontaneous that you managed to make an appointment,' I say drily, picking up my scissors in a bid to keep up professional appearances.

'Point taken. But what I mean is that I'm here partly because I remember you saying where you worked and I knew I was already coming to town on a mechanics' seminar.'

'Mechanics have seminars?' I don't attempt to hide my cynicism. 'What about?'

'Cars.' He shrugs. 'And health and safety stuff.'

'Where?'

'Brent Cross.'

'That's a long way from here.' I'm not letting him off lightly.

'It wasn't too bad, just over half an hour on the tube.'

'But enough about your journey here, *fascinating* though it is . . .' I snip ominously at the air around his ears. 'Why are you really here, because we both know it's not for a haircut?'

I'm not making this easy for him, but I feel he's put me on the back foot by turning up at my workplace unannounced. Also, his appearance has undeniably unseated me, sending my mind into orbit about what's behind it.

'Is there somewhere we can talk?' He shifts uncomfortably in the chair, his voice low. 'It's a bit exposed here.'

I'm not entirely sure I want to hear what he's got to say, but I do know that, whatever it is, I don't want Luca, Angela or anyone else to hear it either.

'Follow me.'

I turn and walk towards the back of the salon, where there's a small overflow room for the ultra-busy days that we never seem to have any more. Either that, or I use it to fire the latest junior, who seems to think that turning up late every morning with attitude is acceptable.

To maintain the flimsy illusion that I'm giving Jason a haircut, I place him in a chair in front of the mirror, but sit to one side of him so at least we're not conversing via our reflections.

'Tom doesn't know I'm here,' he says nervously. 'He'd kill me if he did.'

Ah, that clears that up, then. I feel strangely deflated by this news and realise that perhaps I'd been harbouring a secret hope that he was here at Tom's instigation, to try to convince me that we should be together.

'I see.' I nod sagely, actually seeing bugger all. 'So why *are* you here, then?'

'As his mate really. Because he's so miserable.'

I feel a small stab of panic. 'Has something happened? Daniel's OK, isn't he?' There's the instant recall on that name again.

'No, no, they're both fine.' He smiles reassuringly. 'Nothing has *happened* as such, he's just generally miserable and that's not like him at all.'

I shrug almost imperceptibly. 'Sorry to hear that, but what's that got to do with me?' I have a sneaking suspicion what, but I need to hear him actually say it.

'I know he came all the way to London to see you,' he mumbles, glancing furtively towards the door. 'He told me.'

'Oh, he did, did he?' My tone is feigning disinterest, but I can't help myself, needing to know more. 'And what else did he tell you?'

'That you have a boyfriend.'

He looks at me impassively but I instantly feel self-conscious and, if I'm brutally honest, a little cheap.

'Ah.' I smile ruefully.

'I take it you're still with him?'

It crosses my mind to suggest that it's none of his business but, given the effort he's made to come here, I comply, nodding demurely and resisting the urge to tell him that all may not be as it seems, but I just haven't worked out what I even *feel* yet, let alone what I'm going to do about it when I do.

But even if I decide to end it with Dean, it has to be because it's not right for me, not because there's another option on potential standby.

'Happy?' he asks casually.

Right, now *that's* a question too far. Firstly, because I hardly know the man and, secondly, because I've had a bellyful of that query recently.

'Look, Jason, I appreciate you going to all this trouble, but I really don't know what else there is to say . . .' I start to undo the ties at the back of his neck and lift the black gown away from him. He doesn't move.

'Do you really feel absolutely nothing for Tom?' He stares at me unblinkingly.

'I don't really know him.' I shrug apologetically. 'We had a day at the beach and that's it.' I'm unsure how much he knows and have no wish to inadvertently enlighten him any further. I desperately want him to leave now.

'But you *slept* with him.' His tone and expression are more perplexed than accusatory.

Bowing my head so my chin is near his right ear, I hiss: 'Please keep your voice down!'

'Sorry,' he whispers.

'And by the way, sleeping is *all* we did.'

'I know. But in a way, that's more meaningful than if you'd actually had sex. He liked you enough *not* to, if that makes sense.'

I hold my breath in stunned silence. OK, so he seems to know the full story. I've never really thought of it that way before and a hulking bloke seems an unlikely source for such a romantic perspective.

'Look.' I move to his side again and fix my eyes on his, to ensure he's taking in everything I say. 'It was just a fleeting *thing*.' I resist using the word 'fling'. 'That's all. People have them all the time, especially on holiday.'

'True.' He nods and I feel myself relax slightly. But hang on, he hasn't finished. 'Well, *single* people do anyway, and particularly men. But women in relation-ships having flings? That's not normal behaviour . . . is it?'

My heart starts to beat more rapidly as a surge of indignation powers round my bloodstream. 'Jason, what are you trying to say here? That I'm some sort of slapper?'

He looks genuinely horrified, his naturally narrow eyes widening at the thought. 'God, no. I'm sorry if it seemed that way. All I'm saying is that, maybe, you hit it off with Tom so easily because things aren't right in your relationship.'

OK, so now even a rugger bugger with a lousy taste in jumpers has fathomed the depths of my possible dissatisfaction.

'Know a lot about the female psyche, do you?' I ask sarcastically as a deterrent from the glaringly obvious truth.

'I read a magazine article in the hairdressers . . . when I had this trim,' he grins, pointing to his head. 'And it said that women only have affairs if they're unhappy in their marriage.'

'It's not as simple as that – it never is. And besides, I'm not married.'

'May as well be. Tom says you've been together for six years . . . and you're engaged.'

'We are.' I nod slowly.

Jason is standing now, adjusting the collar of his shirt before reaching towards his coat and lifting it from the back of the chair. 'Look, I'm sorry. I didn't want to come here and make you feel uncomfortable. I just thought that . . .' He pauses and winces ruefully. 'Well, Tom is such a great bloke and I hate to see him so down . . . so I figured it was worth a try.'

'I understand,' I smile benevolently. 'You were being a good friend.'

'It's been nice seeing you,' he smiles warmly. 'And sorry again if I shocked you.'

Having spent the last half an hour wishing he'd leave, curiously I now feel seized by panic that he's about to. Suddenly, there are so many things I want to say and ask.

'Jason . . . what would *you* do if you were me?' I blurt.

He looks at me quizzically. 'I can't really answer that because I don't know anything about your fiancé—'

'Dean. He's called Dean,' I interrupt, inwardly baulking at the 'f' word. 'He's a really nice man, but sometimes it just doesn't feel right. Do you know what I mean?'

'Sort of,' he replies hesitantly, clearly not understanding at all.

'I hear you have a new girlfriend?' I venture, now anxious to keep him talking though I'm not quite sure why.

'Yes, I do. She's really nice.'

'But is she the one?' I tease with false jollity.

'Hard to tell. It's only been a couple of months, but it does feel right, to use your litmus test.'

He extends an arm and starts to pull on his coat, jerking the zip up halfway. Afterwards, he pauses a moment, looking at me pensively. 'I came here today because I felt that you and Tom had a real chemistry going on, something that I never saw between him and Alison.'

I look at him blankly.

'She's Daniel's mum.'

Alison. *That's* her name.

'And his mood since coming to see you tells me that it was more than just a fleeting *thing* for him,' he emphasises, 'but I guess he's alone in feeling that way. Sorry I've taken up your time.'

He raises his arm towards me and I instinctively shake it even though my brain suddenly feels like it has been placed in a blender on top speed.

'You take care.' He smiles wistfully at me, then turns on his heel and leaves the salon before I can even properly compute what's been said, let alone form a response to it.

I stand rooted to the spot, a sudden feeling of coldness creeping up my arms.

Eventually, I compose myself and start preparations for my next client.

After that, it's what I suspect will be an emotionally challenging lunch with Saira. What a day already, and it's only half past nine.

Chapter Twenty-one

'Sorry I'm late. I had a client with hair like a privet hedge after a nuclear winter.'

'No worries. I was enjoying the peace, to be honest.' Saira folds up her newspaper and tucks it into her handbag. 'I can't even sneak off to the loo at home without Rashid tracking me down and trying to sit on my lap.'

'Who else is coming?' I point at the third setting on our little round table tucked away in the corner of Strada pizzeria.

'Ella. She's going to give us the full monty on dumping Philip, but I told her it was one thirty instead of one o'clock so we could catch up first,' says Saira. By 'catch up', of course, she means she can relentlessly grill me with no distractions. 'I have ordered us some bruschetta and olives to nibble on until she gets here.'

So, not even the distraction of looking at the menu and ordering my own starter.

'Now then, tell me more about Tom turning up,' she demands, ruthlessly dispensing with the usual 'so how's life?' niceties. I feel like I'm speed dating.

She has attempted this line of questioning on the

phone a couple of times, but I have always stuck to the description I'm about to utter again now.

'He came, we had a cup of tea, he went.'

'And that's it?'

'Pretty much. As I said, I told him I had a boyfriend, which curtailed proceedings somewhat.'

'And you're fine with that?' She looks unconvinced. 'You haven't spent every waking moment since regretting that you didn't arrange to at least *see* him again?'

'Even if I'd wanted to, it wasn't an option.' I shrug. 'As soon as he knew about Dean, he kind of withdrew. He said that because of his son he needed to know where he stood and didn't want to start anything complicated.'

She looks impressed by this. 'And did you want to see him again?'

'Not at the time particularly, no.'

'And now?'

I smile, studying her face thoughtfully. She's my best friend; lying to her would be like lying to myself, and I know it's time to stop that.

'I'm thinking about him a lot more.' My tone is sad, but inside I feel relief at finally owning up to it. 'Saira, what the hell am I going to do?'

'Only you can answer that,' she murmurs.

'Come on, *tell* me. You're so sorted, so strong . . . and I'm feeling so bloody churned up that I can't think straight. What would you do in my situation?'

She lets out a long sigh. 'I would have ended it with Dean about four years ago. But you didn't do it then and, believe me, you won't do it now either.'

I bristle at this accusation, wounded by my best friend's obviously low opinion of my ability to make a relationship decision and follow it through.

'What makes you so sure?' I huff.

She makes a loud mooing sound.

'What are you doing that for?'

'Déjà moo. I've heard this bullshit before.'

'No you haven't. At most, I have only ever said I felt a little bored. The leap from that to us potentially splitting up was made by you, not me.'

'And now it's different, is it?' she challenges. 'Because there might be someone else waiting in the wings? God forbid that you might find the strength to be on your own for a while. Has *that* even crossed your mind as an option?'

'Yes, it has actually.' I frown slightly, not liking her tone.

'Look, Cam, I'm your mate and I will always be there for you. If you were ill, I would listen endlessly to your woes and sympathise wholeheartedly with every one of them. But there comes a time when a good friend has to tell you a few harsh truths, and this constant deliberating about whether Dean does or doesn't make you happy is becoming just a little tedious.'

I'm simply staring fixedly at her, paralysed by mild shock.

'You want my advice? Well, here it is. It's time to shit or get off the pot.' She clamps her teeth around a large lump of bruschetta, her eyes bulging slightly as she tries to swallow it.

Saira and I have always been polar opposites when it comes to relationships. Prior to Abbas, she had only a couple of boyfriends. But on both occasions, once she had felt even the slightest trace of doubt that they were right for her, she jettisoned them and never repented.

255

I, however, prove picky at the start, then hang on in there for grim death, always thinking the best of everyone, always hoping that if I just give it a little bit longer it might improve. Saira always says I'd give Jack the Ripper the benefit of the doubt.

'Decide what you need to do and bloody get on with it,' she continues, fixing me with a beady stare. 'What's that Mark Twain quote? Something about people waiting and waiting for the right time to do something but by then it's too late . . .'

I purse my lips as if I'm giving careful consideration to what she's said, but inside I'm reeling slightly, my brain shorting with indecision.

'One thing I do know,' she adds, clearly on a roll, 'is that if you *do* decide to end it, it'll be like wrenching a comfort blanket from a child. It's not going to be easy.'

I clear my throat pointedly. 'Christ, talk about piling on the bloody agony.'

'Sorry,' she smiles ruefully.

'But you are right with your quaint analogy about pots and pooing,' I sigh deeply. 'Either way, I *do* need to decide what to do and get on with it.'

'Just suppose you take the path of finishing it with Dean, how will you broach it?'

'Probably instinctively?' I look at her questioningly.

'No, no, no!' She rolls her eyes. 'You have to have *some* idea of what you're going to say, or you'll get talked out of it. You also have to stay very firm, like, "I'm really fond of you and don't want to hurt you any more than I already am, but there's no way I'm going to change my mind" kind of way.'

'Can we swap bodies?' I smile wearily and bite into

my piece of bruschetta, but my mouth is so dry that it tastes like cardboard. I chew disconsolately.

'And what would you do about the flat?'

The question prompts a reflux action and I start to make little choking noises. Saira hammers theatrically on my back.

'Ye gods,' I splutter. 'One trauma at a time, please. Don't panic me even more than I already am. Mentally, I have only got as far as deciding that I have to make a decision; anything after that is a blank.'

'Sorry,' she grins. 'I forgot I'm dealing with a mutant of an ostrich and tortoise when it comes to personal matters.'

I glance up at the clock on the restaurant wall. Five minutes until Ella gets here, unless she's her usual tardy self. In which case, she'll arrive just as they're setting tables for dinner.

'On another note . . .' I pause and pick a piece of toast out of a tooth cavity. 'Do you remember Jason? Tom's friend from holiday, the one who came to the beach?'

'Oh, yes,' she says distractedly, studying the menu for her main course.

'He turned up at the salon today.'

She lowers the menu to the table, registering surprise. 'What did he want?'

'To tell me that Tom is miserable without me.'

She doesn't say anything for a couple of seconds, her lips pursed. 'I see. Well, he's nothing if not persistent. First, he turns up, now he's sent his friend.'

'No, he didn't know about it. It was *Jason's* view that Tom is miserable without me.'

'Or so he says.' She narrows her eyes suspiciously. 'If you do decide to end it with Dean, don't jump straight on the next log floating by. You really need to have some time on your own. You know, get to know *yourself* before becoming absorbed by another relationship.'

Saira is an avid reader of self-help books, not least because she's part of that industry herself.

'I'm just telling you what happened, that's all. I'm not about to go rushing up to Birmingham and leap into Tom's arms.'

'Good,' she says firmly. 'Because someone you've known five minutes isn't going to be the answer to your problems.'

Just as I'm about to contest that I actually *have* any problems beyond a relationship I'm about to end, Ella bounds into the restaurant three minutes early.

'Bloody hell!' I exclaim. 'Have I missed the clocks going forward?'

She ignores me and claps her hands together, her face animated with obvious excitement. 'I still can't believe that I've done it! Philip is history.'

Saira gets to her feet and embraces her. 'Well done! It's great news.' As soon as she says it, her face twists to bemusement. 'Well, not great news in the usual great-news sense, of course, but what I mean is that it's great news that you've managed to do what you set out to do.'

I frown slightly, trying to work out what she's just said, but Ella seems oblivious, flopping in the chair opposite me, her eyes shining.

'I honestly didn't think I had it in me,' she half laughs.

'And clearly you feel it was the right decision,' I surmise from her excitable demeanour, though I suspect there may still be some adrenalin involved.

She nods. 'Absolutely. I slept like a baby after he'd gone, so that's a good sign.'

Saira pours her a glass of white wine and hands it to her. 'There you go. Now spill, right from the beginning, leave nothing out.'

'Well, I phoned him during the day and asked if he could come to the flat. He grumbled a bit, saying he had other commitments, but I stressed it was important and that I'd be home all night so he could pop in when it suited him.'

I resist the urge to interject with 'No change there, then.'

Still panting slightly, Ella takes a large glug of wine and carefully places the glass back on the table. 'So just after nine o'clock, he arrived with a bunch of flowers, like he usually does. I think he was expecting you know what . . .'

I close my eyes and try to blot out the image of Philip and Ella having sex that has just flashed into my mind.

'But I steered him towards the sofa, made him sit down and came straight out with it. I said, "I asked you to come here because I think we need to end this." Just like that.'

She pauses, looking faintly melancholic for a moment before shaking her head from side to side, as if expunging a certain thought, and continuing.

'He didn't seem to take me seriously at first. He kind of smiled knowingly and started kissing my neck, as if it was just some silliness I could be seduced out of . . . but I leant away from him and said I was being serious.'

She delicately pincers an olive between thumb and forefinger and pops it in her mouth, expertly tearing away the flesh and gently placing the stone on the side of the dish.

'He looked surprised for a few seconds, then said he'd been looking at spa brochures because he was going to take me away for the weekend and started trying to kiss me again. This time, I got quite stroppy and told him to stop.'

'Good for you,' Saira interjects supportively.

'It was only then that he seemed to acknowledge what I'd been saying. He asked me why and I said because I didn't feel I was getting anything out of it any more, that I wanted the things you guys have, or are going to have . . . you know, marriage and children.'

I stare down at the floor, wondering at what point during the conversation I should tell her of my ongoing dilemma, if at all.

'And what did he say?' asks Saira, clearly enthralled.

'He said that he respected my wishes and that if that was what I really wanted, then there was nothing he could say that would change my mind.'

'Well, apart from saying that he would leave his wife and have kids with you,' I offer.

'Hmm. Funnily enough, that scenario was conspicuous by its absence.' She smiles sadly. 'Which told me all I need to know really.'

We all ponder this thought for a moment, against the background noise of other customers and the sounds from the restaurant kitchen at the back of the room.

'So how are you feeling?' Saira asks eventually.

'Sad.' Ella shrugs her shoulders, noticeably bony under a pale grey cashmere sweater. 'But also relieved, I think, hence the good night's sleep. Though I may not feel the same in a week's time.'

'Do you think he'll try and fight for you?' I ask.

She shakes her head ruefully. 'No, I don't. Oh, I'm

sure he'll miss me for a little while, but not enough to actually do anything about it. Then eventually, another Ella will come along.'

Would that my situation were that simple, I think, smiling distractedly as Ella and Saira chat some more. Just go home, tell Dean it's over, and we both get on with our lives. But Philip didn't even keep a pair of underpants at Ella's flat. There was barely any trace of him there, apart from a pale blue toothbrush and a can of Gillette deodorant spray, and she'd bought those for him. All he had to do was walk out through the door and it was as if he'd never been there . . . except for Ella's memories of him, of course.

Dean has lived in my flat for over four years now, contributing towards the rent and permeating every nook and cranny with his 'stuff', by which I mean old Spurs football programmes, a signed Harlequins rugby ball, some virtually untouched dumbbells, several patterned polo shirts and cupboards full of his favourite junk food. I have no idea what his position is legally, or whether he would even act on it, but emotionally he has a major investment in the place. It's his home as well as mine.

And what of our shared friends? There are one or two with a clear-cut allegiance, but so many more are involved with us equally. If I walk away from him, will I be perceived as the bad girl, the one who becomes ostracised?

The one saving grace is that our respective families have never really socialised. Dean is quite pally with my brothers, but they only see each other through me, they don't wilfully seek each other's company, and although I don't actively dislike his parents, Roy and Paula, I doubt I'd pine for too long, or at all, if they were suddenly absent from my life.

'Penny for them?' Ella is staring at me quizzically.

'They're not worth that much,' I smile. 'I was just thinking about Dean.'

I look at Saira, hoping for guidance on whether to elaborate, but she's studying the main-course section of the menu again.

'I'm trying to decide if it's over or not,' I blurt.

Ella frowns momentarily, as if she's waiting for me to add, 'Only joking!' When I don't, her mouth falls open. '*Why?*'

'Good question,' I hedge. 'Long, long story.' And one, of course, that she hasn't been privy to, meaning this pronouncement really has come out of the blue and is consequently quite shocking.

'Has he found someone else?'

'No!' I scowl, outraged by her assumption that I'm the one who's been dumped. 'I'm just not sure it's going anywhere.'

'But you live together. And you're engaged to be married. Where else could it possibly go other than having children?' She looks faintly baffled.

'What I mean is that getting engaged has made me realise that, ultimately, Dean might not be right for me.'

Now she's looking overtly confused. 'Are you absolutely sure about this?'

'No, I'm not. Which is why I'm all over the place.'

'No change there, then,' mutters Saira from behind her menu.

'Poor Dean, he must be devastated you're feeling this way,' says Ella concernedly.

262

'No, he's absolutely tickety-boo,' continues Saira, lowering the menu. 'Because he doesn't actually *know*.'

I scowl at her, morphing it into a sheepish smile as I turn back to Ella. 'I haven't discussed it with him because I don't want to hurt him unnecessarily. If I decide to stay with him, then he'll be none the wiser that there was ever an issue.'

She nods slowly. 'But you still haven't answered my question: why do *you* feel there's an issue? You always seem so content with each other. I don't think I've ever heard you argue even.'

There are a million explanations I could give her. How I want so much more than just 'content', how each day just blends into the next, rendered indiscernible by the same predictable routine, how we rarely argue – I dispute 'never' – because we probably don't *care* enough to do so.

But, like Saira, I'm weary of just talking about it now, I need to *do* something without further counsel from anyone.

'What can I say?' I grimace. 'I guess I need to figure out whether there actually is an issue, or whether it's just *me* stopping myself from feeling happy, and nothing Dean does or doesn't do.'

Ella nods thoughtfully. 'And if it's the latter, then what?'

I shrug. 'Then I have to do something about it.'

'This hasn't got anything to do with that bloke from holiday, has it?' she asks suddenly, causing Saira to pull a 'that's-what-I-thought' face.

'No, nothing. *Nada*. Zilch. Zero. Nought. *Nein. Non.* NO! Have I made myself clear?' I glare.

'Crystal.' Ella recoils slightly and exchanges a look with Saira that suggests they both feel they're walking on eggshells.

I know how they feel.

Chapter Twenty-two

'Here you are, darling . . . potato cakes. I've made them just for you.'

Mum proffers a plate towards me, piled high with the speciality I have eaten forty-eight tons of since I was a child. But today, the mere sight of them turns my stomach. For the first time in living memory I'm off my food, thanks to the constant churning feeling in my gut.

I saw Dean only very briefly this morning, as he rolled out of bed and into his work suit, leaving the bedroom without so much as a grunted goodbye. In fairness, most Saturdays I am fast asleep at this hour but today, even though my eyes are still closed, I'm wide awake and have been for the past three or four hours, going over and over things in my mind.

I feel as though I'm standing on a cliff, my toes curled over its edge. Stepping back from it isn't an option, I can only propel myself forward, either into marriage . . . or life on my own. I still haven't quite decided and now here I am, having to face my family *en masse*, at the twins' thirtieth birthday lunch at Mum's house, an event that's missable only by death.

I see James sitting in the corner of the living room and wave. He catches my eye and smiles briefly before returning to what looks like an intense tête-à-tête with Jenny, his girlfriend of almost a year now.

'Where's Josh?' I ask Mum, taking a potato cake so I don't offend her, but simply enclosing it in my hand for hasty disposal in Malteser's direction at the first opportunity. Malteser is Mum's beloved Maltese terrier, who is eight years old and as fat as butter, thanks to her fondness for titbits and our fondness of giving them to her.

'On his way, darling, on his way. He rang about ten minutes ago,' she smiles. 'He's bringing his new girl-friend with him. How exciting!'

'Oh God, not another one,' I sigh wearily. 'I had barely learnt the last one's name before her services were dispensed with.'

'Now, now. This one *must* be serious,' she protests. 'After all, he is bringing her to his thirtieth birthday party, in the bosom of his family. You don't do that if it's just a passing fling, do you?'

With Josh, anything goes, I think to myself. It could easily be a ruse on his part to persuade the poor girl that he's serious and, therefore, she should sleep with him. I've seen it happen plenty of times before. He turns up with some pretty young thing who works terribly hard at being nice to his friends or family. You can almost see the expectation in her eyes. After all, men never introduce you to their inner circle unless you really mean something to them . . . do they?

But Josh isn't like most men. I love my brother, but sometimes I don't like him, particularly for the way he treats his girlfriends. He bombards them with attention, loving the chase, and makes them feel like the centre of his world. Then once they've come up with the goods, so to speak, he gets rapidly bored and drops them. It was perhaps expected when he was eighteen, but now he's thirty it's time he grew up.

Despite being classed as identical twins and seeming as such to those who don't know them, I would say Josh just edges it in the looks department. His eyes are a shade darker than James's and he has slightly straighter teeth. He also has a greater sense of style when it comes to clothes. James is a real sweatshirt and jeans man.

But emotionally, James is a much nicer person and, consequently, the brother I have always got along best with. When Josh was tormenting me by pulling my hair or hiding one of my favourite toys, James would always be the consoler.

Here's Josh now, enveloping Mum in a huge bear hug as she shrieks with delight. She has always claimed that she doesn't have a favourite, but if a gun was held to her head – and if her behaviour around him is anything to go by – then I would say it's him because he can wrap her round his little finger.

Behind him, the most astonishingly beautiful girl is standing with an apprehensive look on her face. She has long, chestnut-coloured hair, pale green eyes and the kind of skin that has never seen a ray of sun in its life, seemingly unblemished. I'd put her age at about twenty-five.

She's very slim and tall, with the slightly gawky gait one associates with a model . . . which wouldn't surprise me, as Josh seems to gravitate towards an awful lot of them.

'Beautiful and stupid,' he always says. 'That's how I like them.'

'They'd have to be stupid to have anything to do with you,' I invariably retort.

In truth, only one or two of them have been cerebrally challenged. The rest have been pretty bright but often insecure or needy, working as they do in an industry where looks matter more than anything else and they face constant rejection.

Then Josh comes along, makes them feel good about themselves for a short while, before rejecting them too. I secretly long for the day he meets his match, falls head over heels in love with her, then she dumps him and gives him a taste of his own, rather bitter medicine. Seeing me staring at her, Josh turns round to his companion, takes her hand and gently tugs her forward.

'Susie, meet my sister, Cam.'

I dutifully shake her hand and she smiles broadly at me, exposing perfectly even, white teeth. They're probably straight from a cosmetic dentistry catalogue but none the less impressive for it.

'And this,' Josh continues, 'is my mother, Liz. Do not, under *any* circumstances, eat one of her undeniably delicious potato cakes. We've got to keep those hips as slim and lovely as they are.'

He places a proprietorial hand on Susie's left hip and I raise my eyes heavenward.

'While we're at it, any chance of *you* getting rid of that gut?' I lean forward and squeeze the skin lying just above his waistband. OK, so I can barely find enough to grab as the protrusion is so minimal, but I want him taking down a peg or two.

To my surprise, Susie laughs heartily and nods her

head. 'She has a point. No danger of *your* eyes being bigger than your belly, eh?'

My immediate thought is that I like this girl immensely, followed swiftly by, What the hell is she doing with Josh?

Whilst Mum takes Susie through to the living room to make the introductions, Josh and I hang back in the kitchen.

'She seems really nice,' I say.

'She is.'

'No, I mean *really* nice,' I emphasise, 'as in far too good for you.'

'Gee, thanks, sis,' he smiles thinly. 'Nice to know you have such a high opinion of me.'

'Oh, come on, Josh. You know I love you dearly, but I don't like the way you treat your girlfriends. I've made that very clear before.'

'It may come as a surprise to you, dear Camomile, but I don't live my life wondering what will or will not please you. Besides, this one's different,' he says over his shoulder as he heads towards the other room.

'Either way, I'm sure you'll manage to screw it up,' I retort childishly. Mum always says that he and I bring out the worst in each other, even now, and she's probably right.

When I walk through, the introductions have already been made and Susie is talking animatedly with Jenny whilst James looks on. He's smiling inanely, like a teenage boy who has never encountered such beauty before. Jenny is pretty, in a windswept, outdoor sports kind of way, all pink cheeks and tousled hair. She's a cute Shetland pony to Susie's sleek, statuesque thoroughbred.

'Right, come along, everyone!' Mum claps her hands together as if we're all six, and gestures towards the dining table. 'Lunch is served.'

The sideboard is groaning under the weight of buffet food: vast bowls of herb and leaf salad, cold potatoes with chives, sliced avocado and mozzarella, a couple of quiches, chicken drumsticks and a large platter of ham. We all take a plate and queue politely.

'Where's Dean?' asks James, idly picking a strand of rocket from a bowl and popping it in his mouth.

I'm just about to reply, 'At work,' which, of course, is the truth, when I hear Mum's voice.

'She's having doubts about whether to marry him or not. Tell her, will you?'

Ah, yes, Mother strikes again. Never someone who will tell a little white lie if the truth will do more damage.

Josh, who is midway through lifting several slices of avocado onto his plate, stops dead, his mouth falling open. James and Jenny look mildly surprised, and Susie has the look of someone who hasn't the faintest clue who we're on about. Which of course she doesn't.

'Mum! I told you that in confidence.'

At which point, Josh throws his head back and roars with laughter. 'Cam, you're not serious? She makes me look discreet, always has.'

Mum shoots him an admonishing glance. 'Ignore him, dear. There's nothing to worry about. We're all family here, we have no secrets.'

'On the contrary,' I seethe, 'I have known Jenny for only about six months and I met Susie all of five minutes ago.'

'Don't worry, I won't tell,' smiles Susie. 'Besides, I don't even know who Dean is.'

'He's Cam's boyfriend,' says Josh. 'Of *six* years.'

'Oh. Quite a big deal, then.' Susie purses her fulsome lips.

'I'll say.' James raises his eyebrows at me. 'What's going on, Cam?'

'Nothing yet.' I want the ground to swallow me up. The notion that they all know I'm harbouring doubts, and Dean doesn't, makes me feel like a complete heel. But then I remember that the blame isn't mine, it lies with the mother I entrusted my supposed secret to.

'So are you splitting up?' James is looking confused.

'No . . . I don't know . . .' I clutch my empty plate, my appetite having faded to nothing now.

'Bloody hell, sis.' Josh's eyes appear to be shining with sensationalism. 'He'll be absolutely gutted if you do.'

Everyone except me has now filled their plate and sat down at the table. I cursorily take a piece of quiche and some salad, and occupy the empty chair between James and Susie.

'So, if it's not too personal, why are you having doubts?' murmurs James kindly. He looks genuinely concerned.

'Doesn't everyone who's getting married?' I reply vaguely. If I was alone with him, I'd go into more detail, but I know Josh is earwigging and I don't trust him not to make a joke at my expense.

'She craves excitement all the time,' trills Mum, filling everyone's water glasses. 'And she finds Dean's dependability a little too predictable. I've told her she's just being silly.'

'Do you remember that girl I dated from the year above me at school?' Josh chips in. 'What was her name? Ah, yes, Greta. God, she was dreary.'

My loathsome brother is now equating my still current six-year, live-in relationship with some passing fancy that lasted about two weeks in 1902.

'Dean is not dreary,' I hiss, my eyes pricking with tears. 'It's just that it feels very, well . . . comfortable, because we've been together for so long. *You* don't date anyone long enough to know what I'm talking about.'

James clearly senses my upset and squeezes my leg. 'Just ignore him. Taking relationship advice from Josh is akin to asking Katie Price for lessons in social etiquette.'

'So I'm dating a complete cretin?' Susie pulls a quizzical face. 'Is that what you're all telling me?'

I smile, grateful to her for seamlessly moving the subject away from me. 'Not a complete one as such, just a partial one.'

'That's reassuring.' She twists her mouth and glances at Josh, who is wide-eyed with indignation but only able to grunt, thanks to a mouthful of particularly glutinous quiche.

'Bollocks!' he eventually splutters, a blob of pastry jettisoning from his mouth and landing in the middle of Susie's plate. 'Aside from the fact that I have just spat food at you, I am the model of good manners.'

We all laugh, a welcome relief for me. I seize the lighter mood as a line in the sand.

'Look, everyone, I appreciate your concern, and I promise I will give you the full story when I feel up to it, but I'd rather not talk about Dean right now and I'd also really appreciate it if you didn't say anything to anyone else, especially him.'

Everyone murmurs their assent and I give what I hope is a winning smile.

'Now come on, dears, there's still vast quantities of food left,' chides Mum. 'Get over there and eat up.'

James and Josh replenish their plates but the women stay where they are. I may be wrong, but I swear the usually jolly Jenny looks apprehensive. My suspicions are confirmed when she shoots James a nervous look as he sits down and he responds with a small nod.

'Um, this seems a bit odd straight after Cam's news . . .' James clears his throat, '. . . but Jenny and I were always going to tell you this anyway, so we may as well carry on . . . We're engaged to be married.'

Mum leaps to her feet, her arms in the air as if celebrating a goal. Thankfully, she resists any hidden urge to pull her jumper over her head.

'Darlings, that's fantastic news! Come here . . .' She gestures towards Jenny, who dutifully stands up and leans in for an embrace.

'Nice one,' grins Josh. 'When's the baby due?'

'Fuck off, Josh,' says James mildly.

'James!' chides Mum, completely ignoring the fact that Josh's comment was far more worthy of her disapproval.

'Come on, details, details,' I smile at Jenny. 'Where did he propose? When's the wedding?'

'He proposed in bed this morning,' she blushes.

'Wow, it must have been a hell of a blow job,' interrupts Josh.

'Josh, don't be so vulgar!' Mum glares at him, and so do I, prompting him hastily to pick up Mum's spectacles and put them on.

'You should never hit a man with glasses,' he grins.

'No, hit him with something bigger and heavier,' I mutter.

'OK,' drawls Susie, 'so now I'm *totally* getting the social-cretin thing.'

'Go on,' I coax to Jenny.

'Well, it was very romantic,' she continues, glancing at James for encouragement, which he gives with a warm smile. 'He brought me a cup of tea in bed, just as he always does at the weekends, and a bacon baguette. But this time, he'd used brown sauce to pipe "Will you marry me?" along the top of it.'

Susie, Mum and I make all the right noises, oohing and aahing in unison. But out of the corner of my eye, I can see Josh wrinkling his nose at what he clearly perceives to be a rather downmarket proposal. No doubt he's about to say something crass, so I dig my shoe into his foot as a deterrent.

'Then he went on one knee and asked me properly. And that's it.' She stops speaking and places her hands between her knees, like a small child embarrassed by everyone's attention.

'Apart from the fact that you presumably said yes?' smiles Susie.

'Or, yes, yes, yes!' chimes Josh, never able to avoid a sexual innuendo.

'Well, congratulations to you both.' I stand up and embrace both of them in turn, lingering longer with James, whom I adore. It gives me immense pleasure to see him so happy, and I know Jenny will be good for him.

'We're just sorry that it's come at such an awkward time for you,' he murmurs in my ear.

'Nonsense! If anything, I should be apologising to you for spoiling your big announcement with my downer. Except, of course, that I didn't bring it up. It was old blabbermouth,' I sigh frustratedly. 'I have always refrained from telling her much about my life, but recently I thought we'd turned a bit of a corner, that I could perhaps trust her.'

'You still can,' he says quietly. 'She doesn't mean any harm. I genuinely think she believes what she said about us all being family. Perhaps you *should* share your problems with us a bit more. It might help. Otherwise, you're just bottling them up all the time.'

'Yes, I could certainly be accused of being a bottler.' I smile ruefully and let out a small sigh. 'What do you think I should do?'

There I go again, up to my old tricks of seeking counsel.

'Only you can answer that,' he bats back.

'But do you think Dean and I make a good couple?'

He shrugs. 'You don't seem to argue much, but that isn't necessarily a good thing. Look, all I can tell you is that I too had doubts about getting married . . . Remember the conversation we had at Stacey's wedding?'

I nod.

'And you said I had to make a commitment to her or let her go? Well, when I contemplated ending it, my fear of losing her far outweighed that of doing something that I didn't necessarily want to do but that I knew would make her happy. In other words, it was the thought of the institution of *marriage* I was baulking at, not the thought of spending the rest of my life with Jen, whom I adore. So I grew up and made the mature decision to propose.'

Tears well in my eyes, though I'm unclear whether my brother's romantic epiphany is the cause, or the fact that

I don't seem to possess this enviable quality to simply make a decision in life and get on with it.

'And once I decided to do it,' he continues, 'I *totally* got into it. It was as if the choice had been what was scaring me, and that once I'd made it, it no longer had any power over me. I have proposed and I haven't spontaneously combusted!' he grins. 'It's such a great feeling.'

'I'm thrilled for you,' I smile.

As he turns back to everyone else and joins in with Mum's toast to his and Jenny's future, I hold my glass aloft but my mind is firmly elsewhere.

Amidst all the angst of recent weeks and all the advice I have sought, it's the seemingly insignificant exchange I have just shared with James that has brought me the clarity I have been seeking.

The fog of indecision has lifted. I now know what to do.

Chapter Twenty-three

It's five o'clock when I walk back into the flat. It's dark and cold, so I yank the central heating thermostat up to twenty-five, and damn the expense.

Strolling through to the living room, my gaze rests on the bookshelf, in particular the bottom section, which houses the three or four photograph albums I lovingly compiled before apathy took over around year two of our relationship.

Squatting, I hook my finger round the first one and pull it towards me, using my sleeve to brush away the layer of dust along the top. As I open the cover, it makes a faint tearing noise as the pages are forced apart after so long.

The first four pictures were all taken on our first date to London Zoo. An odd choice, I know, but at the time I felt it was public enough for me to escape without harm if he turned out to be a nutter, and neutral enough not to give him the impression of romance before I had fully made up my mind. In the event, we'd had great fun and shared our first kiss in a nearby pub as dusk and a winter chill descended outside.

In the first picture, I'm gurning in front of the ape

house; in the second, I'm clutching a small monkey cuddly toy that Dean bought for me in the gift shop. I frown slightly, wondering where it is now, another once-cherished memento probably now rotting at the back of a dark cupboard somewhere.

The others are two separate shots of Dean poking his head through one of those painted scenes you usually find at the end of piers. It's of a huge gorilla and Dean's affecting a roar in one whilst raising his arms, ape-like, in another. If he did it now, I'd probably mumble, 'Don't be so bloody stupid,' and hurry him along, but it was that heady, all-forgiving time when a relationship is brand new and you think everything the other person does and says is wonderful. Equally, you are presenting a unrealistic version of yourself, someone who is forever easygoing, always a pleasure to be with. It's not until later that you allow your edges to be exposed. I sigh heavily at the thought.

When did I start to feel the first twinges of dis-satisfaction? I wonder. More importantly, *why* did I? Is it because Dean stopped being fun? Or was it because I changed and squashed it out of him, that he simply gave up trying to make me laugh because I became so unresponsive to it?

Annoyance is never far from the surface of a long-term relationship. A little grumble here about a tea spillage, a murmured harrumph there because the loo seat has been left up yet again. But deep-seated irritation is quite a another thing, a festering constant that flares up at every imagined slight. Hell, these days, I sometimes only have to hear Dean's key in the lock to feel my hackles rise. Is that his fault, or mine? Perhaps I'm morphing into a right old Victoria Meldrew, and whatever he or anyone else did wouldn't be right. Either way, someone, or something, has to change.

The second page of the album shows us about a month in, when we were still very much in the dating phase but were clearly far more comfortable with each other. There's a montage – taken by Saira, I think – in which I'm grabbing Dean by the neck and trying to lick his face as he winces and laughs in equal measure. We look truly happy, and I was. Then.

I continue, turning page after page, a visual chronology of our relationship as it unwittingly progressed towards . . . what? The edge of the cliff we now find ourselves on. If we'd known the outcome, I muse, would we still have embarked on the journey? I can only answer 'yes' to myself as I flick through yet more photographs that remind me our relationship *was* good. Once.

The next album is primarily taken up with photographs from our first holiday abroad, to Marbella. In one we're sipping comedy cocktails in a bar on the seafront; in another I'm lying on a sunlounger, trying desperately to hold my stomach in; then he's smiling benignly as the sun sets behind him on our hotel balcony. The standard holiday fare.

Towards the back of the album, there's a smattering of pictures from Dean's parents' thirtieth wedding anniversary party. It was the pearl one and, too impoverished to fork out for the real thing, we'd bought them a set of 'mother of pearl' caviar spoons. Like they're going to be eating much of that in their three-bed semi on a wet, windy Sunday afternoon. Mind you, with Paula's lofty ideas, you never know . . .

Thirty years. *Thirty!* You don't get that for murder. And what about all those Golden Weddings I read about in the local paper? Even if I were to meet someone next week and marry them within the year, I'd still be lucky to squeeze in a fiftieth wedding anniversary before slipping this mortal coil. A couple of generations before mine, spending that length of time together was the norm. These days, we're lucky to reach fifty days.

My grandparents on Mum's side were together for forty-five years until he suddenly died of a heart attack at just sixty-five. He dropped dead right in front of her, falling to his knees on the living-room rug one Sunday afternoon. He'd just retired from a thirty-year post as a civil servant with the local council's housing department and they were looking forward to spending their dotage together, pottering around the garden and going on midweek day trips to interesting places, avoiding the unbearably crowded weekends. They'd even ordered the brochures to plan their lifelong ambition of going on a Mediterranean cruise. It was going to be their Golden Wedding anniversary present to themselves.

I had cried so hard at Grandpa Ed's funeral that my swollen face took almost a week to look normal again, but Grandma Eileen had merely stood there impassively, like a stone. Mum reckoned she was in denial, and she remained so until about six months later when I was round there on one of my weekly visits and she collapsed onto the same rug, frothing at the mouth. It scared the living daylights out of me, but the doctors said there was nothing physically wrong with her, it was just delayed shock and a seeming unwillingness to carry on with life.

She'd always been a jolly soul, a daft antidote, if you like, to Grandpa Ed's more sober, sensible character. They complemented each other. He was the capable one who made her feel safe and paid all the bills, and she was the ditsy, fun one who brought unadulterated joy to his life.

After her collapse, she returned home a broken woman, fully accepting that the love of her life was never coming back. She wanted to die too but her body was strong and kept her going, and she was too mindful of the effect it would have on the rest of the family to do anything stupid. So she just existed, really – that's all I can describe it as – until her death two years ago from a particularly nasty bout of pneumonia.

'She's just making no attempt to fight it,' the baffled doctor told me at her hospital bedside.

'I know,' I smiled.

After he'd gone, I placed my cool palm on her feverish forehead and whispered quietly in her ear, 'We're all going to be fine, Grandma. Go to him.'

And she did, that very same night.

Thinking about it now, my eyes fill with tears. Both for the memory of my darling grandma and, if I'm honest, through self-pity that I may never experience that deep level of shared love.

Is it a rare thing, I contemplate, unattainable for all but the lucky few? Or had my grandparents made a decision to love each other come what may, and simply stuck at it, forging a co-dependency? Perhaps the modern-day obsession with independence and personal choice is an affliction that prompts us to give up relationships far too quickly? And, of course, there's no shame in divorce or separation any more, making the decision to leave so much easier.

Closing the album, I place it back on the shelf and pull out the third. From memory, this was about two years into our relationship and, looking at it now, I can see the signs already that, for whatever reason, we're slightly disengaged.

The photographs are from various parties or nights out with friends and we look happy enough. But there's no obvious connection between us. In one, we're posing with Saira and Abbas, but whilst she is touching his arm and leaning in to him, the body language between Dean and me is very much that of good friends or perhaps brother and sister. There's clearly a shared comfort zone, but no obvious sign of a shared intimacy. But then again, perhaps I'm simply being overly critical, actively seeking faults where none exist.

Towards the back of the album there's a photo, taken on my thirtieth birthday, I think, of Dean and I with Mum and the twins. It sets me thinking about their thirtieth birthday lunch earlier today and how Josh and I still seem to rub each other up the wrong way, despite our supposedly mature ages. I have always thought it's because we're so different, with my closeness to James coming from the fact we're so alike.

But now I realise it's the other way round. James is the balanced, stable one, and Josh and I are the fuck-ups. That's why we both look to him for advice and why we repel each other. James is emotionally normal, finding himself a nice girl to settle down with *despite* seeing the bitter fallout from our parents' marriage, but perhaps Josh and I haven't emerged quite so unscathed. The evidence is there for all to see. His propensity to flit from one relationship to another, never hanging around long enough to form any kind of lasting attachment. And me, hanging on in there with a man I may or may not love but who makes me feel safe. Both different manifestations of our deep-rooted insecurity.

I sandwich the album back between the other two and glance around the room that's so familiar to me, such a reminder of how enmeshed Dean and I are. Or our belongings are. There's a joint DVD collection, dozens of books, and framed photos of varying sizes scattered around the place. Then there's the PS3 and its various games, the forty-inch plasma television we both saved up for, the dented sofa we're still paying monthly instalments on, and, in the cupboard, an old dinner service his mum gave us that we've used once when she came round for Sunday lunch.

The phone rings, stirring me from my mental inventory.

'Hello?'

'Hello, dear.'

It's Mum. I feel myself bristling at the sound of her voice.

'I'm just calling to apologise. I shouldn't have told everyone that you were having doubts. It wasn't my secret to tell.'

My mother isn't terribly familiar with the word 'sorry', other than in the context of accidentally bump-ing into a stranger in a crowded street, so I know how much it has taken for her to say it. But I quell my usual propensity to please and resist letting her off the hook with an immediate 'It's OK.'

'No, you shouldn't have,' I say firmly. 'The thought that they all know it and Dean doesn't is an unpleasant and unfair one.'

'It is, you're right. But I have sworn them all to secrecy so he'll never know,' she mitigates.

I glance at my watch and it's as if she reads my mind.

'I deliberately called before he comes home, just to check you're OK.'

'And to make sure I don't do anything I might later regret?'

'No, not really. It's up to you what you decide to do. My opinion shouldn't come into it.'

'It won't.'

There's silence for a few seconds, then she clears her throat.

'Look, I know I haven't set a great example of marriage—'

'It wasn't your fault,' I interrupt.

'But for what it's worth,' she continues, 'I've been thinking, and perhaps it's not you being self-destructive . . . I feel awful for saying that now . . . perhaps it *is* just that you and Dean are incompatible, and that's totally your business to work out which, not mine.'

'Don't worry about it.' I smile into the receiver. 'I'm sure I'll be exactly the same if I ever have a daughter.'

'Whatever you do, I'm sure it will be the right thing.' She sounds relieved that I have forgiven her. 'And if ever you want to talk, you know where I am. I promise I'll keep my mouth shut.'

'Thanks, Mum, I appreciate it.' And I really do.

Replacing the receiver, I stroll through to the kitchen and instinctively flick the kettle on for tea I know I won't drink. Then I sit at the table and stare into space, feeling remarkably calm.

Dean will be home in just over an hour and, for the umpteenth time, I mentally run through everything I'm going to say, followed by the finer details of how and where.

Should I pounce the moment he walks through the door? Should I make tea first, *then* launch into it? Is the kitchen table the right location, or perhaps the comfort of the sofa? All comfortingly distracting stuff.

The nerves only kick in when I hear Dean's key in the lock.

Chapter Twenty-four

'Wotcha.' Dean walks into the kitchen, smiling distractedly as he often does for an hour or so after work, finding it hard to wind down. He particularly hates working Saturdays because, firstly, he misses the football and, secondly, he says it's the favourite shopping day for browsing timewasters who pick his brains on every last detail of a product then leave empty-handed.

He places his rucksack on the table in front of me and glances towards the kettle.

'Is there a brew on?'

'If you like.' It feels like there's a trapped bird in my stomach.

'Good. I've Sky Plussed the match and have managed to avoid knowing the score, so I can watch it as if it's live.'

'Great.' My tone is deliberately flat in an attempt to keep calm.

'You OK?' He glances at me quizzically.

'Not really, no.'

'Let me guess . . . your mum has done something? Or Josh?' He smiles, clearly trying to cheer me up a little.

'No, nothing to do with them.' I smile quickly. 'We need to talk.'

His face drops instantly. Like so many men, those words clearly chill him, invariably leading, as they do, to some deep and meaningful conversation where the woman lays bare her soul and he glances at his watch and wonders if the emotional monologue will be finished in time to catch the footie highlights.

'Oh. Can it wait?' His desperation to watch the match in peace is almost palpable, and after his long day at work, I feel for him. But needs must.

'I'm afraid not.' I stand up. 'I'll make that tea while you get changed out of your work clothes.'

He sighs with such ferocity that I feel it hit my face from two feet away. Looking mightily pissed off, he opens his mouth to say something, then clearly thinks better of it and leaves the room in moody silence.

Pouring water into a mug, I breathe deeply several times, consumed by thoughts of how to open the conversation that will shift the axis round which my life has circled for the past six years. Adding a splash of milk, I stir it and place it on the table in front of the chair he always occupies. A creature of habit is Dean. Same side of the bed, home or away, same chair for meals, same dent in the sofa for TV.

I sit in the only other chair and wait, my fingers drumming on the table to punctuate the silence that discomforts me.

A couple of minutes later, he's back, dressed in his usual 'sports' gear of polo shirt and jogging bottoms, neither of which has ever seen much real exercise. He hovers expectantly at the side of the table, obviously hoping that in his absence I may have experienced a change of heart, but I gesture towards his chair.

'Sit down, then. There's your tea.'

'Thanks.' He reluctantly lowers himself opposite me and leans forward, his elbows on the table. 'Go on then, what's this about?'

Perhaps his awkwardness in dealing with anything to do with 'feelings' should make this easier for me, justify my decision, almost. But it doesn't. Instead, I feel as if I'm about to club a trusting, unsuspecting baby seal over the head. I know subtlety won't work with Dean, I just have to get straight to the point.

'I can't marry you.'

His expression doesn't change, he simply blinks a few times. After a few seconds, he makes a small shrugging movement.

'That's OK. We'll do it later next year. Or the year after that, if you want. I'm cool with that, there's no rush.'

'No.' I shake my head firmly. 'I mean I can't marry you *ever*.'

Again, he seems largely unaffected by this statement and I suddenly realise that he thinks I'm simply anti-marriage and want to stick with the status quo, a position he would undoubtedly occupy with great gusto. He's about to respond, but I cut across him, anxious for no more misunderstandings.

'It's over. Us, the whole thing. I can't do this any more.' I raise my hand and make a sweeping gesture around the kitchen.

Now he gets it, his eyes turning black with shock. He stares at me intently, perhaps assessing whether this is real or simply an attention-seeking exercise that will ultimately be sorted out with a few reassurances and a couple of weekend mini-breaks.

'I mean it,' I verify. 'I'm not crying wolf here.'

During the many times I have imagined this scenario, Dean's reaction has always been either bafflement or quiet anger. So I am completely unprepared for what happens next, his face visibly crumbling before me. He's staring down at the table, and when he looks up his eyes are brimming with tears, his mouth twisted in pain.

'Why are you doing this?' he whimpers. 'I haven't done anything to deserve this.'

I feel a thumping pain in my chest, something I put down to the guilt I feel at hurting someone I'm genuinely fond of. But what else can I do? When James pointed out that he'd realised his misgivings were about marriage itself and not Jen as a life partner, I knew instantly that mine were the other way round. I *do* see myself getting married one day; I positively look forward to it. But I don't see Dean as a life partner.

'I know you haven't, but it's more complicated than that. This isn't a punishment for something *you've* done, Dean. It's about me and my feelings, that's all.'

'I thought you loved me.' His face is obviously wet now, his nose streaming. I should feel sympathy, but to my shame I think of him as too needy and it elicits a feeling of suffocation, thus hardening my resolve. I resist the instinctive temptation to reach across the table to comfort him, not wishing to give him even a faint glimmer of hope that this major problem might be resolved.

'I do love you,' I lie, 'but not in the way it takes to sustain a relationship.'

'What way is that, then?' he asks beseechingly.

289

It's a devastatingly simple question and one for which an articulate answer eludes me.

I shrug. 'All I can say is that it just doesn't feel right.'

'Then at least let me try and *make* it right.'

But I'm already shaking my head halfway through the sentence. 'It's not like that. And it's not your fault, truly. There's absolutely nothing you can do.'

'Then what *is* it? No one throws away six years for no reason . . . do they?'

Perhaps I should have just said that I don't love him any more, I think. In trying not to hurt his feelings, I have backed myself into a corner.

'I love you, Dean, but I'm not *in* love with you.'

'Ah, that old chestnut,' he smiles bitterly. 'Straight from the corny old textbook on getting shot of someone. I thought I might be worth more than that.'

'You were. You *are*,' I correct, 'but I'm just trying to be honest with you.'

'Yes, a bit of honesty is clearly long overdue, isn't it?' He unabashedly wipes his nose on the back of his sleeve. 'This hasn't just come out of the blue, has it? Why didn't you say anything?'

'Well, I kind of did . . .'

'When?'

And he genuinely means it. Either self-preservation has forced a mental block or, as I have long suspected, he has the emotional intelligence of an amoeba.

'Tenerife.' One word and yet evoking such nausea.

'Oh, that,' he says flatly, staring in my direction but with his eyes glazed. It hangs there between us for a few moments before he suddenly straightens his back and focuses on me again.

'Is it him? Is that why you're dumping me?'

I start shaking my head, but he's already on his feet, propelled there by outrage judging by his expression.

'How could I have been so fucking stupid?' He lets out a false laugh. 'He never went away, did he? He's been there in the background ever since your sordid little night together, chipping away at you, chipping away at *us*.'

He's pacing now, backwards and forwards in front of the draining board.

'You're wrong.' I shake my head firmly. 'It has nothing to do with him.'

Dean stops dead in his tracks and narrows his eyes at me. 'Have you been in touch with him since I asked you not to?'

With a little bit of artistic licence, the answer, of course, is 'no'. After all, it was he who pitched up on my doorstep; I didn't solicit it. But I have always been a lousy liar and guilt is obviously written all over my face.

'You have, haven't you?' he shouts, his face etched with disbelief. 'I should have fucking *known*!'

'I didn't get in touch with him, he came to see *me*,' I protest feebly, knowing I'm clutching at straws.

'He came here?' He clutches his head at this information overload. 'Jesus Christ, it's all coming out now, isn't it? Did you shag him in our bed?'

'Dean, don't. He only came here because he couldn't understand why the emails had stopped. Once I told him about you and that we were getting married, that was the end of it. He left and I haven't heard from him since.'

'Except that we're *not* getting married now, are we?' he practically spits.

'No, we're not. But it's not because of him. You have to believe me.'

'Believe *you*?' His contempt for me is undisguised. 'Why the hell should I? You didn't even tell me he'd been here.'

'Because I didn't want to upset you,' I mitigate.

He makes a scoffing noise. 'You seem to be doing a pretty good job of it now.'

'Better now than later,' I mumble, but he doesn't seem to be listening, continuing to pace up and down whilst slowly shaking his head from side to side.

'You go on a girls' holiday and sleep with a complete stranger, I forgive you . . . fuck, I even ask you to *marry* me, and then you throw it all back in my face . . . Why should I trust anything you say?'

'Because I'm telling the truth,' I say wearily. 'It doesn't change anything, but it's important to me that you don't think this is about him.'

'Ah, diddums. Protecting your new boyfriend, are you?' he retorts childishly.

I close my eyes, then open them again slowly. 'Can we keep this conversation on a mature level, please?'

I flinch as he lunges towards me, stopping when his face is barely an inch from mine.

'I will say *what* I fucking want, *when* I fucking want. Got it? You are not occupying the moral high ground here.'

Nodding, I stare at the floor, not trusting myself to look at him. Now I have delivered my bombshell, I want out of here. The rest is just painful padding. But I know I owe him the chance to vent his spleen, so I stay put.

'So, if I suspend disbelief for a moment and accept that your decision has nothing to do with what's-his-name—'

'Tom,' I venture helpfully.

'I prefer what's-his-name,' Dean snaps. '*If* I choose to believe you, then spell it out for me again why this relationship is ending? Because I don't mind admitting that I'm fucking baffled by it.'

'I guess we just got too set in our ways, too comfortable.' I shrug.

He affects a heavy shrug, obviously mimicking me. He looks very angry now and for the first time in our relationship, I wonder what he might be capable of.

'Too comfortable?' he sneers. 'Oh, yes, God forbid that we'd ever be *that*. How fucking *dreary*, eh?' He uses his hands to push himself away from the draining board and over towards the kitchen door, then swivels to back face me again. 'What do you want, then, Cam?' he challenges. 'Massive arguments? Is that it? How about actual fist fights? A front seat on the roller coaster of emotional torment. Would that be uncomfortable and exciting enough for you?'

I visibly flinch in the face of his anger. 'You're wilfully misinterpreting what I'm saying.'

'No I'm not. I'm *trying* to establish exactly why you're chucking six years away on what seems like a fucking whim.'

He noticeably tries to calm himself with a couple of pronounced breaths, then after a few seconds pass, his expression changes to a more conciliatory one. He sits back down in the chair, giving me a rueful smile that doesn't reach his eyes.

'Everyone craves excitement from time to time, Cam; I totally get that. And I also get what you're saying that we're a little set in our ways, particularly me.' He reaches across the table and grabs hold of my hand before I can move it out of temptation's way. 'But I thought we were working on that by doing more things together. We had a laugh at the wedding show . . . didn't we?'

I nod and smile. 'We did. But it's not enough. It feels like we're in a rut.'

'Maybe. But it's a nice rut and I quite like it there.'

'Then we're not the same kind of people.'

'What's so bad about it?'

'It's not bad,' I falter, knowing I'm sounding ridiculously picky. 'But it's not good either. Sometimes, I feel as though we have little in common except that we both live under the same roof.'

He tightens his grip on my hand. 'We'll do more exciting things, I promise. Just don't chuck this away without giving me the chance to be the person you want me to be.'

As he says it, I feel a burning sensation in my chest as if my heart is literally searing in two. Clearly I still care about him enough to feel genuine pain at the hurt I'm inflicting, but not enough to stop doing it.

'You mustn't change,' I murmur. 'You're fine just as you are. I'm the one with the problem, the one who should change, but I don't think I'm capable of it.'

'Capable of what?'

The truthful answer is 'capable of settling for someone I suspect isn't right just because they're a nice person', but I fudge it.

'Capable of just being happy in the moment, of not constantly hankering after adventure. Perhaps I need to go up the Himalayas and find myself,' I smile sadly.

'Let's save up and go together! We could do it next year.' His eyes are shining at the thought. 'We can go on lots of adventures.'

I shake my head slowly, knowing I have to continue to be cruel to be ultimately kind. 'It won't work. Nothing will.' I pull my hand away from him and turn sideways in my seat to justify the action. 'Sorry, but my mind is made up.'

He starts to cry again, huge racking sobs this time. He looks at me with such hurt in his eyes that I fleetingly contemplate saying, 'OK, let's give it one more go,' just to put an end to his pain. But I stop myself. I have done the deed and I know it's the right thing to do, so to capitulate now would just be prolonging the inevitable.

'Dean, I am truly, truly sorry that I have hurt you so badly, but surely you wouldn't want us to carry on as we were, with me living a lie?'

'I'd rather that than lose you,' he sniffs, extracting an old tissue from his sleeve and blowing his nose.

'You're not losing me. I will always be your friend.'

'Ah, yes, the consolation prize,' he sniffs petulantly. 'I'm not sure I can be your friend.'

'Well, that's your decision.' At last, something I can lay at his door, however minor.

Silence descends for a few seconds, him staring over my shoulder and out of the window, me scraping my thumbnail back and forth across the table.

'So who knows about this?' he says eventually.

The question takes me by surprise, trifling as it is in the grand scheme of things.

'No one.'

He seems to believe me. He stops crying but his nose is still red, giving him the look of someone with a heavy cold.

'What are you going to tell them?'

'What would you *like* me to tell them?' I feel I owe him that.

'That we're not splitting up.'

'Dean . . .'

'OK, OK,' he sighs irritably. 'Let's just say that we've decided to take a break for a while.'

'A break? But then they'll be expecting us to get back together,' I hedge, knowing full well they probably won't.

'That's what I want to tell them,' he says obstinately.

'OK, fine.' I shrug, hoping to God he doesn't encounter my blabbermouth mother anytime soon.

Silence again, the only sound the drip, drip of the kitchen tap he said he would try to fix about six months ago. Yet another example of his lacklustre attitude to life.

'So what happens now?' He looks at me questioningly.

I inwardly wince, anticipating that this part of the conversation might be even more awkward and uncomfortable than the actual break-up.

'Well, I suppose you need to find somewhere else to live,' I say hesitantly, before adding as a supposedly uplifting afterthought, 'but don't worry, I'll help you look.'

'Big of you,' he fires back sarcastically. 'So let's get this straight, you're pulling the rug from under my feet both metaphorically *and* literally?'

'It is my flat.'

'Oh, suddenly it's *your* flat now, is it? Does that mean I can instantly stop paying half the mortgage and half the bills?'

'Yes, of course it does.' I feel a thump of financial dread at the thought. 'And what I meant was that it's my name on the deeds, that's all.'

My knowledge of law doesn't extend far beyond what I have learnt from TV crime shows, but I know enough to realise that, legally, I'm on very shaky ground here. When Dean first moved in, it didn't cross my mind to get him to sign a waiver document or a short-hold tenancy agreement. After all, not very romantic, is it? 'Darling, I love you and, by the way, can you just sign this piece of paper that means you won't get half my stuff when I dump you?' But now I may live to regret it.

'After six years, I must have *some* legal rights,' he ventures, narrowing his eyes at me. 'I could refuse to move out unless you pay me a lump sum.'

I nod slowly. 'Yes you probably could.'

'But I won't,' he sighs. 'You know I won't.'

And I probably do know that, I think. Not just because he's too disorganised or lazy to do anything about it, but because it's also not in his ostensibly nice, uncomplicated nature to be deliberately obstructive.

'You don't have to move out straight away,' I smile reassuringly. 'It can wait until you've found somewhere you like.'

'Something tells me you'll be working very hard to find me that place,' he mutters sulkily. 'And in the meantime, what about the sleeping arrangements?'

'The sofa's very comfy,' I nod, resisting the temptation to add, 'Christ knows, you spend enough time on it.'

'Good. Because I wouldn't like to think of you being uncomfy on it,' he smiles weakly, valiantly trying to put on a brave face.

I laugh theatrically, completely out of proportion to the calibre of the joke, anxious to maintain the light-heartedness now it's reared its head.

'More tea?' I ask with all the brightness of a children's television presenter on Prozac. I stand up to indicate that, as far as I'm concerned, the worst is now over and we should return to normality, albeit one with different boundaries.

'Yes, please.'

He stands too, but still seems apprehensive. He opens his mouth to speak and my heart sinks, expecting him to seek yet more validation for my decision.

'Is it OK if I go and watch the football now?'

Chapter Twenty-five

'The things you see when you haven't got a camera!' laughs Ella.

'Or a gun,' I smile wryly.

We're dressed in ridiculously unflattering outfits of blue towelling shorts with matching tank top, thick ankle socks, leg warmers, gloves and woolly hat. We resemble post-menopausal cheerleaders.

We are waiting to enter the cryotherapy chamber at Champneys spa in Hertfordshire, an icily cold treatment designed to help with wide-ranging conditions such as psychological stress, rheumatism and psoriasis. Though if we're honest, our expectations are purely cosmetic ones, hoping it will tighten up our facial skin.

Saira is sitting to one side of us, still wrapped up in her cosy spa dressing gown, having swerved this one on medical grounds. She's pregnant again, you see. Six months pregnant, to be precise, and now looking bloody marvellous on it after an initial three months of almost continual vomiting. She's the only pregnant woman I know who managed to actually *lose* weight. But now she's over the worst of it and her face and body have filled out a bit. Sadly, so have her ankles.

I peer into the small window at the front of the chamber and see the previous three victims – sorry, I mean, willing participants – trudging round and round in a circle, patting their arms and legs in the minus-100-degree cold.

'Remind me again why we're doing this?' I wince.

'Because it releases our endorphins,' replies Ella, who is a bit of an addict.

'Meaning?'

'It will help with any aches and pains.'

'And will I look like you when I come out?' I add, peering enviously at her peachy skin.

'No, you'll just be a slightly bluer version of yourself, but believe me, it will give you such a rush,' she enthuses.

The door cranks open and a cloud of liquid nitrogen billows into the room, closely followed by a woman whose face appears frozen in an expression of mild pain. Reassuringly, her two friends are smiling, though I'm unsure whether they simply entered looking that way and have been frozen into remaining so.

'Right!' The instructor turns her attention to us. 'Ready?'

'I may regret saying this, but yes,' I nod. Ella follows suit.

The woman explains to me that we will be in the first chamber for a minute, acclimatising to the cold at minus 60 degrees, and will then move in to the minus-100-degree chamber when we feel ready for a further two minutes.

'If at any time you want to come out, you can.' She opens the door to the first chamber and gestures for us to go in. I throw a tortured look over my shoulder at Saira.

'Have the warm towels and hot toddies ready. We're going in,' I intone with all the gravitas of a military commander.

She makes a salute gesture, then instinctively pulls her fluffy robe tighter around her. 'Aye, aye, Captain.'

Once we're inside, the instructor closes the door on us and instantly the cold hits the exposed sections of my arms and legs, giving the feeling of dozens of little needles being prodded into my flesh. Imagine the chill of wearing a bikini down your local High Street on a bitterly cold November night and then double it. It's *that* cold and we're not even in the second chamber yet.

After what seems like an eternity, the instructor gives a thumbs-up sign through the window and we give one back, indicating we're ready to move through to the minus-100 zone. My legs and arms already feel red raw and I know my face has atrophied into a permanent expression of surprise, but the good news is that I'm already so numb from cold that the drop in temperature seems to make little difference. Also, because there's no wind or moisture accompanying it, it feels fairly bearable.

I look across at Ella, who looks just as she always does. If it wasn't for the daft outfit, she could simply be strolling through a park on a mild autumn day.

When the exit door eventually opens, I am first through it, frantically rubbing my bright red thighs. I look up to see Saira practically wetting herself, which doesn't take much in her condition.

'You look like a Smurf with high blood pressure,' she shrieks.

'Fuck off,' I say amiably, hastily removing the blue woolly hat.

To add insult to injury, Ella saunters out looking exactly the same as she did three minutes ago.

'Invigorating, isn't it?' she gasps.

'Er, yes. Can we go to the bar now?'

But first the instructor insists we do a few minutes on exercise bikes and Power Plates to warm ourselves back up again. Again, Ella executes the task effortlessly whilst I'm puffing like Thomas the Tank Engine with emphysema.

I've never liked exercise, finding it inutterably dreary. The one and only time I ever ventured into a gym, I merely sat on an exercise bike, eating a full butter croissant and watching MTV on the screen positioned above my head. Which may go some way to explaining why the 'shape' I got myself in is round.

'Right, can we do something *relaxing* now?' I whinge in the changing rooms afterwards, gratefully jettisoning the rest of the Smurf suit and pulling on a fluffy white robe.

'How does lunch sound?' says Ella.

'Unbelievably good idea!' I feel my spirits lifting, then instantaneously fading again as a thought enters my head. 'Is it proper nosh or something that resembles the bottom of a budgie's cage?'

'A bit of both. Come on, follow me.'

I link my arm through Saira's and we tag along behind Ella towards the restaurant. As we enter, the *maître d'* actually trips over a bump in the carpet in his rush to be at Ella's side.

'Ms Powell, how lovely to see you again. How long are you staying with us?'

'Just until tomorrow.' She gives him a killer smile and he visibly shivers with excitement.

'Such a short time! Can we not persuade you to stay longer?'

'Can we not persuade him to let us sit down and eat?' I hiss quietly in her ear. 'I'm in danger of passing out here.'

She reaches to one side and grabs a plate from a small pile nearby. 'Here you go. It's self-service.'

Oh, joy of joys. I *love* self-service, having perfected the art of expertly building a Mount Everest of food on even the daintiest of plates. The food looks good too. No burgers or chips, sadly, but managing to be healthy and imaginative . . .

As I make my way to our table, I walk very carefully, anxious not to disrupt my delicately balanced food mountain. Placing it on the table, I glance up to find Ella scowling at me. In front her is a plate with a small piece of salmon and a few lettuce leaves. You can still see the pattern on the plate, for God's sake.

'Cam, this isn't a one-stop, all-you-can-eat buffet,' she says scathingly. 'You can go up as many times as you like.'

'You can?' I look down at the glut of food on my plate and suddenly feel like a complete fool. Correction: greedy fool. 'Oops,' I grin. 'You can take the girl out of the ghetto, but—'

'Ghetto?' snorts Saira. 'You're from a semi-detached in Bromley. It was hardly the Bronx.'

I place a gherkin in my mouth as daintily as I can, and decide to distract their attention away from my gluttony.

'So, how's your love life, Ella? Pointless asking about yours.' I gently prod a finger against Saira's swollen belly. 'At least one of us is getting it.'

'Yes, six bloody months ago.' She pulls a face. 'Abbas

is terrified that having sex might harm the baby, so he's barely come near me since.'

I turn back to Ella, awaiting her usual answer of 'non-existent', and see that she's blushing slightly with a faintly smug smile.

'Oh my God! Who is he?'

'It's very early days,' she mitigates.

'How early?' demands Saira. 'Have you had sex yet?'

'Saira, please!' Ella looks genuinely shocked at the outburst.

'Sorry,' she mumbles sheepishly. 'I have to get it vicariously these days.'

'Well, the answer is no, anyway. I have only been seeing him since last week.'

'Details, details,' I splutter through a mouthful of brown rice.

'Well, he's called Luke,' she smiles broadly, 'and he's *lovely*.'

'We kind of guessed that.' Saira unconsciously rubs a hand up and down her belly. 'What we want to know is, where did you meet him? How old is he? What does he do? Is he—'

'Married,' Ella interrupts. 'No, he's not. Well, unless he's lying to me.'

'I was going to say, "Is he good-looking?" actually, but that's reassuring to know.'

Ella stares up at the ceiling, as if trying to remember the questions. 'Um, I met him at the gym, he's thirty-five, and he lends money, I think.'

'Ooh, could be useful,' I pipe up.

'He lends money to entire *countries*, Cam, not spendthrift hairdressers.'

'He might make an exception when he gets to know

me,' I sniff. 'So I take it you've been out on a date already?'

'Two, actually. First of all we just went for coffee after a gym session, and then he asked me out for dinner.'

'A low-carb one, I presume?'

She pointedly ignores me and addresses her next remark to Saira. 'As I said, it's early days but I'm having great fun.'

It's nice to see her so relaxed about a man after the tense couple of years involving Philip. After she dumped him, she never heard from him again. Not a visit, not a phone call, not even a note. At first, she'd been quite bullish about it, maintaining that she was pleased by the distance because it meant she could move on with her life more easily. But after a couple of months and still no word, she drunk a little too much one night and the self-doubt poured out, notably a slurred monologue about how foolish she felt at spending two years of her life with a man to whom she clearly meant nothing.

We reassured her, saying that Philip was probably heartbroken but forcing himself to stay away from her out of respect, because she'd asked him to. Also, that he was doing it to ensure that she would move on more quickly and find the happiness she deserved with someone else. He loved her *that* much.

We said all of that, but as Saira and I admitted to each other later, we didn't really believe it ourselves. And besides, Ella probably didn't either. Fact was that Philip was a prize shit who had taken what he could, then barely given her a second thought once she'd lost patience with the stalemate. No doubt he had already moved on to some other sucker, if you get my drift.

By complete contrast, I have heard from Dean several

times since the day he finally walked out of my flat for good. In the end, the search for a new place for him had taken only a couple of weeks, aided and abetted by four thousand pounds loaned to me by Mum and Dad – two thousand each.

Dean didn't want to take it, but I had insisted, primarily because I felt it was only fair after he'd contributed so much to the mortgage, but also because I knew he'd need it for a deposit and perhaps some furniture in his new home. So it wasn't for entirely altruistic reasons.

I fully expected to be the one who found and arranged a visit to the new place, but to my astonishment, Dean came home one night and announced that Gary, his colleague in the mobile-phone shop, was looking for a new flatmate and that he could move in the coming weekend.

The day he left was a bit of a damp squib, with him simply pecking me ruefully on the cheek and sauntering out stage left with a couple of large, borrowed suitcases and a few carrier bags. I don't know what I expected after six years – a few tears maybe, or at the very least a quivering lower lip.

I didn't cry either, but when he'd gone I did get the most crashing depression for the rest of the afternoon, wandering disconsolately around the flat, not knowing what to do with myself now I was footloose and fiancé-free. But Saira reckoned I was simply mourning the loss of something so familiar to me, not particularly Dean as a person.

And she was right. About a week later, the blackness lifted and I started to feel liberated by the new sense of space in my life, of being able to do what I wanted, when

I wanted, not answerable to anyone. Not that Dean was ever particularly demanding of my time . . . In fact, he happily watched TV alone on many occasions whilst I got on with other things, so perhaps the feeling of being answerable was a millstone I hung round my own neck. Whatever, it wasn't there any more and it felt good.

But staying away from Dean wasn't an option for me. I felt too guilty, too mindful of his feelings and wanting to know how he was coping without me. Perhaps there was a little bit of insecurity and self-obsession wrapped up in there too, of needing to know he was pining for me.

So when he called on what I assume was the pretext of asking if I'd seen a particular CD of his, we agreed to meet in a pub halfway between our homes. At first, we made polite conversation about what we'd been up to, but after a few drinks he became maudlin and said he missed me, found his new life empty without me in it. Not to mention the fridge, probably.

I responded that I *was* still in his life, just not in the same way as before, and that he could call me whenever he wished. An offer I soon regretted when he started calling once a week, every Sunday night, for 'a catch-up chat'. Then it became twice a week and suggestions were made about meeting up. When I resisted, he started buying tickets for my favourite bands or the latest film and casually asking if I wanted to go with him 'just as friends'. But I knew it wouldn't be, so I initially made excuses, eventually becoming more brutal and giving a firm 'no', explaining that I didn't feel it would be appropriate.

Ella thought I was being too harsh, but Saira thought it was the right thing to do. Her only worry was that

Dean might feel I was staying away because I couldn't trust myself to keep my hands off him. Whatever, he must have got the message because I now haven't heard from him for about four weeks.

'So when are we going to meet this Luke chap?' Saira's voice breaks into my thoughts.

Ella raises her eyebrows. 'As I said, I really like him. Meeting you two so early on might prompt him to run for the hills.'

'Charming.' I have started to tackle the east face of my food mountain and manage inadvertently to spit out a small piece of beetroot, which lands on Ella's plate. 'Ooh, careful, that's got a couple of calories in it.'

She jokingly pokes out her tongue at me whilst using a paper napkin to remove the offending object from her plate. As she does so, my phone starts ringing in the depths of my handbag and several women on a nearby table shoot me a murderous look.

'This is supposed to be a place of relaxation!' hisses Ella. 'At least put it on bloody silent.'

As I hit the 'ignore' button, I glance at the caller ID and wince.

'Oh God, it's Dean. I was rather hoping he'd given up on me.'

'Or maybe he was simply playing hard to get in the hope that it might inflame your passion,' suggests Saira.

'Well, either way, it hasn't worked.' I click on voicemail and press it to my ear.

'Hi, Cam, it's me, Dean. Can you give me a call, please? There's something I need to tell you.'

'Blimey.' I pull a face. 'He sounds really serious. Something must have happened.'

They both look immediately concerned, Ella waving her hand at me, shooing me towards the door.

'Go outside now and call him.'

I do as I'm told and head out through a set of French doors at the back of the restaurant. The impressive gardens stretch out before me, but I simply move to one side and settle myself in a small wooden chair, clearly placed there by someone having a crafty fag between exercise sessions.

As I punch in Dean's number, I wonder what on earth could have happened. One of his family has fallen ill, perhaps? After six years together, it would be only natural that he'd want me to know. Or what if there's something wrong with *him*?

I shiver involuntarily.

'Hi, Cam,' Dean answers almost immediately.

'Hi, are you OK? Your message worried me.' I realise that my swift reply might be misinterpreted by him as deep feelings of concern betraying my wish to reconcile, but it's not really the time for games.

'Yeah, yeah, I'm fine.'

'And your family?'

'Fine too. It's nothing like that.'

I let out a long breath and feel my shoulders relax slightly. 'What is it, then?'

'I don't quite know how to tell you this, but . . .'

I'm suddenly tense again. What the hell is he going to say?

'. . . I've got a new girlfriend.'

'Sorry?' I croak.

'I've met someone else. I felt it only right that I should tell you.'

A silence descends whilst my brain computes that

neither Dean nor any member of his family is dying or even faintly unwell. Not even his mother's bloody cat. No, the urgency and grave intonation were all because the man I no longer want for myself has found someone else to inflict his habitual ways upon.

After a few seconds, he clears his throat.

'Are you OK?' he asks concernedly. 'Sorry if it's come as a bit of a shock.'

'It isn't a bloody shock,' I retort irritably. 'I thought there was something wrong with you, *that's* why I'm speechless. From the tone of your message, I thought it was something really important, not simply an update on your frigging social calendar.'

A waiter comes out of the French doors with a packet of Silk Cut in his hands, but seeing an angry, red-faced woman on the smoking chair, turns on his heel and goes straight back inside again.

'It's a little more than that,' mutters Dean petulantly. 'I just wanted to tell you myself . . . you know, before someone else did.'

I long to scream back that even if Saira or Ella or anyone in my family knew this supposedly startling revelation, they would probably place it behind a runny poo in rank of importance, knowing as they do how pleased I am to be out of the relationship. But I don't say it, feeling calmer now and not wishing to be deliberately cruel.

Besides, I'm starting to feel slightly chilly and want to curtail the conversation so I can return to the warmth of the restaurant.

'Well, I'm really happy for you.' And for me too, I think, liberating me as it does from the burden of residual guilt.

'Really?' He sounds faintly disappointed.

'Yes, truly.' I stand up and pull the robe tighter to my body, peering through narrowed eyes at the gloomy sky. I know I should now feign interest and ask him questions, like where did he meet her, what's her name, what does she do . . . but I just don't have the energy or the inclination for it.

'She's called Louise,' he offers.

'That's a nice name,' I observe lamely.

'She came in to buy a phone.'

'And walked out with a boyfriend,' I quip.

'You should meet her.'

I snort loudly. 'Don't be a twat.'

'What? She's got to understand that you're a very important part of my life.'

I suddenly feel overwhelmed with weariness. '*Was*, Dean, was. We have to move on, and me having cosy suppers with your new girlfriend isn't going to help any of us.'

He doesn't reply and I know he's sulking. But it's not my problem any more, it's hers . . . Louise's.

'Look, I have to go. I'm standing outside and I'm freezing. Thanks for calling and let's speak soon,' I add, more as a sop to him than through any genuine compulsion to revisit this awkward conversation.

After ending the call, I place the phone in my pocket and go back inside, my expression sombre as I walk back towards the table.

'Is everything OK?' asks Saira pensively.

'It's bloody fantastic!' I grin, launching myself into a cartwheel and narrowly missing a waiter.

The look on their faces is a greater tonic than any spa treatment.

311

Chapter Twenty-six

Tapping on the hotel-room door, I smile broadly as he opens it dressed only in his shirt, socks and, thank the Lord, underpants.

'I can only pray you're not going up the aisle like that.'

'Possibly,' he winces. 'I put my trousers in one of those overnight press thingies and they've gone all crinkly.'

I pick them up from where they've been slung on the back of a chair and inspect them closely. 'Oh dear, I see what you mean.'

His eyes follow me anxiously around the room as I start opening cupboard and wardrobe doors and peering inside.

'There has to be an iron in here somewhere . . . a-ha!' I pull it out triumphantly and plug it into a wall socket. 'One pair of well-pressed trousers coming right up.'

'Sis, you're a star.' James lets out a heavy sigh. 'Jeez, this wedding lark is very stressful.'

I burst out laughing. 'You've done piss all except turn up. Jenny has done everything else.'

'I hired my own suit,' he grins.

'Yes, and look what you've done with it,' I grimace,

kneeling on the floor to tackle a particularly stubborn crease. 'There, I think that's done it. Now come on, the bride is supposed to be the fashionably late one, not you.'

As he tugs on the trousers and threads his belt through the waistband, I pick up the white rose corsage Jenny has organised for him and pin it to his jacket lapel.

'Do you think everything's going to be OK?' he asks nervously.

'Of course it is. Jenny is a delightful girl and you love her to bits – what can possibly go wrong?'

He rolls his eyes. 'Not that, of *course* I'm fine about Jen. I'm talking about Mum and Dad.'

'Oh, *that*.' I purse my lips. 'They'll be fine. Besides, even if they weren't, they'd hide it so they don't spoil your big day.'

'When have you known Mum to hide *any* feelings?' He looks at me with raised eyebrows.

'OK, point taken. In that case, I promise I'll have my stiletto poised over her windpipe for the entire day, just in case she flares up.'

'Now you're talking,' he laughs, adjusting his tie slightly. 'Right, how do I look?'

I take a step back and study him. At six feet two, he's an athletic shape, his broad shoulders accentuated by the cut of the well-tailored morning suit.

'Bloody gorgeous. If you weren't my brother, I'd marry you myself.'

As he heads off to the bathroom for a last-minute spruce-up of hair and teeth, I'm left standing in the middle of the room, contemplating my own wedding day that never was. If I hadn't baled out when I did, how would I be feeling if this was *my* big moment, pulling on the dress and the various accessories that every little girl dreams about at some time in her life?

At worst, sick. At best, numb. That's how I'd be feeling. Because none of the romantic trappings could have disguised the fact that I was about to bond myself even more restrictively to a man I wasn't in love with.

James emerges from the bathroom with his hair slightly wetted and slicked to one side.

'Ugh, you look like Mother has spat on her hand and styled your hair ready for Sunday school.' I advance towards him and tease his hair back into its usual, slightly tousled look. 'Thank goodness I'm here to stop you making a tit of yourself.'

'Gee, thanks, sis. You're all heart,' he quips, kissing the top of my head. 'Right, come on, let's get going.'

The church is already packed by the time we get there. As James walks towards his seat in the front pew, shaking various hands along the way, I peel off and scour the rows for Mum.

Dad is sitting near the back with Ava, wearing what can only be described as a dented hubcap on her head, but there's no sign of Mum anywhere.

Spotting Josh on his way in with Susie, I grab his elbow and drag him to one side. 'Mum's not here. Have you seen her?'

'Calm down,' he drawls. 'When have you ever known Mum to be on time for anything?'

'Well, I thought she might make an exception for her own son's wedding,' I hiss. 'If she arrives after the bride, I *will* kill her.'

He strolls off, leaving me anxiously peering out of the

door as the last straggle of relatives and friends make their way to their seats.

I'm just getting my mobile out of my bag to call her when I spot Mum walking briskly up the path and I heave a sigh of relief.

'Cutting it fine, aren't you?' I scowl, tapping my watch. 'Jenny is due here any second.'

But she doesn't seem to hear my protest, merely looking at me pensively whilst smoothing down her skirt.

'How do I look?'

And it suddenly clicks. Mum is late because she has probably been spending the last couple of hours trying on different outfits and redoing her make-up and hair, fretting that she won't match up to Ava.

'You look beautiful,' I say truthfully. 'Very classy.'

She's wearing the pale beige Jaeger skirt suit I know she has spent a small fortune on, along with matching shoes and a chic wool beret. Her usually wiry hair has been blow-dried into a smooth wave and she is wearing minimal make-up that enhances rather than ages her features.

I link my arm through hers and gently tug her towards the aisle. As we walk past, Dad and Ava are facing forward and don't see us, but I know she's seen them as her body palpably tenses up.

'She's not a patch on you.' I squeeze her arm reassuringly and she gives me a warm smile, noticeably raising her chin as she takes her place near the front.

The ceremony is over and we're now doing the pre-dinner mingling bit at the conference hotel James and Jenny have chosen for their reception.

Of course, the happy couple are the centre of attention for most guests, but for three of us – me, Josh and the groom himself – the main event has yet to come: our mother bumping into Dad after more than ten years. And of course, his, ahem, rather effervescent new wife.

Because Mum arrived at the church late and left before them in a separate car, they have so far managed to avoid each other. But there are only sixty guests in one room here, so the circumnavigating can't go on for much longer.

Since my 'full and frank' with Mum all those months ago, the twins have seen Dad a couple of times. Apparently she rang them individually a few days later and said that *if* they felt they needed her permission to contact their father, then it was granted.

I won't say they're bosom buddies with him, or perhaps ever will be, but being quite a traditionalist (hence the morning suit) James felt it only right that his father, and consequently Ava, should attend his wedding. But not before checking with Mum first.

I sidle up to Josh. 'Ever get the feeling there's an elephant in the room?'

'Oh, come on, Ava's not *that* large. She's cuddly – isn't that what they say these days?' he grins.

'Ha-ha.' My smile vanishes instantly. 'Oh God, they're coming this way.'

But as they get closer, Ava peels off in the direction of the ladies' loo, leaving Dad going it alone.

'Hello, you two,' he says amiably, giving me a peck on the cheek and shaking Josh's hand with a warm smile. 'Where's your mother?'

'She's in the loo . . . Oh shit!' I clasp my hand over my mouth as realisation dawns. 'Excuse me . . .'

I run as fast as my painfully tight stilettos will carry me in the direction of the toilets, ignoring the attempts of a passing distant aunt to say hello.

All seems quiet on the cistern front as I enter the small room of five cubicles, and I hover expectantly, not wishing to call out and alert either of them to each other's presence. After a few seconds, there's a flushing sound and a door is unlocked. I position myself in front of the mirror opposite it, looking for all the world like a woman checking her make-up.

Mum appears and is about to greet me when I pull a face and place my finger against my lips, miming a ssshhh.

'What?' she says out loud, prompting me to indulge in a spot of head-and-eye-rolling.

I jab my finger towards the only locked cubicle and mouth 'Ava' at her.

'Ever?' she says even more loudly than before. 'Cam, darling, have you been drinking? What are you talking about?'

At that moment, the other door unlocks and Ava's breasts edge their way out of the cubicle at least a second before she does. If she has sussed what was going on outside her cubicle, she doesn't show it.

'Ah, Cam sweetie,' she gushes, 'there you are. Wasn't it the most simply gorgeous ceremony?'

'It was,' I smile weakly, knowing there is now no other option than what I'm about to do. 'Ava, this is my mum, Liz.'

I extend my arm in Mum's direction and simultaneously turn my head to find her staring at Ava with the mix of incomprehension and horror I used to display in algebra lessons. True, Ava is quite a sight, with the aforementioned dented hubcap (actually a silver flat cap) plonked on top of her wavy red hair, and a low-cut frilly white blouse teamed with a skin-tight black pencil skirt and crimson-red platform ankle boots. But Mum's stunned expression suggests she is naked except for three well-placed tassels.

The myriad gold bracelets on Ava's arm jangle loudly as she extends her hand towards Mum, who shakes it, her innate politeness clearly overriding her trancelike state.

'Hello, Liz. I've heard so much about you.'

I flinch slightly, expecting Mum to fire back with a torrent of sarcastic abuse along the lines of 'Well, you would, wouldn't you, because you stole my bloody husband.'

But to my surprise, Mum simply says meekly: 'Nice to meet you.'

'I was just saying to Cam what a lovely ceremony it was,' continues Ava. 'You must be so proud of James. I was never able to have children, but if I had, I would have loved to have had a son just like him.'

OK, so one's regrets over the failings of one's reproductive system isn't the usual fare for a first-time conversation with someone, but I think I know what Ava is doing. She effectively 'stole' Mum's husband, even though he walked of his own accord, but she's putting Mum in the position of control by pointing out that she has children, something Ava could never manage. Clever.

And it seems to work.

'Thank you,' smiles Mum, seemingly genuinely. 'Yes, he's great. All my children are.' She leans to one side and envelops me in a theatrical hug whilst I struggle to keep the surprise from my face.

A slightly awkward pause ensues, with both women smiling at each other warily.

After a couple of seconds, Mum moves to the sink and starts washing her hands and Ava stands alongside her. They start chatting about the ceremony, how lovely the flowers were, the hymns and so on. To anyone walking in here right now, they might seem like old friends.

Shaking her hands first, Mum pulls a paper towel from the dispenser and passes it to Ava before grabbing one for herself.

'I haven't seen Jim yet,' says Mum casually, as if referring to a distant uncle rather than the man she shared twenty-five years of marriage with.

'He's talking to the twins, I think,' replies Ava amiably. 'Shall we go and find him?'

Involuntarily, my shoulders tense at the mere thought, but Mum is already heading towards the door.

'Yes, let's,' she says brightly, holding the door open for the woman about whom she hasn't uttered a single nice word in all the years she's known of her. 'Are you coming, dear?' she adds as an afterthought in my direction.

I shuffle out meekly and follow them to the distant corner where Dad is still chattering away to Josh and James. He has his back to us, but Josh clocks the advancing posse and his expression morphs into disbelief. Dad turns round to see what's caused it and is greeted by a sight rarer than Halley's Comet. His two wives simultaneously smiling broadly at him.

'Look who I've just bumped into,' says Ava, standing to one side and doing a 'ta-dah' motion towards Mum.

'Hello, Liz. Long time no see.'

Dad stretches both his arms towards Mum and takes

her hands in his, smiling warmly. There doesn't appear to be any awkwardness between them, but I feel it acutely, wishing this meeting was taking place somewhere a little more private. Not so much for Dad, who I believe dealt with any issues arising from it a long time ago, but for Mum, to whom the forgiveness bit is still shiny and new. Instead, she has me, the twins and Ava all gurning at her obsequiously like new parents indulging their one and only child.

But she seems to take it in her stride, taking a step forward and kissing Dad politely on both cheeks.

'Hello, Jim. You haven't changed a bit,' she murmurs.

Dad blushes. 'Very kind of you to say so, but also a complete lie.' He pats his ample abdomen. 'This is sizeably larger than when I last saw you, and this . . .' he pats the top of his balding head, '. . . is considerably thinner.'

They start talking about the ceremony and what a handsome couple James and Jenny make, and I tune out, feeling a little weird. Their tone is that of casual acquaintances who perhaps worked together years ago, meeting for a polite catch-up on what's happened to each of them in the interim. But these are my *parents*, two people who also once stood at an altar and swore lifelong allegiance to each other and who bore three children together. It's surreal that they are now talking as two people who barely know each other any more.

James catches my eye and pulls a 'this is going well' face and I smile wistfully.

Yes, I suppose it is, I think . . . as meetings with embittered ex-wives go. Especially when the main object of that embitterment is present too, in all her brassy glory.

Speaking of which, Ava touches Mum on the arm and asks her if she'd like a drink from the bar.

'A white wine, please,' Mum smiles, turning back to Dad as Ava totters off in search of alcohol.

'You look incredible, Liz,' he smiles. 'I mean it.'

'Oh, nonsense,' she flusters, but I can tell she's thrilled to hear it. All those hours of fretting about her appearance have paid off.

'You never could take a compliment,' Dad sighs, and I see Mum's smile fade slightly, clearly stung by this small yet incisive criticism. But she swiftly rallies herself and brightens again, albeit probably falsely.

'Cam says you're living in West Sussex now. That's a beautiful county.'

'Yes it is. Indeed it is.' Dad rolls backwards and forwards on the balls of his feet, starting to look faintly uncomfortable.

It pains me to say it, but I suddenly realise that the only thing these two people standing before me have in common now is their three children. Nothing more. And I wonder at this moment whether that was all they *ever* had in common.

'Right!' James cuts through the awkwardness by clapping his hands together. 'As the groom, I think I should be mingling a little before the ritual humiliation of the first dance.'

'Yes, yes, you go on,' says Dad. 'I might even throw some shapes myself later.'

Josh and I groan simultaneously. He dances like a puppet whose strings are being methodically cut off, one by one. The David Brent watercooler moment doesn't even come close on the cringeometer.

'Dad, please, no,' I beseech. After all, you're never too old to be embarrassed by your parents. Or, indeed, your stepmother, who is teetering back in this direction clutching two enormous glasses of white wine and wantonly displaying her red bra straps to all and sundry.

'There you go, Liz,' she says chummily, handing Mum a glass and taking a slurp of her own. 'Get that down you.'

Much to my shock and horror, Mum does precisely that. Dutch courage, for sure, but also a cast-iron guarantee that things could get very messy later on.

'Right, I'm going to mingle a bit too,' I pipe up, looking directly at Josh. 'Coming?'

Josh nods thankfully and we link arms, our sibling rivalry forgotten in our mutual desperation to get away. Forging our way across the room, we head towards where a desperate-looking Susie has been cornered by one of Jenny's inexorably dreary uncles with wandering-hand syndrome.

'Do you think they'll be all right?' says Josh, jerking his head back towards Mum and Ava.

'Who knows?' I sigh. 'But I suspect we're about to find out.'

'Penny for them?'

OK, as chat-up lines go, it's right up there with 'Do you come here often?' but the enquirer seems pleasant enough so I resist the temptation to say something obnoxious.

I had noticed him earlier, actually, talking to Jenny and James at the side of the dance floor. He's quite striking to look at, tall and slim, with black hair and blue eyes.

I smile welcomingly and he clearly takes this as an invitation to sit down next to me at the table, empty of other people but full of post-wedding dinner debris.

'I was just thinking that my mum and Ava are getting on extraordinarily well,' I slur distractedly, the effect of far too much Chardonnay.

'Oh.' He follows my gaze across the dance floor to where two middle-aged women are currently back to back and singing Abba's 'Waterloo' at the top of their voices, their arms above their heads. 'Is that unusual, then?'

'*She* . . .' I point towards Ava, or at least I try to, '. . . is my dad's second wife, and *she* . . .' I move my finger slightly, '. . . is my dad's first wife.'

'I see.' He looks as confused as Adam and Eve on Mother's Day. 'So is one of them your mother, then?'

'That one, of course!' I blurt with anger disproportionate to the 'crime' of him even *thinking* that blousy Ava might have spawned such a perfection of womanhood as me from her loins.

He seems unaffected by my outburst, extending a hand in my direction to shake. 'Alex. Pleased to meet you.'

'Cam.' I shake it and smile hazily.

'Drink?' He doesn't wait for an answer, topping up my wine glass from a bottle of white on the table. 'So how do you know the happy couple?'

'He's my brother. A twin.'

'You don't look alike.'

'No, he's a twin. But not with me.' I frown slightly, unsure if that made sense. 'What about you? Bride or groom?'

'I went to school with Jenny.'

323

Putting him at five years younger than me, I swiftly calculate, despite my inebriated state.

'Just schoolmates? Or something more?' I tease. Oh God, am I actually *flirting* here?

'Strictly platonic,' he grins. 'Sadly, despite my best efforts, she wasn't interested in anything more.'

It might be my imagination, but I swear he's moved slightly closer to me. I can definitely feel his breath on my neck and I have to admit, it's rather pleasurable. It's been eight months since I was even close to a man, and six years before that since I've felt the frisson of something new and unknown. Discounting Tenerife, of course.

'Do you have a boyfriend?'

Yep, even though I'm pissed I can surmise that he's definitely coming on to me now, his hand resting lightly on my knee. He's looking at me questioningly, a sleepy smile on his face.

'Nope, not any more. We split up.'

'That's a shame.' His hand is resting a little heavier on my knee now and his thumb is circulating it. It feels nice. 'So you're young, free and single.'

'Well, definitely the last two,' I murmur, feeling a little out of control now. He's attractive, I've had way too much to drink, and weddings always make me feel amorous.

'How about we go somewhere quieter?' he whispers in my left ear, the touch of his mouth sending an involuntary shiver down my back. 'So we can get to know each other a little better.'

I know full well that he just wants sex from me and then, in the morning – if he even stays that long – it will be bye-bye. But what's so wrong with that? I muse.

Maybe sex with no strings attached is what I need? After all, better that than yet another relationship that starts well and tapers off into dull routine.

I think about it for all of three seconds before coming to the very obvious conclusion that a fun, but ultimately meaningless, liaison with Alex – or indeed with *any* man – is not the way forward for me. I may be tipsy, but I'm not about to repeat the mistake I made in Tenerife, of throwing moral caution to the wind and hating myself for it. Some women can flit from man to man with ease, enjoying the moment and never tormenting themselves with 'what if?'s. And I envy them, because I know I simply can't do it without feeling consumed by insecurity.

'Nice idea,' I smile, wishing to let him down gently, 'but I'm not that kind of girl.'

'Damn!' He grins endearingly. 'How about changing the habit of a lifetime?'

'No. I like myself just the way I am,' I fire back. And for perhaps the first time ever, I realise that I actually do.

'Oh well, it was worth a try.' He stands up and wanders off, presumably in search of someone else to try his luck with.

I fleetingly consider changing my mind as I study his muscular bottom retreating towards the back of the marquee, but I know he's not the answer to the strange pang that I'm feeling right now as I sit and survey the straggle of partygoers still going strong. It's not sex I'm craving, though it wouldn't go amiss in the right circumstances. No, I'm lonely. Or at least I think that's what it is.

Sure, I have wonderful friends and a tolerable family, but it's not the same as having a special someone to talk to when you get home each night, the one you're the first to call when something good or exciting happens in your life. Dean wasn't that person either, but since he left, I have been telling everyone that the single life is wonderfully liberating. And it has been. I've enjoyed every second of the past few months and discovered that yes, I *do* like my own company. But I'm fast realising that the right relationship should feel liberating too, that if it's right you can have the best of both worlds.

I sneak out through a side exit, avoiding the goodbyes and potential cries of 'Don't leave yet', knowing that no one will be quite sure when I actually left anyway. Tomorrow, I'll do my usual spiel about how I looked everywhere for them to bid adieu but to no avail . . .

As luck would have it, a black cab is passing and I hop gratefully in the back, closing my eyes and drifting off until the jolt of the arrival at my flat wakes me up.

Once inside, the power nap has sobered me slightly and I sit nursing a cup of coffee for around twenty minutes, deep in thought about my life and where it's going. My job prospects flit in and out of my mind, most notably the dream I have always had of owning my own salon and whether I'm ever going to stop just fantasising about it and actually *do* it. So too does the momentous event of my mother finally meeting Ava and whether, in the cold light of tomorrow morning, they will remain as friendly as they seemed in the fog of alcohol and Abba.

But there's another subject too, one that has entered my mind quite a bit lately. This time, it stays, lodged firmly at the forefront of my thoughts, refusing to budge. Time, perhaps, to act on it.

Emboldened by a rush of caffeine, I flip open my laptop lid and stare at the screen as it loads, ignoring the niggle of nerves fluttering in my chest. Creating an email, I take a deep breath and start to type in the address that has seared itself into my memory, figuring I now have nothing to lose.

Dear Tom . . .

Chapter Twenty-seven

The cup of coffee sits untouched in front of me for two reasons. Firstly, it resembles the water that sits in the base of a dishwasher when there's a blockage and, secondly, I'm way too nervous to eat or drink anything.

I have flicked listlessly through the freebie paper left on the seat beside me and exchanged the word 'sorry' with the man opposite when our feet accidentally collided, and that's it. The rest of the journey has been spent staring out of the window but not really seeing the scenery, just deep in thought about what I'm going to find when I reach my destination.

I'm wearing my favourite pair of old Levi's, comfortable but not too shapeless, and a white T-shirt with a pale pink cashmere-mix cardigan over the top. The effect, I hope, is feminine but not too girly, effortless but not too sloppy. I even got Luca to blow-dry my hair yesterday, so a night's sleep on it would make it look less try-hard. Believe me, it's taken me *hours* of hard work to look this casual.

My phone beeps and the woman in the adjacent seat gives me a scowl that suggests I am marching up and down the central aisle playing bagpipes. We're in the 'quiet carriage', you see.

I might understand her reaction if it had indeed been an oasis of calm up to this point, but it has been anything but, with the Tannoy cracking into life every three minutes whilst some train guard who loves the sound of his own voice drones on about the station we've just left, the type of ticket you need to be on this train, the station we're about to get to and how pleased he is to have us on board today. At one point, he was even describing the contents of the bloody sandwiches in the buffet bar. Shut uuuuup.

I glance at my watch for the nth time in an hour and see it's now a few minutes until we arrive. Time for yet another dash to the loo to check my hair and, ahem, minimal make-up. Well, made to appear minimal anyway.

By the time I re-emerge, people are standing in the corridor, poised to alight the moment the train shudders to a halt. Peering over someone's shoulder, I see us slowly pass a sign saying 'Birmingham New Street' and a rush of nervous adrenalin courses through my veins. Here we go.

I perfect what I like to think is a confident stroll along the platform, not reluctant but not desperate either, a woman pleased to be here but not cloyingly keen.

As I near the ticket barriers, I scan the area beyond and there he is, hands in his pockets but smiling reassuringly at me. At the moment our eyes meet, I know that, for me anyway, I have done the right thing in coming here.

People talk of thunderbolts and I have always smiled indulgently whilst secretly thinking, Cobblers, but now I

329

get it. There's nowhere else I'd rather be right now than here with him. The only potential spanner in the workings of my mind is that he may not feel the same way.

'Tom, hi!' I smile rather formally, hovering uncertainly in front of him. Do I kiss him? Shake his hand? He answers for me by stepping forward and giving me a polite kiss on each cheek.

'You look well. How was the journey?'

He said 'well', not lovely, great or even good. And asking me about my journey is right up there with 'What's your favourite colour?' Clearly, he's not giving anything away regarding his inner feelings about my visit.

The instigation was all mine, made during the email sent after James's wedding two weeks ago. Despite my maudlin mood, I had been careful to keep the tone ambivalent in a 'long time no speak' kind of way, and had fabricated an afternoon hairdressing course as a reason for visiting Birmingham the Saturday after next, casually adding would he like a quick lunch beforehand?

It had taken him precisely thirty-six hours and ten minutes to reply (not that I was fanatically checking my emails or anything) and he was equally ambivalent, saying that yes, that would be nice and that he'd meet me at the station to save time. So here we are.

'I thought we'd go round the corner to a little Italian place that's cheap and cheerful,' he says. 'How long have you got?'

'No rush,' I smile.

'But I thought you had a course to go to?' he says matter-of-factly.

Shit, shit, shit. 'I do, but it's very casual.'

330

'What, as in you could come all this way and not bother to go at all?' His face is still impassive so I'm not sure if he's pulling my chain or not.

'No, I do have to go, of course,' I burble. 'Just not for long. It's like a pop-in-and-say-hello-to-the-organisers kind of thing.'

Blatant rubbish, of course, but he clearly decides to let the matter rest and simply jerks his head in the direction of one of the station exits.

'Come on, then, let's crack on.'

Sounds like he wants to get rid of me asap, I fret, following behind and trying hard to quell the dogged nag of insecurity by telling myself he wouldn't have agreed to meet in the first place if that was the case.

The restaurant is small with subdued lighting, a family-run oasis in a sea of soulless chain of shops all competing for the transient attentions of passing travellers. A small sign above the door reads 'Established 1954', so clearly they own the building outright and don't have to worry about rental overheads. Just as well, because aside from us, there's an old man – possibly a tramp – in one corner and what I assume to be a mother and daughter in another, huddled in deep conversation. Tom leads me to a wall table midway between the two.

Once we're settled, with coats over the back of our chairs, orders made, menus taken away, he places both his elbows on the table and cups his chin in his hands, studying me intently.

'So why are you here?'

His tone is lightly enquiring rather than confronta-tional, but his directness still takes me aback. I'd forgotten how straightforward he is.

'Um, I just thought it would be nice to catch up,' I bluster.

He lets out a controlled, low sigh, like a parent giving their teenager a second chance to tell the truth. 'Cam, on what basis are you here?'

As ever, I could prevaricate for Britain, but I sense his appetite for that would be zero.

'On what basis would you like me to be here?' I lower my eyes as I say it, then look up at him in what I hope is a coy way but fear simply looks shifty. This is my hopeless attempt at flirting, but it's painfully apparent it's cutting no ice.

'Let's cut the crap, shall we?' Now he seems faintly impatient with me, mildly cross even. 'You emailed me and suggested we meet . . . why?'

The arrival of our starters buys me a little time to think. My natural instinct is always to hedge my bets, childishly assuming that this will in some way protect me should rejection come my way. But I know that this is probably my one and only time to tell Tom what I feel, and that if it leads to a rebuff, then so be it. That's a better price to pay than returning to London with so many things left unsaid.

Once the waiter has retreated, I open my mouth to speak but Tom gets there before me, his expression and tone resolute.

'Look, Cam, I don't play games. I told you that before. You're the one with the boyfriend and when I came to London to find you, it was quite clear you were sticking with that set-up. To be honest, it's against my better judgement that I have even agreed to meet you today.'

I pop a garlic mushroom in my mouth and give the appearance of chewing thoughtfully. But inside, I'm in full panic mode, so far outside my comfort zone that I feel like I'm skydiving without a parachute.

Six years of Dean, the emotional safety net, followed by eight months on my own. Now here I am, placing my beating heart in the hands of a man who may well be just about to hurl it right back. I feel emotionally stripped bare, exposed to the icy elements of someone who is clearly very pissed off with me. Every fibre of my being wants to withdraw from this situation, to retreat to the safe terrain of being home alone, to forget it ever happened.

But I can't. I *have* to do this, *have* to know. The alternative would be emotional cowardice, and I've wasted far too much of my life on that already.

'There *is* no hairdressing course,' I say eventually.

He raises his eyes heavenward as if I've just told him that bears do indeed shit in the woods.

'And I haven't come to Birmingham to see the sights.' He looks pointedly at his watch.

'OK, OK!' I wince. 'But help me out here. I was in a relationship for six years, I'm out of practice on this kind of stuff.'

'You said "was".' He narrows his eyes.

'Sorry?'

'You said, "I *was* in a relationship."'

'Yes, that's right. It's over.'

'How long?' he asks quickly, studying me intently as he waits for an answer.

'About eight months ago.'

He nods thoughtfully, pursing his lips. 'I see. What happened?'

'Nothing really. I just realised it . . . or he, rather . . . wasn't what I wanted. So I asked him to move out and he did.'

'What, just like that?' He looks sceptical.

'Pretty much, yeah.'

'I see.' There's a small muscle twitching in the side of his right cheek, but no other sign of possible emotion. 'And were you right to do it?'

'Absolutely. He has a new girlfriend now and is blissfully happy, and I've been on my own ever since. I needed to do that.'

'And now you're here,' he says coolly. 'Why?'

'Why are *you* here?' I throw right back at him.

'You're being evasive again, but I'll play along with it.' He looks faintly irritated. 'I'm here because you asked to meet with me.'

'So you're just being polite,' I smile, though inside I'm feeling very shaky indeed. This man unsettles me.

'Yes, I suppose I am.'

This isn't going how I pictured it at all. In my mind, I was going to come up here, we would have a coffee and a bit of a laugh, then fall into each other's arms.

'Look, Cam . . .' he leans towards me a little, his face intense, '. . . what exactly do you want?'

OK, this is it, I tell myself. Say it, say it, say it. Or fudge it, return to London and for evermore regret it.

'I think I want you.' There, I've said it. The little secret that has dominated my thoughts of late is now out in the open. It has been uttered to another human being, albeit in the tone of someone ordering extra ham for their pizza, but perhaps a lack of emotion is advisable at this delicate stage in proceedings. Regardless, it is now a reality to be dealt with. Oh God, I feel sick.

'I see.' His body language stays firmly in neutral mode, his hands interlinked on the table in front of him.

Despite this, I stay surprisingly calm, my rampant

insecurity lying blissfully dormant for now. It's probably rendered immobile with shock.

I don't know what else to say, so I tuck enthusiastically into my garlic-mushroom starter even though I'm not in the slightest bit hungry. I notice he's not touching his minestrone.

'It'll go cold,' I blather obviously, nodding towards it. But he ignores me, leaning forward on his elbows.

'Trouble is, I'm not sure if I want *you* any more.'

Bang. My insecurity breaks through the shock barrier and surges forth, filling my veins with ice. It feels as though every hair on my body is standing to attention.

'Um, right. Well, then,' I stutter, my eyes flitting around the room, trying to focus on anything but him. 'At least I know now. I didn't want to die not knowing.'

'Not knowing what?'

'That I didn't at least try to let you know that I was now single and . . .' I trail off miserably.

'And what?' he persists firmly.

'What does it matter now?'

'You see!' He shoots backwards in frustration, his chair making a loud scraping noise on the wooden floor. 'You're incapable of giving a straight answer to anything. It's infuriating.'

I look directly at him now, my eyes belying how wounded I feel. 'I'm sorry if I frustrate you, and I'm sorry I didn't tell you that I had a boyfriend, and I'm sorry about the email business, and I'm sorry for wasting your time today . . .' I can feel I'm on the edge of tears and close my eyes momentarily to try to gain control. 'But most of all, I'm sorry you don't want me, because I have wanted to be with you ever since I met you . . . it just took me a while to work that out. And now that I have, I'm here to tell you, but it seems you've moved on. There,' I finish flatly, 'is that non-evasive enough for you?'

'It is, thanks,' he smiles sadly. 'And I didn't say I've moved on. Perhaps I should have chosen my words better. I do still want you, in fact I'd have sex with you right now, right here on this table if I could . . .'

I smile at this; I can't help myself. But I swear you could fry an egg on my face right now.

'What I meant was that I'm not sure if I want to have a relationship with you.'

The smile fades. 'Oh.' I can't trust myself to say anything else, but the expression on my face must leave him in no doubt of my crushing disappointment.

He pushes his untouched soup to one side and leans in closer still, his voice low. 'Look, in normal circumstances, people meet, start to go out and see how it goes . . . but we met on holiday, we live in different cities *and* I have a kid. We were on the back foot before we even started.'

I nod my head slowly in agreement. It's all true.

'But even *then*, I felt there was something about us that was worth pursuing, so I came down to London and . . .' He pauses and lets out a long sigh.

'And discovered I had a boyfriend,' I finish for him.

'Yes. And sorry, Cam, but it made me feel that I can't trust you, and if I can't trust you, then however attractive I find you, it's never going to be anything more than a fling because of Daniel. He's my priority and I couldn't risk him getting to know someone who's emotionally unreliable.'

I frown, slightly irritated now. 'Hang on a minute. It's totally up to you if you've written me off, but I have to defend myself against the slur of being branded emotionally unreliable. I was with the same man for *six* years, a man who wasn't right for me in the end, but no one can say that I didn't give it my best shot for a long time. And yes, I *did* go on holiday and end up in bed with you, but it was totally out of character and there was just something about you that I trusted. It was *one* mistake, Tom, but it seems that, in your eyes, my punishment is to be written off as unsuitable to be near children! How little you know me.'

I stand up and start to pull on my coat, tears of indignation filling my eyes. Rummaging in my handbag, I pull out a ten-pound note and throw it on the table.

'That's for my food.'

'Stop being so bloody melodramatic and sit down.' His voice is resigned but firm.

'There's nothing more to say.'

'Yes there is,' he sighs. 'There's plenty. *Sit* down.'

I do as I'm told, albeit reluctantly. But I keep my coat on and my handbag firmly clamped under my arm.

'Look,' he says softly, 'it's not terrible sexy, but when you have a child you have to compartmentalise any relationships. Is it just a fling that you can easily keep well away from them? Or is it something more? In which case you introduce them and pray that it lasts the course. My dilemma is that I don't see you as a fling – my feelings for you are already way past that. But after everything that's happened, I honestly don't know how we'd fare long term either. I mean, you're great fun, but you have a life in London, not here, you're as stubborn as hell, quite insecure and seemingly incapable of making emotional decisions . . .'

'And you're cold, equally stubborn and bloody insufferable,' I interject crossly.

To my surprise, he bursts out laughing. 'We're quite a pair, aren't we?'

I relax slightly and place my handbag on the table in front of me.

'The thing is,' he continues, serious again, 'I'm not saying that Daniel would have to be in on any relationship from the word go – of course he doesn't. And if you lived up here, then it would be easy for us to go on a few dates and see how it goes . . . But you don't.' He leans back in his chair and sighs. 'You live in London, which means there would be quite a lot of effort involved in us seeing each other, and it would therefore be more time-consuming too. I'm not saying I'm not prepared to do that, but after everything that's happened, I'm just wary of emotionally investing in someone who might be a bit, well, flaky.'

'Oh, so I'm flaky too now, am I? Gee, thanks.' I fold my arms and stare sullenly into the middle distance.

'We all are from time to time,' he smiles. 'My point is that the odds seem rather stacked against us and, with a young son to think about, jumping in feet first without knowing how deep the water is just isn't an option for me any more.'

'Fair enough,' I say softly, looking straight into his eyes. 'Obviously, I came here because I think there's something between us and I wanted to at least go on a few dates and see what transpires. I totally respect that you're doing what you think is best for your son, but sometimes I think children are more resilient than we give them credit for. I also think that, as long as you're happy, he will be.'

I stand up and extend my hand towards him. 'Now I really *am* going to go. I can get the four ten train. Bye, Tom.'

He stands up too and takes my hand, looking faintly perplexed. Then he moves round the table and pulls me in for a hug. I close my eyes, savouring the faint vestiges of the aftershave that evokes so many memories and, until now, so many hopes.

'Bye, Cam.' He pulls away and smiles down at me. 'I hope you eventually meet someone who makes you happy.'

'Me too,' I reply wistfully, and head off towards the station.

Chapter Twenty-eight

I settle myself into a seat by the window and place my bag on the one next to me, hoping to deter any potential travelling companions of the kind who pack their own egg and cress sandwiches or have rampant BO.

What just happened back there? Right now, I feel numb, but I know it's going to hit me later. On the journey up, I was shaking with anticipation at the prospect of seeing Tom again and introducing the new me – single, emotionally honest and very much interested in dating him. On the way back, I feel horribly exposed and desolately empty.

I suppose I had suspected he might make it slightly difficult for me, but total rejection hadn't really entered my mind, particularly as he had agreed to meet up.

I let out a long, low sigh and press my cheek against the cold window, staring out of it but seeing nothing. The Tannoy crackles into life and I brace myself for the latest bout of verbal diarrhoea.

'Ladies and gentlemen, the train is about to leave the station. If you are not travelling with us today, then please vacate now. And all those remaining on the train should check that they have the correct ticket for this journey, or you will be asked to leave at the next stop . . .'

Yada, yada, yada, I think mutinously to myself.

'May I remind you that the buffet car is located towards the centre of the train, between first class and coach G, where a number of drinks and hot snacks are being served . . .'

Kill me now.

'And finally, for passenger Camomile Simpson, who I believe is travelling with us today . . .'

I sit bolt upright as the train starts to move, straining to hear the rest of the message above the hissing noise of brakes being released.

'. . . Tom Jarvis has asked me to tell you that he's changed his mind and, if you'll still have him, he would like to give it a go after all.'

The Tannoy clicks off and I swivel my head, glancing around the carriage to see if anyone is approaching with a camera and a contract for some *You've Been Had* TV show. But the man opposite is studiously reading his newspaper and the woman in the seat in front has her iPod on full blast so I doubt she even heard the message.

Once the initial shock has subsided, and I'm thinking more rationally, I instinctively grin to myself like the Cheshire Cat, knowing that only Tom could have placed that message. And, of course, he has a track record for using the airwaves to communicate with me . . .

I lean back in my seat and stare at the ceiling, still smiling broadly. So what now? Do I call him straight away? Do I wait until I get home and send him a considered email stating that, yes, I do still want to have him. Boy, do I.

'Excuse me, but is this seat taken?'

I turn towards the voice, and it's him, smiling nervously. My heart lurches at the mere sight of him.

'Yes it is, I'm afraid. I'm expecting my new boyfriend to arrive at any second.'

'I see. Well, if you don't mind, I'll just sit here until he does.' He takes my bag off the seat and lowers himself down. I get a small waft of the aftershave again.

'So,' he says softly.

'So,' I grin.

'Did you get my message?'

'Loud and clear.'

'And?'

I toy with the idea of making him sweat a little, but dismiss it as quickly as it pops into my head. No games, time to get serious.

'And, yes, I'll still have you.'

'Good.' He looks immeasurably relieved.

An awkwardness descends, him looking at me expectantly and me wondering what the hell happens now. A busy train carriage hardly seems the place for a passionate kiss, so I do what I do best and keep talking.

'What changed your mind?'

'What you said about Daniel, you know . . . that he'd be happy if I was happy . . . that struck a real chord with me,' he says. 'But mostly, when I said that I hoped you'd meet someone who would make you happy, I felt sick.'

'Was it the minestrone?' I say, po-faced.

'Ha-ha.' He pokes his tongue out. 'Besides, I didn't eat any of it. No, it was the thought of you being with someone else, and also the fact that *I* could be the one to try and make you happy and I'd just blown it.'

'I'm happy right now,' I smile, pressing my cheek against his shoulder.

'Good.' He looks down at me thoughtfully. 'Much as I'd like to, I know I can't predict the outcome, and you can't either, but shall we at least give it a go and see where it takes us?'

'I thought you'd never ask,' I grin, feeling a swell of unadulterated joy.

Instinctively, he lays his hand on mine and it feels like the most natural action in the world. My whole arm tingles with pleasure.

'It's going to be weird, isn't it?' he adds. 'You know, working backwards.'

'How do you mean?' I ask vaguely, struggling to concentrate as his thumb starts to make a circular motion on the back of my hand.

'Well, here we are talking about *starting* to see each other and I've already seen you starkers.'

'Ssssssh!' I look over each shoulder to check no one heard before turning back to him and wincing. 'That was *totally* out of character.'

'Yes, so you keep saying,' he teases. 'And ditto for me too.'

'OK, so can we make a pact, then? Just say we do get on well and things do progress and people start to ask us how we met, can we come up with something socially acceptable?'

'What, instead of "We both got rat-arsed in a Tenerife bar and woke up naked together"?'

'Precisely.' I feel the heat of my shame burning my cheeks. 'I'd rather say we met at a BNP rally than *that*.'

'OK, how about a nightclub?'

'Yeuch, way too cheesy.' I pull a face.

'Um, the gym?'

'Do I *look* like I go to the gym?'

'I know! On a train . . . we met on a train.'

'Very *Brief Encounter*. I like it!'

The sandwich trolley rolls towards us and I suddenly feel rather hungry, tucking into a BLT with all the gusto of someone no longer in a state of nausea-inducing apprehension. I still feel slightly jittery, but it's the more pleasant, nervous excitement variety, anticipative of what might happen next.

'So what did you really think when I suggested we meet up today?' I grin. 'Go on, be honest.'

'That you had tried to forget me but couldn't. My animal magnetism was too much for you to . . . ahem . . . bear.' He makes a low growling noise.

'Very good! Spot on, in fact.'

'Easy one,' he smiles, 'because I felt the same way. It was my sensible *head* speaking back there in the restaurant, not my heart.'

'After Jason turned up at the salon, I kind of allowed myself to hope that you were feeling the same as me.'

'*Jason* came to see you? He didn't say anything . . .'

He looks genuinely shocked and I'm taken aback that Jason didn't tell him about it after the event.

'Yes. He was just being a really good friend,' I add hastily. 'He said you were a bit miserable and he thought it might have something to do with me.'

'The cheeky sod.' Tom's mouth drops open in mock outrage. 'Mind you, he was right. But now I'm feeling altogether more cheerful.'

He leans sideways so his nose is just inches from mine. My insides lurch with pleasure.

'I'm glad you came today,' he murmurs.

'Me too.'

The anticipation is killing me, but having been the one

to send the email, get on a train and admit that I'd like to start dating, call me old-fashioned but I feel *he* should be the one to make the next move. However, I *am* prepared to assist him by imperceptibly drifting forward a few centimetres . . .

Our lips brush lightly and he stares into my eyes with an undisguised mix of lust and smugness. Eventually, he applies pressure . . . or is it me? – at this proximity, it's hard to tell – and we lose ourselves in a lingering but gentle kiss.

'Ladies and gentlemen, we are now approaching Coventry. That's Coventry, next stop.'

Tom pulls himself away from me, looking reluctant. 'I'm sorry,' he winces, 'but I have to be at work by six so I need to get off here and find my way home.'

'Don't worry,' I smile. 'I understand completely. I'm just glad you came this far.'

He leans down and grabs my face, kissing the end of my nose.

'I can't make any promises, Cam, and we're going to have to take this really, really slowly at first, because of—'

'Daniel,' I interject softly. 'I know. I'll follow your lead.'

'Thanks.'

Seconds later, he appears outside the window, blows me a kiss, and is gone.

Chapter Twenty-nine

'Aren't you just the cutest little thing?' says the elderly lady, a gloved hand tickling under Mysha's chubby chin. 'How old is he?'

'*She*,' replies Saira pointedly, 'was a year old last week.'

She waits until the lady has said her goodbyes and wandered out of earshot before pulling a face. 'Bloody hell, I know she hasn't got any hair, but quite how obvious does it have to be that Mysha isn't a boy?'

She has a point. Mysha is dressed in a bright pink babygrow with a pink bow clipped on to the one, barely perceptible sprout of hair right on the top of her head.

'Clearly, a baby has to look like bloody Rapunzel before anyone makes the leap to possible femininity.'

I smile as Mysha extends her arms towards me, drawing her in for a cuddle. She loves to play with my hair, twirling her index finger round it whilst sucking her thumb on the other hand. I love Rashid too, but there's something extra special about the closeness I have with this little one, be it simply because she's a girl and I perhaps have a greater affinity with her, or maybe that I'm just more mellow these days and finally understanding the allure, and yes, responsibility, of motherhood.

Shortly before taking Mysha from her mother's arms, I was pushing her empty buggy and allowed myself to imagine, for a few seconds, that she was mine. And you know what? After many years of feeling bile rise in the back of my throat at the mere thought of what I saw as such a burden, it felt entirely natural, comfortable even.

We have just been to the swings near Saira's house and we're now walking back for lunch, probably in the garden, as it's such a gloriously warm, sunny day. Ella is meeting us there.

It didn't work out with Luke, but she's not unduly bothered by that, seeing him as a pleasing distraction after the unsatisfactory tensions of life with Philip. Luke wined her, dined her, and helped her move on, but when it became clear he was getting serious, she had gently ended it, saying she wasn't ready for commitment. Well, she is, just not with him.

She's a changed woman now. Oh, she still exfoliates for Britain and rarely has a hair out of place, but there's something slightly less fussily perfect about her appearance because she's finally stopped trying to please.

Philip's compliments were always conditional or with a subclause attached, like 'That dress looks stunning on you, but I'm not sure about the boots.' But Luke adored her, plain and simple. She could be wearing denim dungarees and jackboots and he still thought she was a goddess in human form.

During one of our chats recently, she told me that she finally feels in control of her life, no longer someone else's whim. She's working as a teaching assistant in a local primary school and planning to take the examinations so she can one day be in charge of her own class.

As we approach the house, she pulls up in her cute little Fiat 500, a thirty-sixth birthday present to herself.

'Hello, scrumptious!' She completely ignores Saira and me and swoops Mysha from my arms, lifting her into the air and down again to wiggle noses. Mysha shrieks with delight.

'And good afternoon to you too,' I say amiably, following them all through the house and into the garden.

Minutes later, Ella has placed Mysha down on a blanket with a selection of multicoloured toys dangling above her head and we each have a glass of chilled rosé in our hands.

'All for one, and one for all.' Saira raises her glass in the air and we both do likewise. 'Isn't this lovely?'

Truth be told, it's been a while since we've done this, the three of us together in one place. We still talk on the phone a lot, but physically in the same place at the same time? It's been a good few months now.

First of all, Saira has had a new baby to contend with and is only just starting to raise her head above the social parapet again. And secondly, Ella has been throwing herself into her new job, and various dates, of course, so nights out midweek are less likely. Oh, and I have recently moved to Birmingham, making them even *less* likely.

Sorry, didn't I mention that? Yes, I've given up my job at the salon, bid *arrivederci* to Luca and the others, and found myself a senior stylist's position with the second city's 'top' hairdresser, a local celebrity called Gino

Governato. Yes, this one really *is* Italian. And I'm telling you all of this without feeling even the faintest twinge of panic.

Ever since Tom and I decided to give it a go, I have been leading an exhaustingly peripatetic life of working during the week, then hanging around station concourses every Friday night, either waiting to catch the train to Birmingham or to meet one. For the first few months, we alternated, and on Tom's weekends here I discovered a London I barely knew existed, seeing it through the eyes of a newcomer. We visited galleries, enjoyed exotic drinks in a variety of side-street cafés, took riverboat rides, made spontaneous trips to matinée performances at theatres and sometimes just stayed in, snuggled up warm against the lashing winter rain. The only thing missing from this twee montage was 'Love Is in the Air' as background music.

Tom showed me what a vibrant city Birmingham is too, but after six months he suggested I start to get to know Daniel, so our outings became more child-centric.

The first meeting was in a café at their local park, where I was introduced as 'Daddy's friend'. For raw apprehension, it surpassed any experience of my life, including exams, job interviews or even meeting someone's parents. Getting the approval of someone's child is so crucial yet so impossible to manufacture.

I had been careful to remain neutral in Tom's company that day, very much 'a friend' and anxious not to present a challenge to the bond he shares with his son. But as we walked away from feeding the ducks, Tom had held my hand in front of Daniel as if it was the most natural thing in the world.

'You're holding hands!' Daniel had sniggered.

'Yes, that's because Cam is my *girlfriend*,' his dad had replied. And that had been it. Nothing more complex than that.

But the first time Daniel had stayed over when I was there, I had suggested to Tom that I sleep on the sofa.

'Nonsense,' he'd said. 'If we act as though it's the most natural thing in the world for us to be in the same bed, that's how he'll view it. Seven-year-olds don't look at things sexually.'

In the three months since first meeting Daniel, I feel like I have been on a crash course in child management, taught by a leading expert. Tom would be the first to admit the guilt he feels that his relationship with Daniel's mother didn't work out, but he's determined his son won't be damaged by it and their enduring bond is the most important thing in his life. A lot of women might feel challenged or slightly ostracised by that, but luckily I don't. It just makes me love him even more.

Once I'd met Daniel, it became the pattern that it was easier for me to travel to Birmingham each weekend, particularly as Tom had him for only one night during the week, depending on his work shifts, and on Friday nights and up to Saturday lunchtime. Eventually Tom had mentioned that perhaps all the travelling was getting a little tiring for me and weren't there good salons in Birmingham that I could perhaps work at?

'You can move in with me,' he'd added casually, with characteristic straightforwardness.

It was a big leap, both emotionally and geographically, but at thirty-seven, and having prevaricated for Britain over my last relationship, I just went with my heart *this* time. So I rented out my London flat to a young couple and bid a fond farewell to my family, particularly Mum, who wept as if I was emigrating to flaming Australia.

'I'll get settled, then I'll be back to visit in a few weeks,' I consoled. In fact, I'm seeing her later today for the first time since leaving.

In truth, our telephone conversations have been enough to sustain me, and I haven't missed her one little bit, knowing as I do that she's only a short train ride away. The one I have missed more than any is Saira, with whom talking on the phone is a poor substitute. That's why it's so wonderful to be here with her now.

'So, missing us yet?' she asks, as if reading my mind.

'Yes,' I smile, glancing from her to Ella. 'But it's worth it.'

'No regrets, then?'

I shake my head effusively. Saira was very dubious when I had announced my intentions to up sticks and head to Birmingham, not because she doubted my and Tom's relationship, but because she felt it was me taking all the risk.

But I countered that Tom had made a huge emotional investment by introducing me into Daniel's life and that it was far easier for me to make the move than him.

She was also worried that I might be leaping in with both feet and doing everything far too quickly, therefore hastening the likelihood of me becoming bored again. But I assured her that everything about this relationship felt different, that Tom challenges me, not in a bad, destructive way but in a constantly fascinating one. Also that we've been dating for nearly a year and where is it written that two or three years is a more socially acceptable period of time to pass before deciding to interlink your lives? When you know, you know. Right?

It's been only six weeks since I moved in, but already I feel sure it was the right decision to have made.

Ours is not a tempestuous relationship, one where I'm mistaking constant friction for the excitement of passion. We rarely disagree about anything. Tom is so calm, so kind, and immensely supportive towards me, a *comfort* to me, if you like. He sees so many atrocities in his job, so many examples of the excesses of ugly human behaviour, that his priorities in life are centred round Daniel and me, and making it all work.

When it's just the three of us, bunkering down with a takeaway and a DVD, I don't want to be anywhere else in the world. With Dean, the prospect of a quiet night in would prompt a desire to dilute his company, perhaps by inviting others round. Or better still, by going out myself to meet friends.

'I was thinking . . .' I top up own wine glass; then refill Saira's and Ella's too, '. . . we should go on another holiday. But this time, let's take the men and kids too.'

'Here she is!'

Mum descends on me in a cloud of freshly applied Chanel No. 5, her arms drawing me into a stifling hug.

Behind her, already seated at the immaculately laid lunch table, are James and Jenny, Josh and a girl who most definitely isn't Susie and, believe it or not, Dad and Ava.

To be honest, I could have stayed much longer at Saira's, drinking wine and gossiping long into the afternoon. But I'd promised Mum I'd be here for two o'clock and it's already a quarter past, hence everyone clearly chomping at the bit to start eating.

I kiss and hug everyone I know around the table, then

find myself lingering in front of Josh's latest arm candy.

'This is Adriana,' he grins. 'She's not long arrived from Poland so she doesn't speak much English.'

'Ah, just your type. Dependent on you *and* a language barrier,' I instinctively snipe before I can stop myself. But straight away, I regret it and add, 'Sorry, forget I said that,' and, for once, Josh lets it rest.

When Tom first met Mum and the twins during one of his weekend visits to London about three months into our relationship, we were driving back to the flat when he asked matter-of-factly, 'What is it about Josh that annoys you so much?'

I cited a litany of his supposed crimes, such as arrogance and promiscuity, and Tom listened thoughtfully before saying, 'But so what? How does that harm you?'

He went on to explain gently that what would otherwise have been a pleasant family gathering had in effect been ruined by my and Josh's constant sniping, or rather, by *me* goading and him retaliating.

'Why does he need your validation for how he chooses to live his life?' he said calmly. 'He's not breaking any laws. Just let it go.'

His words are ringing in my head right now, as I see my family for the first time in six weeks and have already risked poisoning the atmosphere with an unpleasant knee-jerk comment. Luckily, there isn't a cat in hell's chance of Josh's new girlfriend having understood it.

'Pleased to meet you, Adriana,' I smile widely, shaking her hand before taking my place at the table between Mum and James.

'So how's married life?' I smile at him and Jenny, who's the other side of him.

'I absolutely love it,' he enthuses. 'It's a doddle.'

'It's only been a year,' laughs Jenny, raising her eyes heavenward. 'Plenty of time to get sick of it yet.'

'What happened to Susie?' I whisper to them from the corner of my mouth, jerking my head across the table to where Josh is asking Adriana if she'd like wine in a booming, staccato fashion that suggests she's either deaf or stupid.

'She dumped him just last week,' winces James. 'Said she felt they were in different places in life, etc., etc. The usual cobblers.'

'True, though,' I say ruefully. 'She was so sparky and beautiful, I rather wonder what she ever saw in him.'

James says nothing, a tactic he frequently adopts when I'm criticising his brother, but Jenny nods in agreement.

'He was heartbroken, though,' she confides.

'Yes, clearly.' I look across to where he is now excavating Adriana's ear with his tongue. 'Still, each to their own, I suppose.'

Mum has now sat back down after she and Ava handed out the starters of French onion soup. In the centre of the table is a plate piled high with great chunks of white, crusty bread.

'I never thought I'd see the day,' I comment, watching as Ava settles herself at the other end of the table, fussing over Dad and making sure his napkin is covering his lap.

'What day, dear?' Mum takes a sip of soup and pulls a face that suggests it's too hot.

'The day that you and Ava would not only be in the same house together, but behaving as though you might actually be friends.'

'Oh, she's not so bad.'

'I'm not saying she is,' I answer. 'I'm referring to the

fact that, up until a year ago, you wouldn't even acknowledge she was on the planet. Now you're ladling out soup together . . .'

'My new-found philosophy in life is that no one can drive us crazy unless we give them the keys,' she smiles.

'Like it!' I nod.

Josh is telling a loud story about the time James once did a detention for him at school because they look so alike, and James is chipping in with observations too, so Mum and I have a chance to chat surreptitiously.

'How's Tom?' she asks, seemingly idly, but I know it's a loaded question.

She likes Tom, but when I first told her I was moving to Birmingham, she beseeched me to rethink, saying pretty much the same as Saira: that it was too soon and the compromise seemed to be all mine. She also added in her extra two penn'orth that, given more time, I might find myself a man who was less 'complicated', as she put it. What she meant, of course, is one who doesn't have a child.

'That's his first-born,' she said. 'You'll never be able to compete with that.'

'I don't feel the need to,' I responded.

'He's good, thanks. Really good,' I say now. 'And Daniel is well too,' I add, even though she hasn't asked.

'That's nice to hear,' she smiles. 'When am I going to meet him?'

That's one of the greatest challenges about being a 'stepmother', I find. If Daniel was mine, Mum would have been on the doorstep either during or immediately after his birth, her involvement in his life being completely instinctive and natural. But when the child isn't yours, there's a protocol to be followed, a consultation process with others, who then deliver their verdict. To me, bringing Daniel here seems like an obvious thing to do, but I know that before it happens, his mother will have to be asked her permission.

'Soon, I hope,' I hedge. 'He's such a sweet little boy, I'm sure you'll love him just as much as I do.'

'So it's serious, then?'

'As serious as I've ever been about anything.' My eyes well up with tears at the thought and I blink hastily, trying to control myself. 'I'm just really . . . really . . . *happy*. There's no other way of putting it.'

'That's wonderful, darling, truly it is.'

She places a reassuring hand on my arm, her expression one of palpable relief. I realise that, despite our differences over the years, my happiness, or lack of it, has been bothering her.

'And how about you?' I look down the table to where Dad is trying to extract a sizeable crust of bread that has dropped into Ava's cavernous cleavage. 'How's your brave new world of harmonious relations with old Bonnie and Clyde down there?'

She laughs, simultaneously nodding her head. 'Good, actually. Cathartic, even . . .'

'In what way?'

'In that it's made me hold a mirror up to what our marriage was actually like, rather than the imagined version I was harbouring inside my head all this time. The shock of his leaving made me build up the marriage into something it had never been.' She lets out a small sigh. 'He hasn't changed a bit, you know.'

'Apart from the bald patch and wrinkles.'

'I mean his character. He's *exactly* as he was when we were together and I realise now that all the things

356

that irritated me about him are what she loves him for.'

'Such as?'

'Oh, the daft practical jokes . . . I just don't find any of them funny,' she murmurs. 'Never did, never will. And his constantly chirpy outlook on life . . . I convinced myself afterwards that I missed it, but actually that drove me nuts too. There was never light and shade, it was always "let's have fun, fun, fun" and to be honest, I found it rather wearing. I wanted to be allowed to feel miserable once in a while, without the "smile, it might never happen" mantra being endlessly rammed down my throat.'

I look at Dad, who, even as we speak, is on his feet and doing his old Michael Flatley routine, hands on hips and knees bouncing up and down like pistons. Adriana is laughing uncertainly and Ava's head is thrown back in gales of guffaws as if it's the funniest thing she's ever seen . . . for the hundredth time.

'I rest my case,' smiles Mum as I turn back to face her. 'And funnily enough, now I'm no longer married to him, he doesn't irritate me any more. I can see him for what he is – a perfectly nice, relentlessly cheerful man who just happened to marry someone with a completely different outlook on life. It doesn't make either of us wrong, just unsuited.'

'That's exactly the same as I felt about Dean, apart from the relentlessly cheerful bit,' I laugh. 'We just weren't suited and now we've each found someone else who suits us far better. Saira bumped into his sister, Stacey, recently and apparently he's now living with Louise and blissfully happy, so clearly I did him a huge favour.'

'Likewise Ava to me,' admits Mum. 'Funnily enough, I've become quite fond of her. We don't see each other much, but we talk on the phone every so often.'

'About what?' I ask incredulously.

'About stuff, really. What we've seen on TV, a recipe we may have read and liked, the weather . . . nothing revelatory. Although she did ask my advice on something to do with your father the other day. *That* felt a little weird.'

'I'll bet it did. What did she ask?'

'She said she was worried he was drinking too much but that he wouldn't listen to her. She thought he might take more notice if I said something to him.'

I widen my eyes, unable to keep the smile from my face.

'I know. I wasn't sure if it was a compliment or whether the unspoken message was that I was more schoolmarmish and might have more of an impact!' she laughs.

'And is he drinking too much?' I cast a concerned eye down the table and note that he's on red wine.

'Generally? No, not really. But for a sixty-two-year-old man whose last blood test showed he was borderline type 2 diabetes, then probably, yes.'

'So have you said anything?'

'Not yet. But I've promised her that I will when the right time presents itself.'

'What a turn-up for the books, eh?' I shake my head, smiling ruefully. 'To paraphrase Bette Davis in *Whatever Happened to Baby Jane?*, "Do you mean all this time you could have been bloody friends?"'

'No, I don't think we'll ever be *proper* friends,' she says slowly. 'But at least we're not enemies any more.'

We stop talking and our attention drifts down the table to where Dad is raising his glass in a toast.

'To Liz. Thank you for your delicious food and generous hospitality.'

'Hear! hear!' we all chorus, except Adriana, who is smiling beatifically.

'It's an extra pleasure to come here,' continues Dad, 'because I'm now married to a woman whose cooking is so bad that even the dog goes to the neighbour's house to eat!'

Again, Ava guffaws uproariously whilst the rest of us make a charitable attempt at laughter.

Families are like fudge, I conclude. A few nuts, but mostly sweet.

Chapter Thirty

It's 8 a.m. on a Saturday and I'm up, which is a miracle in itself. I'm also dressed, albeit casually in jeans and a V-neck jumper, with carefully applied 'natural' make-up. Why? Well, because Tom's ex, Alison, is about to drop Daniel off and, whilst I have no reason to feel threatened by her in any way, I don't want her to think I'm a dishevelled minger either. Human nature, I guess.

Tom normally collects Daniel from school on Fridays and he then stays with us until just after Saturday lunchtime, when Tom delivers him home again. So up to now, my contact with Alison has been limited to the few occasions she's phoned for Tom and I've picked it up. But last night, Daniel was invited to a friend's house for a sleepover and Tom hadn't wanted to spoil that for him by insisting he stick to the routine.

'If it means we don't have him this weekend, then that's the price we pay for him having a normal childhood,' he shrugged.

But in the event, Alison suggested she collect him early today from his friend's house and bring him here and to stay tonight instead.

One of Tom's police colleagues is off sick and, as he's

chasing another promotion and wants to look keen, Tom's offered to cover a few hours extra, going in at five this morning and not due home until late afternoon. So I'm holding the fort.

The doorbell goes and I check my reflection one last time in the microwave door. Here we go. I clamp my best smile in place and throw open the front door to find Alison with an equally forced expression of unbridled joy. Her shoulder-length brown hair is scraped back into a ponytail, but I note that she too is wearing enough make-up to enhance her features but not enough to look desperate.

'Delivery for Cam,' she says amiably.

'Do I sign here?' I deadpan, pretending to scribble on Daniel's forehead.

'Aaaaargh!' He wriggles from my grasp and moves inside the house, waving casually over his shoulder. 'Bye, Mum. See you tomorrow.'

'Bye,' she smiles.

I expect her to move away, but she doesn't, hovering expectantly.

'Do you have to head off straight away, or do you fancy a quick cuppa?' The words have left my mouth before I even realise I'm saying them.

'That'd be nice, thanks.'

She steps inside and I wonder fleetingly if she's been in here before and whether I have inadvertently over-stepped some invisible line in the sand drawn by Tom. But immediately, her demeanour tells me that this isn't new territory. She's not scanning the room, she seems comfortable here, as if it's familiar to her.

Daniel has already switched on the Cartoon Channel with practised ease and doesn't seem to notice as she and

I move through to the galley kitchen, where I fuss about theatrically with cups and teabags and she leans seemingly nonchalantly against the oven. I notice she's enviably slim, unconsciously holding in my stomach as I do so.

'So, are you going out tonight?' I ask with the deep originality of the hairdresser that I am. It's such an innocuous question when asked of a complete stranger, dull even.

But I instantly fret that it may seem rather prying when directed at my boyfriend's ex-wife.

'Yes,' she smiles, showing no sign of being offended by my temerity. 'That's why it was rather helpful that you guys are having Daniel,' she adds with endearing honesty.

'Happy to oblige.' I'm dying to ask where she's going, but instead busy myself by pouring hot water into the cups.

'I'm going out on a date,' she volunteers.

Now, I know that Alison started dating someone shortly after she and Tom split up, and that it lasted only a few months. But since then I have no idea what she's been up to. I have casually broached the subject with Tom a couple of times, but he always shrugs and says he hasn't a clue. Most importantly, Daniel has never mentioned anyone, so even if she has been seeing someone, they haven't yet been introduced to her son.

'Sounds fun,' I murmur vaguely, unsure what else to say. I'm dying to know more but don't wish to appear nosy or as if I'm fishing so I can immediately report back to Tom.

'Well, we'll see. It's very early days,' she sighs. 'In fact, it's our first proper date. We've met for a couple of coffees up to now, but tonight we're going for dinner.'

'Anywhere nice?'

'A new Greek place that's just opened in Erdington. His idea.'

'Lovely.'

Oh, sod it. Pretending to be disinterested is all well and good, but it's not natural, is it? To hell with appearances.

'Where did you meet him?'

I swear a faint blush creeps to her cheeks and she affects a wince.

'He's a dad from Daniel's school.'

'Not a married one, I hope?'

After years of dealing with Ella and Philip, it's a kneejerk response that I instantly regret when I see her shocked expression. 'Oops, sorry,' I cringe. 'My close friend was dating a married man for a while and I have just opened my big mouth without putting my brain into gear. Something I do often . . .'

'Don't worry.' She looks visibly relieved that there seems to be a feasible reason behind my outburst rather than it being a harsh judgement of her. 'No, he's not married. He's divorced, like me, but he's got two children.'

'How old?'

'Thirty-seven.'

'I meant the children,' I laugh.

'Oh!' Her eyes widen and she clamps a hand over her mouth. ' Um, eight and nine. A boy and a girl.'

I pass her the cup of tea and gesture for us to move back into the living room. As I follow behind, my mind is fast-forwarding to a time when, if the relationship develops, she might be introducing Daniel to two potential off-the-peg siblings, and how he might feel about that. And, not for the first time, I wonder why she and Tom split up when their estrangement meant such upheaval for their child, irrespective of how adultly they have handled it.

I have always believed that, once I had children with someone, it would take something monumental to happen – like violence or hopeless alcoholism – for me to break up the family home. But now I wonder if that's a little unrealistic. For example, just suppose I had accidentally fallen pregnant with Dean's child, who was now two or three years old. Would I still have ended our relationship, or would I have slogged away at it purely for the sake of our son or daughter? Hard to say.

But did things become so bad between Tom and Alison that she felt there was no other option than to walk away and potentially subject their son to new relationships on both sides? Or was it simply the idealism of youth, of assuming the grass would be greener elsewhere then realising it wasn't and regretting it?

No matter, I muse, because he's with me now and I have no intention of giving him up. So we'll just have to muddle on through with whatever life throws at us.

'Are either of the kids in Daniel's class?' I whisper, making sure he can't hear.

She shakes her head. 'No, one is the year above, and the other the year above that. He'd probably recognise them from the playground, but they're not friends as such.'

I nod sagely to compensate for not knowing what else to say. Discussing the personal life of my boyfriend's ex-wife is new territory for me.

'Besides, it's early days,' she repeats. 'He doesn't need to know about any of this.'

'No, of course not.' I jerk my head in Daniel's direction. 'Anyway, he's so engrossed in the TV, I doubt he even knows we're here.'

'I'm not talking about Daniel.' She looks at me intently. 'I mean Tom.'

'Oh.' I'm rather taken aback by this little turn of events, not particularly because I was going to pounce upon him as soon as he returned from work, declaring gleefully, 'Have I got gossip for you,' but more because I don't like the idea of having a secret between me and his ex that he is excluded from. The dynamic is all wrong.

But equally, I don't want to upset Alison when we seem to be getting along so well.

'Look, I'm not going to volunteer the information,' I say carefully. 'But he's going to know you came in, because Daniel will tell him, and if he asks me what we talked about, I'm not going to lie. I'd feel uncomfortable doing that.'

Blimey, did I really just say that in such a calm and reasonable fashion? Clearly, Tom's straightforwardness is starting to rub off on me.

'Fair enough.' Her tone is soft and she shrugs resignedly. 'But it probably means that you and I can never be proper friends.'

'Well, I guess we both have enough of those already, don't we?' I smile. 'I'm happy to just settle for being friendly *towards* each other . . . if you are?'

She smiles back but it's faintly wary. 'OK, so be it, then.' She stands up and places her empty cup on the table. 'Right, I'd better be off. Thanks for the tea and tell Tom I'll be in touch tomorrow morning sometime.'

She kisses a distracted Daniel on the top of his head as she passes, then lets herself out of the front door.

I put my hand on it to close it behind her, but she pauses with one foot still on the step.

'It's never ideal when you split up from the father of your child,' she says slowly. 'There are all sorts of obstacles to overcome, not least any new relationships and how they might affect Daniel. But for what it's worth, I'm really glad Tom is with someone as principled as you. And Daniel really seems to like you, which helps.'

'Thanks.' I give her a genuinely warm smile. 'That means a lot. And also, for what it's worth, thank you for not being the ex from hell and feeling threatened by me. Rest assured, I will never knowingly tread on your toes.'

She gives me an 'understood' salute and starts to walk away.

'I hope it goes well tonight,' I call after her. And I mean it wholeheartedly.

'Right, about fifteen minutes should do it.'

I gently place the baking tray of rock cakes in the oven and close the door, turning back to face Daniel. As I do so, a cloud of powder hits my eyes. 'Hey!'

Moving swiftly but blindly in the direction of the worktop, I fumble around until my hand alights on the bag of flour and I bury my fingers deep inside it, scooping up a fistful, which I hurl in his direction.

It makes contact with his chest, exploding across his arms and lower neck and prompting him to shriek with delight.

Soon, we're throwing flour with gay abandon across the kitchen until we both resemble abominable snowmen, and the beige-tiled floor is carpeted in white powder. As I tip the last vestiges of the bag over Daniel's head, I turn round to find Tom leaning against the kitchen doorframe, grinning bemusedly from ear to ear.

'I don't know, I leave you two alone for just a few hours and look at the trouble you get into.'

'She started it!' yells Daniel, removing a small lump of flour from his jumper and flicking it at me.

'That is such a big fat *fib*!' I retort, lunging for the butter dish and smearing a huge blob of it in his hair.

Before Daniel can retaliate, Tom has grabbed hold of both his hands.

'Come on, you, time for a shower.' He gently shoves him out of the room. 'And I'll deal with *you* later.'

He leans forward and kisses me, leaving a residue of flour around his mouth. When he's gone, I start the arduous task of cleaning up the mess but figure it's a small price to pay for such bloody good fun and a bonding exercise bar none.

I know that Daniel will never be considered *my* son in the eyes of some because he already has a mother, but I can honestly say that I'm incredibly fond of him. I won't pretend that it's easy all of the time, particularly when Daniel is playing up and I feel Tom lets him off too lightly, but I have learnt to keep my mouth shut and offer advice only when it's sought. After all, with no children of my own, it's not like parenting is my specialist subject.

After Alison left, *E.T.* came on the television. Daniel had never seen it before.

'What's E.T. short for?' he asked.

'Because he's only got little legs,' I joked, then we

curled up together on the sofa, sharing a blanket, and watched it right through to the end, which gets me every time.

'Don't cry, Cam,' Daniel beseeched me. 'It's a *happy* ending really because E.T. actually wants to go home.'

'I know,' I blubbed. 'But he won't be able to see his little friend any more. That's sad.'

'But his friend loves him enough to let him go,' he added.

This simple yet worldly-wise statement from such young lips set me off again, howling heartily into my already soaked tissue.

Realising that Daniel was looking rather alarmed by this bloated, red-faced apparition before him, I suggested baking rock cakes as a jolly distraction. And rather conveniently, the light covering of flour worked miracles in toning down my puce complexion so Tom hadn't an inkling about my sobfest when he arrived home.

Daniel suddenly appears in front of me, all scrubbed clean with his wet hair combed neatly.

'Dad says it's your turn now,' he says matter-of-factly.

Leaving Daniel in front of *Tom and Jerry*, I wander upstairs to find Tom standing outside the shower cubicle, folding a wet towel and placing it over the radiator.

'What's he up to?'

'Watching *Tom and Jerry*.'

He moves behind me and closes the bathroom door, flicking the lock across.

'Good. That means we've got five minutes.' He pulls my jumper over my head and starts to unbutton my jeans.

'What will we do for the other four?'

I let out a loud shriek as he strips off and bundles us both into the shower . . .

'What do you fancy for supper?' I snake a hand idly across the back of the sofa, skimming the top of Daniel's head as I squeeze Tom's shoulder.

'Not your concern,' yawns Tom, who has slept through most of *Scooby-Doo*. 'Daniel and I are cooking tonight, aren't we, chum?'

Daniel nods and leaps off the sofa enthusiastically. 'Can we do it now?'

'Yep.' Tom stretches his arms and legs and gets to his feet. I attempt to follow him but he pushes me back down. 'We don't need any help, thanks. You just relax.'

They go into the kitchen and pointedly close the door, so I happily get the message and lie across the whole sofa, idly flicking through the channels. The phone could ring right now, with George Clooney on the other end saying, 'Come to Italy with me for the weekend,' and it would be a resounding 'No, thanks.' I can't think of anywhere I'd rather be than lying here whilst 'my boys', as I like to think of them, are in the next room preparing me a culinary treat. After years of feeling faintly agitated at the thought of a night alone with Dean, and how I might be missing out on something more exciting elsewhere, I now totally understand the feeling that, irrespective of what's going on across town, you're right where you want to be.

I close my eyes and doze a little, aware of whisperings in the background and the sound of cutlery being laid at the table. Eventually, perhaps ten or twenty minutes later, I feel a little hand on my shoulder, shaking me awake.

'Dinner is served,' grins Daniel, clearly very pleased with himself.

Bleary-eyed, I stand up and focus on the table, all laid out with a white cloth, paper napkins and a couple of candles. In the centre is a small vase with a clump of wilting dandelions.

'I picked those,' he says proudly. 'And I laid the table.'

'Then you are a very thoughtful *and* clever boy. Not to mention a very handsome one.' I kiss the top of his head and sit down in the place bearing a ragged piece of paper with my name scrawled on it. 'And place names too. How posh!'

Tom comes through from the kitchen, his oven-gloved hand clasping a lasagne. It's in a tin-foil tray and is clearly professionally prepared . . . by someone at the swanky new deli that's just opened down the road . . . but I don't care. He pours us a glass of chilled white wine each, and Daniel has blackcurrant squash.

'To the chefs.' I hold my glass aloft. 'This is such a treat, thank you.'

As we tuck into the lasagne, Tom tells us about his day and how he got called out to someone's house because 'they'd had an argument'.

As he's now part of the murder squad, I know it was undoubtedly an argument that resulted in someone being killed, but Daniel is too young to be given such a dose of harsh reality yet, so his father skirts round it.

'What did they argue about?' he asks. 'And why couldn't they sort it out themselves?'

'Because sometimes people need others to intervene,' answers Tom.

'What's inter . . . interv . . . ?'

'It means to get involved and try to help people work through their problems.'

'So did you and Mum have someone to help with yours?'

The question clearly takes Tom by surprise and he stops mid-chew, blinking rapidly.

'Mum and I didn't really argue,' he lies.

Daniel's brow furrows. 'Then why did you split up?'

I suddenly realise I have been unconsciously holding my breath throughout this little exchange, and have to pant slightly to catch it again. Tom shoots me a curious look, then turns back to his son.

'Because we didn't really love each other any more, we just became *really* good friends instead. But we both love you more than anything else in the world.'

It's straight out of the 'how to handle children in a divorce' textbook, but it seems to work. And the new girlfriend is totally seduced by it too. God, I love this man. His strength of character, his intelligence, his calmness and his utter devotion to his son. Nice bum too.

'Can I get the pudding now?' asks Daniel, as if the previous couple of minutes haven't just happened.

'If you like,' smiles Tom, grimacing at me about the tricky questions as soon as Daniel has left the room.

He returns seconds later with a plate of the rock cakes we made earlier, placing them on the table in front of me.

'Oooh, now let's see.' I waggle my finger above them, pretending to be unsure of which one to choose, but Daniel gently bats it away.

'That's yours.' He points at the one nearest me, which looks slightly misshapen.

I'm momentarily stunned by what I perceive to be his bossiness and lack of manners, and wait for Tom to admonish him like he usually does when he steps out of line. But he's simply smiling at him indulgently.

'Oh, OK.' I'm still too unsure of my territory to tell him off when Tom is present, so I dutifully take the rock cake he has assigned to me and place it on my plate. They each take one too.

'Go on, then. Taste it.' He pushes my plate closer to me.

As we both snaffled one earlier when Tom wasn't looking, I'm unsure why Daniel is putting on such a display of enthusiasm at me eating the damned thing, but I play along, biting into the side and making all the right 'yum' noises.

As I chew, he stares intently at me, looking fit to burst.

'It's soooo good,' I enthuse lamely, unsure what's expected of me. It's only a bloody rock cake, after all.

'Take another bite,' he demands.

I look across at Tom, but he simply smiles sheepishly and makes great play of lifting the crumbs from his plate with a damp finger.

As I take the second bite, my front teeth clash with something hard and my eyes instinctively close tight.

'Ow!'

The offending object is still in the cake and I form a pincer movement with my thumb and forefinger to pull it out. Far from looking concerned as to what it could be, both Tom and Daniel appear to be grinning nervously.

As I tug at it, the cake falls away and suddenly I'm looking at a crumb-covered circle of metal that looks suspiciously like a . . . Oh my God, it *is* a ring. And it's a diamond solitaire, which can only mean one thing . . . can't it?

As I look up, Tom nudges Daniel in the ribs, prompting him to move round the table to my side.

'Cam?' he squeaks, standing next to me uncertainly, before clearly remembering what he's been coached to do and falling awkwardly onto one knee. 'Dad and I were wondering . . . will you marry us?'

He hovers expectantly, placing an arm out to steady himself as I stare down at him, my mouth gaping open. Suddenly, in a rush of emotion that makes the *E.T.* upset look like a trifling sniffle, the tears are pouring down my cheeks and I'm emitting such huge, gulping sobs that poor Daniel starts to look alarmed.

He gets to his feet and steps backwards, nearer to Tom. 'Dad, is she all right?'

'She's fine, son. I'm not an expert, but I think they're happy tears.' Tom inclines his head slightly and peers at me. 'They *are* happy tears, aren't they?'

I nod frantically between racking sobs, struggling to find the breath to speak.

'Yes,' I croak eventually.

'Yes they're happy tears, or yes you'll marry us?' smiles Tom.

'Both,' I gush, lunging towards them and enveloping them both in a wet yet heartfelt hug.

As I stand here, glued together with my new, ready-made family and all the responsibility and possible awkwardness it may bring, I feel not one small shred of uncertainty, not even one nagging doubt.

When you know, you know. That's what they say. And *now* I finally get it.

This feels right. This is where I belong.

The Second Wives Club

Jane Moore

'A *fabulous* read!' Sharon Osbourne

It's Alison's wedding day, her gorgeous husband Luca is by her side, and everything is just perfect. Perfect that is, until Luca's first wife gatecrashes the reception and makes it clear that she's going to remain very much part of his life.

A stunned Alison soon finds an ally in Fiona, a founding member of The Second Wives Club and similarly plagued by her husband's ex. There she's introduced to Julia, whose husband has stayed best friends with his first wife – to Julia's intense irritation – and to long suffering Susan whose entire life is surrounded by reminders of her partner's saintly former wife.

For the women, The Second Wives Club is a refuge and a lifesaver: somewhere to bitch and to gossip and to share horror stories about the exes' latest excess. But maybe if they all have the same problem they can work together on a solution? For enough is enough: it's way past time for the Second Wives to stop settling for second best.

Read on for an extract . . .

A first wife is for life, not just for Christmas

Letting out an ever-so-pretty little sigh that didn't cause her bosom to erupt from her corseted dress, Alison cast her eyes up and down the top table, letting her gaze linger on the eye-catching arrangement of lilies from one of London's top florists.

The fact that hundreds, if not thousands, of identical lilies were available from far cheaper outlets was neither here nor there. As she had told Luca on the numerous occasions he had questioned the validity, not to mention expense, of it all, she wanted *the best*.

If she'd had her way, they'd have been married in St Paul's Cathedral with a hundred-strong choir and Dame Kiri Te Kanawa warbling the bridal march. But the small matter of Luca's previous marriage had limited them to Windsor Register Office, and his refusal to shell out for any more 'London prices' meant the reception was being held at a nearby conference hotel of the kind usually associated with a Corby trouser press and complimentary bourbon biscuit in every room.

But looking at it now, she thought, you could never tell that the day before it had been a drab old room frequented by the sales team of a double-glazing company. The maroon Draylon-upholstered chairs were disguised with white cotton covers, gathered in by a red velvet bow tied round the back, and the four seventies-style pillars propping the ceiling up were now unrecognisable, peppered with red rosebuds and fronds of trailing ivy.

Alison had employed the services of an event organiser, but being the offspring of a mother who was such a fanatical perfectionist that she put newspaper under the cuckoo clock, she was also a control freak. So she'd overseen every last detail herself, adamant that her wedding was going to be the fairytale perfect day she'd always imagined as a little girl. So far, she hadn't been disappointed.

Turning to her left, the subtle smirk of satisfaction skewed slightly into one of dismay as she clocked Luca's six-year-old son Paolo smearing his foie gras terrine from one side of his plate to the other. Resisting the temptation to inform him it cost £10 per serving, she extended a gloved hand and patted him on the head, hoping to distract him from his messy task.

'All right, soldier?' she said gently, feeling him recoil slightly under her touch. He made an angelic pageboy, a vision in midnight blue velvet pantaloons with matching soft cap. At least he'd kept his on, she noted.

His four-year-old brother Giorgio, sitting to his left, had dispensed with his in a muddy puddle hours ago.

'When are we going to the park?' he whined.

'The park?' Alison looked puzzled.

'Yes, Daddy said he'd take us. Today.' Paolo's big brown eyes looked at her imploringly.

'Not now, darling,' murmured Alison. 'Another time, eh?' The bloody park indeed. What on *earth* was Luca thinking of, promising them that?

The sound of a finger being rapped against the side of a microphone broke into her thoughts. It was David Bartholomew, getting ready to speak. He'd been Luca's best man at his first wedding to Sofia, but despite Alison's keenest efforts to get him jettisoned from this in favour of someone new, Luca had flatly refused.

'I can't just change my best friend to suit you,' he'd growled, so she'd finally let the matter drop.

Luca and David knew each other through their love of football. They had met through a friend of a friend several years earlier, discovered a mutual passion for Chelsea, and – bingo! A firm friendship was formed on the terraces of Stamford Bridge. It was very much a season-ticket relationship, restricted to match days only.

Alison had only met David a handful of times, when he'd popped in for a quick coffee while dropping Luca home. She knew he was married to someone called Fiona, but other than that the details were patchy. Like most men, Luca was very unforthcoming on the minutiae of other people's lives. Not because he was being discreet, simply because he wasn't interested enough to ask.

'Well, here we are again.' David's voice boomed out of the speakers at the back of the room to a polite ripple of laughter.

Knowing all eyes were on her, Alison clamped on a beatific smile, but inside she was seething. She wanted this to be *her* day with Luca, their own special bubble where they could pretend his life began the day he met her. And David had already ruined it all with an opening gambit that reminded everyone present that Luca had been married before. It got worse.

'We're here to celebrate the union of a man who signs his wedding certificates in pencil,' he boomed, grinning at Luca who grimaced back.

Everyone in the room was tittering and Alison had to resist the urge to lunge for the six-inch knife lying idle by the side of the cake.

'He's the only guy I know who hires his wedding rings!' David ploughed on, waiting for the laughter to end before delivering his next hugely unoriginal joke that made Luca out to be a serial Lothario with a 'Next' label in his underpants.

Suddenly a door slammed at the back of the room, somewhere near the dreaded table nine. 'Dreaded' because it was where Alison had seated the ghastliest of Luca's seemingly limitless relatives, supposedly out of harm's way. There was his Uncle Mauro who still pointed at planes and his second cousin Maria who, to put it kindly, was only knitting with one needle.

Alison scowled in the direction of the table, aware that a commotion had started there and was gradually rippling across the room in a Mexican wave of sharply indrawn breaths. She craned her neck to see what it was, but a hideously large hat on table eleven obscured her view.

David, seemingly oblivious to anything other than the small podium in front of him, was halfway through some lame old anecdote about when he and Luca had both fallen asleep on a train and accidentally ended up in Cornwall, but no one appeared to be listening.

By now Alison could see that a brown-haired woman was advancing unchallenged across the room, her face twisted in fury. As she moved closer and her features came into focus, Alison felt a slight chill start to prick at her forearms.

She couldn't be sure as she'd only ever seen one grainy photograph, but . . .

'Luca?' she began tentatively. 'Is that . . .'

'Mama!' Giorgio shot up from his chair and started to scramble under the table, brushing past Alison's ankles as he did so. Emerging the other side, he clamped himself to Sofia's left leg as if she was rescuing him from some horrific ordeal. Paolo had the foresight to take a couple of chocolates with him before swiftly following suit.

By now, David had stopped speaking, his face frozen with apprehension. There were over three hundred people in the room, but Alison had never heard a silence like it.

Sofia was now standing within two feet of her and Luca, her dark, Italian eyes burning with a look that could curdle milk.

'So thees is what you call going to ze park, huh?' She ignored Alison and looked defiantly at Luca who just shrugged nonchalantly.

'You lied to me!' she shouted, pushing her face forward so it was just inches from his.

Luca recoiled slightly but his own face remained impassive. 'Let's get real, Sofia . . .' He spoke so softly that a woman on table three had to crane her neck to hear. 'I had to lie or the children wouldn't have been able to come today, would they? Even though I'm their *father*, you would have forbidden it.'

For a few seconds they glowered at each other across the table before Sofia made a sucking noise with her teeth to illustrate dismissal of what he'd said. Drawing herself up to her full height of 5'6", her ample bosom heaving with a palpable sense of injustice, she stuck her chin in the air in defiance.

'What mother *would* want her children dressed like performing monkeys while their father marries some dirty *whore*?' For the first time, she actually brought herself to look straight at Alison as she emphasised the last word.

A chorus of gasps and 'Ooh, I says' swept through the guests who rapidly returned to silence in case they missed the next bit.

'Excuse *me!*' Alison stood up, her hands placed indignantly on her hips. 'How dare you call me that in front of my family and friends? You don't even know me.'

Sofia's lip curled into a sneer and she waved one slim, tanned arm dismissively. '*Your* family and friends? I see very few people here that I didn't see at my own wedding. You think you're the cat with ze cream, but you have a second-hand day.'

She paused a moment and pointed one finger towards David, whose terrified expression suggested he thought it might be loaded. 'A second-hand best man . . .' the finger moved to Luca '. . . a second-hand husband . . .' then finally Alison '. . . and what looks like a second-hand dress. You've even had to borrow my children.'

'Well, not anymore.' Sofia clamped an arm round each boy's shoulders. 'They're coming with me.'

Her insides churning with humiliation and indignation, Alison looked to Luca to do something. But he stayed silent and motionless apart from yet another Latin shrug. It was a habit she'd found incredibly sexy when they first met; now it was overwhelmingly irritating.

'See what you've married?' scoffed Sofia, jerking her head towards her ex-husband. 'Luca has never stood up to anyone, he always takes the easy option.' A child clamped to each leg, she resembled someone in dire need of a double hip replacement as she jerked her way across to David's podium. Grabbing his microphone and turning it towards her, she tapped the end of it like a true professional, checking that what she was about to say would be reaching the entire room.

'My ex-husband is a coward and she's welcome to him.' Her voice seemed to hit the back wall and bounce back again, filling every corner. 'But she's not having my children.'

With that, she began to guide Giorgio and Paolo back towards the door she had burst through just minutes earlier, close to Uncle Mauro who was now grinning broadly and pointing at her.

About halfway across the room, Sofia walked past a table of the shellshocked bride's friends and family. Alison's sister Louise rose tentatively to her feet.

'Excuse me,' she said, with the unerring British politeness that suggested she was about to ask where the lavatories were, 'but you can't speak to my sister like that.'

Sofia stopped in her tracks and fixed her with a death stare. 'Oh, yes, I can. And I have. And I will again if it suits me to do so. Got that?'

Louise sank back into her seat and shrugged at the others around the table. Emboldened by the sight of her sister's embarrassment and her enemy's retreating back, Alison bristled into action, swivelling to face her new husband. 'Luca, they're *your* children too. Go after her and bring them back.'

But Luca stayed where he was and just sighed. 'It doesn't work like that. The mother has all the power.' He watched Sofia as she snaked her way to the back of the room, the guests parting before her like the Red Sea. 'Let them go. At least they were there for the ceremony,' he added as an afterthought.

'Well, hoo-bloody-rah, put out the frigging bunting!' Alison's face now matched the roses decorating the pillars in front of her. 'Is this how it's always going to be?'

'You should have asked that question *before* you married him, love.'

Alison's head swivelled to where she thought the woman's voice had come from, but everyone on table two was looking like butter wouldn't melt. If idiots could fly, she thought mutinously, this place would be an airport.

Sitting back down in her chair with a heavy thump, it suddenly dawned on her that she had spent so much time planning her fairytale wedding that she'd never actually stopped to think about the reality of what she was taking on. A man with a determined and ferociously bitter ex-wife and two children already poisoned against her.

She loved Luca dearly, was probably even a little obsessed by him if the truth be known. But now the subterfuge of their initially illicit relationship had been stripped away, would her passion for him endure throughout all the mini-dramas resulting from his past? She'd just have to wait and see, hoping that it would.

Sofia had finally disappeared from view and the room started to fill with noise again, the guests obviously discussing the theatrics they'd just witnessed. Alison knew that in most people's eyes, probably everyone's, in fact – including her own friends' – she had wilfully stolen Luca from Sofia and therefore deserved everything she got.

Speeches over, the band Zorba, or 'Ex-zorba-tant' as Alison referred to them after writing a £2,000 cheque for their services, struck up the first few notes of Elvis Costello's sleepy ballad 'Alison'.

With all eyes on them, Alison smiled and extended her hand to Luca who led her to the dancefloor.

"*Aaaaaaalison, I know this world is killing you . . .*"

Not to mention my husband's ex-wife, she thought mutinously. As they swayed slowly to the music, she tried to forget about Sofia, instead burying her head in Luca's neck and inhaling his Fahrenheit aftershave, the musky smell that had first attracted her to him. As she closed her eyes to block out everyone's gaze and let her mind wander, she could convince herself that everything was going to be all right. And it probably would if it was just the two of them.

Trouble was, there were three gigantic complications in the shape of his two young children and their ferocious mother, all of whom were here to stay.

'"*Oh, Aaaaaalison, my aim is true . . .*"'

As the music trailed away, Luca took a step back from her to acknowledge the applause of the onlookers and Alison's bubble was broken. Leaving him to take the floor with a favoured aunt, she refused all offers of other dances, pretending she needed to visit the loo.

Heading in that direction for authenticity, she reached the door and bumped chests with a smiling woman whose brown curly hair was falling into her eyes. She looked dishevelled, but in a sexy rather than a slovenly kind of way.

'Hi, Alison.' She grinned.

Alison smiled back though she had absolutely no idea who this was.

'I'm Fiona.'

She extended her hand and Alison took it, still looking blank.

'David's wife. The best man?'

Alison theatrically slapped her palm against her forehead. 'Oh, God, sorry. I guess I'm still a little shellshocked from . . . well, you know what.' She shrugged apologetically.

'Yes, I certainly do.' Fiona pulled a face. 'I wanted to talk to you about that, actually.'

'Oh?' Intrigued, she jerked her head towards an empty sofa positioned to one side of the foyer. 'Shall we?'

They wandered over and sat down, Alison smoothing her dress under her and scooping her train to one side. Fiona took a quick glance around then fixed her grey eyes on the bride's face.

'That was pretty ugly back there.' She tilted her head towards the reception room in a reference to Sofia's outburst.

Unsure where this woman's loyalties lay, Alison simply shrugged. '*C'est la vie*. I understand why she did it.'

'Really?' Fiona looked unconvinced.

'Why, don't you think it was justified?' Alison threw the ball into her court, testing the water.

Wrinkling her nose, Fiona sighed. 'Tricky one. Upset about the breakdown of her marriage? Yes, I sympathise.' She checked over her shoulder again. 'Causing an embarrassing scene at her husband's wedding in front of their two children? Nope, sorry. That's *so* wrong.'

'Do you think so?' Alison studied her face for signs of potential betrayal but saw none. She knew any of her own friends present would wax lyrical about how disgraceful Sofia's behaviour had been – in fact, many had done so already. But she desperately wanted allies in Luca's camp too. Or at least someone with an objective view, and Fiona might be that person.

'I must say, it has made me slightly apprehensive about the future . . . if that's the way it's going to be,' Alison said tentatively.

Fiona sighed. 'Tell me about it.'

'You sound like you've been there?'

'Sort of. David . . .' She broke off as someone advanced towards them. It was Alison's mother, Audrey.

'Darling, I've been looking everywhere for you. Are you all right?'

'Mother!' Alison raised her eyes heavenward. 'That's the tenth time you've asked me that. I'm fine, really.'

Audrey looked unconvinced. 'That dreadful Sofia needs to move on with her life, don't you think?' She glanced at Fiona but didn't wait for an answer, turning back to Alison again. 'Anyway, your father wants another word. Stay here, I'll get him.' She drifted off on a cloud of White Linen.

Fiona raised her eyebrows. 'She's formidable.'

Alison smiled. 'She's also on another planet. The other day, a homeless man came up to her in the street and said he hadn't eaten for three days, and she said: "Dear chap, you must force yourself!"'

Fiona burst out laughing. In the distance, they could see Audrey bustling back into view with her husband Alasdair in tow.

'Look, I won't keep you on your big day,' said Fiona hastily. 'I just wanted to give you my number.' It was already scribbled on the piece of paper she handed over.

'Thanks.' Alison wasn't quite sure what this meant, but she was grateful for the gesture.

'It's just that a couple of friends and I have this little club, and I thought you might like to join. It's a kind of self-help group, I suppose.' Fiona smiled reassuringly.

Alison looked baffled. 'What, like a weight loss thing?' She looked down at her own enviably slim hips.

Grimacing at her own wide girth, Fiona laughed. 'No, although I could probably do with joining something like that . . . no, this is a sort of secret group founded by me. We've only got three members so far, four if you join us. We get together once a week for moral support.'

Intrigued, Alison's mind was racing over all the possibilities.

'What are the criteria for joining?'

'You just need a small scar running from here to here.' Fiona used her forefinger to trace a line from the corner of her mouth down her chin. 'It comes from years of biting your lip.'

Alison was starting to feel like someone whose pilot light had gone out. 'Sorry? I still don't get it.'

Fiona smiled benevolently. 'Welcome to the Second Wives Club.'

THE POWER OF READING

Visit the Random House website and get connected with
information on all our books and authors

EXTRACTS from our recently
published books and selected
backlist titles

**COMPETITIONS AND PRIZE
DRAWS** Win signed books,
audiobooks and more

AUTHOR EVENTS Find out which
of our authors are on tour and
where you can meet them

LATEST NEWS on bestsellers,
awards and new publications

MINISITES with exclusive
special features dedicated to our
authors and their titles

READING GROUPS Reading
guides, special features and all
the information you need for
your reading group

LISTEN to extracts from the
latest audiobook publications

WATCH video clips of
interviews and readings with
our authors

RANDOM HOUSE INFORMATION
including advice for writers,
job vacancies and all your
general queries answered

Come home to Random House
www.rbooks.co.uk